# THIS IS NOT THE END

by chandler baker

**HYPERION**

Los Angeles New York

First Hardcover Edition, August 2017
First Paperback Edition, August 2018
10 9 8 7 6 5 4 3 2 1
Printed in the United States of America
FAC-025438-18173

This book is set in Avenir LT Pro, Bembo MT Pto, Futura LT Pro, Helvetica LT Pro, Orator Std/Monotype; Jelena Handwriting, Matchmaker, Mrs. Eaves/Fontspring

Designed by Tyler Nevins
Title lettering by Molly Jacques

Library of Congress Control Number for Hardcover: 2016033381
ISBN 978-1-4847-9009-0
Visit www.hyperionteens.com

The SFI label applies to the text stock

*For Rob, we've created some*
*wonderful things together*

# *PROLOGUE*

The most formative memory of my life isn't even my own. It doesn't matter that I wasn't there to see it happen, that I didn't feel the rip of pain or hear the solitary shriek followed by silence, I've still managed to live that moment a thousand times. One thousand times I've told myself the story from his perspective. One thousand times I've tried to rewrite history and failed.

Here's what I recall.

Big, soggy clouds hanging low in the sky, the last drizzle having been wrung out of them. It's not an important detail, but if it hadn't been a rainy day, we would have been on the back porch or down on the shell-y stretch of gray beach behind our house. I know the rain must have made Matt bored, because usually I was the one climbing things and getting scraped-up knees those days, mainly because

Matt was too old. He did still read to me about talking lions and magical queens that turned the world to ice, but I also caught him talking on the phone to girls occasionally, and I didn't like it.

In the memory, I've tried to edit the weather, but it never works. The story won't hold together without it.

Our neighborhood has a palm tree infestation, which is to say that there are palm trees everywhere and their roots try to choke out any plant that dares to grow nearby. They can make other kinds of trouble too. The tall ones that mark the property line around our house have to be supported at the base with wooden beams so that the giraffe-like trunks don't topple over and gouge holes in our roof.

So it's notable that we have one of the only oak trees in a one-mile radius. Since nobody can climb palm trees, I can attest to the fact that looking at a nice, solid oak does tend to give you the urge to hike an arm over one of the branches and climb it. In other words, I get where Matt was coming from. I just wish for the thousand-and-first time that I could change it. But, like I said, he was bored and must have just finished a book—actually, yes, I remember that, one of his books about aliens or sorcerers—and that oak tree is right outside his window. Maybe if the previous owners hadn't planted it there or if Matt and I had swapped rooms, maybe none of this would have happened. But they didn't, we didn't, so we're stuck in it.

Matt went outside. He rubbed his hands on his pants and over the bark. The air smelled like damp wood with a hint of seaweed, since we're so close to the shoreline. He could see bits of sand trapped in the tree's crevices because, of course, sand gets everywhere—even in our ears sometimes. There are times when I relive this story that I find myself wiping my own hands, and then I realize that I'm not in the memory and Matt's hands don't work anymore.

He had a new paperback shoved in his back pocket, and he'd decided to read it from up in the tree, like one of the boys in *The Swiss Family Robinson*. So he stretched onto his tippy-toes until he could reach the lowest branch. The bark stung the inside of his arm as he hoisted himself onto the lowest branch. He enjoyed the sensation of his dangling feet and climbed higher so that there was more air between his shoes and the ground.

The branches creaked under the soles, but there were fat, sturdy limbs above him. So Matt scaled farther up the oak, careful not to slip on the wet wood. This is the part where I try to tell Matt to stop. End the story here. Turn back. Go no farther.

The last branch that he hooked his arm over looked like all the others. He didn't see the gash between the limb and the trunk. He didn't feel it give under his weight until all of it was already pressing down and it was too late.

I wish I didn't remind myself of this so much. Then maybe I could un-remember the memory.

Too late.

The sound was the cracking of bone. Flashes of leaves and twigs that tore at his shirt and neck. His stomach shot up to his throat as his torso fell unevenly toward the dirt, which was packed hard from the rain. Time stopped. Just like it does in the movies. Everything else crawled into slow motion.

It felt like he was falling forever.

Then, when his back hit the ground, it seemed like there would never be breath in his lungs again, and his spine splintered like thin ice under a footstep, forking off into spidery veins that fractured the world—into *before* and *after.*

**BUREAU OF HEALTHCARE RESEARCH & QUALITY**
**RESURRECTIONS DIVISION**

Application for Resurrection

Name of the Resurrection Holder: ______________________________

Resurrection Holder's Birthdate: ______________________________

Resurrection Holder's Social Security #: ______________________________

Name of the Resurrection Candidate: ______________________________

Resurrection Candidate's Date of Death: ______________________________

Cause of Death: ______________________________

Sworn Affidavit Regarding Cause of Death:

I, ______________________________, represent under penalty of law that the death of the aforementioned Resurrection Candidate was the result of neither suicide nor assisted suicide.

______________________________

Signature

**IMPORTANT INSTRUCTIONS (sign below)**

I, ______________________________, understand that I must arrange for delivery of the deceased to the Designated Resurrection Site (see pamphlet instructions). Cremated cadavers will not be eligible for resurrection. I understand that this resurrection choice is made in compliance with the Pickering Regulations and will be my only choice. I consent to conferring my sole resurrection choice upon ______________________________, the Resurrection Candidate.

**PLEASE FILL OUT REVERSE SIDE FOR CANDIDATE INFORMATION**

# chapter one

## 23 DAYS

When I was eight, I watched a woman jump from a bridge while my mother and I were stuck in traffic. Her arms spread out like a bird's wings, and for a moment she was suspended, the wind catching her blouse like a sail. Then the moment snapped and she fell from the air. Her body cracked against the water. And her existence was snuffed out. Gone.

So for as long as I can remember, I've known that water's strong and solid enough to kill. I think of an early memory of my brother standing on the shore behind our house while I picked my way barefoot across a stone jetty that protruded out into the sea. "If you fall," he said, "I'll bring you back." He had puffed out his chest and pushed his crop of sandy-blond hair out of his eyes, squinting into the sun that reflected off the water. He was so unbroken then, his forehead crumpled into a worried knot of skin at the top of his nose as he tried to sound brave. I've always been the daredevil between us.

I watch the water now frothing against the rocks below me like a rabid animal. My toes hook precariously over a jagged rock face. The distance is thirty-odd feet, far enough to send needle pricks through the soles of my feet, not far enough to crush my bones on impact. I consider this a happy medium.

Then there's the thwack of bare soles behind me. A shadow crosses. A foot plants inches from mine. "You snooze, you lose, suckers!" My boyfriend, Will, tucks his bronzed legs into a cannonball. His hair—which at this stage of the summer now matches the color of his skin—spikes up and trails after him, fluttering in the furious rush of wind as he plummets into the ocean. Behind him, a white plume of water gushes up and he disappears below the surface.

I glance back. "You're next." I gesture to Penny, who stands three carefully measured feet from the ledge. She is so *not* a daredevil. More the yin to my yang.

From that vantage point, I imagine she can see the horizon, but not the drop waiting below.

"No." She shakes her head, swishing a so-blond-it's-nearly-white ponytail across her shoulders. "I can't. I want to. I really do. I just . . ." She has this way of bowing in her knees like she has to go to the bathroom, literally shrinking into herself. I know this as the first telltale sign of chickening out.

I lean on one leg and peer back over the ledge where Will has resurfaced. He treads water and tosses his head so that ocean spray flies out and plasters his hair over his right eyebrow. He cups his hands around his mouth and calls up to Penny: "Get it together, Hightower."

We discovered this point two months ago while we were swimming offshore of the public beach. From the surface, we took turns diving as far down as we could, trying to see if we could touch the bottom to find out whether it was safe enough to jump. It was Will who had tried it first. I had held my breath, waiting for a scream—or worse, nothing. But Will had come up laughing and baiting us in after him. Will and I have been coming back once a week like kids circling the line at an amusement park.

Staring down, my pulse thumps in the webbed skin between my thumb and pointer finger. The feeling of my stomach leaping clear into my throat is there even before I step into thin air.

I look back at Penny, who is quivering in a turquoise triangle-top bikini and using her eyes, the color of sea glass, to plead with me. I consider myself the definitive expert on all things both Will and Penny, and this, I know, will be good for her. With just a few weeks left of our last summer together, her chances to conquer her fear of heights are dwindling.

"Think about it this way," I tell her. "You just start from there and keep on walking. One step, that's all you have to commit to and then—*poof!*—no turning back."

"Keep on walking... off a *cliff*," she says. Goosebumps pop up all over her skin, even though the air is the temperature of a Jacuzzi. "You forgot to mention that part."

"If all your friends jumped off a cliff, wouldn't you?" I quirk an eyebrow and hold out my hand. "We'll do it together."

She closes her eyes and takes a deep, soothing breath, pinching her thumb to her middle finger. It's what she calls her "centering" ritual, and since she's not looking, I don't mind rolling my eyes. Penny is a devotee of yoga and Eastern meditation, much to the confusion of her Jewish parents. As for me, I'm more act first, think later. Penny, on the other hand? Think first . . . and then think some more.

After a moment, she swallows and nods, then gingerly steps closer to me. Her palm locks against mine, hot and damp, covering up the silvery crescent-shaped scar on the side of my hand left over from where a dog bit me a couple of years back. Between heights and fang-toothed fluff-balls, I'll take the death-defying drop any day.

Penny peers down her nose at the water below. The waves break in white crests, slamming up against the rock face, but I'm not worried. Penny's a good swimmer. It's the jumping she needs work on.

"The only way the bottom gets closer is if you get farther from the top," I say. "You ready?"

Her lower lip quivers. "You're *sure* this is safe?"

I squint. "I'm living proof, aren't I?" At this she looks me over as if to double-check that I am, in fact, alive and therefore suitable evidence. She squeezes my hand tighter. "Okay. On three. One . . ." I bend my knees. "Two . . . three . . ." I swing my arm and lunge out into the open air. Penny's fingers immediately slip from between mine, and all of a sudden I'm grasping nothing but wind. I try to turn to see if she's with me, but I'm falling too fast. The air whistles in my ears. Sky and sea roar around and through me. It's a split second before the ocean stabs my legs and the tough skin on the bottom of my feet.

A gush of salt water rushes into my nostrils. My sinuses burn. I squeeze my eyes tighter and kick. Bubbles pour out my nose and the tide drags me back and forth horizontally while I struggle up, up, up.

I fight against the undertow and the water grows warmer, which is how I know that I'm headed in the right direction. My mouth breaks the surface and I gulp air down. My hair clings to my head and neck and I'm grinning, shaking the water out of my ears and swishing my legs furiously to tread water.

I glance up and there's Penny waving at me from the top of the cliff. "I couldn't do it!" Her voice echoes down the cragged face. "I'll meet you guys down there."

"Pen—" But splashing is coming from behind me and before I can get a word out a weight pushes down on my shoulders and water charges through my parted lips. Sinking back under, I work to pry the calloused fingers away. Then, twisting, I give Will a sharp jab to the ribs. He swims backward and I come up coughing and laughing before whacking my arms against the water and splashing him square in the face.

"Truce! Truce!" he calls, dog-paddling toward me. I let a few sips of salt water fill up my cheeks, and then when Will's hands are on the straps of my bikini bottoms and he's leaning in for a kiss, I spit a fountain of water at him, giggling and retreating with a backstroke for safety. "Hey! I called truce!" He runs his hand over his eyebrows and down his face. "A blatant violation of the rules of engagement." He snatches my ankle just as I'm almost clear of his reach and tows me back where he plants a wet kiss on my cheek. I scrunch up my shoulders and make a show of not liking it even though it's obvious to us both that I do.

"Let's hurry up. I'm so hungry I could eat a woolly mammoth," I say.

"Why not just an elephant?" Will asks.

"An *elephant*? But they're adorable." I dip my head underwater, wetting my hair so that it slicks straight back. "God, Will, I'm not a monster."

Will swims in front of me and I wrap my arms around his neck so that he's giving me a swimming piggyback ride. "I could eat a pterodactyl. I bet they taste like the chicken of the sky," he says grandly.

"We're strange, you know that?" I rest my chin on the crook between his neck and shoulder. He smells like seaweed and coconut suntan lotion.

He shrugs. "Three more weeks until your great, big, epically magnificent, cowabunga awesome birthday surprise. Have any guesses?"

I feel the steady beat of his legs underneath me, kicking calmly toward shore. His broad shoulders tense and relax with each stroke.

"Does the birthday surprise have a nickname? Because that seems like a bit of a mouthful."

"Oh, that *is* the nickname. That's how awesome the surprise is." Will doesn't do understated. Sometimes I worry that if we ever get married, Will's proposal will involve a large-scale choreographed dance number and singing animals, if he can swing it.

"Let's see. Last year you took me on a helicopter ride during which I puked in a bag. The year before that you rented a party bus to take us all to see a cheesy horror-movie marathon. So, that's land and air. I'm going to guess water this year. A boat! You're taking me on a boat!" I squeeze him harder around the neck.

He lifts a hand and wipes water from his eyes. "I'd tell you, but then I'd have to kill you."

"But then there'd be no one left to bring me back." I jut out my lower lip. "I think that'd sort of defeat the whole birthday-surprise hoopla."

"Then I guess I'd better not tell you." He tickles the bottom of my feet. I cringe and curl my legs more tightly around him. Penny, Will, and I all have summer birthdays—Penny thinks that's part of why we all get along so well, and as much as I scoff at her stargazing horoscope babble, she may be on to something, because all three of us could basically live on the beach, and that's one of my favorite things about us. I mean, I'd die if Penny made us go hang out at the mall or something.

The two of them have both turned eighteen already—their birthdays are only a week apart, with Penny being the older one. Their closeness in age is why their moms are best friends. Neither Penny nor Will used their resurrections on anyone. There are rumors that a few kids in our class might be using their resurrection choices this year. Penny thinks her aunt resurrected somebody back when she and Penny's mom were teenagers—back before the Pickering Regulations passed to control population growth by only allowing one resurrection choice on a person's eighteenth birthday—but none of us know if it's true or not. I don't think I personally know anyone who's used their choice. The thought makes my stomach clamp down on itself like a steel trap.

Because there it is. The countdown. Ticking away in the back of my brain. Just over three more weeks until my eighteenth birthday, and then . . .

"How about a hint?" I ask, because I want to focus on the good part of my birthday, the part where I get to spend it with my two favorite people in the world. Nothing else.

"So greedy."

"Come on, a pre-pre-birthday present."

Will pauses. He spits some seawater from his mouth. "Your wish is my command." And then he just stops. I feel the grin in his cheeks.

"Yes . . . *and* . . . ?" I prod.

"That's your hint."

I splash him in the face but manage to get myself in the nose just as much as I get him. The salt burns. "That's not a hint, you cheater."

He shrugs and readjusts my weight on his back. "Guess you'll just have to finish the hunt to find out."

I groan. This is so Will. "What kind of hunt?" I whine. "Are we talking treasure, Easter egg . . . *deer*?"

He laughs. "*Deer?* And risk the wrath of Penny?"

The sinking sun spreads golden fingers of light up to the beach. The water grows shallower and I can feel Will bouncing along on his toes to keep our heads above water. I dip a toe down, but it's still too deep for me to stand, so I lay my cheek on Will's warm, sunburned shoulder and close my eyes. "You know you're not as charming as you think you are, Will Bryan," I say with a sigh.

But really all this talk about my great, big, epically magnificent, cowabunga awesome birthday surprise has done is get me thinking of my birthday and what it means. How I'll have to sit alone among strangers in the waiting room, scan my fingerprints, fill out my paperwork for the resurrection, arrange for the body to be brought to the resurrection site, wring my hands while that body lies on a cold metal gurney and is injected by faceless doctors with the lifeblood, then try to breathe while the vitalis process restores the dead cells until they're completely undamaged. I've run through the steps in my mind a thousand times.

And none of this is Will's fault. He doesn't know what I'm planning to do on my eighteenth birthday.

One resurrection, one choice, one person, and unlike Will's and Penny's, mine is already spoken for.

# chapter two

## *23 DAYS*

I unfurl my arms from around Will and together we crawl up to shore. Penny reversed the Jeep so that the wheels are backed up to the sand. She honks the horn and sticks her hand out of the roof, waving us in. Penny has the kind of Jeep without doors or a roof and instead just a roll bar on top. During the summer we practically live in this car, like a band of sand-crusted beach bums.

Will and I trudge up the rest of the shore and climb into the Jeep, sandy feet and all. I take shotgun next to Penny, and Will scoots to the center seat in back so he can poke his head through. Penny wouldn't mind if I sat in back with Will, and I know we're lucky for that. She's not the type of friend to tell us to get a room or to lay off the public displays of affection even though there've been girls at school who've made sidebar remarks to me about how it must be annoying for Will and me to have to cart around a "third wheel" all the time, comments that I'm sure Penny's heard before too. And that's exactly why none of them are my best friends.

Penny has never once made me choose between time with her and time with him. Not that I could possibly. The three of us are like our own little self-sustaining island. We once spent an afternoon negotiating a fake custody arrangement for Penny in case Will and I ever broke up, and I only won primary custody by a hair. The whole exercise made us laugh until Penny peed a little in her shorts and had to run to the bathroom. I mean, Will and I are an institution.

"I can't believe you chickened out." I gently shove Penny's shoulder from my spot in the passenger seat. This is nicer, I decide, than saying *I can totally believe you chickened out, you big chicken*, since Penny's skittish about spiders, global warming, the potential of contracting a deadly virus, and basically anything else I can think of, which is funny since what she doesn't find frightening is sporting fashions that have never been in style, well, *ever*, or making impassioned pleas to save the whales to a roomful of her peers while they are playing Minecraft on their phones. I prefer to let my actions do the talking—it's way simpler.

Penny flicks her gaze to the rearview mirror and slides her unpainted nails down the base of the steering wheel. "I'm like a fine bottle of wine, Lake, I'll be ready in my own time."

I reach over and begin to flip through the radio stations.

"What do you think's going to happen exactly?" I ask. "I mean, you watch us jump. Do you think you're just going to spontaneously combust in midair?"

From the backseat, Will puts his toes up on the console between me and Penny. Penny wrinkles her nose and pushes them back onto the floorboard, then sighs, putting the Jeep into drive and pulling out of the small beach-access road onto a rarely trafficked two-lane highway. "I don't know. I'm scared I'm going to spaz out or not jump far enough, and then I'll just plummet straight down the side of the cliff and, yeah, die. That's the scenario. I'm going to die a gruesome, bloody death. That's what I see every time I step up to the edge," she says, sliding a pair of cat-eye sunglasses over her nose. "Now is that really so far-fetched?"

"Yes," Will and I both answer in unison.

Penny tosses her hair over her shoulders and waves us off. "What took you guys so long anyway?"

Will leans between us. "We were discussing Lake's great, big, epically magnificent, cowabunga awesome birthday surprise. She was trying to pry hints from me, but as you all know, I've got it under lock and key like it's a goddamn national treasure." Will settles himself back into the seat. I look back to see him looking smug. We all know Will is the actual worst at keeping secrets. Far too excitable. In fact, I give him a week on this whole birthday thing, tops.

That's why it's Penny who sneaks a sideways look at me, then reaches over and squeezes my hand. Penny's the only one who knows that, for years, I've been approaching my eighteenth birthday with a sick sense of anxiety. Because she's the only one who knows my resurrection has been earmarked to be used for someone who's not even dead yet.

I squeeze back twice so that she knows I'm fine. I have the two of them.

Penny follows the curve of the road, and the wind begins to air-dry my skin and hair. As if to echo my thoughts, though, we pass a billboard on the side of the road that reads: ARE YOU PREPARED? SUMMER SAVINGS ON CRYOPRESERVATION FOR THE WHOLE FAMILY! The billboard, which features the left half of a beautiful female model's face—skin frosted with beads of ice, frozen crystals glittering from her hair and eyebrows—wasn't there last week. In the last few decades, facilities specializing in cryonics, the process of low-temperature body preservation, have multiplied, giving families a low-cost means to preserve their loved ones while they wait for a member of the family to reach resurrection age. Parents even purchase cryonics insurance for their kids. But lately, I've wanted to ignore the resurrections. They only remind me of death. And so I'm thankful when the advertisement disappears in the distance behind us.

I stare out at the white jasmine that lines the side of the road, interspersed with red and orange wildflowers. We're whizzing along the stretch of road when I feel a tap on my shoulder. I turn to see Will unbuckling his seatbelt.

"What are you—?" I ask.

He tucks his legs underneath him, and pushes himself to stand on the seat, his fingers wrapped around the Jeep's roll bar, gripping tightly.

Penny does a double take in the mirror. "Will!" She stretches her arm back and tugs on his ankle. "Will, get down from there. You're going to make me get a ticket."

But Will tilts his face up to the sun like he's praying.

"Not funny, *William*." Penny looks back at the road. And I can tell she kind of means it. Penny rarely gets mad. Occasionally she and Will get into it about something dumb—bound to happen after eighteen years of friendship—but overall, when it comes to minor annoyances, she's, like, some sort of Zen master.

Will reaches a hand down for me. "Come up here," he says. Fine bits of salt crinkle into the folds of skin around his eyes as he squints in the sun. Sometimes I think that I love Will so much that my heart will combust. It actually embarrasses me, because I know that it's the type of thing that if I tried to put into words would just sound weird and stupid and make both of us uncomfortable. So then I get this feeling of trying to carry it all around in my chest, a feeling that's too big to fit, like a balloon on the brink of being filled with so much helium it pops. Luckily for both of us, Will's the one who's good at this sort of thing, at grand romantic gestures and sappy words that, even though they make me blush or even occasionally cringe, somehow fit him. More than that, they make Will *Will.* Something about the tone and rhythm in the way he speaks that makes it all sound confident, casual, earnest, and innocent at once.

My heart performs a little tap dance in my chest. The air is warm. The water has evaporated from my skin, leaving behind a layer of sea grime. The sky is so saturated with blue, I swear if I could reach up high enough, my finger would come away dripping with it.

And I'm seventeen. There's only three measly weeks left in my life that this will be true. I'm seventeen and this is our last summer together, at least like this, and in three weeks, after my resurrection choice, it'll all be different.

I swallow down the sick feeling that wells in the back of my throat every time I think about my birthday, and grab Will's hand. He'll be starting senior lacrosse practice in a few weeks too, and everything we do has the weight of the last days of our last high school summer ever coloring it. He pulls me to my feet and I grab the bar for support.

The wind blows back my eyelashes and the corners of my mouth, and I can't help but smile because up here it feels as if we've been untethered from the world. I look down into the Jeep's cabin and Penny is shaking her head. But then I feel her hand, warm from the baking steering wheel, snake around my ankle, anchoring me to the spot protectively.

Another car sweeps past us in the opposite direction, honking its horn. Will and I let out rowdy whoops after the car, our voices carried away. Penny digs her fingernails into my ankle and I relent. I latch my hands onto the ledge at the top of the windshield and drop back into my seat. I've learned to listen to Penny when she tells me I'm about to take a stunt too far, because when I haven't, I've wound up with stitches, broken toes—once I nearly knocked out a tooth. A couple of seconds after, Will lands safely in the backseat. I can feel the happy flush in my cheeks as I click my seatbelt into place. Will spreads his arms across the top of the entire backseat and puffs out his bare chest like he's king of the whole car.

Penny turns the music down a few decibels. "My mom will freak out if I get pulled over, you guys," she says in her calm but meaningful voice. It's true, Tessa is wonderful, but you do not want to cross her.

"Sorry, Pen." I squeeze her shoulder and the crease in her forehead disappears. Because in the same way she's there to make sure I don't go too far, I make sure she lives beyond the confines of that beautiful brain of hers. The world just isn't as scary as she thinks. "From this point forward, we'll keep our butts planted firmly in our seats."

The road back to town is twisty, the kind that, if you're prone to motion sickness, turns your insides to slime.

"Where's your phone?" Will leans between us and asks Penny when the song changes over to a hair-removal commercial. "Put on that playlist I made."

"What playlist?" I ask.

Penny sticks her hand into the cup holder. "I could have sworn it was in there. Shoot, I hope I didn't leave it on the—" Penny pops open the center console and torques her back only a fraction to look into the cubby. "Found it," she sings out, retrieving her cell.

It's a split second. That's all it takes. Her hand shifts the wheel to the left. At the same time, half a ton of metal in the shape of a silver Lexus is barreling toward us in the opposite direction.

"Penny!" I shriek. But she jerks the wrong way and the other car charges toward us like a bull.

We're going to hit it. The thought is so obvious and sharp in my mind, it's as if someone has said it out loud. I feel Will jolt to attention behind me.

The moment stretches. I never knew how long a single moment could be even as it occurs to me that if it were any amount of time at all this situation—this *problem*—could be fixed.

A horn wails. The sound of screeching tires fills the perfectly warm blue-blue sky and I know that this is going to hurt with a certainty that drills down into my still-intact bones. The space between the two pairs of headlights vanishes.

When the hoods make contact, my head slams forward. Glass splinters. Screams ring through the roar of crunching hardware. We spin to the side and I'm reminded of the tea-cup rides at the fair. There's a violent lurch. On my end of the car, the wheels jump off the pavement and the Jeep flips onto its side. I throw my hands over my head.

Pain shoots through my wrist and elbow as we flip upside down. Something clamps over my chest. Hard, jagged edges rake the top of my scalp. My vision goes blurry. At last, the movement stops, but the melody of tinkling glass lingers even as the last sliver of conscious thought is wiped from my mind and I sink down into nothing.

# chapter three
## *22 DAYS*

This is not the end, I tell myself as I struggle for the surface, kicking and fighting against an invisible weight. If I were dead, there'd be no pain, I figure.

So I hold tight to the deep, throbbing ache in my arm and the soreness that encases my whole body like a straitjacket.

If I were dead, there'd be no beeping. I listen to the electronic chirp of a machine and, once convinced, I open my eyes to find that I've guessed right and that, yes, I'm alive.

And as my eyes adjust to the light, I spot the lump of my legs underneath a thin blue sheet. Baby blue. I always thought hospital sheets were white. Across the room there's a sink and a biohazards waste dispenser fastened to the wall below an illustrated poster of a nurse washing her hands.

Seafoam-green curtains hang from a single window. The ceilings are speckled white tile. A clear tube snakes out of my arm. I cling to each of these details as evidence that the room I'm in is real, that I'm real. I'm pleased at how quickly I recognize where I am. I take this as a good sign. My brain works.

It takes another second to realize that this also means the accident was real.

My mind keeps going fuzzy and in and out of focus like a camera lens. I feel very light on the mattress. The only image I can conjure from the last day is of glass glittering off the asphalt.

It hurts when I swallow. It also hurts to sit.

I stare at my toes and tell them to wiggle. When they do, I breathe a sigh of relief that scrapes at my raw throat.

The whir of a wheelchair sounds like a robotic bee approaching. I think I must be too doped up to startle. My brother puffs into the contraption to guide his chair since he doesn't have the use of his arms or legs. The whole apparatus spins to face me, and for a second my heart no longer feels like it's being choked out and I'm a little sister again with someone there to protect me.

"Hi," I say, weakly.

"Don't worry," he says, and the feeling of security vanishes so that it's like I'm being dropped flat and hard onto a cold surface as I remember who it is the two of us have become. "You haven't turned out like me."

I peer back down at my toes. "I wasn't—" I begin to protest, but Matt rolls his eyes, his favorite—okay, one of his only—expressions.

"Please. I still go for the toe wiggle myself." He peers down his nose. "Nope, nothing. Ah, well, there's always tomorrow, right?" His left cheek dimples with a sly, cruel smile that I should be used to by now. He's wearing a heather-gray sweatshirt that's baggy around the chest and arms. The blond in his hair disappeared a long time ago, as though someone had colored over it with a darker crayon, and now only his eyelashes, pale against even paler skin, are leftover reminders of a boy who spent summers on the beach and autumns out on his dinghy collecting crab traps.

"Where are Mom and Dad anyway?" I ask, staring straight ahead at the empty wall in front of me.

"They went downstairs for coffee. They're going to piss their pants when they find out they missed you waking up."

I attempt to scratch my nose and discover that a plaster cast covers my left arm from my knuckles to an inch above my elbow. That explains some of the throbbing.

"How long have I been out?" I ask, ignoring the piss statement. I tend to keep things formal when it comes to my brother. Conventional wisdom says we're supposed to be extra nice to people with disabilities, which means that when it comes to Matt, I should be a saint. He's a C-2 complete quadriplegic, practically the king of disabilities.

"Eight hours or so," Matt says. "Gave me a real scare, Lakey Loo." He uses the nickname he gave to me when I was a kid. I mask a wince. It sounds mocking when he says it now. "Don't forget. Without you, there's no resurrection for me. You're my golden ticket, Willy Wonka."

I let my head fall to the side and glare at him. "You'll get your resurrection, but thanks a lot for the concern." He knows I hate to be reminded of the deal he made with my parents. If he lived until my eighteenth birthday, they would help him die so that I could use my resurrection choice on him and he could return able-bodied thanks to the restorative work of vitalis. After he'd attempted to self-destruct by driving his wheelchair off a flight of stairs more than once, they agreed. I wasn't asked my opinion.

He stares back, his expression unreadable. Matt has a way of going blank when he wants to, as though his face were paralyzed along with the rest of him. It's infuriating.

I go back to looking at the wall since that at least seems preferable. It turns out this day totally sucks. If Penny's mom was going to kill her for getting a ticket, she's going to freak when she finds out Penny flipped the Jeep.

*The Jeep.* I drum the fingers of my good hand against the plastic rail of the hospital bed. RIP.

I groan at our misfortune. Our parents will look at us and say, *It could have been so much worse.*

I hate that. It could always be worse. We could be starving kids in Africa. That doesn't change the fact that we made a lot of great memories in that car and now it's going to be junkyard food. We won't even get to give it a proper sendoff.

Tears well up in my eyes. Stupid, I tell myself. Stupid, stupid, stupid. Penny is going to be *so* upset. I bite down on my tongue until I can taste blood like nickels in my mouth, and the tears vanish before they can spill over onto my cheeks.

"When can I see them?" As soon as I ask, a pounding starts up behind my eye sockets.

"Who? Mom and Dad?" The signature smart-aleck laugh creeps into Matt's voice. "I'm sure they'll be back in, like, five seconds. Chill. You're still their favorite child." You would think that Matt's condition would have made him ultrasensitive in times of crisis, but it's the exact opposite. It's like he called dibs on all the world's bad luck and no one else is entitled to feel sorry for a damn thing.

"No." I jut my jaw out and speak through gritted teeth. "Will and Penny. Are they here too?" I push the heel of my left hand between my eyebrows and close my eyes, mimicking one of Penny's deep, cleansing breaths. Maybe I got the worst of it and they didn't have to come to the hospital at all. I'd heard of that happening. People walking away from car wrecks without much more than a scrape and a couple of bruises.

I feel a wave of nausea. My pulse rams into my temples and nasal cavity. I try to shake it away. Is there a call button? A nurse? Someone to bring pain medication?

Matt watches, observing me. I catch a hint of an expression that is unknowable to me and has been for years now. I have no way of perceiving what would make him happy or sad anymore since everything just makes him angry. Faster than I can memorize it, that brief, very human expression disappears.

"Seriously?" He scoffs and looks off to the side, like, *Can you believe this girl?* "You do realize you hit a car dead-on, right? I mean you were *there*. Doctor What's-His-Face said you were probably conscious through most of it. I figured you already knew."

"Knew what?" My tone comes out snappy and peeved. I regret it instantly. It's an unwritten rule in my family: when it comes to Matt, we don't retaliate, we tolerate.

A quick frown that I might have missed if I hadn't known him for almost eighteen years crosses his face. Then the creases at the corners of his eyes flatten as I hear his familiar, sarcastic laugh. His brown eyes turn hard beneath the shadow of his cap. "They're dead," he says, and it's as if a fist has punched through a brown paper bag, and with it my chest crumples.

"You're lying," I tell him. "You are *so* lying."

He doesn't argue. Instead he sips and puffs at the sippy straw, moving the wheels of his chair backward and forward in tiny measured increments.

The handle on the door turns. Mom comes in first, a muffin in one hand and a to-go cup of coffee in the other.

Her hands are full, but she uses the one with the muffin to cover her mouth anyway. Crumbs scatter to the floor. "You're awake. Oh, honey." Every familiar wrinkle on her face cuts deeper, becomes more pronounced. My mom wears her hair pulled into a ponytail with a large barrette made of shiny white shells. "We're so sorry we weren't here."

All the while there's a pressure building in my chest like a teakettle and I know she must misread my expression, because she looks so happy—weepy, maybe—but genuinely joyous and I sense that this is wrong. All wrong.

Before my dad can shut the door, I reach my boiling point. "*Dead?*" I shriek. "They're *dead*?"

Their faces freeze in matching masks of horror. Mom's hand begins to shake and coffee burbles out from under the lid of the cup. There's a flash of disgust when she peers down her nose at my brother, but it's gone too, before I can take a mental snapshot. "Why, Matthew," she says, flatly.

My dad isn't a tall man. In fact, he's the same height as my mother, slight and sinewy from miles of flat-road biking on the weekends, but he draws himself up to his full stature. "Lake," he says, his voice deeper than normal. But he doesn't need to finish. It only takes that one syllable to know it's true. They're gone.

I fold my body in half. The needles buried in my skin tug at the veins in my arms when I sink my head into my hands.

"Lake, listen," Dad says. There's a weight on the mattress beside me, and the smell of sandalwood aftershave. "They did everything they could."

And all of a sudden it's there. A fully formed snapshot. Penny thrown from the car. Her leg splayed at an unnatural angle. Will pinned by the waist underneath the side of the Jeep, a sickly red creeping out from his back that I tried hard to mistake for the flashing red lights of the ambulance.

Mom rubs my back. "The paramedics brought Will back to the hospital, sweetie, but there was too much damage. There was nothing they could do." Her tone is soft and soothing, like she's singing me a lullaby, and I wonder if that's the thing that will haunt me forever. That delicate singsong voice that crooned to me my worst nightmares.

My chin snaps up. "Will's here?" This means that Penny had died on the scene, but Will still might be near.

My parents look through me to each other as if I'm a little kid. "Yes, but—" my dad begins.

"Where? Where is he?" Now I do sound like a child, a petulant, naughty child, and I slam my fists into the mattress so that both my parents bobble for balance. Pain shoots through my right elbow.

Dad clears his throat, trying to assume his position as head of the household. "He passed away, Lake. He's gone."

"I want to see him," I say. "Get me out of these." I pick at the tape holding the IVs in place. My dad flattens his hand over mine to stop me and I feel the familiar bits of sticky residue left over from the grip tape of his handlebars. I glare down, tears blurring my vision. Droplets fall from my nose, leaving splashes of salt water on my paper gown.

Mom's hand is on my shoulder. I flinch. The need to see

Will is overwhelming. The fact that he's dead is somehow beside the point, but to explain this to my parents would require more words than I have in me.

What I need is to hold his hand, to press my cheek to his, to lean down and smell salt water and coconut. The moments of Will in his perfect Will-ness are slipping and I don't know where he'll go. He's the only rope left to latch onto.

"Just let me go." I hurl my body to either side. Both my parents grunt on impact before Dad grabs hold of me in a tight hug.

"Will's family needs to . . . they need to be alone right now." There's a hitch in my dad's voice that makes my entire body go limp. *But I'm part of his family*, I want to say. *Me.*

But my muscles are sandbag heavy and I slump into his arms instead. The fight drains out of me as I snot and sob into his shirt. The machine attached to me continues to beep incessantly, which is the only way I can convince myself this isn't a horrible dream.

A hiccup racks my chest. I wipe the slug trail coming from my nose with the back of my hand. "I'm going to bring them back," I say. "They're going to come back and it'll be okay," I continue while rocking in place. "I'm almost eighteen." I glance toward the window, through the angled blinds. Slivers of thin light X-ray the morning clouds, and I count the days until my birthday.

Mom's palms are warm on my cheeks. She holds my face and looks me squarely in the eyes. "Lake," she says. "You know you can only have one."

"No," I say. Tears drip from the sides of my nostrils. My chin trembles. "No, Mom, there's an exception. There has to be an exception." She tries to lean in to kiss my forehead, but I tear myself away. "Give me my phone. Where's my phone? Did you bring our tablet? We need to start doing research. Dad, help."

I feel around the hospital bed, searching for the cold, slick glass of my cell phone. Maybe there is some kind of application. Some seminal court case I've never read about. Some instance where, I don't know, twins died and it was deemed too inhumane to bring back only one.

The bed's empty. My dad brings my head into his chest and holds the side of my face to him. I can hear his heart beating underneath his shirt. "There aren't any exceptions, Lake. That's the law. You can only choose one. Just one. Always."

"But how do you know?"

My dad sighs. "Trust us, Lake. We know." And he sounds very sad when he says this, because despite all the strides that science has made, despite the fact that what's known as the "lifeblood," injected as part of the vitalis process, can regenerate fully dead cells to health, it has still managed to fail my brother and now the process will fail me too.

He doesn't let go of me. I try to match my breaths to his. Try and fail. In the background, I recognize the robotic buzz of my brother's wheelchair and, when my dad releases me, I look over to see that Matt has turned his back to us and is now waiting at the door.

# chapter four

## *1,582 DAYS*

I didn't know that people could break until Matt was already broken.

The actual breaking, as in the fracture of the bones, happened sometime in the last few weeks. I can't pinpoint the timeline anymore. The details feel hazy the farther we get from the event, like I'm trying to nail down something small on my calendar and I can't remember exactly which day I did it on.

It feels as though I'm outside bulletproof glass that's ten feet thick while the rest of my family is on the inside. For endless days my parents have busied in and out of Matt's room. Often they'll gently tell me to stay out of the way. It's a sensitive time after all. And they treat me like I'm an acquaintance who has brought a tuna casserole to a funeral instead of their daughter and Matt's only sister.

As a result, the days are long and boring. Mom breaks

the news to me that I'll be on some sort of bereavement leave for the rest of the school year and I'll have to study independently for my finals. When I tell her I don't want to take time off school, she says that it's for the best, and the discussion ends there because I don't want to be a pain about it.

In regular life, we play along with reruns of *Family Feud* on Thursday nights. The winners get desserts, the losers have to serve them. This Thursday, we don't.

Mom always comes to read magazines on my bed in the morning while I take a shower and get dressed. But now she's never there.

Instead, the three of them talk in Matt's room for hours, in low murmurs that never crystallize into words. Nobody invites me to this new family of three. Jenny finds a new best friend since I'm not at school anymore and, without my parents to drive me around, we both stop trying to stay in touch.

I scroll through web pages, reading all the articles on quadriplegia that I can find. That's the diagnosis for Matt since the accident. The specifics are bleak. Total loss of function for all four limbs. Impairment in controlling bowel and bladder movements. Spasticity. Loss of sexual function. I try to gloss over that last one.

The prognosis—that's the medical term for Matt's disease forecast—is even worse. Bed sores. Frozen joints. Respiratory complications and infections. Something they're calling deep vein thrombosis that I don't quite understand but which sounds terrible.

But none of these things seem real to me because I can't see Matt.

I don't know what day of the week it is, only that it's mid-May, and the humidity has already been gradually creeping indoors, where it leaves a slippery film of sweat on every surface. I get up the guts to knock on the door. The voices behind it stop, but no one answers to let me in. My mom, my dad, and Matt are all in one room and nobody calls for me to join them.

My throat goes tight and my eyes prick with tears. I wait five, ten minutes before retreating.

The house feels extra big with everyone but me living in Matt's bedroom. I'm alone with an ache in my chest that won't go away.

Tonight, I lie awake in my bed, idly turning over the inhaler in my hands. I haven't needed it since I stopped going to soccer practice, a change that happened when I quit going to that school. I've been able to breathe deeply and easily even after I've been crying for a couple of hours.

I'm waiting for my dad to turn off the television and for my mom to get her last glass of water for the night. When my eyes start to close, I pinch my arms to stay awake.

Eventually, it's just the sound of the ocean outside. A relentless roar. Mom used to say that what she loved about the ocean is that each morning it brought along a fresh start. Whether you left footprints, a sandcastle, or words printed in the beach, the next day they'd be gone and what you'd be left with was a clean slate, like the beach had scars the water could heal. In science class they taught us that this process was called "erosion." The water wasn't healing the beach at all, but tearing bits of it away. I like Mom's version better, and I listen to the sound of the waves, wishing that they could heal us too.

I crawl out of bed wearing a big sleep shirt that goes down to my knees. The long hallway between my room and Matt's is spooky. The tile is cold under my feet. Tucked underneath my armpit is a paperback copy of *The Chocolate War.* The book's been earmarked at page 176. It's not that I can't read it myself. I'm thirteen. I know how to read. But I've never been much of a reader. This only changes when Matt chooses a specific book for me and when it's something we do together. Funny that with my stuffy lungs and asthma, I'm the athletic one and Matt's the sibling with his nose always in a book. I have a sick thought that I wish instantly to take back. What I think is that maybe the universe knew what it was doing when it made Matt the way he is—an *intellectual,* as my dad would say. But that would mean that Matt was meant to get paralyzed, and I know that can't be right.

I'm nervous in a way that I've never been to see my brother. I knock softly on his door, three times. There's no answer. I'm afraid that if I knock again, Mom and Dad will wake up and tell me not to bug him.

So I turn the knob and slip through the dark crack. His room smells unfamiliar, like old rubber and medical equipment.

In the corner, I can make out the bulky outline of the new robo-technology wheelchair, creepy in its emptiness. It even has a robotic arm that Matt is eventually supposed to be able to use to pick up basic items, but he hasn't learned how yet.

"Matt?" I hiss through the darkness, careful of where I step. No answer. "Matt?" I tiptoe to the far side of his bed, where the open curtains allow a trickle of moonlight to paint swatches of his bed sheets silver. It's still quiet. The lumpy form under the covers doesn't move. I place my hands gently on his chest and shake him. Matt still doesn't move. "Matt, wake up."

"What, Lake?" I can't tell whether his voice sounds groggy or not.

I draw back my hand and clam up. I remember a time when I was only five or six and Matt had the flu. Mom didn't want me catching it, so she kept shooing me from his room, but I had painted him a picture that I wanted him to have. So I snuck in when she was doing laundry, only for some reason when I got there, I became deathly shy all of a sudden and dropped the picture on his lap and ran. I glance at it still pinned to the wall behind Matt's desk and try to be brave. This time I can't catch what Matt has, but it's so much worse.

"It's me. Lake," I say, when saying something becomes preferable to saying nothing at all.

A small laugh.

"I had to come see you," I say.

"Oh." His voice is a whisper in the dark.

"I'm going to crawl up. Hang on." I have to push past the awkwardness before literally pushing him to the side. The bed is taller than I'm used to. He has a mattress that mechanically raises and lowers now, the same as the ones in hospitals. His legs and arms are floppy when I move them, but after some grunts and groans on my part I've made enough room to nestle in beside him.

We both just lie there for I don't know how long. For some reason I thought his body would feel cold and dead and am relieved to find that it's warm next to mine.

"Does it hurt?" I ask at last.

He grunts. "Sometimes."

"Like . . . where?"

A pause. "Like, everywhere."

"Matt." I turn onto my side. The mattress creaks beneath my weight. "Nobody will tell me what happened. Mom and Dad keep treating me like a little kid or something."

He sighs an impatient *Why are you here?* sigh. "What do you think happened, Lake?"

"You had an accident." This is the only thing I know. *Matt's paralyzed. He won't recover. We have to take care of him now.* That's all my parents told me. End of story.

"I . . . fell."

"Doing what?" I ask.

"Does it matter?"

"Yes."

He sighs again. Why is he so annoyed with me already? "Out of a tree, Lake. I fell from a tree."

I swallow so hard, I know that we can both hear it. Matt must feel dumb for falling out of a tree and that must be the reason he sounds so irritated, not because of me, I tell myself.

"It's going to be okay." I put my hand on his hand, but I'm not sure whether he can feel it. I hadn't thought to look that part up.

"Easy for you to say." He lets out an angry laugh I haven't heard before.

I'm hurt, wounded, but I try to think of the stupid tree, not myself. Matt *will* be okay. Maybe not in the way he wants to, but he will be. He has me. I push closer to him until it feels like our sides are sewn together and we could be one person.

"You know they were trying to cure paralysis?" Matt

says out loud, even though I'm not sure he's really talking to me. But then again, who else would he be talking to?

I hadn't considered this possibility. "They will!" I say excitedly. "Of course they will."

"No. When they discovered the vitalis process. It was an accident. They were trying to cure *paralysis*. How fucked up is that?" I've never heard my brother say the F-word. "They thought, 'Hey, if we can just regenerate the cells in the disabled nerves, then whoop-dee-doo, we'll be able to get a body working again.'"

We don't get to study resurrections until eighth grade, and everyone has a different opinion about them, so my parents say it's not something I should bring up in polite conversation, like politics and religion. "But . . . doesn't it regenerate dead cells?" I venture, confused.

"Sure." There's the angry laugh again. "But it doesn't stop there, it spreads and regenerates every fucking cell it touches until it's wiped the whole body. Kills the live ones, cures the dead ones. Hooray for science."

I don't know what to say. I think what Matt needs is time. And hope. And probably me. I shimmy to a sitting position, excited that I came equipped with my very own distraction. "Guess what? We're not finished with *The Chocolate War*," I interject.

"Lake, I can't read it to you."

"Sure you can." I reach over and flip on the lamp. I hear Matt wince. He squeezes his eyes shut. Without meaning to, I let out a small gasp. A catheter bag filled with Matt's urine is sitting on the other side of the bed from me. There's no way Matt can cover it himself. More than that, he looks pale, with deep grooves cut into the hollows of his eyes. His hair is greasy. My voice rasps. "Nothing's wrong with your eyes, Matt."

He opens them and stares up at the ceiling. "I said that I can't."

"Fine." I split the spine open to the dog-eared page. "Then I'll read it to you."

"I didn't invite you in here." There's a snap to his tone that stops me cold, mouth open, ready to begin the first word of chapter twenty-five. "You just busted in."

"Yeah, because Mom and Dad wouldn't let me in to see you."

"It wasn't Mom and Dad, Lake."

"But—" His meaning dawns on me too late.

"*I* didn't want to see you." My mouth goes dry. "There's nothing you can do to help. There's nothing anyone can do to help. I'd be better off if... if I were dead." He chokes on the word. "Now can you please... Can you please just get out, Lake? You're annoying me. Don't you get that? I'm tired right now. I just... I just want to be alone."

There are no words. I try to tell myself that this is just the dumb tree talking. That Matt will get over it. He'll have time to heal on the inside and things will be different. Quietly, I close my book and slide off the bedside.

And as surely as I tell myself that Matt needs time, I know that my heart has already begun to fracture—irreparably—just like his spine.

# chapter five

## *19 DAYS*

I wonder if for the rest of my life, I'll be haunted by beautiful days. I wonder if I'll look out on a cloudless sky splashed with sunshine, hear the roar of the ocean, feel wind tickling my face—then just when I start to fill up with happiness, stop short on a single moment. I'll remember the blood and the gore and the sadness and the death that the nice day might be hiding just underneath its sparkling surface, waiting to spiral and spread like a drop of red in water before it taints the whole glass. And almost everything will look like a mirage, wavering and waiting to disappear the second I get too close.

From the breakfast table I stare out over an uneaten bowl of oatmeal at the beachfront behind our house. Splashes of water turn to foam between the jetty rocks. I'm trying to cling to snapshot images of Will and Penny, alive and happy, but each time I try, they keep dancing away, as fleeting as the whitecaps that dot the sea.

*"Lake?"*

My elbow hurts. My back hurts. My neck hurts. My heart hurts. And not in that order. I stir the congealed oats before letting the spoon clatter into the bowl. *"Lake?"* I've been hearing Will's words as an echo since the accident: *Your wish is my command.* How many days has it been, anyway? Three, four, maybe five? I wish for you to be alive, Will. That's what I wish for. *Your wish is my command.* That's the only thing that I wish for. I pick up the spoon from the bowl and watch the oatmeal fall plop, plop, plop.

"What do you think he meant?" I murmur out loud.

My mom clears her throat. "What do I think who meant by what?"

I blink. My vision adjusts from the faraway plane to the one two feet in front of me where my parents stare from a couple of seats away at the table. Have they been hovering this whole time?

I exhale. "Will. Just...something he said." Because I can't expect them to have the answer. "Something to do with my birthday." I glance between them and wrinkle my forehead. "What's today?" I ask, trying to remember. "Is it a weekend? Shouldn't you be biking or at work or something?" I say to my dad.

Dad stopped golfing with his friends after Matt's accident, but he found an old road bike in the garage and he started riding that—obsessively, it seemed—for hours on end. But when he'd get back from his routes, he'd be calmer, friendlier, and so Mom kept taking care of Matt during those hours too, even though she had to do it all week as well.

That's why her clothes are always several years out of style and she never updates her haircut.

It sounds bad to say this, but I understand my dad more for his bike outings than my mom for her unflagging ability to care for my brother.

"It's Tuesday," he says.

Then my dad touches Mom's elbow and it seems to give her the courage to speak. "Honey." She's using her Matt voice on me. "Maybe those questions can wait. Your father and I want to talk to you."

I blink again. I can't seem to focus on these two. I return to staring out the window. I imagine Penny and me out on the stretch of private beach doing cartwheels until we get dizzy.

"Sweetie, we need you to try to focus." I can tell Dad's trying to strike a balance between gentle and stern.

"Sorry," I say.

My mom puts her hand over mine and pulls it into her chest. "Lake, please, we know this is an extremely sensitive time, but there were some things you said in the hospital about resurrecting Will and Penny and we just want to make sure that... well, that you know that's not possible."

*This.* It would be easier to swallow shards of glass. But of course they're right. *One.* I'm going to have to make a choice.

"I know," I mumble and glance down at the table and then at our clasped hands. I can't have them both, I add silently. *This* is my new reality.

Her smile is small and weak, but there's a hint of pride there too. "We don't want anyone to get the wrong idea."

I shift to the edge of my seat. My mother's eyes are

gray this morning, and sad. It's early and I know she'll have already changed Matt's catheter bag and given him a sponge bath in bed.

"Who do you mean by 'anyone'?"

She grips my fingers more tightly. "Lake, we love you so, so much. We're here for you." She looks up at my dad and he wraps his arm around her shoulder and squeezes her arm before returning the full weight of his attention to me. Meanwhile, a coldness spreads underneath my ribs. "What we mean to say is, while we know Will and Penny were your best friends, Matt is your brother."

My gaze hardens. The chill turns icy and begins creeping out into my limbs.

Dad must decide that it's finally time to take his turn, because he starts talking. "In the hospital, you mentioned resurrecting Will or Penny." Calm, methodical, laying out the facts for me. "We know the news was a shock to you, but we also know that *you* know"—he tilts his head toward me—"that you've already promised your resurrection choice. Isn't that right?"

My mouth is numb. "To Matt?"

The right answer. Dad nods. Pleased. "Yes, to Matt." But then he must catch my expression—honestly, it's a mystery to me what my face looks like, but I'm guessing it's not good. "We've had this agreement." His voice goes down an octave.

Matt. Dead. Me. Alive. The thought of my brother killing himself on purpose because *I* said he could has always made me feel sweaty under my arms. But now it's making me downright nauseated.

"But... but... that was before, though."

His Adam's apple bobs in his throat. "Yes, that was before Penny and Will died, we know."

I shake my head. "*No*, that was before Matt told me my two best friends died, the same way—the same way he might have told me my *goldfish* had gone belly up." My pitch is rising. I feel my cheeks turning hot. I set my cast on the table and it bangs loudly.

I know in the depths of my soul that these are the words that have been brewing, but I am surprised to be able to say them out loud so easily. The truth is, I'm not even sure I *love* Matt. Not after everything.

"But—" Mom curls her now empty hands into her lap.

I bolt from my chair. I would bolt from my skin if I could, but I'm stuck in it, so I make do. It feels good to tower over them. "Matt's *alive*. There's a big difference. If he wants to live his life as a complete ass-face, well then that's his business, but at least he's breathing. At least he has a chance."

Mom takes a sharp breath. "You don't understand—"

"*You* don't understand. Lots of people are disabled, Mom. And they have perfectly happy lives."

"Yes, and lots of people are—"

"Don't." Dad cuts over her. I'm breathing hard, but I let him speak. "Lake, I know these are tough choices." His reasonableness makes me want to punch him in the nose.

"Yeah. Yeah. They're tough choices." I jab my thumb into my sternum. "They're *my* tough choices. I should never have let you try to make them for me in the first place." My face is wet now.

Mom covers her mouth. She's shaking her head slowly

and I'm watching her face break open like an egg. "Lake, Lake, honey." She opens her arms like she's ready to wrap me up and pet my hair the way that she used to, and now I'm just wishing she had never stopped reading magazines on my bed while I got ready in the morning. "We're sorry. We—we're sorry."

I don't go to her. I just stare, mouth open. However I feel about Matt, I do love my parents, deeply, because I know they're only doing their best. But all of a sudden, loving them and loving Penny and Will feel like currents pulling me in opposite directions.

Dad looks to her. He places his hand on her shoulder. She sinks into the seat back. I catch a small nod. "You're right, Lake." His voice is gravelly. "You're . . . absolutely right. But—" I tense and he holds his palm out to stay me. "Bear with me. Will, Penny, or . . . well . . . you're going to be dealing with loss. We've spoken with your doctors and we think it's important for you to see a therapist." I start to protest. I'm sensing a trap. He cuts me off. "Right away. You're young. This kind of trauma, it's very real."

"I don't need to talk to a stranger to know that."

"Maybe it will provide some clarity for you."

I soften. He doesn't mention Matt. He doesn't insist on the promise I made. The promise I already know I'm not keeping. Matt is alive. My friends are not. There can't be a more stark distinction. Meanwhile my head is spinning, with nowhere to land.

"Please," he says. "This one thing. For us." And that's the line that gets me.

My jaw clenches. I want to talk to Penny, not some

shrink who knows nothing about my friends, who knows nothing about anything. But despite everything, despite how for years it's felt like Matt, my mom, and my dad have formed their own family and forgotten to ask me to be in it, despite that, I *still* don't want to hurt them. "Fine," I say. And then I add, "But that's the only thing I'm doing."

# chapter six

## 19 DAYS

I need some air. And some space. Miles and miles of each if I could get it. I can't. Or, rather, even if I could there's no running away from what's happened.

So, it's a small thing, but I convince my parents I can drive myself to the therapy appointment that it turns out they had already booked for me. A few days ago, when I needed to get away from my family, I could run to Penny and Will. Now there's only this. I can tell my parents are trying to do "the right thing" and are struggling to figure out what exactly that means. I don't blame them. There's no handbook.

The heat fumes off the asphalt and snakes around my ankles. I drop my sunglasses into the seat behind me before I close the door and squint up at the sky, which is exactly as blue as it was on the day of the car wreck.

That's the problem. None of this seems real, because the

world's not cooperating. I keep getting this feeling, like I'm just waking up from a nightmare, when actually I'm still living in it. Even the building of Garretson, Smith & McKenna looks more like a law firm than a psychology practice. I'm already starting to sweat by the time I cross the lot and push through the glass door into a blast of air-conditioning.

I have to blink several times to adjust to the artificial light, and I'm rubbing at my eye sockets as I approach the linoleum countertop with the sliding window. A middle-aged woman slides open the Plexiglas between us. "Name, please?"

"Lake Devereaux?" I say it as a question. My heart rate has already picked up its pace to that of a brisk jog. I try to relax by pinching the pressure point between my thumb and pointer finger, another Penny technique, but I've had what doctors call "white coat syndrome" ever since I was a kid and so my blood pressure skyrockets the second I'm in a doctor's office. Even one where there are no needles involved.

The woman tap-tap-taps her keyboard. "First visit?" she asks without looking at me.

I shift my weight in my sandals. "Yes, ma'am." I rest my cast on the countertop in front of me and pick at the cottony inside near the knuckles while she finishes finger pecking. Finally, the woman slides a clipboard in front of me. She frowns at my cast. "Can you write with that, hon'?" she asks.

I nod. "I'm right-handed."

"Dr. McKenna will take that from you when she calls you back." The glass slides into place, like a limo divider, letting me know that the conversation's over.

I find a seat in the waiting room, which is empty but for one person, a boy around my age bent over a magazine.

I choose a chair along the opposite wall so that two rows of chairs separate us. This feels like proper waiting-room etiquette. Particularly in a therapist's office.

I slip the pen from the top of the clipboard balanced on my lap and begin jotting down answers.

*Current medications?* I hesitate, then write *None.*

I used to carry an inhaler with me everywhere I went, but I haven't needed it in years. My parents say I must have outgrown it, that when I quit playing soccer my lungs had a chance to recover.

*Anti-depressives? No.*

*Suicidal thoughts? Never.*

*Self-harm? Never.*

*Family history of clinical depression?*

I think about Matt. Does it count if he had extenuating circumstances? Depression hardly seems genetic when it stems from paralysis. I quickly scribble *No* as my response. Because I suppose becoming a world-class jerk is a different thing from being depressed . . . right?

God, I'm already regretting agreeing to this.

From the other side of the room there's a rustle of pages, footsteps, and then a shadow crosses on the ground in front of me. Without lifting my chin, I glance up from my clipboard to see that the other waiting-room occupant has moved to a chair just across and one to the right of mine. He has reopened his magazine and is now hunched over with his elbows on his knees flipping through the glossy insides. Dark hair falls down over his forehead.

Okay . . . I think, shaking my head and returning my eyes to the questionnaire.

How many items are on this thing anyway? I lift the page and peek underneath. Double-sided.

The boy sitting across from me clears his throat. I jot down another answer. Then, he clears his throat again. Keeping my head down, I close my eyes and pull in a deep breath. The aisle between us is narrow and his body feels close, like he's punctured the carefully drawn boundaries of my personal space. Obviously *he* knows nothing about waiting room etiquette. By the third time that he clears his throat I press the clipboard down onto my lap and sit up, startled to find a pair of blue eyes trained on me. It takes only another quarter second for my own eyes to trace the outline of an angry red birthmark that covers the top quadrant of his face, from the middle of his forehead and down the bridge of his nose until it falls off to the left, cuts partway down his cheekbone, and recedes into his hairline, just below the temple. The effect reminds me of a picture book that my mom used to read to me as a kid featuring a dog named Spot.

*Damn,* I think. I *know* this face.

I press my lips into a thin line, the way I do when I make eye contact with somebody I don't know in the grocery store and quickly glance away. Too quickly, I realize.

But he won't recognize me, I tell myself. It's been too long, too many years, and I don't have a mark as easily recognizable as his.

The boy sitting opposite me is one I went to elementary school with very briefly. All the kids in our class pretended he had some infectious disease because of the birthmark on his face. Nobody would go near him except for this weird smelly girl with constantly dirty tights that you could always see because she kept taking off her shoes. What are the odds?

I can still feel his stare on me and it makes me fidget in my seat.

*Psychopath*, I want to say, but instead I curl my legs into the chair underneath me.

"They don't really read those, you know," the boy says, giving no indication that he knows we've met before.

"Oh?" I raise my eyebrows before turning back to the long list of questions that fill the page. This time, I'm careful not to stare at the birthmark.

I try to focus on the next question, begin to write an answer and then scribble it out.

"I'm telling you." I hear the magazine flip shut. "There's no point. Dr. McKenna—you're with Dr. McKenna, right?—will take the clipboard from you and set it on her desk, never to be looked at again. End of story."

"Is that so?" I say, instantly annoyed. I bite my tongue and soldier on through the next series of checkboxes, if for no other reason than as a semipolite means to avoid having a conversation in the waiting room of my soon-to-be therapist.

"You're wasting your time. . . ." He clucks his tongue and raps his fingers across the closed magazine.

I sigh and, relenting, look up. "How do you know?" I ask, this time unable to avoid looking at the raspberried skin. I don't recall whether he was this annoying back in grade school. Probably that's why he didn't have any friends, I muse, making myself feel the tiniest bit better about being a shallow kid some-odd years ago.

He glances down at his lap for a split second and then angles his face slightly away, like he had noticed me noticing.

"Well, for one, I'm *pretty* much an expert in all things psychotherapy. Not to brag, of course. For two, I filled out the entire questionnaire as though I were Count Dracula. Medication: 'O' Negative. Allergies: Garlic, the sun, holy water. She never said a word." He sits back and looks directly at me again. "Same thing at the other place I used to go to. Dr. McKenna's way better, though. Trust me."

"Interesting." I nod. "Or maybe she just didn't want to give you the satisfaction." And then I pointedly return to filling out the column of checkboxes.

"Ah, I get it," he says. "You must have OCD or something. Is that why you're in here?"

I set the pen down hard on the clipboard. "No," I say through gritted teeth. "I'm not . . . obsessive-compulsive. I'm just *following* instructions." *And I'd like to be left alone,* I add silently, although I think my tone more than implies it.

"Okay." He tosses the magazine in the empty chair beside him. "What are you in for, then?"

"Excuse me?"

"What are you in for? What's gone so haywire up here to land you in the pristine offices of Garretson, Smith & McKenna, PhD, LPC, CRC?"

I shift my weight in my seat and hug the clipboard tighter. "Well, that's overly personal," I say. "Not to mention rude. I don't even know you."

"You're Lake . . ." He snaps his fingers repeatedly, like he's trying to conjure up the answer. Then I see him peer down his nose at my scrawled handwriting. I snatch my clipboard and hug it to my chest. He rolls his eyes. "Okay, so I can't remember the last name. Lake Something-or-Other. Relax, you went to Oceanview Elementary with me." Busted.

He wears a light checkered shirt unbuttoned over a cotton T-shirt and yellow shorts and he smells, well, kind of amazing. In fact, I find myself wanting to lean in just a touch closer to catch another whiff of— What is that? Aftershave? Cologne?

I'm about to open my mouth when I stop myself. It's been years. He doesn't still go by—he can't still go by—

"Ringo." He grins and extends his hand out for me to take. Pine trees with a hint of vanilla. Odd combination for a person. "It's been a while."

"I—I—I didn't recognize you."

It's not a complete lie. It seems sort of amazing that the boy sitting in front of me is the same one who years ago hardly spoke above a whisper. Actually that's why he'd been held back a year, so that he was in my grade. No one knew if he was slow or just shy, only that he tolerated Smelly Ellie— Maybe that's why he's so intent on the good cologne now? That, and he sat inside every day when it was time for recess.

My gaze moves to the ring around his eye that had reminded me of Spot the Dog. Crap. This is just my luck today, running into someone who I probably more or less ignored, even perhaps rudely, ten years earlier. I had no idea what happened to Ringo after that one year when we shared a classroom. A new school? Homeschooling? I hadn't cared, but to be fair, I didn't even keep up with my former best friend, Jenny.

"Really?" He looks at me skeptically. "You see a lot of faces that look like this walking around? Damn," he says. "And here I thought I was unique."

I let out a small laugh that sounds more like a hiccup.

"So, see, now that we've gotten *that* out of the way," he continues, "are you going to tell me what you're in for?"

"I—I still think—" I begin to protest. Then, I shut my eyes and exhale. "What the hell. I was in a car accident. A few days ago. My best friend and . . ." My voice rasps over the ridges in my throat. "Um, my boyfriend, and they, well—they both died."

Ringo strokes his chin. "Yikes. That *is* rough. Well, how old are you?"

"I'll be eighteen this month."

"Shit."

"Shit," I agree. "So what are you in for?"

His brow line drops lower. I notice that the birthmark makes his eyes appear uneven, like the ringed one is sitting lower on his face. "I'm not telling you that," he says. "That question is entirely too personal. And quite frankly, rude. Besides, I hardly even know you."

My lips part and I'm about to snap at him, when the door on the other side of the waiting room opens and a woman calls my name. "Lake Devereaux?"

Ringo picks up his magazine from the seat beside him and reopens it in his lap.

I stare hard at him but stand up. "That's me," I respond to the woman.

"Welcome," she says in a flight-attendant voice. "We'll be right back here."

And when I glance back at Ringo, half expecting him to look at me with a sly grin and eyes that appear crookedly set but aren't actually, he instead keeps them trained on the pages of the magazine as though that's what he'd been doing all along.

# chapter seven
## *19 DAYS*

Dr. McKenna has blond, chin-length hair and wispy bangs and wears a smart skirt-suit that reminds me of one of the prosecutors on a procedural television show. I follow her through the doorway into an office, where I'm relieved to find no couch. Having never been to therapy before, I've been picturing exactly the setup that I've seen on television, which includes me lying down on a black leather sofa and being forced to spill my deepest, darkest secrets to a doctor with a thick notepad. Up until this very second, I'd become particularly hung up on whether I should take my shoes off before lying down on the couch. It seemed like the sort of thing everyone else knows how to do except for me.

Stuff like that gives me a lot of heartburn. Like when I go to the doctor and they tell me to take off everything from the waist down, I always have this momentary flash once the nurse is gone when I worry that I haven't heard her right. As though I'll strip down, and when the doctor comes in, he'll wonder why the heck I've taken my pants off. I don't know. It's just one of those things about me. The way Penny was scared of both global warming and heights, in that order. Or how Will was afraid he'd end up like his dad. I wonder if this is the sort of thing I should be telling Dr. McKenna. Or maybe it's completely irrelevant and she'll think it's weird if I bring it up. In therapy, do people talk directly about their problems or do they circle around them until they have a "lightbulb" moment? Here I go again.

When I hand Dr. McKenna the clipboard, she sets it down on her desk without looking at it. I think of Ringo and his knowing smirk, and feel a little too irritated, considering he's someone I hardly even know.

"First of all," she says, taking a seat on the opposite side of her desk and rolling the chair closer until her elbows are resting on the surface. I run my fingers over the ridges of my cast. "Can I just say that I'm very sorry for your loss? Your parents provided me with a bit of background, and I know that is the most trite, cliché thing I could possibly say." She rolls her eyes toward the ceiling. "But I'm afraid even psychiatrists aren't given magic words for these types of situations. We're stuck with the exact same ones that the rest of the world is."

And with that, I think that I like Dr. McKenna instantly.

"How would you like to begin?" she says.

"I—I don't know. It wasn't my idea to come here in the first place." This comes out more snappish than I intend.

She nods sympathetically but doesn't say anything more.

I fidget. "My parents say I can only bring back one person. I guess that's true. I mean everyone knows that. It's just . . ."

Dr. McKenna doesn't try to finish the sentence for me. Instead she leans back in her chair and says, "Why don't you tell me about your friends."

## 1,444 DAYS

Summer has passed and I've turned fourteen now, with nothing to show for an entire season of my life. My brother and I didn't pick crab traps or dive for sand dollars. Instead, I tried to fill our time with new things, diligently researching all of the activities we could do now together—a zero-gravity salt spa, the aquarium, IMAX theater, a one-man comedy act about defending cavemen—but Matt either wasn't interested in doing anything or wasn't interested in me. (Unfortunately it still seems to be a healthy mixture of both.)

Mom and Dad have both decided that I will attend a new school. The decision is made in one of those family meetings to which I'm no longer invited. One day it's just: "Good news, Lake, we've gotten you a spot at St. Theresa's," and then the next I'm standing in an ugly navy-blue sweater vest with nowhere to stash my brother's old skateboard, which I became at least halfway proficient at riding during my ample alone time these last months, weeks, whatever they were.

Modern History, I read on my schedule. The ink has begun to smear from where my sweaty thumbprints have mashed the paper against the scratchy grip tape of my board. I tuck both the board and the schedule under my arm. I'm holding on to the skateboard like a security blanket, because in the last few weeks it's kind of become one.

Just go in, I chide myself. This shouldn't be half as scary as dropping into a six-foot ramp, but this thought does nothing to calm me because *should* and *shouldn't* just don't seem to apply anymore. My hummingbird heart thrums against my ribs. "It'll be good for you," my parents had said. I sighed, remembering. Broccoli was good for me. Private school? That was debatable.

With the current state of my home life, I'm both starved for companionship . . . or have possibly lost my appetite for it—it's impossible to tell which.

I'm hovering outside the classroom, already twenty-five minutes late for class. Mrs. Savage: not the most promising name for my first-period teacher. I smooth the pleats of my skirt, check that my crisp white button-down isn't bunched beneath the crest-emblazoned vest, and at last open the door.

Eleven pairs of eyes snap into focus and I immediately long for something to do—skate, dive, surf, *anything*—other than stand there reddening under the heat of their collective gaze. I shuffle over to Mrs. Savage and fish the pink slip from the front office out of my pocket. "Hi, I'm new here?" I add the ridiculous question mark on the end like I'm not sure. It's possible that in only one summer I've managed to completely forget how to interact with humans.

She scans the slip, then turns to the class. "Everyone, this is Lake Devereaux. She's a new student. Please welcome her accordingly."

There's an exaggerated cough and in the middle of it I can clearly hear the word "Boner." My neck blazes.

Then a boy sneezes and the word "Sexy" comes out.

"Enough," says Mrs. Savage without much force. "Unless a few of you have suddenly come down with the flu and need to be sent to Principal Nazari's office?" Silence. "That's what I thought." She resumes a smug smile. "Lake, we were just about to break into debate groups to discuss what will be our semester project this year. The class will be holding a mock congressional session to either pass or vote down the Pickering Regulations." I nod and try to avoid eye contact with any of the other students. "Since Harrison was so *vocal,* why don't you join his group with Maya and Peng."

Harrison the Articulate Sneezer raises his hand. I thank Mrs. Savage and make my way toward the empty seat nearest the group while Mrs. Savage explains the assignment, which is to work with our group to represent an interest group, then debate its side of the argument as if we were trying to draft the legislation surrounding resurrection rights. No resurrection history is included in any school curriculum until eighth grade. I used to be excited to finally get to study it when I was younger. It seemed so grown-up.

Now I can't think about resurrections without thinking of Matt and the promise my parents made him only a week ago. I'd been the one to find him. Blood had been seeping out of his mouth, running down from the corners. It dribbled down his chin. He'd tried to bite through his own tongue to choke, a tactic he'd seen in a movie that Dad let him watch when Mom left to get her hair cut.

"Alexis Angel," the girl named Maya says to the two boys. The group is turning their desks to face one another. She ignores me entirely, instead staying busy punching buttons into her phone, as I push my skateboard under one of the desks and rest my saddle oxfords on it. "Too pretty. Too perfect. Guarantee it," she says without looking up.

Harrison rolls his eyes. "You're just jealous. Lead singer of Dante's Playground."

Peng throws an eraser at Harrison and hits him squarely between the eyes. "Come on, everyone knows that one. All his fans are death groupies."

"I've heard he's actually not." Maya glances up. "He's just saying he is to push his image. Oh!" She leans forward. "Somebody told me, I can't tell you who, that Principal Nazari is."

Harrison guffaws. "But he's so . . . feeble." He does a crooked, bent-over impression of an old man walking.

Maya raises her eyebrows and shrugs, pushing her thumb hard into her phone screen many times over.

"Um." I sit up and give a small wave. "What exactly are we doing?"

"Sorry, hi." Maya shakes her head like she's a little embarrassed. She sets down her phone. "I just programmed a cheat code to this new game and I'm *ob*-sessed." I make sure to look impressed, given that I can hardly save contacts to my phone without getting frustrated. "Anyway, we were just guessing resurrecteds—who is, who isn't. Potter Goodwin. What do you think?"

"I . . ." My eyes shift around for somewhere to land. "I don't know who that is."

Maya smacks her tongue to the roof of her mouth impatiently. "You know, that congressman, the one who is all, no resurrections, they're a sin against God the Father, the Son, and the Holy Spirit?"

"Yeah." I use the toes of my shoes to roll the skateboard underneath me. "I guess so." The name did sound familiar.

"Sorry, it's not important. What's important is you. You're the first new kid we've had since sixth grade," she says. "It's super strange."

Harrison flips his notebook closed. Not a promising sign for our group project. "Yeah, but that was Michael Glaser and he's weird and definitely not hot."

"Yeah, Michael's a real boner killer." Peng snickers.

"So." Wanting to steer clear of all topics involving male anatomy and my relative hotness and do something other than stutter, I click open a pen and make a show of preparing to jot down some notes. "What interest group have we been assigned?"

Maya scrapes a paperclip on her desk. "Resurrecteds." She points around the room at the different clumps of students. "They're pharmaceutical companies, and they're the naturalists. Personally I think we got the best one. Peng even suggested we could dress up like commune members in white linen on the day of." She shrugs like she doesn't care one way or the other. I've seen the eerily serene members of one of the nearby communes only once before. They were gathered for a peaceful protest in support of resurrected rights, dressed head to toe in their creepy white linen. I can't imagine that if I got a second chance at life, I'd want to live it tilling the earth and without Sephora. The commune members, though, are a small but substantial subset of resurrected people who feel they've been spiritually enlightened as a result of having died and come back to life. I don't know if there's any truth to it, but it's at least easy fodder for the late-night talk-show hosts.

I write the word *Resurrecteds* at the top of my page.

Harrison leans over his desk toward me. "I'm a lifeguard, you know." I'm getting the picture that schoolwork is not going to be a top priority here.

"No, I didn't know that." I scribble another note on the paper. "Seeing as I only met you twelve seconds ago." I mumble that last part. I hear a snort of laughter behind me and turn to see a girl with hair so blond, it's nearly white, covering a grin with her fist. I turn back to Harrison.

"Yeah. Over at Miller Beach," he continues. "A bunch of us go out there and drink in the lifeguard stands on Friday nights. You should come."

"And feel free to bring any of your hot friends," Peng adds, tapping his pen on the desk. He reaches across with his other fist and bumps knuckles with Harrison.

"A generous offer." I resist the urge to roll my eyes at someone on my first day, and then, out of nowhere, I suddenly have this giant pang of longing for *Family Feud* nights with Matt and my mom and dad and for the giant bowls of popcorn that accompanied them and for the times when my brother and I chucked pieces of popcorn into each other's mouths because, like, it'd be one thing if I was going home to that.

But Harrison leans back in his chair and gives me an appraising once-over. "Just trying to be hospitable."

There's a screech of a chair behind me. Then I look up to see that I've been flanked by the lithe girl with the nearly white-blond hair and piercing green eyes.

"Hello, Harry." The girl with the angel hair pats Harrison congenially on the shoulder. "I see you've met my old friend, Lake." She flashes me a grin. Her mouth is pink, like she's been eating strawberries all day. "Our moms were close when we were young. We lost touch a bit when Lake went to a different school."

Peng clears his throat. "We were just inviting Lake to the lifeguard shack this weekend. You know there's always room for you, Penny." He clears his throat. "On my lap." He scoots back his chair and splays his legs wide and vulgar.

*Penny.* She stays cool as an ocean breeze. She tilts her body toward me, looks down, and subtly lifts her blond eyebrows. I shake my head a tiny fraction of a degree. No, please, no. She glances over my shoulder. "Do you want to ask your boyfriend if he wants to go?" she asks. "Will?"

I follow her gaze to where it lands behind me. On a boy with a tan so golden, it glows, and shaggy surfer hair that reminds me of a beach at sunrise. "Sorry, Harry, my boy," he says, and tilts his chin, a cocky, self-assured gesture that makes me feel ten instead of fourteen, and continues reading from the open notebook on his desk. "We've already got plans on Friday." Then there's one quick flash. He looks up at me and, well, not all boys can pull off the wink, but I'm here to report that Will Whose-Last-Name-I-Don't-Know can.

I clench my fists and place them in my lap, trying hard not to blush too obviously, because surely the girlfriend of that boyfriend wouldn't blush at all. I've never had a boyfriend. Has Penny?

I start to worry that maybe I'm the butt of some weird joke and actually Penny is Will's girlfriend and everyone's making fun of me, but then her smile is so warm when she looks down at me and we've shared that secret look and I don't know what it is about her but she just doesn't seem mean.

"Too bad about the lifeguard stand," Penny says. Even in uniform she looks different from all the other girls in the class. She has an armful of gold, purple, and ruby bangles that jingle when she talks and there's an infinity symbol drawn in black marker on the back of her hand.

"Whatever." Peng shrugs and sinks lower in his seat.

Penny gives my arm a gentle squeeze. "Just wanted to say hi. We'll catch you later." She spins. Her ponytail is so long that it brushes between her shoulder blades.

"If you ever decide to stop being a vegetarian, Penny, I've got some meat right here in my pants for you," Harrison says.

"Vegan, Harry," she says without turning back around. "And thanks, I believe you've just committed me for life."

Harrison snarls and hunches over his notebook, and for the rest of the class neither one of the boys bothers me at all. After we've made a list of all the reasons resurrecteds should also be entitled to a resurrection choice, I pack my bag and check my schedule for the next class. I pack quickly, but when I finish, Penny has already vanished from the classroom. In the past, I haven't done much talking to boys other than Matt. At least not in person. Instant messaging is its own thing.

But Will is still putting his things neatly in his bag, so I decide to stand awkwardly close to him while waiting several seconds too long to say something. When he looks at me I stammer out, "Thanks."

He grins. His smile is friendly but not quite as warm as Penny's. "I'd apologize for all men everywhere, but honestly, I'm not sure those two have evolved past Neanderthal."

"Yeah." I shift my weight on my feet. "I'm not quite sure what all that was about, but I appreciate it."

He glances at the skateboard, which is tucked back under my arm, and then he's right back to eye contact. A nice change from where Harrison and Peng had been training their stares. "Don't worry about it," Will says. "Penny"—he shakes his head good-naturedly—"she just can't resist a charitable undertaking."

My mouth opens but no sound comes out. I don't know what to say to that. Was I—*am* I a *charity* case?

But if Will meant it as an insult, it doesn't show in his body language. He extends his hand out to me and, still mute, I take it. Then we shake like we're two businesspeople meeting at the office. "See you around, Lake."

And all I can think is, I hope that happens soon.

# chapter eight

## 19 DAYS

My appointment ends promptly on the hour when Dr. McKenna scribbles something on a pink prescription slip and passes it across the desk. I look up and see the second hand hitting the five. Not even a minute over.

Still, I emerge from the small offices of Garretson, Smith & McKenna, PhD, LPC, CRC, like a bat from a cave, half blinded from the sun. When my eyes adjust, the first thing I notice is the hunched-over figure of Ringo sitting on the curb. His checkered shirt is stretched tightly across his back and his fingers toy with the laces on his shoes.

I hover, unsure whether to stop or pass by. Only, it's not like I have anything else to do. I'm both best-friendless and boyfriendless. It's amazing how quickly a fatal car crash can clear a girl's schedule.

"What are you doing here?" I ask. My shadow crosses over his feet.

He turns to peer up at me and I can see only the side of his face that's unmarred by the birthmark. It's then that I'm struck by how handsome it is. Smooth skin. Dark eyebrows. Nothing like the kid I remember from elementary school. Or maybe I'm just so desperately lonely that I am seeing him as handsome in order to fill a Will Bryan–size space in my heart. Honestly, the human mind can be a total warp. "I thought you were waiting for your appointment?"

"Well," he says. "My appointment was over two hours ago."

"Two *hours* ago?" I glance back at the glass door, where our reflections are distorted. "But—then what are you doing now?"

"Now, I'm waiting. Something I'm *very* good at." He leans back and gently rests his elbows on the sidewalk behind him. He closes his eyes and tilts his head up toward the sky. "Behold. One of my many talents."

I try not to stare at the birthmark, but with his eyes closed, I find myself lingering over it like I'm snooping through someone's belongings. "For how long?" I turn my bulky, plastered arm over and scratch underneath the padding.

"For however long it takes my ride to decide to come get me."

I shift my weight, wondering if I should have passed by after all. The heat has begun to snake up around my ankles again. A real scorcher. "You're older than sixteen," I say.

He opens one eye, squinting up at me, and I quickly glance away from the mark on his face. "Nineteen."

"Then how come you don't drive?"

"Oh, I do. I just don't have anything to drive *in*. And

I've found that's an important part of the equation." He shuts both eyes again, and his hair falls away from his forehead.

I stand awkwardly, unsure of what to do now. My car is one of only a few in the lot. "Do you . . . I don't know . . . want a ride?" I ask.

He pushes himself upright and dusts off his elbows, which are now red and dimpled from the pavement. "*You're* going to give *me* a ride?"

I wince. I'm guessing I didn't talk to him much back in our third-grade class. I shrug. "I'm offering. Yeah."

He thinks for a second and then heaves himself onto his feet. "Okay, then. Sure, that'd be great. I'll just text my ride and tell them not to come."

I'm still not sure whether he ever really had a ride as I lead him to my car and unlock the doors. The inside of the cabin is stuffy with the kind of heat that could kill a dog left inside it in under an hour. When I turn on the air conditioner, it blasts us with a desert wind that only dries the sweat without cooling anything off.

"Um, so . . ." I drum the steering wheel. "Where to, Ringo?" I buckle my seatbelt and wait to make sure that he does the same.

"Southshores. Do you know the neighborhood? Right near the Conch Burger and the old boatyard."

I nod. Our town's not exactly large. We have two big high schools and my private one and a whole bunch of tourists.

He settles his head back on the headrest and lets out a long, charged breath.

"What?" I ask.

"Nothing."

I feel my neck tense the way it does when I have to speak to Matt. Why had I agreed to drive Ringo clear across town? As if I don't have enough on my plate already, this is hardly the time for charity projects. I blame Penny for this. Or maybe it's Will. All I know is that before them, I wouldn't have gone out of my way to talk to anyone. I pull out onto the main road and, at the first stoplight, begin chewing on my thumbnail.

"You can't just *breathe* like that and then tell me it's *nothing*," I say at last.

"I can't breathe?"

"No." My glance flits sideways. "I said you can't breathe like *that*."

He clucks his tongue and shakes his head. "Okay, then. Your car, your rules." He starts taking short, shallow breaths like he's beginning to hyperventilate. I snap my chin in his direction, feeling my eyes bug.

"Jesus, are you all right?"

"Is this a better way to breathe? I want . . ." He continues to heave. "To make sure . . . my breathing . . . is pleasing . . . to you."

I relax. If I knew him better, if he'd been Will, I would have punched him in the arm. But I feel the corners of my mouth inch upward. "Is this *always* how you make a first impression?"

"Ah, but you're forgetting. It's not a first impression."

*It sure feels like one,* I want to say. But instead I say, "You know what I mean."

"It depends, then," he says, thoughtfully. "What kind of impression do you have?"

"One of a smart-ass."

"Then no. Mostly people just notice my face."

I stare straight out the windshield, not sure of how to respond. So I decide to say something noncommittal, which turns out to be "Oh?" I think it sounds stupid.

"You did too. Notice my face. First, I mean. Back in elementary. Now. It's okay, though. Everybody does."

"That's not—"

"It is." He cuts me short. "It's just a birthmark. In case you were wondering. No real tragedy behind it." He puts air quotes around the word *tragedy* and I wonder what that's supposed to mean. Like, does he think it *should* be considered a tragedy? "I was born a healthy eight-pound, six-ounce baby boy. No crippling diseases. Ten fingers, ten toes. I just happened to have this big blotch around my eye, so . . ." He trails off as if I should know how to finish that sentence. "No need for it to be the ugly elephant in the room or the car or wherever."

I actually do relax and feel a tiny bit less fearful to look at him for longer than a split second. Ringo is so completely changed from when I first met him. If therapy is to thank for his newfound confidence, then Dr. McKenna must be one hell of a good therapist.

I adjust the dial on the air-conditioning. The knots in my shoulders unwind. "It's not ugly," I say. "It's unique. My mom once told me"—I smile at the memory of my mom when she used to be more *my* mom and not just Matt's—"that birthmarks are what's left over from angel kisses."

And I hope this sounds like a compliment, but worry that what it actually sounds like is a motivational poster that would be taped up in a school nurse's office. Worse, when my eyes accidentally flit over to his face, all I can see is the marred skin.

He rolls his eyes. "Great, guess an angel decided to make out with my face then."

"I only meant—"

"I'm kidding. Chill."

The untouched side of his face is invisible to me. Light catches the blue iris of his eye, turning it glassy and translucent. The curve of his skin from nose to lip forms a small, perfect ski slope. His profile is much more boyish than Will's square-jawed, salt-sprayed surfer look. In the moment that I'm caught staring, I feel a pool of sadness rise and take shape: that his birthmark had to destroy something so lovely.

My cheeks flush with warmth. What a mean thought to have. Jesus, what's wrong with me?

I settle back into my seat. "How long have you been seeing Dr. McKenna?" I ask, changing the subject to shared ground.

"About a year."

I let out a low whistle. "Wow, you must be *really* messed up." But I allow a crack to split my voice so that he knows I'm joking.

He laughs. "I wouldn't throw stones in glass houses."

There's a long pause that I don't know how to fill. We're cutting through our town's main drag now. Through a wall of condominiums I can catch glimpses of the ocean. The water looks more green than blue today and not at all gray. There are virtually no whitecaps dancing along the surface. The ocean, I've found, has moods. Today it's turned calm. Serene. And I wonder if it's doing that to mock me.

Ringo breaks the silence for me. "So . . . cut the crap. Who are you going to pick?"

I lose the patches of ocean as the balconies of the cheap, non-sea-facing rooms take their place, building after building. Mostly unoccupied this time of year. The summer is the off-season. June through September are too swelteringly hot. It'll be another few months until the northerners flock to our city for the winter.

"Your boyfriend, right?" Ringo jumps in again. "You're just going through this whole therapy shtick so that it looks like you actually considered your best friend?"

A lump grows in my throat. "No."

"I mean, don't get me wrong," he says. "I respect it. Go through the motions. Pretend like your best friend actually has a shot at resurrection. But let's face it. You're a seventeen-year-old girl with a boyfriend. You've probably been practicing your signature with your first name and his last since before you had your first date." He pauses and glances over and I feel the heat spread all the way up to my hairline.

"That's so *not* true." Except that a part of what he said echoes the feelings that have already been parading through my chest for the past twenty-four hours. I love Will. How could I not bring him back?

My mind conjures an image of the cowlick on the right side of his forehead and how he hated the way I licked my palm and tried to flatten it down.

"That's what I thought," Ringo says triumphantly.

And now I'm stuck with him, traveling inside a sixteen-square-foot box, and I'm really, truly starting to loathe my big mouth. "Can we please talk about something else?"

"Sure," Ringo replies a little flatly. Only he doesn't volunteer a change of topic and neither do I.

Instead, he eventually begins to hum and I'm tempted to turn on the radio to make him stop, if that wouldn't seem overtly rude.

I sigh. "What's that?"

The melody stops. "What's what?"

"That song that you're humming. What is it?"

He hums another bar. The melody isn't familiar. I'm not much of a music buff, though. My selections are basically limited to what plays on the radio.

"Oh, that?" He hums a little louder. "'Across the Universe.'" I furrow my eyebrows. "Seriously?" he asks. "The Beatles." I scratch my temple. "You don't know who the Beatles are?"

"I know who they are! Well, I've heard of them, anyway."

Ringo shakes his head. "Tragic."

I cock my head, annoyed. "Okay, so what? We don't share a taste in music. Knock that off the topic of conversation list."

"As though the Beatles are a matter of taste."

The condominiums have become too thick and they now hide the ocean completely. Patches of sand creep up through the parking lots, though, and skirt the blacktop.

I've only looked away for a second, but when I glance back at the road in front of me, my eyes catch silver. A dark windshield. A Lexus emblem. My whole body goes rigid. The silver barrels toward us on the opposite side of the median. The borders of my vision creep inward, narrowing my focus. I feel my teeth begin to chatter. Then my breaths begin catching painfully in my chest, as if they're rubbing up against a nail.

"Lake?" The voice is distant.

It's replaced with the sound of crunching metal. Glass that explodes and rains down like glitter. I know that I'm screaming. Blond hair streaks in front of me. I want to reach for it. To pull it back. But my seatbelt strangles me.

I feel myself wrenched sideways. The steering wheel is stripped from my hand.

"Brakes! Hit the brakes!" The voice smashes through the grate of twisting steel. My eyes fly open and my heart comes to a full stop for one single moment. I slam my foot into the brake.

I lurch forward. My hands stop my forehead from hitting the steering wheel. My car jerks short and I'm slammed back into the headrest. My heartbeat has resumed and it's now thundering in my chest like hooves in the Kentucky Derby. I stare up at the rustling fronds of a palm tree, inches from the front emblem on my car.

"What..." Ringo pants beside me. His hand slips from the steering wheel. "Was... that?"

"I—" I blink, bewildered by the easy sound of traffic behind us. "I'm sorry," I stammer, open the car door and stumble out. "I just have to—I have to get out of here."

"Wait. Where are you going?"

I kick off my shoes and begin following the narrow path of sand to where I know it will broaden. I trace the smell of the ocean, let the salt fill my lungs. When I hear the other door slam, I don't look back. I cut between two white condos and the sea comes into view.

Walking on thick sand is more challenging than any other kind of walking. My feet start going more sideways than forward and I'm forced to concentrate, to engage my thighs and my torso muscles to continue pressing onward at the same pace. When I'm firmly on the beach, halfway between the condominiums and the ocean, I give up and plop onto the sand. It's hot and I bury my feet up to the ankles and wrap my arms around my knees.

Tears run over my lips, mixing with the salt already starting to gather on my skin from where the wind has touched it. A few minutes later, I feel grains of sand being kicked up nearby and look up to find Ringo beside me.

"I thought I was okay." I sniffle. "I hadn't expected—"

He sits quietly, still wearing his sneakers. His knees fall to the side and he swirls his finger in the diamond-shaped window of beach between his legs, drawing spiral after spiral.

"It was a silver Lexus," I offer. "The car that Penny hit. It was a silver Lexus and we hit it and then they were both dead." I drop my chin and shake my head. Something about the way I phrased this feels final. Like the period at the end of a sentence at the end of a paragraph at the end of a page at the end of a novel. And when I reach the end, I feel as though my insides have been turned upside down and emptied out. "I don't know. I guess when I saw that car on the road coming toward us, I just sort of... lost it." The driver of the Lexus died too, I'd later found out. Her daughter was in the backseat. The little girl survived.

*"Hmmm."* Ringo murmurs. He's sitting on my right side, which means that when I look over, all I can see is the red blotch blighting that side of his face. The skin looks so damaged, it hurts me to look at.

I fake a laugh and wipe away the smear of tears spreading down my cheeks. "Bet you're wishing you didn't take that ride now, huh?" I flick sand over my toes. A shudder runs down my back and I'm able to release the final shreds of the accident memory. "You know I didn't, like, plan to almost kill us. Sorry."

He shrugs. "It's not like I had anything else on the schedule." His voice is a little too sad, as though he's saying that dying today wouldn't be more traumatic than anything else that could occur on a given day. He pulls his knees back up together and lays his cheek on one to look at me. "It blows, you know."

"Yeah . . . I know."

"No, I mean, like it really, truly sucks. Like I'm talking the world's largest Hoover-vac suckage. No, wait, the universe's biggest black hole. That kind of suckitude." He pauses. "Anyway, sometimes I think you just need someone else to recognize it too. How cosmically unfair life is."

"Nobody ever said life was fair." I take on an authoritative voice as though I'm reciting a phrase I've heard a thousand times before because it *is* a phrase I've heard a thousand times before.

Ringo sits up straight. "See, *that* is the garbage people say to make themselves feel better about their good luck. Your situation is balls, Lake."

My shoulders jerk with a puff of laughter that's gone before it starts. "Thanks," I say, using my fingers to sift through the sand for bits of shell. "It totally is . . . balls." Maybe it's the ocean, or maybe Ringo's right that it does feel better to have someone acknowledge how bad I have it, but I do feel just the tiniest bit calmer.

"Balls!" Ringo yells out toward the sea. He raises his eyebrow at me in challenge.

I glance around. A few families dot the shoreline. I take in a long breath. "Balls!" I scream. "This. Is. Balls!" I listen to my voice as it's carried off by the wind. The screaming has quieted my thoughts. At least for the moment.

He lies back, stretching out his legs, and rests the back of his head straight in the sand and stares up. "You've got to decide somehow, though."

I wipe tears and snot with the back of my hand. At least Ringo isn't someone I care about impressing. "Yeah, somehow. Any ideas how?" I consider telling him about Matt and about my plan to betray my family's trust, but the moment passes and I let it.

"So it's really not just an automatic boyfriend pick?"

I think for a moment. "No. I don't think so."

"Okay, then."

I look over and catch a small but noticeable smile playing on Ringo's skyward-tilted face. He looks more than a little pleased. Not that I'm surprised. Ever since I hit puberty, guys have been into me. I don't think that's cocky of me to think either. I'm not one of those gorgeous girls who doesn't know how pretty she is. I know exactly how pretty I am, but it's just another fact about me, like being right-handed or a decent surfer or above average on a skateboard. But maybe it's not just Ringo that's changed. Maybe I seem different to him too. I reach over and give him a semigentle smack in the gut with my nonplastered arm. "My boyfriend is *dead,* need I remind you? It's terrible."

Ringo grunts and pulls his knees up. "Jesus! I know, I know. But, you know what they say, there's no right way to mourn." He props himself up on his elbows. There are specks of sand dotting his hair and he's wearing the same sly smirk that he sported in the waiting room. This time, though, despite the fact that I actually had smacked him, the urge to do so is less strong.

"Did Dr. McKenna teach you that?"

"Yeah." He dusts sand from his elbows, and some sprays onto me. I squint to avoid getting it in my eyes. "I really think you might need some tutoring in this whole therapy thing. Frankly, you're way behind." He switches to sitting cross-legged beside me. All business now. "All right, so, choosing. You need a methodology." I look over at him, confused. "My mom was a professor," he explains. "What I mean is, you need some sort of system. Criteria that you can use to make your decision."

"That sounds so . . . impersonal." I call up images of Will and Penny. Will with his shaggy hair and sunburned cheeks, plus his ridiculous desire to make everyone happy in the grandest way possible. Penny, earnest and well meaning, who would get teary any time she saw either of us cry—and trust me, she'd seen it plenty. I can hardly consider splitting them up into a series of checkmarks and categories: Penny—humanitarian. Will—brave. No, that isn't going to work.

Ringo shakes his head. "It doesn't have to be. Think about it for a second." He holds up a finger. "What's one thing you think you'd need in order to make your decision?"

I glare at him. I might as well have lost something, and he's the person standing there asking me where the last place was that I had it. But he holds my stare, and it's me that breaks first.

"To talk to each of them again," I say at last.

He nods. "Okay, but how about something more within the realm of *possibility*. I'm not a goddamn magician, Lake."

I close my eyes and think so hard, it hurts my brain. "Will . . . my boyfriend . . ." I say, eyes still closed, concentrating. "He was planning this thing for my birthday. I wish I knew what it was."

"Like a cake?"

I let my eyelids open a sliver and peek out at him. "Will would *never* do just a cake. Unless it was twenty-tiered, with a conga line dancing out of it." I take a deep breath.

"Okay, so you think if you just knew what it was it would be *like* Will speaking to you again?"

"Yes . . . no . . . I don't know." Geez, Ringo really has been to a lot of therapy. "He gave me a hint. He said it was a hunt. And he was talking about . . . wishes."

"So, wait, like a scavenger hunt?"

I look up, surprised. "Exactly like a scavenger hunt." Now *that* is a plan with Will written all over it. "And the wishes." The last word barely escapes above a whisper because I haven't phrased the two pieces in my mind like this before. But now a memory is bubbling up of Penny, Will, and me. "There was a full moon right before my fifteenth birthday," I begin. "Penny had insisted we go camping for the night so that we could hike these trails she'd read about. We stayed near this old cougar's den that was actually really cool and Penny forced us to do some weird friendship ritual that Will and I thought was dumb but we went along with anyway. Then at the end, we each . . . we each had to make a wish. For our life."

I run my hand through my hair. I don't care that my fingers are sandy.

"I'd completely forgotten about them," I continue. "I bet

that's what would've been at the end of the scavenger hunt." I scrunch up my forehead. "I don't remember exactly what happened to them. But I think maybe one of us kept them. As a time capsule or something."

"Wishes, huh?" He doesn't sound impressed. "What was yours?"

"I . . . have no idea actually." I feel my eyes beginning to dance with excitement. "But maybe, maybe if I knew what each of them wanted with their life, it would . . . it would be like . . ." I shake my head, trying to break something free up there. "I don't know what, but it would help."

But all I can think of is finding this lost piece of Penny and Will, a part of them that is only rightfully mine. It feels big and important. It feels like a map back to them.

Ringo scratches under his chin. "That's great and all, but I was thinking something, like, more internal to you maybe?"

"No, you were right." I drop onto my back. The sun doesn't feel sweltering anymore.

"I just don't want you to get, you know, all your hopes pinned on—"

"No, Ringo, this is it. This is perfect."

He sighs and drops back next to me. "Okay, then, um, yeah, it's perfect."

I listen to the crash of waves on the shore, to how the shells tinkle musically as the tide pulls them out toward the horizon. The sadness is still burrowed deep inside me, but I try for a moment to feel what it would be like for the weight to hover just above my skin, barely enough, just so that I can do what I need to do, navigate the next few weeks and make the hardest decision of my life.

If I don't think about it too long, perhaps it's possible I can get through this. After all, I've already made one gut-wrenching decision and that was not to help Matt. The thought makes my stomach cramp in pain. I try to convince my pulse not to ratchet up, up, up again.

I roll onto my side and stare at Ringo's profile. Maybe it wasn't the worst thing in the world that I'd nearly killed us. Then I realize that of course it wasn't, because the worst thing in the world already happened.

"So, I guess it's official," I say. "We're both crazy?"

"Batshit," he says. "But since I'm slightly less so"—he pauses to wait for a protest, which I don't make—"you should probably let me drive." And after a while he starts to hum again, and I listen to him and the ocean, waiting for my pulse to return to normal and the shaking to leave my joints. "Definitely an 'Across the Universe' day," he says.

And I say, "Sure, whatever that means."

# chapter nine

## 19 DAYS

I let Ringo drive, but that still leaves me with the way home. I drive eight miles under the speed limit, mind the yellow lines between lanes, and jump whenever any car honks or moves to pass me—which, on account of my slow speed, is a lot. I've never been scared of anything physical that I can think of—new people, being ignored, social niceties, sure, but *this?*—and yet there's fear coursing through my veins like the aftereffect of hard drugs and I have to keep talking myself down to rational thinking.

By the time I do get home from dropping off Ringo and yet another near-death experience, the panic has overwhelmed the excitement over my newfound plan—my methodology—and has been replaced by a thudding headache that's taken up residence behind my eyeballs.

I think the weather is conspiring against me, because it's

changed too. Bits of ocean have now crawled past the shore and into the air, turning it muggy. It tries hard to suffocate me as I trudge up the steps to my front door. Many years ago, my house was pink, but now it's the color of a used Band-Aid. It sits uncared for at the end of a narrow avenue that dead-ends into the other properties with an ocean view. Bits of stucco crumble onto the tiled porch and stay there for ages. Moss and vines grow up the trunks of slender palm trees, strangling them until the leaves turn brown.

I stick my key in the rusty lock and twist.

"Lake?" my mom calls before I can even shut the door. "Is that you?"

I swallow hard, uncomfortable with how we left things this morning. "Yeah, it's me."

"Oh good," she says. "We're in the kitchen. Can you head this way?" My mom's voice echoes in the high-ceilinged atrium. The sound of waves crashing against the rocks outside booms. No matter the time of day, my house always smells like the inside of a seashell.

I follow the corridor to the right and find Matt and my mom.

Mom gives me an unexpected hug, patting my back and squeezing me tightly. "How was your appointment?" she asks. "You were gone a long time." There's a worried note hidden in there.

"It was . . . fine." I clutch my elbows to keep from falling apart. I avoid looking at Matt. Mom looks too hopeful, so I add, "It didn't fix anything."

She frowns but in an understanding sort of way. I notice that her car keys and wallet are sitting out on the marble-topped island. She slides them off. "Can you please sit with

Matt and feed him dinner? I forgot that we're out of milk, so I need to run out to the store."

"I can run out—" I interject quickly, not wanting to be left alone with Matt. She must know that.

"No, no." She waves me off. "You stay here. I'll be right back." She's desperate to leave me here, but whether it's because she needs a break from my brother or because she thinks spending time with him will change my mind, I can't tell. "There's leftover pasta in the fridge, or some chicken-tortilla soup, if he'd rather."

"But—"

I see another flash of desperation in her eyes. Like a caged animal. "Thanks, Lake. See you in a few." She tries to say this lightly before she disappears down the hall, but we both know she's fleeing. I could have easily picked up milk for her on my way home. Mom wanted an excuse and I feel both manipulated and sorry for her all at once.

I turn slowly around to face Matt. His wheelchair sits near the window. He's doing the thing where he wipes his features clean of any expression. Recently, Matt's started to refuse haircuts. When Mom tries, he'll toss his head, which is practically the only movement of which he's capable, and last time, her scissors left a bloody gouge in his left ear. Since then, his hair has grown out to his chin and, without the sun, turned a dull bronze. Shaving him is the one thing he'll let our dad do because the scruff tickles his nose when it gets too long.

"How's it going?"

"Swell." He gives up nothing. Not yet. I try not to look or, even better, *feel* guilty about the latest broadcast of my decision to Mom and Dad. Has he heard? Again, I can't tell.

But what he has to understand is that there's a difference between him and my friends, the major one being that he's alive and they're not.

"So." I try to keep my voice conversational, but it comes out false and Matt's a shark for that sort of thing. "Hungry?" I ask, determined to press on. "Would you rather the pasta or the soup?" I open the fridge and pull out two Tupperware containers. "Or both, I suppose. Not sure how well they go together."

"Soup," he replies.

I nod and put the container of pasta away. "Excellent choice." I pull out a bowl. In go the broth and chicken and tortilla strips. I then pop it into the microwave, already wishing that he'd chosen the pasta. Feeding Matt is a messy affair. There's the cutting up into small bites of any solids, and if liquids are involved, half of the contents are sure to wind up on his chin. At least when I do the serving. My parents are better.

"So . . ." I look back. Matt's wheelchair trips over the tile grout as he pulls closer, crowding me. Expression, voice, still blank. But the sense of foreboding grows inside me and, like a scene in a horror movie, I feel the suspense growing in the tense knot at the back of my skull. "Did the shrink change your mind?"

A familiar edge creeps into Matt's question and I feel an unpleasant tingle run up my spine, like I'm watching a spider slowly creep toward me.

"About what?" I've decided to play dumb. Maybe I'm a chicken for it. So sue me.

"Did you really think that Mom and Dad wouldn't tell me about your little Lakey hissy fit?" I flinch, stung, then try to cover by gritting my teeth. Of course the three of them would have talked behind my back and called a meeting that I wasn't a part of, and I'm sure Matt knows that this lack of VIP access bothers me.

"It wasn't a hissy fit," I say smoothly. "But that's fine. That they told you, I mean. I suppose you should know sooner rather than later."

"You know that's why Mom and Dad are sending you, right? To the shrink?"

I listen to the hum of the microwave. "She's a *therapist.*" I emphasize the nonderogatory word. "It wasn't the worst experience in the world. You should try it sometime." It's my own jab, but I doubt it makes a dent. "Anyway, Mom and Dad were right. It actually was kind of helpful to talk to someone."

Matt scoffs. "You think they really care about that?"

I spin. "Yeah. Maybe I do." Alarm bells are sounding in my head. Experience has trained me to appease my brother. Always pacify him. Don't do anything to anger him. This is the code I'm used to living by and now I'm finding it harder to break than I thought.

I turn back and stare, stare, stare hard at the microwave. At the slow rotation. At the sinking minutes and seconds until the digital clock flashes. The microwave beeps. I pull out the bowl of soup. The ceramic scalds my thumb and forefinger and I snatch it back to suck on the stinging skin. "Damn it." I wave my hand before grabbing a dish towel and move the bowl over to the breakfast table.

"Oh, stop being such a baby," says Matt. "Some of us don't even have the use of our hands."

I shoot him a sharp look, then push the wheelchair over

to the table and sit down across from him. "Open up." The spoon scrapes the inside of the bowl.

Matt opens his mouth robotically and I guide the spoon into his mouth. His lips close around the silver and I slide it out while he gulps down the mouthful. His eyes don't leave my face and I feel my cheeks heating up. "This little grieving phase you're going through? They're only trying to hurry you through it so you can get back on track and hold up your end of the deal."

I focus hard on the silverware wobbling in my grip. This time, broth dribbles down Matt's chin and I have to dab down his neck to clean the mess. "It's not a phase," I mumble.

"If you ask me, I think they're being entirely too delicate about it, treating you with kid gloves, sending you to see a fancy psychiatrist." I shovel in another spoonful, hoping to shut him up. "I get it, I guess. They hope you'll come to the right conclusion on your own. But in the end, it doesn't matter. Because you already promised, Lake," he says, his voice flat and serious this time.

"I know what promise I made," I say softly.

"Mom and Dad, they told me. You told me—"

"Told you what?" I snap.

"That if I lived until your eighteenth birthday, your choice would be me."

"As if you had another choice." But that's not exactly true. I remember the time before our parents cut the deal with Matt. How Dad caught him trying to drive his wheelchair into the ocean, only the wheels got stuck in the wet sand. How many attempts before he'd figure out a way to do it?

Matt's eyes go hard. "He was a high school boyfriend. You would have broken up anyway." There's a weird tingly sensation in the back of my throat. "And you would have gone off to college and lost touch with Penny. There's a whole big world out there, Lake. Trust me, you're not losing as much as you think."

He pauses to maneuver the robotic arm of his wheelchair to pat me condescendingly on the head. It's about the only thing he's able to do with that wheelchair arm of his.

The heat in my cheeks transforms into something solid, a veil that creeps into my line of vision and I can hardly see except through pinhole slits to a world colored in rage. The spoon clatters to the table and I don't know whether I threw it down intentionally or whether I lost my grip. Droplets land on Matt's nose and forehead. I make no move to wipe them off.

"You're jealous." My voice quakes. "Jealous that I loved them and that they loved me. Jealous that anybody loved me when you're so . . . so . . ." I search for the right word but can't find one that would cut deeply enough. I can just make out Matt's face through my anger—and through what I realize now are tears. He's once again mopped his features clear of expression. He's gone unreadable again and it infuriates me. I stand up, knocking over my chair. "I . . . could never . . . miss you a fraction of the amount that I miss them."

I stare down my nose at him. My brother looks very small and frail. I wait, heart pounding, for the regret to seep in. Usually when Matt goes on his tirades I suffer an odd sort of double vision. I see the old Matt hovering behind those cold eyes like a ghost. The one before the accident, the one who used to sit on my bed at night and read me *The Lion, the Witch and the Wardrobe* and make sandcastles with me in the morning.

But I've never spoken to him this way. I've never allowed myself to form the words even in my head. But as I wait, I find nothing inside but hatred. He's spent the five years since the accident tearing any bond we had apart and I'm done trying to figure out why.

"Get your own damn soup," I say, and leave my brother at the table to starve.

# chapter ten
## *19 DAYS*

When my mom gets back I tell her that I'm going to see Penny's parents and Will's mother alone, though the plan had been for us to go together. Matt doesn't rat me out. But she takes one look at the full bowl of soup and must know. Maybe that's why she doesn't argue about me leaving her there, even though I sort of want her to. For once, I'd like her to look at her two children and choose me. But she looks too tired to argue, and besides, how many times has she met Penny's and Will's parents anyway—like, twice?

I tell myself it's better this way as I change into the appropriately selected all-black outfit she's laid out on my bed, and get back into my car. Plus, I need to look for the first scavenger hunt clue, so it's an added bonus that Mom won't be getting in my way at Ms. Bryan's house. I get a flutter in my stomach when I think about what the first clue might be.

Will always knew the right thing to do in every situation. I am especially thankful for that part of my boyfriend, now that he may have left me the only bread crumbs back to him and to Penny.

As I stand on Ms. Bryan's doorstep, a pair of black flats blocking half the message on the doormat that reads NO PLACE LIKE HOME, I feel nervous for the first time since Will first introduced me as his girlfriend. Ms. Bryan and Penny's mom—Tessa—are best friends. They're both like second mothers to me. In the past few years, I've probably spent more combined time at the Bryan and Hightower residences than my own home.

I pull down the hem of my dress. It's too long and it keeps bunching over my stomach. The fabric is wool, and since it's ninety degrees out, the dress feels itchy on my skin, like tiny ant mouths are biting me. I use the fingers sticking out of my white cast to clack the brass knocker. Then I reach down and scratch my ankle through a thick pair of hose that seemed like a respectful gesture at the time but are now just turning me all sweaty.

Ms. Bryan comes to the door in no time at all and I barely get my foot back to the ground without toppling over. She's been expecting me.

My whole body is numb. Will's mother ushers me into their home through a tiled foyer and into the kitchen, where his older second cousin, Jeremy, stands at the counter holding strands of cooked spaghetti in his grubby fingers and dropping them into his mouth. Jeremy rents the basement downstairs. He's okay, kind of a screwup, and his half of the family doesn't get along with the Bryan half. At least that's what Will told me. Having him there helps Ms. Bryan out with the mortgage, though, and, according to Will, it gets Jeremy off his own mother's hands. Every family needs a black sheep and, although I suppose Jeremy is the Bryans', I've always kind of liked him.

"Jeremy!" Ms. Bryan scolds him, turning pink in the cheeks. Considering that her son is dead, I personally don't think it matters what Jeremy does with spaghetti.

Jeremy shrugs and slurps a noodle. "Hi, Lake," he says, mouth full. I wave my giant white cast monstrosity and instantly feel guilty. I have a broken ulna, a fractured elbow, a rib contusion, and a colorful array of bruises, but at least my heart's still beating.

"How's Matt doing?" he asks. My brother and Jeremy are the same age and used to be friends at the public high school I would have gone to if I hadn't gone to St. Theresa's instead. I don't blame Jeremy for not keeping in touch. It's not like they were best friends, more just guys who ate lunch together and occasionally watched weird movies that nobody else liked. Friendship with Matt now is tolerable only for those that also enjoy trying to pet a cactus or a rabid porcupine.

"He's . . . Matt," I say, and Jeremy nods as if he knows exactly what I mean. Jeremy is twenty-two. Over the last few years, his recreational drug habit seems to have become less extracurricular and more of the main event.

Ms. Bryan slips her hand into a pair of green oven mitts. "How are you doing, Lake?" Ms. Bryan is one of those people whose whole identity screams *mom*, from her haircut to her jeans to her biweekly cookie bake and ostensibly no first name. And this despite the fact that she has a full-time job as a paralegal. "Have you been getting any sleep?"

I relax a little. I climb up onto one of the barstools like I've done so many times before and rest my elbows on the cool granite. It's always been Ms. Bryan who's been there to ask how my school day was. Sometimes with Tessa, Penny's mom, while the two of them crowded into the kitchen sharing a wine spritzer and trying to get Penny and me interested in going to see the latest movie adaptation of their favorite sappy romance novel.

"Yeah, some," I say. "I'm still taking some pain medication. It makes me sleepy. But my parents don't want me staying in bed all day."

"Smart." She swirls a wooden spoon through a bubbling pot of meat sauce. I notice that the lines around Ms. Bryan's eyelids are bright red, so I know she's been crying. There's no Mr. Bryan. Well, there is, but not one who Ms. Bryan can stand having in the same room for more than three minutes.

I glance over at the four place settings around the table. Everything in the house is uncomfortably normal and doesn't seem to fit with the reality that her son's abdomen was recently crushed by an SUV.

I can't seem to stop thinking in such morbid terms. When I try to process the accident, I haven't once been able to soothe myself with standard clichés such as *My friends have passed away* or *My friends have gone to a better place.* Instead, it's the spreading pool of blood under Will's back and the sickening angle of Penny's leg that play over and over in my mind.

"Does your arm still hurt, then?" Ms. Bryan asks me, removing the oven mitts to fill glasses of water. She motions for Jeremy to carry them to the table, and as she does, nods at my cast. "I broke my wrist when I was a little girl, rollerblading. I had to get pins in it. But, to be honest, it hurt nearly as much when I found *out* it was broken as it did when I actually broke it." She smiles, close-lipped. "Probably not you, though. Will's always bragging about how tough you are."

I force the corners of my mouth to curve upward. I don't feel tough. It's true, I've skateboarded down disastrously steep hills, surfed right up until the first bolt of lightning, and skated from behind the bumper of Penny's Jeep. But I've never been as deeply afraid as I am now. Today, the fact that I nearly killed Ringo at the mere sight of a Lexus has confirmed the fear that I've felt slowly seeping in.

"It could have been a lot worse," I say. Which is true. There's a pause and I know I'm supposed to say something to fill it. I've said the wrong thing. Stupid. "I'm sorry.... It's hard...." I wring my hands together. "What I mean to say is that I'm sorry about what happened." I stare down at my depressing shoes. I want to say more about how I can fix this, but when I start, something inside me twists like a lock.

"It's only been a few days," she says. "But it feels like so much more, you know? And also like nothing at all?" I follow her to the table as she carries a bowl full of spaghetti. She gestures to a chair, which I pull out while she goes back for the meat sauce and Parmesan. Jeremy is already plopped down with his elbows on the table. "Like today, I found a pair of his sneakers at the bottom of the stairs where he'd left them...." Her lips disappear into a thin line and she waves her hand as though the thought had been silly.

I feel a knot form at the base of my throat.

Jeremy reaches over the table and grabs himself a slice of garlic bread and the pronged ladle for the spaghetti. "Can we please, like, press *pause* on all the sad stuff until after we eat? Full-time mourning works up an appetite." The whites of his eyes are red and glassy, and I suspect that smoking pot works up an appetite too.

"Is Tessa on her way?" I ask. "Is Simon coming too?" There are only four place settings, and apparently Jeremy's joining us for dinner. The fact that Penny's dad may be skipping out on dinner worries me. Is he too upset to leave the house? What could be so important that he can't make it?

It feels good to be back in the Bryan household, where it smells like Will and feels like home. I can already tell my parents were wrong to keep me from the Bryans at the hospital. Ms. Bryan would have wanted me there.

She checks her watch, then looks down at her lap and takes extra care when neatly creasing her napkin there. When she looks up, her eyes are sparkling, but she's put on a misshapen smile. "Actually, I'm not sure Tessa's coming." Her eyes flit to the door and then back to me. She seems nervous. "Please, help yourself." She pushes the bowl toward me.

Confused about the shift in mood, I dollop out a heap of spaghetti that I'm not at all hungry for, right as the front door swings open. From my spot at the table, I can see Mr. Bryan's head poke inside. He sees me and waves. My pulse quickens as in walks the fourth place setting, which is not Simon Hightower and is definitely not Tessa.

"Sorry I'm late," he says. "Maddie's going through this phase where she screams bloody murder any time Linda or I try to leave the house. The neighbors must think we're ripping out her toenails." He drops down into his seat at the table. "We're even seeing a baby psychiatrist about it," he says with a note of pride.

My mouth has gone dry. I wrap my fingers around the

cool glass of ice water and imagine the expression on my face, the same as a deer caught in headlights. An ambush.

Mr. Bryan—Logan, as he likes us to call him—thumps Jeremy on the back as he takes a seat beside him and across from me. Will's father is wearing a gray button-down shirt with the sleeves rolled up haphazardly. I wonder if that's because he's only half in mourning, since Will is only half his family now. The other half, the one he made with his secretary, *Linda,* lives across town.

His chair screeches as he pulls it closer to the table. He then lifts his finger to point out my cast resting on the table next to my plate. "Ouch, that's got to hurt." Will hated comparisons to his dad, but it's tough to deny the same campaign-trail smile pulled out whenever they want to flash that Bryan charm. "You going to get your friends to sign that or are you too old for that kind of thing now?"

My face feels tight, like the skin is pulling toward the center and the functioning of my lungs has reached a full stop.

"She doesn't have any friends, Logan," says Jeremy, tearing into another slice of bread with his teeth. My mouth falls open, but no words come out.

*"Jeremy,"* Ms. Bryan hisses. My best guess as to why Jeremy's here now is that, one, Ms. Bryan didn't want to risk being alone in a room with Logan and, two, the dinner table feels a tad less empty with a young male presence.

I'm not angry, though, because Jeremy's right. I'm completely friendless. And everyone is staring around the table at one another knowing that it's true.

"I—I'm so sorry for your loss," I spit out too abruptly.

Logan gets very still. "Thank you, Lake." His voice gets gruff. "Thank you, I appreciate that. I know what you mean.

But, the truth is, there's no need to apologize for things that weren't your fault, Lake. That Penny on the other hand—"

My face flashes hot. "It wasn't Penny's fault."

Logan shakes his head and looks down at his fork. He has a handsome crop of salt-and-pepper hair. "That's not what the accident report says." How did he get his hands on the accident report and why hadn't I seen it? Had I even been asked what had happened? I can't remember.

*"Logan, don't say that,"* Ms. Bryan hisses. "That's enough." Ms. Bryan's silverware clatters to her plate.

"It wasn't her fault," I say more slowly this time.

Logan's jaw clenches. A vein protrudes from his forehead. "Aren't I entitled to be upset, Jolene? Aren't I ever allowed to be upset about anything? He was my son too."

I share a look with Jeremy.

"I know he was your son too. That's why you're here," Ms. Bryan shoots back.

At this they both immediately drop eye contact with each other and switch to staring at me. I think, for a second, they've forgotten that I am in the room. *That's why he's here*: I turn the phrase over in my mind.

"Smooth," says Jeremy, shaking his head and making thatch marks with his fork in the red pasta sauce smeared over his plate.

"Wait, where *is* Tessa?" I ask for the second time tonight. "Was she even invited?" I feel sick. I haven't spoken to Penny's family since the accident. My parents said I would see them here and that I needed to respect their space. Do they think I'm avoiding them?

Ms. Bryan ignores my question. "I guess you know why you're really here, then," she says. I feel painfully idiotic, because in fact I didn't realize why when I first arrived, but I do now. "I—*we*—wanted to talk to you about your birthday. It's this month, isn't it?"

"Yeah," I say. "It is."

"Right. Well, we know you and Will loved each other very much and so we assume . . . but wanted to be sure that . . ."

"I told Jolene that we shouldn't assume anything," Logan says. "So, excuse me for being so blunt, but we want to hear straight from you that you're planning to use your resurrection on our son."

"No pressure," Jeremy adds.

Underneath my dress and my stupid, sticky hose, I've become a human sweat faucet. The best thing about black, I'm learning, is that it doesn't show armpit stains. I cast about for something to say, something to make me feel less trapped. "But what about Maddie?"

"Maddie's a baby," Logan says. "The idea of being without Will—well—for any amount of time—"

"It's unbearable," Ms. Bryan finishes.

They're right. Maddie's only an infant, so if they depended on her to use a resurrection choice on Will on her eighteenth birthday, then Will would miss almost seventeen years of his life. Once he was resurrected—if he were *ever* resurrected—I'd already be thirty-four years old while he would have stayed eighteen. Would I look different to him? Would I feel different?

"And paying for one?" I ask. The question is distasteful and I flush to even suggest it. The buying and selling of resurrections is illegal. The commoditization of life was the grease atop the slippery slope on which our population currently found itself. After all, that was how the debates began. Was vitalis a right or a product? If left only to those who could afford it, then could we live with the demographic the life-blood would inevitably create, with the powerful more powerful and plentiful and the poor left to dwindle and die? But there are ways, I've heard, if you know where to look and aren't afraid to ask. . . .

I look at the Bryans with their current but sale-rack clothes, their mortgages, their used cars, and know they could never afford a resurrection on their own.

"Even if we sold both houses . . ." Logan's voice trails off.

Ms. Bryan exhales loudly. "Sorry, we don't mean to be insensitive. We know you've just been through a terrible trauma and your mom says you're already seeing a therapist—we think that's great, don't we, Logan?—but I'm sure you'll understand."

"Of course," I respond on autopilot. My ears are ringing.

"Then it'll be Will." Logan says this as a statement. There's a certain authority that comes with devastatingly good looks, and he wields it like a movie star.

Ms. Bryan isn't even looking at me anymore. She's cupped her hand over her mouth and is staring out the window, which, in the darkened night, now reflects our images back to us. There are fresh tears brimming so close to the edge that I can't believe they stay balanced there.

Meanwhile, I knit my eyebrows. Heart pounding. "I . . . don't know. I mean, I think so. I just—" The sight of Ms. Bryan sitting there shaking her head at nothing and of Logan's eyes boring into me feels like a rope being wrapped around my neck. I should have let my mom come. She could have dealt with this. It was a mistake to come alone. Suddenly I feel like I can't sit here a moment longer. I'm screaming at myself not to overpromise, not to promise anything. "I'm feeling a little sick, Ms. Bryan." My voice sounds convincingly frail without even trying. "Can you excuse me for a second?"

My thighs ram the underside of the table as I bolt out of my chair. The water in all four of the glasses sloshes onto the place mats. I take quick steps down the hall and, without looking back, climb the carpeted stairs to the second story, past the framed school pictures of Will.

Upstairs, it's graveyard quiet. My heart thuds against my chest. My ears are still buzzing and I stuff my fingers inside to try to make them stop. Through the floor, angry, muffled voices have begun to rise. I can't make out the words, but I know they must be about me. I wait to hear the thudding weight of someone following me, but instead, I find myself completely and utterly alone.

I massage my temples and stretch my neck, trying to shake loose the feeling of claustrophobia. How could Ms. Bryan have gone behind Tessa's back like that? At the same time I know I've probably been naïve not to see it coming.

The Bryans, they're just desperate, I tell myself.

But so am I.

It has been an overwhelming taste of what I can expect to be dealing with for the next few weeks. Penny or Will? An impossible choice to begin with, and I've only been focused on how it affects me. On my eighteenth birthday I'll be giving one family back their child and the other... nothing.

I now know with sinking certainty that the family whose child I don't choose won't be in my life anymore and

I'll have lost not just one of my two best friends but another set of parents as well.

The burden bears down on me like a heavy meal sitting undigested in the pit of my stomach. I push the door to Will's room closed behind me with a quick snap and collapse onto his bed.

There, I take several deep breaths into the fabric of his comforter—sucking in the scent of coconut suntan lotion—before pulling my face from it so that I don't cover the whole thing in snot.

My chest rises and falls in shallow puffs as I stare down my nose. *I'm in Will's room.* For a boy's room, it's clean if not neat, and it's clear Ms. Bryan hasn't done anything to tidy it up in the last couple of days. *I'm in Will's room.* I pull myself up into a sitting position. I'm blinking, eyes wide now. I scurry off the edge of the mattress. The turn of conversation has chased all thoughts of the scavenger hunt from my mind, but here I am. Will's great, big, epically magnificent, cowabunga awesome birthday surprise. For a second, it feels almost too easy, too fortuitous, and I imagine Will up here leading me to the answer, because surely this must mean that I need to find the wishes, that they'll work their magic somehow. Why else would Will have chosen a scavenger hunt? Of all years, why this one?

If only I'm smart enough to figure out the trail to where he wanted me to go.

I cross the room and let my fingertips trail along the length of his desk, which is crammed against the window. There's a paperback lying facedown. I put my thumb in the spine to hold the page and flip it over. The book is a copy of an old Joe Hill novel called *The Heart-Shaped Box*. The open page is three-quarters to the end. Quietly, I read the last few lines that Will must have read before he died, searching for some clue as to what he was thinking.

I quickly set the book aside and lean back against the desk. I haven't gone a day without speaking to Will in over a year, and now I've gone two and it's like he's simply been lifted out of the world and I'm struggling to pull him back.

After fifteen minutes of checking in drawers, under the bed, in his closet, in the dirty-clothes hamper, and between the books in his shelves, I'm no closer to finding the hidden wishes or to figuring out the first step in how to get them. I'm frustrated, hungry, desperately sad, and borderline angry when a knock sounds on the door. "Lake, are you in there?"

I pinch the bridge of my nose, close my eyes, and count to three.

"Come in!" I say and try to rearrange my face into something suitable for the parents of my dead boyfriend.

# chapter eleven

## 1,444 DAYS

In the last ten days I've become a Will and Penny anthropologist. Maya asks me to eat lunch with her and I do, but we don't have much in common, given that she's kind of a tech-nerd and has a weird obsession with playing Dragon Con 6 on her phone. Most of the time I zone out and watch Will and Penny.

I can't figure them out.

They *aren't* dating, but they *do* act like a married couple. From afar, I see Penny snatching a Snickers bar from Will's lunch, hiding it, and trying to slyly replace it with something unappetizing, like carrot sticks. They argue. Penny usually wins. It's . . . confusing. I've never been friends with a boy aside from my brother, and I'm aware that totally doesn't count.

On the surface, Penny and Will don't even seem like they'd hang out, let alone be inseparable. Everyone loves Will, teachers, students—upperclassmen, lowerclassmen, it doesn't matter. He tends to make small talk while using expressive gestures and I even witnessed him remembering the janitor's birthday with a card and candy from the vending machine. Penny is confident and unbothered, but she tends to keep to herself unless she's making signs for Greenpeace or recycling or endangered animals.

The two of them just have this aura. People listen to them. For instance, Peng and Harrison haven't bothered me since Penny shut them down.

Neither of them has spoken more than two words to me at a time since my first day of school. Short of stalking—okay, a little stalking—I have spent my free time searching for my opening, hoping they would invite me to sit with them or hang out after school.

I realize I could make the first move, but I don't want to be an intruder, I want to be part of them. The desire to belong within a friendship that close fills me with a longing I didn't know I had until I stumbled on it between the two of them.

That's why I'm surprised to find Penny alone. It happens so fortuitously, I'm half convinced that I should take it as a sign. Class is already in session, and I'm headed back from the office, where I've been wrestling with a school administrator once again over the details of my schedule.

I'm walking through our school's breezeway when I notice Penny a short distance away, kneeling beside a clump of trees. I slow down to study her, one of my new favorite hobbies, and it's then that I hear the telltale sniffles of crying.

*Crying.*

I glance around, thinking Will must be nearby before

realizing that he's not and she's alone. I take a deep breath, unsure of what I'll do or say. I've never been exactly good with girls my age. I think that's why I've tended to gravitate toward physical activity—if it involves a thrill that makes talking either impossible or irrelevant, that's even better. I mean, I don't even talk to my previous best friend, Jenny, anymore, and when I did, it's not like we shared big secrets or I'd tell her when I was sad or anything. Those things had been reserved for Matt or my mom.

I step off the path, cutting across the crunchy grass toward Penny.

I gently call her name. "Are you . . . Are you okay?"

She turns to look at me. "Oh, hi, Lake, it's you." She doesn't seem either surprised or disappointed. Instead, she looks like she's had pinkeye for three weeks straight. Her nose is dripping two slimy rivers that fork off over her lips. I'm instantly fearful. Something is deeply, deeply wrong.

"What happened?"

She is toying with the braided leather necklace and amethyst charm that dangles from her neck. "It's dying." She looks away from me and her eyes flood with new tears.

"What is?" But I see the spots of pink blood on Penny's fingers and try to stave off the rising panic. "You're *bleeding*, Penny. God. Here, I'll help you to the nurse's office." I hold out my arm. I'm not sure where she's hurt or what's taken place, but she is clearly a girl in distress.

She shakes her head, then bends down to the ground. When she stands back up, she's cradling a small bird in her hands. I flinch. The bird's feathers are twisted—some pulled out to the stem—and coated with blood. Its head hangs limply against Penny's fingers, an oozing gash in its throat.

The bird's membrane moves slowly and horizontally across its eye like it's blinking, and the needle-thin beak appears to chatter.

"He's a sandpiper." Penny holds the bird close to her chest, her chin tucked to her collarbone, staring down at it. "I don't know how it got over here." She strokes the bird's brown speckled wing. Tears dribble off the tip of her nose. "A cat must have gotten it. Or maybe a fox . . . or a lawn mower." Penny chokes. "I don't know what to do." She sobs.

I try, but I don't think I feel as badly for the bird as I do for Penny, who seems almost broken over a tiny animal that has never loved her back, not even for a day. "We could take it to a vet?" I suggest because I want to add something.

But we both stare at the bird. It's opening its beak methodically now, staring into nothing. The breaths are labored, wings still.

"It's in pain," she whispers. "It's in so much pain." Penny gasps for air between silent sobs, and again, it's her pain that I feel, her pain that I want to go away.

This girl with her bangles and her quirky braids and inner confidence is completely flattened out in the face of the bleeding bird.

Penny's eyes seem to plead with me. "I texted Will," she says, voice still quiet. "He's not responding."

I close my eyes because my throat has started to get all tight the way it did when I used to have asthma. "I could . . ." Then I shake my head furiously. "No, I'm sorry, I was just thinking out loud and—"

She looks at me, eyes bright and intense. "Please, Lake?"

The bird is pressed against her and Penny is crying, crying, crying. "It's in pain," she says.

I don't even know what to do, not for sure, but I reach out for the bird and scoop it from Penny's breast. There's a spot of blood on her crested sweater vest. "All right," I say. "I guess I can."

I have never been a person that scares easily. I remind myself of that as I feel the barely there weight of the dying bird in my hands. I lay it gently on the ground. Penny turns away, dropping her head into her hands. My pulse slows. There's nothing in my head. Loud silence. As I take the heel of my shoe, balance my weight, pause to focus and aim for what I know has to work—*must* work—on the first try. Then I bring my heel down hard and fast and without hesitation on the bird's head, where at once it stills underneath my foot.

The sound comes rushing back into my skull. I'm dizzy to the point of nausea, but Penny buries her face in my shoulder and hugs me. Will shows up as if out of thin air, though I imagine it was actually from the hallway.

He sees me. He looks down at the ground. Frowns and nods. He wraps his hand around Penny's back and then another grips the back of my neck, giving it a gentle squeeze. And eventually the roaring in my head slips down into my heart, where it turns into something much warmer and simpler and good.

# chapter twelve

## *18 DAYS*

When I wake up, my sheets are doused with cold sweat and my heart is pounding against my ribcage. The last thing I remember is falling. My eyes are peeled wide open, but I'm not seeing anything in the real world. I'm still hovering somewhere amid the in-between.

And then I'm remembering the dream. It had started with a crash or—no—maybe the crash had come in the middle, after Matt had begun climbing the tree. I thought it had started with the crash, with the crunch of metal and blood, but now that I'm awake and breathing again, I'm getting my orders mixed up. I can see a hazy Matt, scaling the tree—tan arms, blond hair—but when he falls, it's not to the ground, but into a raging gray sea. And then the blood returns. From the car crash.

I pry myself from the soaking mattress and kick the blankets off my legs. There's nothing more boring than hearing about another person's dream, but I have this insatiable urge to tell someone the whole sequence of events, as though by telling, it might relinquish its weird hold on me.

Then I realize the person who I'd tell—Penny—is dead. And here I am, fully awake and queasy. The start of the fourth day since the accident.

I crawl out of bed. My neck's still sore from the crash. The bone beneath my cast throbs and the skin itches. I try sliding a fingernail under the plaster, but can't reach the spot, so I work on ignoring it, the same way I'm working to ignore the ragged hole in my chest where my heart used to be and the growing sense of dread.

Without bothering to check the mirror, I slip on the pair of flip-flops stowed beneath my bed and tread through the quiet downstairs hallway. I don't know exactly why, but before I know it, I'm outside in the glaring sun where the sweat on my back dries almost instantly. None of the neighbors are outside to bear witness to my embarrassing pajama attire. My drawstring pants are baggy in the backside and have Santa-clad pigs on them.

I shuffle down the driveway to stand beneath the oak tree in our yard and do something I've never done before. I stand directly underneath it and stare up into the branches. When Matt fell, I thought that my dad swore he'd have it chopped down, but now I can't remember if I had been the one who asked him to do that. Or maybe it was my mother. I'm not sure.

The branches' leaves are brown at the edges where they've been baked in the summer heat. I trace the limbs sprouting from the trunk and look for the stub of the one

Matt fell from. All these years, I thought I remembered exactly where it was. But it's not my memory. I wasn't there.

I walk up to the base of the trunk. The first real branch, one that would hold the weight of a person, is a few feet above my fingertips, which are stretched over my head. Matt was only a couple of inches taller than me at the time of the accident. Wasn't he? And I've grown since then. I frown and remember that the tree too must have grown. It seems like an awful lot for a tree to grow in a few years, though. In the messy tangle of twigs, there are several shoots of baby leaves and branches sprouting from the trunk. But none looked as I imagined the remnants of the terrible broken branch would.

I stare down at my toes, at the worn grass carpet at my feet, and try to imagine Matt lying in it. A prickle works its way up the length of my spine, notch by notch.

I look up at the house and see a subtle brush of movement in one of the first-story windows and feel someone there, watching me, behind the sheen of the glass. Perturbed and unsatisfied, I turn my shoulders away and trudge through the oppressive heat back to the house.

Inside, the air-conditioning smells mildew-y as it blows through the vents. I retreat to my room, feeling dazed, probably the end result of days of crying that have turned me into an emotional prune. I am no closer to choosing between Penny and Will, except that yesterday I felt that I'd have to choose Will and then today I'm furious with myself for not giving Penny a fair shot.

I have nothing to show for the days since the accident and I'm beginning to feel the constant nothingness like an ulcer drilling a hole through the lining of my gut.

"Well . . ." I jump at the voice and then at the warm body occupying the back corner of my room. "Have you figured it out yet?" Matt sits in his wheelchair, eerily still, as always.

I wait for several heartbeats, my knuckles boring into my chest as the organ underneath drums, drums, drums furiously. "Christ, Matt, you scared me half to death."

The sun pours through the window, turning my brother into a silhouette. "We wouldn't want that, now, would we? Not the golden goose, the holder of the magical ticket to Wonderland."

Matt likes to make odd references, allusions to books that he listens to—hundreds of them—in his ample spare time. Often the literary connections are mismatched. Sometimes they aren't. Sometimes it's difficult to tell.

I glare at him, keeping the bed between the two of us. "Have I figured what out?" I ask, in no mood for his riddles, but my mind flits back to the oak tree and its tall branches and the tough sandy dirt barely hiding underneath the grass there.

With Matt, every question doubles as a test. I already feel as though I'm failing, but it's important not to step on any land mines, especially the kind that will leave you without a foot or a hand.

I tuck my hands deep into my armpits. I seriously wish I'd thought to put on a bra.

More proof of how much has changed. I remember when Matt and I used to come down for tea in the morning and drink it out on the beach, both of us with hair still a mess, teeth not brushed. But now I hardly ever see Matt unless I'm fully dressed for the day. He feels too much like a stranger and I have the sense of needing to put on my armor before dealing with him.

I take a step closer, just so the light shifts and I can see him clearly. The toes of his socks are stretched out and they hang awkwardly down past the wheelchair stirrups. A pang of guilt knocks me in the stomach as I think about how I'd left him hungry in the kitchen. I bet Mom's angry.

"The hunt," he says, matter-of-factly.

My attention snaps into focus. "What are you talking about?"

His grin is wolfish. "Okay, so you *do* know about it at least. I wasn't sure. I don't know if you're aware, but your good looks have made you painfully slow. Mentally."

I grit my teeth. Be quiet. Don't engage. That's what he wants. "But—" I say, thickly, not doing myself any favors in terms of refuting Matt's point.

He cocks his head and his dull-brown hair obscures his eyebrows. "But—but—but—" he mimics. "How do *I* know about the hunt? Lake, really. What kind of big brother would I be not to involve myself intimately in the love life of my little sister?"

I narrow my eyes. "The kind that I've been living with for the last five years?"

"I'm hurt."

"Spare me."

I feel sorry for Matt. Of course I do. But it's hard to have a relationship with someone who wants me to be as miserable as he is. Does he not remember the dozens of times that I tried to forge a new relationship with him? Does he not recall when I bought us tickets to see a marathon of all the

Tolkien movies? Or the time when I bought us that high-tech version of Trivial Pursuit, even though I'm terrible at trivia? He wanted nothing to do with me. *Nothing.*

And I moved on because I had to move on, and we got on with the inevitable business of not liking each other.

But now here we are. *Speaking.* Sort of. My head feels swollen. Maybe it's a belated side effect of the accident. I've heard of whiplash pain not revealing itself until days or even weeks after a car wreck.

But I fight the sensation and instead give in to his game out of sheer necessity. "Yes. I know about the scavenger hunt. And I know what's at the end of it. What I don't know is how to get there."

"Then I imagine it's going to be hard to get very far without the first clue."

"Yeah, thanks, I've figured that much out too." I sound peevish and hate that I've so obviously allowed him to get under my skin. Again. God, it could be so different between us. If only he'd tell me how sorry he was that I've just lost my two best friends. If only he told me what I did to make him hate me. But the truth is I'm not sure what's on the other side of those "if onlys" anymore. Maybe nothing. "Why are you so interested anyway?" I say, wishing he'd get the hell out of my room and leave me alone like he has been for the past five years. "You don't even care that they're dead."

Matt adjusts the angle of his chair using the straw-like contraption. The motion casts his face in shadow again. Dark screen. Unreadable. *"Au contraire,"* Matt says flatly. As a byproduct of having nothing to do, Matt has listened to the complete sets of Rosetta Stone for Spanish, French, German, and rudimentary Japanese. "It's practically the only thing I care about right now." At this, I soften. My eyes search his for signs of my big brother. "Your friends dying went and screwed everything up. More specifically it screwed *you* up. And that is something I care about *immensely*."

I notice that he doesn't say some*one* and my temper flares so white and hot that I can't speak.

"Honestly, teenagers, cars, it's so obvious I'm practically kicking myself—" He pauses. "Notice I did say *practically*—for not anticipating this sort of disaster in the first place."

"I'm glad this is all so amusing to you." I've heard enough. My keys are on my nightstand and I cross the room to get them. We're done here.

"Wait," Matt snaps with a sharpness that feels as though he's bitten me. "I can help."

"Can? Will? From you those are two different things." My hand closes around the mini surfboard I use for a keychain.

"I can tell you the first clue."

I freeze and turn slowly to him. "What did you say?"

"I know it."

"How?"

"Because I found it."

"*How?*" I repeat more loudly and slowly, as if he can't understand English.

"Because I was here when your dopey boyfriend showed up to hide it in your room and swore me to secrecy. Good secret keeping, huh?" He winks.

I scan the room. The clue. It's been in here. Here. All along. "Where is it, then?"

I snatch up the corner of my bedding and tear it from the mattress. I shake the blankets and look for something to tumble out. But nothing does. I search around for the next thing to tear apart.

"It's gone," he says. "I destroyed it."

"You *what*?"

"I destroyed it."

Like I hadn't understood him the first time. It's a good thing there's a bed between the two of us. "You *psychopath*." I reach my hands up and tear at my hair. Pain shoots through my elbow. Matt's eyes go wide. "What is *wrong* with you?" I screech. "That is maybe the last message I'll receive from Will ever, and you—you—" I catch my reflection in the full-length mirror nailed to the wall. Red splotches dot my cheeks. "You *took* that from me."

"Stop, Lake," he barks at me and for some odd reason I obey. "I needed . . . insurance. And," he scoffs, "let's face it, clearly, I wasn't wrong. But, I've memorized it. Okay? Calm down. I know the whole thing by heart."

I feel uncomfortable, like all of a sudden my clothes are two sizes too small. "Memorized it," he says.

The words aren't computing. Why? How?

I begin to pace, panting and agitated. I consider the effort it must have taken to use that damn robotic arm that he has hardly bothered to learn to maneuver since he first got that wheelchair. It could have taken him hours. That's how much he hates me. Right there. *Remember this, Lake, if nothing else.*

Matt's eyes don't waver from my face. Not even for a moment. "I'll tell you, but I'm going to need something in return first."

"No. I'm not promising you my resurrection."

He laughs. "No, of course not. You already promised

that, so a new promise of your resurrection would be altogether redundant, don't you think?"

I close my eyes and think about sweet Will and how he painstakingly put a scavenger hunt together to lead me to something because he thought it was important, and now I do too.

I open my eyes and there's Matt. Cruel. Bitter. Mean. Matt.

"Don't you want to know what I want?"

I stare hard at him. Testing, thinking, *Think, think, think,* Lake.

Mom pops her head in to my room. I haven't even heard her coming. "Everything okay in here?" The corners of her eyes show worried creases.

"Everything's fine," we both say in unison.

When we don't say anything more, she just taps the doorframe. "Lake, I'm going to make some chamomile tea. I'll make you some." And then she disappears.

And as soon as she's out of earshot, I tell Matt to go to hell because I don't want him going anywhere near Will and Penny. Because their memories, at least, are still mine.

# chapter thirteen

## *18 DAYS*

Before I even consciously know where I'm headed, I've almost arrived at Southshores, a white-stucco apartment complex with red-tiled roofs and a massive parking lot. I'm pleased to find that anger and adrenaline get me most of the way there at a normal rate of speed and that, while my heart has taken up residence somewhere at the top of my throat, the fear of driving hasn't seemed to have gotten any worse. At least not yet.

For the first time since becoming friends with Will and Penny, I felt like I had no escape hatch. And it sucks. Because every time I need my family the most, I'm reminded of how the air between us, stuffed into that ocean-view home, has condensed into a hotbed of need and dysfunction. In that moment before I grabbed my car keys, I truly believed that if I breathed in one more lungful of that air, the toxic fumes would smother me dead.

And then I happened to think of Ringo and it felt like finding the release valve on a teakettle, and it was here or drive around or home and so I chose here.

I pass through the white-painted wrought iron gates of the community and drive straight to Ringo's building, where I knock on the door.

"Ringo! It's me, Lake!" I call. My pent-up anger has me bouncing on the landing out front of his apartment, number 102. I'm relieved that after only a few seconds there is shuffling behind the door, the clink of a chain being slid back, and then Ringo's half-and-half face peering out at me from the crack. "Tell me again that my life sucks." I stomp my foot and curl my fists into balls at my side.

"Lake," he says. "What are you doing here?"

I press my hand against the outside door, push it open, and barge inside. "You were right. Cosmically unfair. Have I mentioned that I hate everything? Because if not, I feel like I should mention it again. I hate everything." Just like on the beach, it feels good again to say this, out loud, and to Ringo. He is the only person whose face I have seen in the last four days who hasn't wanted something from me. No, *needed* something from me, and it turns out needs are at least ten times more oppressive when applied to somebody's soul.

Ringo hovers near the entry. "You should have called."

But I already feel lighter now that I'm unloading some of that added weight onto him. I spin on my heel. "My *brother,* do you know what he did? He destroyed the first clue. *Destroyed* it. Do you know how messed up that is?" Ringo's cheek twitches. He's not moving into the apartment with me. I look over my shoulder, suddenly self-conscious. There, in the small, poorly lit living room is a middle-aged woman sitting on the couch staring fish-mouthed into the television. "Oh. I'm sorry." It's midweek during the day. "I didn't think—"

Without blinking or taking her eyes off the screen, the woman reaches for a Big Gulp sitting on the TV tray next to her, finds the straw with her mouth, and takes a long sip.

She doesn't acknowledge me.

"Are you going to introduce me?" I ask Ringo through gritted teeth, nervously twisting the hemp bracelet around my good wrist.

He sighs, finally taking a few steps toward me. "Sure thing. Lake, this is my mom, Renetta Littlefield. Mom, Lake Devereaux."

"Nice to meet you," I hasten to say.

Nothing. No signs of life but for the squeaking of the straw in the lid. Ringo raises his eyebrows at me. One disappears into the angry red birthmark.

I bite my lip and shift my weight. "Did I come at a bad time?"

He gives a noncommittal shrug. "You should have called." I remembered now Ringo entering his number into my phone before he got out of the car following our near accident. Then he told me to take care and was gone.

Well, that's what I'm trying to do. I'm trying to take care of myself, I'm trying to stay afloat, to cling on to the only lifeboat there is. But now my clumsy fingers clutch around the shape of my cell phone stuffed into my back pocket.

"I—I—" I press my palm to my forehead. "I'm *so* sorry. I'm an idiot. What is wrong with me? Just showing up like this."

Ringo is more tense than when I last saw him and he has

a sour look on his face, like he's just swallowed five lemons whole. "No, it's fine." He casts a sidelong look at his mother. "Let's go somewhere else to talk, though, okay?" He's keeping his voice low.

The actors on the television babble on against the backdrop of dramatic instrumental music.

I nod, relieved. Ringo too seems to collect himself. He takes a deep breath and puts his hands on both my shoulders. He lowers his head to look straight into my eyes. "Just... wait here, all right?" He tilts his chin to gesture at the couch next to his mom. "Five minutes. Promise. I just... I need to put some shoes on and—" He pinches the flimsy white undershirt he's wearing. I blush. "Get dressed." Then he mouths "*Five*" and holds up one hand, fingers spread wide while he backs away. "Promise!" he calls as he disappears down a dark hallway.

I swallow, uneasy, then sink carefully down onto the sofa cushion next to Ringo's mother, worried that in my attempt to escape one suffocating atmosphere, I might have jumped right into another.

"Hi," I say. "Your, um, apartment, it's lovely." Not a word. Ringo's mother has a pooch of fat above the waistline of her pants on which crumbs have gathered, giving the impression that she doesn't move from here often, but she is quite pretty, her face smooth, with high-arched eyebrows and dark eyes. "Have you lived here long?"

She unwraps the plastic from a Twinkie and stuffs one end of it into her mouth. "I can't hear my soaps," she says. A few cake morsels fall into her lap, where she leaves them.

My jaw clamps closed. I don't even dare utter the words of an apology. Instead, I resort to the coping mechanism of awkward people everywhere and pull my phone out from my pocket.

Up until now, I've been too scared to check ChatterJaw, an app that lets kids in a particular social circle post anonymously. I usually check into our school's ChatterJaw at least once a day, more during the school year, when I feel like idly checking out whatever gossip is sweeping St. Theresa's or if I've forgotten the night's assignments for a particular class that I don't share with Will or Penny.

But for the past week, I've been consciously avoiding the application because, well, I already know what the gossip of the day will be. I haven't been immune to the pull of seeing it firsthand, though. So, maybe just a peek now. While I won't have time to think about it. Perhaps it won't hurt. Much.

I click on the icon and wait while the loading spiral swirls and swirls. I sneak a look at Ringo's mom. She's taken another bite of her Twinkie and set it down in favor of the giant soda cup.

The app loads. My fingers are sweaty with anticipation. I don't have to scroll to find evidence that news of our car accident has reached the St. Theresa's crowd. The thread *R.I.P. Will Bryan & Penny Hightower* has been upvoted 137 times, so it appears at the top. I tap the thread and the screen populates with dozens of anonymous messages. I scan through a few:

> Only the good die young

> Will and Penny, your lives were taken too soon. I will see you in every butterfly, every springtime flower, every rainbow. Rest in Peace

Really makes you appreciate the small things . . .

Be real, guys, they thought they were better than everyone else

Ass

Has anyone talked to Lake?

I heard she was in the car too. She's not listed as a fatality so . . . there's that

The messages are basically what I'd expect—some that wax poetic, others that are mean, plenty that are just curious. I wish I could stop there, because I can handle those messages, but it's the next thread that grabs me by the throat and strangles the air out of me.

*Virtual Bookie: Over/under—who will Lake choose?*

*"Damn,"* I mutter.

"Hush," Ringo's mom snaps and I shrink closer to the armrest on my side of the couch.

The first message in the thread is:

Lake turns 18 this month. Who wants to take bets on her resurrection choice. Serious takers only. We'll go private to exchange the $$

"Going private" refers to the private-message feature through which ChatterJaw members can send each other messages only visible to a single other member in their social circle.

Despite my conscience screaming at me not to, I read the messages that follow:

> Will—$20
>
> Will—$45
>
> Will—$15
>
> Will—$155
>
> You guys are crazy. #Teampenny all the way! Penny—$40 #hoesbeforebros
>
> Will—$60 #teamwill
>
> Penny—$120 #teampenny
>
> Lake's not resurrecting Will. No way. Haven't you checked out the Spilled thread? #Doyourresearchbitches #troubleinparadise #teampenny $200

I read the last message again. What is the poster talking about? "Trouble in paradise?" What "research"?

"You ready?"

I jump and jam my finger into the lock button on my phone. My screen goes instantly dark. "Huh?"

Ringo is standing in front of me, dressed in a pair of gray

shorts and a navy polo. "Keys, phone, wallet." He touches his pockets. "Yep, good to go."

I realize I'm meeting him with only a dumb stare. I'd nearly forgotten where I was. He looks at me quizzically, the stained patch of his face wrinkling. "Um, yeah, yeah—" I shudder, shaking the cruel messages away as best I can. "Where are we going?"

"Coffee shop. Down the street. We can walk." He says this like he knows it will be a relief.

He offers me his hand and pulls me out of the crater I leave on the flimsy sofa cushion.

"Nice to meet you," I call to Ringo's mother before I hurry after him, out of the cramped apartment. Ringo's walking quickly and I have to trot to catch up. He's leading me across the vast parking spaces and back through the white iron gates. "I . . . thought you said your mom was a professor?" I ask in my best innocent voice.

When we're out of the gates, Ringo's pace slows and he adopts the easy, relaxed posture that I admired when we last met. "Was," he says. "She's retired." He puts that in air quotes.

"Are you two in some sort of argument?" I think of my own family, where we're literally battling over promises of life and death, but it's still not as awkward as it was between Ringo and his mom.

"We had a falling out. About a year ago, give or take," he says.

"It's been like that for a *year*?"

We walk along the steaming road in the direction of a strip mall, which is drawing nearer by the second.

"Pretty much."

"Oh." Ringo seems like he's finished talking about his mother. Our steps fall in sync and we walk along the road in silence.

"I'm not trying to be a jerk," he says. "I like to keep my worlds separate. At home and, well, basically everything else."

"Me too," I say, and mean it.

"Your life is cosmically unfair," he says, and I catch him looking sidelong at me with a crooked smirk creeping the curve of his mouth up. "Total balls."

"Thank you." The constant knot in my chest seems to untangle itself by one loop at least. I try to imagine Will in the same position as Ringo right now. What would he say to me? It's hard to imagine that he would say anything was cosmically unfair. Will was an eternal optimist. Even when his dad left, sure, he cried, but he was already busy making plans to be nothing like Logan. He wouldn't have said that anything sucked. Nothing sucked for Will Bryan. Nothing except for dying.

Ringo leads me into Neville's Coffee Shoppe. On the outside, it's a simple, run-of-the-mill, strip-mall storefront, but once inside, I find a busy cafe. Round community tables dot the center of the room. Hanging above them are outlet strips where patrons have plugged in their laptop computers and cell phones. There are other seating options too. A nook with loveseats and squishy armchairs. Schoolroom desks. High-top counters. Conspicuously absent is any sign of the beach at all. The decor is all deep gray and crimson without any of the sky blue and white, the coastal colors that businesses in our town typically favor.

I follow Ringo to the coffee bar and the baked goods display. A barista with a tight shirt, tattoos, and a white towel slung over his shoulder greets us. "Ristretto macchiato, dry?" he asks Ringo, already pulling a small cup from underneath the counter.

"Come here much?" I tease. The barista doesn't linger over Ringo's split-personality face or glance away.

"And what it'll be for the missus?" he asks, using the towel to dry the inner rim of the mug he's already holding.

"Actually, I don't like coffee," I say.

The barista raises his eyebrows to Ringo. "What is this, witchcraft?"

"Pure heresy," Ringo agrees. "How are you running? Battery power?" He arches back as if to look for a pack or an outlet between my shoulder blades.

"All natural, I guess." I flip up my palms apologetically.

"Ringo's veins are highly caffeinated," says the barista.

"We can fix this." Ringo draws out his wallet and lays a credit card on the counter. "Make it a cup of Neville's house blend, double-double."

"But—"

"You'll like it," Ringo insists, daring me to challenge him.

When the barista comes back with a sloshing mug and a small cup, both with saucers underneath, he pushes Ringo's credit card back toward him. "First-timers and their enablers on the house," he says. Then to me, "We run on the addiction model. When you need your next hit, you'll know where to find me." He slaps the towel over the countertop and then heads off to tidy up around the espresso machine.

"This way." Ringo jerks his head and we both try to

balance our overfull cups as we snake our way to a corner of the shop I can't help but notice is already occupied.

A hunched-over girl with purple cat's-eye glasses and a curly black ponytail glances up from her keyboard. "Hey, Ringo, didn't expect you here so early today."

"Emergency evacuation," he says, taking a sip of his espresso, then jerking away when it turns out to be too hot. "Lake, this is my friend Margaret Zee. Margaret, this is Lake."

"Howdy," she says, continuing to type at an alarming rate of speed.

"Margaret codes software a few days a week to earn extra cash," he explains. "Then there's our proverbial old married couple, Vance and Kai—" Two reedy boys with skin tones on the opposite ends of the spectrum look up and give a short wave and a smile. They are leaning into a single pair of headphones that is plugged into a clear plastic case with a miniature vinyl record spinning inside. "Simone, she works here but is on break; and Duke, as in Ellington, but he'll answer to his real name too, which is Daljeet." I take in the list of people rapid-fire. Simone's blunt-cut bangs frame an angular face where it's peeking out from a black-and-white magazine featuring a photograph of Frank Sinatra on the cover. And finally: "I'm sorry, who's Duke Ellington?" I ask.

"Duke's that guy." Ringo points over to a tubby Indian boy wearing a black T-shirt with a smiley face on it. "Duke Ellington is a famous jazz musician. No relation unless you count their fantastic taste in music."

"Right," I say, rocking back on my heels. "Quite a crew you've assembled." I feel a flush of self-consciousness, realizing how insulated and how homogenous and *white*

St. Theresa's—the world I've been committed to since eighth grade—is.

And then there's the fact that, of course, I've assumed Ringo would be a loner. Why, because of a stupid birthmark on his face? God, I really am a jerk.

"Can we crash here?" Ringo asks Margaret while at the same time pushing a large stack of textbooks from one of the chairs at her table.

"How do you two know each other?" I ask Ringo, but it's Margaret who answers.

"I used to be an assistant for Professor Littlefield. I sort of adopted Ringo after that."

"Topic of conversation," Ringo begins to Margaret, "is how much Lake's life blows."

"I'm intrigued," she says. "Ceiling fan, breeze, or gale force?"

Ringo looks to me for an answer. "Hurricane," I say. "Category five."

She frowns, impressed. For the first time, she stops typing, leans in on her elbows, and waits for me to continue.

I chew the inside of my cheek, unsure that I want to spill my guts to Margaret. But Ringo leans back in his chair and takes a long sip from his cup. "Go on, Margaret can be trusted."

So I do. I catch Margaret up on the car accident, then tell them both about the ambush by Will's parents, and end with the destruction of the only known note-slash-clue left over from my dead boyfriend, which was destroyed by my older brother. In the process I learn that *double-double* means double sugar, double cream, and actually start to like the house-blend coffee that Ringo ordered me and the pleasant buzz of energy that seems to help me think more clearly. The only things I don't tell them are about Matt's paralysis and my promise to him and, most importantly, about how I've already broken it.

"So," I finish, "I have to resurrect one of them and people at my school are taking bets and the problem is I have no idea what I'm going to do or how I'm going to figure out where Will was trying to send me."

Margaret finishes listening to my story. She pulls her cheeks in taut and lets out a long low breath. "That . . . *sucks.*" She adjusts the glasses on her nose. "Like . . . an octopus tentacle . . . or . . ." She scratches her temple.

"A space vortex," Ringo says.

"Exactly." Margaret resumes typing—*bang, bang, bang* against the keyboard. "Resurrections are . . ." She glances up from the screen. "Have you told her?"

"Told me what?" I pivot toward Ringo.

"*Nothing,*" he says, and shoots Margaret a dirty look, which she doesn't catch since she's already returned her attention to the glowing blue screen in front of her. "We're talking about you, your problems," Ringo continues. "That's enough ground to cover." I narrow my eyes, but he presses on. "So draw straws," he says.

"Be serious."

"I am."

I glare at him.

"Fine," he says.

Kai moves between tables and drops a sheathed record in front of Ringo, who says a quick *thank you* before Kai returns to his headphones.

"You need a new way in," Ringo continues. "If this

search for the Holy Grail that your boyfriend has laid out for you is the only way you feel you can make a decision, then you have to get to the end of it. Just think—what's going to lead you there?"

I twist my fingers in my lap. "Yeah, you're right. I guess. I don't know." Matt said he wanted something in return that wasn't my resurrection, but I don't know what it is that he's asking for. Ringo seems to be telling me to open Pandora's box and find out, but I'm not sure I want to. I sigh. "There's another thing. I found this anonymous post on our school's ChatterJaw account. It said something I didn't understand about how I wasn't going to resurrect Will because there was trouble in paradise."

"Were you in a fight?"

I'm quickly discovering that Ringo is the easiest person to talk to that I've ever met and I try to weigh how much I should watch my tongue before saying, "No. Of course not." Will and I did bicker with each other plenty, usually about stupid things, like when he talked too loud in movie theaters or how he always had to make small talk with strangers. Penny was always our tiebreaker. In a few quiet Penny sentences, she could tell us which one of us was right without making either of us feel wrong. "But . . . it's bothering me. Like why does someone think that they know Will's and my relationship better than I do?"

"So ask the person who posted it," Ringo says.

"It's anonymous."

The *clack-clack* from Margaret's keyboard pauses. "I'm offended," she says. "You are sitting in front of the wizard."

"Gandalf, Dumbledore . . ." Ringo lists them.

"Merlin," she says.

"You can find out who posted it?" I ask. "Anyone?"

She twists her mouth and pinches one shoulder to her ear. "Almost anyone. It has to be tied to a traceable e-mail address that the user has logged in with. So, like, there are limitations. If someone didn't use their normal account, used an alternate IP address, maybe if they went private, but otherwise, yeah. Show me the post."

And so I do.

"Need another one while we wait?" Ringo points to my empty mug.

I give him a thumbs-up, then lean over to him and say softly, "I like your friends." I scan the crowded corner. I'm not even sure what half of them are doing, but I've never been someone with a large group of friends. Obviously, since my entire social crowd has been wiped out in a single car wreck. It's lively and the relationships seem more fluid and less intense than I'm used to.

Ringo winks and it wrinkles the uneven skin around his eye. "Be right back." He raps the table twice with his knuckles and disappears toward the front counter.

Despite what I had just said, my chest instantly tightens as I look around at the group of faces with whom I know I don't fit in. The swell of being on the outside, of not belonging, grows inside me, like yeast rising up my throat and closing off my airways. The terrible part of it is that I had thought I was past this. I believed that Penny and Will would always be around to insulate me from this very feeling. That it was okay for me to never have to start a conversation with anyone new because Penny didn't feel awkward anywhere she went, because Penny would be there all day every day.

Penny and Will were my miracle when I had no one else, and here I am alone again and I am starting to wonder if anyone will notice if I get up and run.

But then Kai, who is straddling the back of his wheeled chair, plants his feet on the concrete floor and pushes toward me. He comes zooming over in one athletic arc and catches himself on the side of the table.

He grins, flashing blindingly white but crooked teeth. "What kind of girl are you?" he asks, rubbing his chin into the hand that's resting on the seatback. He stares up at me with dark eyes. His black hair is buzzed into a high-top fade with not an inch of fuzz at the line where it reaches his ears.

I reach for the mug of coffee and take a sip, realizing too late that it's empty. "That's, um, a loaded question."

He narrows his eyes and looks me over like he's trying to guess my measurements. "Liz Phair, I bet," he says. "No, no." He holds a finger up like an exclamation point. "Wait, something with a little more gumption. And girl power!" He claps. "Letters to Cleo?"

He waits and it dawns on me that I'm supposed to have a response. "Are those . . . bands?" I venture, biting my lip. He widens his eyes and gives me a perfunctory nod as in, *Hello, of course they are.* "I don't know, I guess I'm more of a Top Forty girl?" I wince, knowing full well that this is the wrong answer.

Kai clutches his neckline and stretches out an open-palmed hand dramatically. "Jesus take the wheel!" he cries out in a theater voice. "Please, please, please, tell me you have not told our Ringo that. That boy is fragile as my mama's wedding china and that may break him."

"My . . . musical taste?"

The confusion and concern must be obvious on my face—Ringo, fragile? And would he really care what I listen to on the radio?—because Vance drags his chair over to us. Vance is just as thin, long-limbed, and bony as Kai, but he has the complexion of a vampire. His dark hair is tucked into a knit cap, and black-rimmed glasses frame an angular face.

"Excuse him." Vance nods at Kai. "His mother sent him to theater camp at a tender age and now we have this."

Kai makes a show of being offended. "Excuse *you.* The camp circuit is *still* buzzing over my debut as the Artful Dodger in *Oliver Twist.*"

Vance's eyebrows lift above the frame of his glasses.

Simone glances over from behind her thick crop of bangs. "Are these two harassing you?" she asks.

"I don't think so," I say quickly, but Simone gives them each a stern look anyway.

"A makeover!" Kai bounces on his seat. "That's what we'll do." He must see that I look skeptical because he says, "Oh god no, you're gorgeous. A musical one. And Christ, just because I'm gay does not mean I can do hair."

Vance puts his hand on Kai's knee, a gesture that seems loving and as though he's trying to quiet his excitable boyfriend all at once. "He's trying to indoctrinate you," Vance says. "You know, we accept her, one of us, gooble-gobble, gooble-gobble, that kind of thing."

Kai squinches up his face and then rolls his eyes. "It's a quote," Kai explains with a dismissive wave. "He likes old movies too. Not one of his finer qualities."

"Not when you fall asleep by seven o'clock during the opening credits," Vance snaps back.

"Please, when I'm thirty and have a face like a baby's bottom, we'll see who's complaining."

"Still me," Vance replies. I bounce between them like I'm watching a tennis match. Neither Duke Ellington nor Simone seems to take notice at all, so this kind of back-and-forth must be a regular occurrence.

I've almost forgotten what I am doing here and what I'm waiting for when Kai looks past my shoulder and says, "Give us the song for today," and I turn back to see Ringo handing me a fresh cup of coffee.

He smiles down at us. He has a nice smile, wholly untouched by the mismatched hues of his skin, and I think again about what Kai said, about Ringo being fragile, and wonder if it can be true.

"'Come Together,'" he says.

"I . . . still don't know that one," I confess, but Vance is already retrieving his laptop and handing me one of the earpieces he had been sharing with Kai. He scans down a list on the screen, selects the *play* button, and I try to relax to the new sound of the Beatles, to live just for a moment as if the weight of everyone else's expectations and my own need for Penny and Will weren't crushing the air from my lungs.

I listen until Margaret slides a scrap of paper with a name on it over to me, and the lovely tune that had been drowning out my worries turns off-key in my ears, and the juggling balls of Ringo's coffee shop friends come crashing down around me.

# chapter fourteen

## *1,343 DAYS*

In middle school, my best friend was Jenny. A best friend was an important thing to have in middle school. Anyone who was anyone had a best friend and Jenny was a good one to have because she bought us matching bracelets, linked arms with me whenever we walked to class, and called me her BFF in a loud, brassy voice that made people pay attention. But I didn't really like her. If I spent longer than two hours with Jenny, that loud, brassy voice began to drive me insane. And she was always wanting to choreograph dance numbers to songs that I didn't like. In fact, given the choice between hanging out with my mom and hanging out with Jenny, I'm embarrassed about how often I'd choose my mom.

That wasn't the case with Penny and Will. Penny has this theory that soul mates don't have to be romantic, and so that's what the three of us are. Soul mates.

Three months after I started at St. Theresa's, we're

huddled together on the floor of Will's bedroom. My back's pressed to the closed door and I'm listening to the muffled sound of his parents' screams.

"Her name's Linda," I report back solemnly.

"*Linda?*" Penny wrinkles her nose. She's seated cross-legged with the backs of her hands resting on her knees, like she's meditating. Her printed silk pants drape onto the carpet. Her bangles are silent. "Linda," she repeats. "That name has a very cold energy, doesn't it?"

"I've never really spent much time on the energy of the name Linda," I whisper. Penny mouths the name *Linda* again, like she's still considering it.

Will drops his head between his knees. "That's his secretary. God, could he *be* any more cliché?"

Penny and I share a worried look.

"I think this calls for the snack stash," I say.

"I'll man the door," Penny volunteers.

I crouch on my knees and pull out a plastic tub from underneath Will's bed. A limp sock comes out with it and I chuck it back under the dust ruffle. I toss the bags of powdered donuts and potato chips into the center of the space between Will and me and hand the dehydrated kale chips and almonds over to Penny.

"Thanks," Penny says in a hushed voice, popping a kale chip into her mouth.

I watch her munch as I tuck my knees under my chin. Something happened earlier today, something I haven't told either of my friends. Matt spoke to me. It was right as I was finishing getting dressed to come over to Will's. Matt seemed nervous. He made small talk, something about a pelican he had watched dive into the ocean and come up with I-can't-remember-what in its mouth. I was in a hurry, barely listening, trying to get over here because Will, I knew, was in crisis. But Matt had memorized the night's showtimes at the local movie theater, memorized them so that he could tell them to me, so that we could go see a movie together. And I didn't pay attention. I realize that now on the floor of Will's room with the lights turned off. "I'll be back later tonight, Matt, or tomorrow," I told him as I scooted around his wheelchair to leave. There's a spoiled-milk feeling in my stomach when I linger on the image of Matt's face too long.

But as I watch Will, sitting inches from him—the boy who has been there for me and made me feel like I belong somewhere—I think, What else could I have done?

"I hate him," Will is saying and I try to tune back in. Because *we* are a family too. "How can he leave my mom like this?" There's a crack in Will's voice. I scoot nearer to him so that our hips are pinched together. I let my head fall against his shoulder. Penny gives me a sad smile. Will sniffles and I push the thoughts of my brother aside for the sake of the people who don't make me work so hard, or make me feel so terrible, just for the privilege of loving them. That's what family is. Will's and my families have just somehow forgotten. "What if it's, like, hereditary or something?" Will says. "Being a lying cheat. What if it is?" I know that what's happening is a tragedy in Will's life and I feel terrible about it, but at the same time I have a deep sense of rightness because he feels he can reveal this side of himself to me and to Penny. It's my most promising sign that the weeks we've had since the bird won't be just a passing phase. Will and I are here to protect Penny and I'm just now learning that Penny and I are here to protect Will.

"It's not," Penny says softly.

I feel Will shift underneath me and I move my head from his shoulder. When I do, I see that his deep-brown eyes are trained on me. "Promise me that I'll never be like him."

My tongue sticks to the roof of my mouth. A shiver races up my spine. I tried with Matt until I could no longer try any harder and when I stopped I found this. "I promise." My words are almost too soft to hear. And right then, I know that it's official. I'm falling in love with Will Bryan.

"*Ssssh, sssssh,* you guys." Penny flaps an arm at us. She leans in and presses her ear to the door. She's holding up a finger, telling us to wait. The finger slowly lowers. "Will, you're going to have a sister," she says.

# chapter fifteen
## *18 DAYS*

Margaret figures out the name of the anonymous poster in under an hour. I don't need to take the scrap of paper on which she'd written it. I'm not going to forget a name I already know: Harrison Vines.

He's the same year as me at St. Theresa's. It's common knowledge that he's had a crush on me since the second I set foot on campus and that *I* think he's a sexist pig. As far as I know, this in no way makes him think we are any less compatible. So there's a better than 80 percent chance that Harrison has made up the whole thing because he hopes that Will's death will leave a vacancy . . . in my pants.

But then again, that would be pretty dark, even for Harrison.

I decide to stop by the public beach on the way home, where I know Harrison lifeguards full-time during the summer. When I reach the public beach, the late afternoon has just begun to melt into the evening hours. The sun has gone orange and smolder-y, its outer edge gently kissing the horizon where it will slowly continue to melt into the world's largest puddle. European tourists with their tight Speedos and sunscreen-painted noses are collapsing their umbrellas and preparing to drag them up to the parking lot, which won't be bearable to walk on without sandals for another hour.

I kick my shoes into the thick reeds growing near the boardwalk and cross the beach toward the blue lifeguard stand near the shore. A green flag flutters in the breeze, letting beachgoers know that the water is calm and there have been no signs of aggressive sea life. But as a local, I never swim at dusk on account of the fact that it's dinnertime for sharks.

"Harrison!" I yell through cupped hands as I get closer. "Harrison!" The surfboard and orange rescue buoys are buried halfway in the sand, so I know the guards are still on duty. "Harrison Vines!"

A head pops over the railing of the stand—a small hutch on stilts that is painted blue. The boy lifts his reflective sunglasses and nestles them into a thick crop of dirty-blond hair. "Lake?"

"I'm coming up," I say, and scale the sandy steps of the ladder, my palms scratching against sun-baked wood on the way up. Harrison is waiting for me, wearing a tank top and a pair of white shorts with a red cross on the side. A whistle dangles over his chest.

"Is everything okay?" he asks in a way that sounds like he's genuinely concerned.

"*No*, everything is *not* okay."

"Right." He puts his hands on his hips and nods, understanding. "I heard."

"I know you heard," I say.

He pinches his chin between his thumb and forefinger until it dimples. "Listen, I'm on duty for another ten minutes. Until then I'm not supposed to have visitors on the stand. Would you mind, like, waiting inside the hutch?"

I roll my eyes. "Seriously?"

"Believe what you want, but I'm good at my job, okay? So in or down, pick your poison."

I huff. I don't like Harrison, but I'm also remembering how I haven't really talked to him much in the past four years. In fact, I haven't talked much to anyone other than Penny and Will, and that's exactly the way I've wanted it.

I move past Harrison into the hutch. He stands in the doorway, looking out at the ocean. There are a few swimmers still paddling in the shallows. He drums the wood with his fingers. "We keep a cooler," he says. "*Not* for while we're working or anything." He meets my eyes as if to make clear that he means it. "But there are a few beers in there and wine coolers. You can help yourself."

I start to object. I don't drink. Here and there a few sips, maybe a glass, but then I remember that my only two friends are dead, my brother hates me, and my life blows like a category five hurricane, so I fish in the ice until my fingers freeze and I come up with the slender neck of a tangerine wine cooler. I borrow the bottle opener from on top of a stack of crates that doubles as a desk and settle into an open lawn chair to wait.

The taste of fruit and alcohol is tangy and delicious on

my tongue. I notice that I'm halfway through the bottle and that the fizz is already traveling to my head before I remember I have to drive and force myself to stash the remainder underneath my chair, out of sight.

At last Harrison blows his whistle. He takes the flag out from its holder on the railing, gives it a ceremonial wave, and then lays it horizontally on the wooden landing outside.

He ducks into the hutch and we stare at each other like we're each from some alternate universe and are recognizing alien life for the first time. Harrison removes the whistle from his neck and hangs it on a nail.

"Am I supposed to guess the reason you're here, Lake? I'm sorry about Will and about Penny. The team's planning on doing a memorial or something for Will, but, well, they're waiting to see what happens." Harrison and Will are on the school's lacrosse team. They don't hang out much, but it's impossible not to like Will, so I know the two get along and I believe Harrison when he says that he *is* sorry.

"Why did you say I won't choose Will?" I ask, and to my surprise I don't sound that pissed, more like curious. Like *Please, tell me the answer, tell me why I choose Penny instead.* As if Harrison Vines is some kind of oracle.

"What are you talking about?" But Harrison angles his muscular shoulders away from me.

"On ChatterJaw. Why did you make that post? Trouble in paradise?" I repeat and let my hands fall in exasperation to my bare tan thighs.

His brow line twitches down for a split second. "ChatterJaw is anonymous."

"Not, it turns out, if you know the right people." It

feels good to be in control of the situation, even if it's one step in a completely crazy out-of-control process. "So don't bother messing with me, okay? We both know I'm on a short timeframe here."

Harrison sighs and leans against the crate. He has pale sunglasses-shaped tan lines around his eyes. "Why do you think?"

"I don't know, you have some crazy, weirdo stalker crush on me? You're mean? You like to torture small animals and dance on headstones?"

He lets his head droop and stares at me, deadpan. "I've been dating Maya for a year, Lake."

"Oh." I press my lips together. "I didn't know. Congratulations. Maya's nice."

He lets out an irritated laugh. "Yeah, she is." Then he runs his hands through his hair and it stays put from all the air's sea salt. "I shouldn't have posted it. I'd take it down if I could. It was stupid." ChatterJaw posts are permanent. Whatever goes on the virtual bulletin board stays there. Period. One of the reasons the drunken Saturday night threads are so good to peruse on Sunday morning.

"But you did," I press.

"I—look, I don't know what I saw. Maybe it was nothing. Maya thought it was nothing. She kept saying that I was butting in where I didn't belong. But, I don't know, it was just this one day, I was in the locker room, running late for practice because I had to tape up my knee. Will must have just set his phone down on the bench because the screen was still on and all these messages started coming through. From ChatterJaw. His phone was blowing up. I wanted to know what was going on because I figured, I don't know, maybe it was something big. I couldn't help it—okay, fine, maybe I could have—but you know it alerts you when there's a response to a thread you posted on. Well, I checked the thread and there were only two people responding to this one. I read through some of the messages and they just seemed—well, it's hard to say, I guess."

"They seemed what?"

He pinches the bridge of his nose. "I don't know, Lake. Will was a good guy, one of the best, so I'm not saying there was anything, like, scandalous. I figured you probably knew, honestly, but then—look, you can read the thread for yourself. Check in the 'Spilled' forum, about a month back. The title of it was *Love is for Fakers*." The title alone makes me sit up straight in the chair. "I think they went private," he says.

"Who?" I ask.

"How should I know? It's anonymous."

My lips purse. I don't know what to say. *Love is for Fakers?* Will Bryan wouldn't be caught dead in a thread like that. Unless he was joking or arguing or I don't know. Harrison Vines didn't know Will. I did.

I stand to leave. "Thanks for the drink," I say.

"Lake?" He stops me as I'm about to take the first step down the ladder and onto the beach. "If it helps, my uncle, he was resurrected. You could talk to him, if you need to. About it."

I swallow. "Right, I . . . appreciate that, Harrison."

The sand prickles my bare feet against the wood.

"People can grow up, you know," Harrison says to the back of my head. "If you give them a chance."

I shrug, knowing what he means but not being sure what I can do about it now. I take the long way back to my

# chapter sixteen

## *18 DAYS*

*Love is For Fakers*

I'm a mosaic made from sharp edges and broken things

As long as no one looks too closely—not even me—none of the ugly bits show through

Those parts that want to smash love and tear holes in hearts

But I'm still made up of the broken things

Even if nobody knows

I still feel them

Ripping into my soul

Did you write that?

A part of me did, yeah

Is it true?

I think so, a lot of the time anyway

Well, when you said it, did the ugly parts show through?

Yes

Maybe they're not as ugly as you think

Or maybe they're even uglier

I feel like that sometimes too

Feel like what?

Like everything's just an act. Like what's the point?

Like none of this stuff

is who I am on the inside

Like I'm constantly on stage performing

The part of great guy

Are you not a "Great Guy"?

Maybe not a Great Guy

But I'm a decent one I think

I wanted to be a GG but

I think maybe I'm just a phony instead

It's

.....

Exhausting?

Kill me, I'm whining

Stop. That's the GG talking

Just be the decent one today maybe

The thing is

I don't know that I can start that now

You kinda already are

I'm hijacking your thread

You're the only one reading it

Still.

How long have you been writing poetry?

Is it poetry? I think they're just words.

You're lucky. You can write the true things

On an anonymous message board . . .

It helps I think. Even if nobody reads it

I know I'm there somewhere on the page

Where I can find me

I'll read it

Do you write?

No. I draw. Stupid cartoons mainly

I'd like to see one someday

If you're lucky

I thought we already established I am ^^

# chapter seventeen

## *17 DAYS*

"Fine, you win." I stare down my nose at my brother, wheelchair parked in the corner of his room, eyes fixed on a made-up point beyond his window while listening to an audiobook in French. I click *pause* on the media player. "I want you to give me the clue. So tell me your terms."

I've given up. I'm exhausted. Last night, I managed two hours of sleep. The words in my head from the ChatterJaw thread would not stop whispering on and on and on until I would have pulled my hair out by the roots if it had made them go away.

Matt puffs into the straw and spins to face me. He stares hard in that unflinching way he has that makes you feel as if he's uncovering some inner part of you that you'd rather keep hidden. I wait for the shift, for the flash of my brother before the accident, the one who sometimes appears so vividly on his face that I half expect him to stand up and declare that his paralysis has been some elaborate game of make-believe. But that alternate-universe brother of mine isn't there, not even for the most fleeting of instants. In a way, it makes all this easier. "You have to promise to take me with you," he says and there's no hard edge of laughter in his voice now.

"Where?" I ask.

"On each stop of the scavenger hunt." He enunciates his words like a professor.

"And why would you want to do that?"

The only reason my brother leaves the house is for doctors' appointments, and it's an ordeal. There's the loading of him into the car. The exhaustion that takes hold of him so easily, he's hardly able to withstand a trip for more than ten minutes before he's cursing with fatigue and irritation. Not to mention he hates the outside world.

"Closure," he says.

*"Closure,"* I repeat. "For who?"

"You."

"That makes it sound like this will be the end of Penny and Will for me." I narrow my eyes to slits. "It won't. But even so, what's in it for you?"

He blinks slowly, deliberately, refusing to rush even as he knows the minutes are barreling past me and my birthday is drawing closer and closer and closer. "I get the chance to make my case," he says. "An audience, as they'd say in medieval times. To convince you that I am *still* the right choice."

I peel my glance away to stare out the window. Yeah, except I'm not sure Matt was ever the right choice.

When I was younger, I used to pick my nail beds bloody,

worrying about the day when my parents would stage an accident to help kill my brother. Even at fourteen I knew there'd be no coming back from that. Not as a family. Whether he drowned or fell from a balcony or they bludgeoned his head or he accidentally overdosed, they would willingly pull the last thread that held us together and they and my brother would no longer be the same people I loved. I was supposed to be a part of that.

"I'll take you," I say. "On the scavenger hunt. Just give me the first clue so that I can get on with this thing." Before I was worried that if I let Matt be involved, I'd be giving a piece of Penny and Will away. Now I worry that if I don't, I won't get any pieces of Will or Penny back. So I vow not to let it happen. He'll be a passenger and that's all.

"Every stop of the way?"

"Every stop of the way." I can't find a way, not without the first clue. And I need it now more than ever. Because of what Harrison told me. Because she—whoever *she* was—had known something about Will that I hadn't. He'd shared something of himself with this anonymous girl—assuming it even *was* a girl—that he hadn't shared with Penny or with me.

After I spoke to Harrison and read the thread that turned everything upside down for me, I went back to Neville's to see if Margaret could uncover the other user. I didn't even care if I was overstepping my bounds and asking too much of a relative stranger or that the shop was twenty minutes out of my way back home. But Margaret and Ringo were both gone and I was left with a thousand questions and no answers.

For now, I wanted to set the universe right. I wanted

to find those wishes. To hear Will speak through the words written on the scraps of paper. To know that Will and I aren't just an institution, we're the real deal.

I won't lie, though. I feel guilty when I tell my mom that I'm taking Matt out. Only because she looks so damn hopeful and it makes me want to cry that I can't make her heart whole and fix mine at the same time. We have to take her van because it's the only vehicle we have that's outfitted for Matt's wheelchair. I've heard that there are quadriplegics that can drive by using hand controls, but unfortunately Matt's not one of them, and I wonder sometimes when I catch myself still thinking about such things how just one small change to Matt's condition like that, how a break in his spine just a single vertebra lower might have changed the quality of his life entirely.

Mom asks a bunch of questions about where we're going and what we'll be doing and when we'll be back. I guess Matt's already thought it through, because he has answers for everything. We're going to the library. There's a speaker this afternoon. Something about the Civil War. Mom keeps looking at me all, *You sure?*

She even interjects and says that I have a lot on my mind and maybe it'd be better for me to stay close to home, but I say that I'm fine and I need to get out of the house.

I suppose it's hope and the fact that I don't have any friends left that make her believe I'd want to get out of the house with Matt.

Matt won't recite the first clue until we've finished the whole loading process and driven away from our street. I pull to the shoulder of the road, where the tires of Mom's van crunch the broken seashells scattered there. The smell of rotting seaweed seeps in through the closed windows.

"Well?" I push the gear into park. "You'd better not have forgotten a word."

"Do you want it or not?" Matt asks from the back.

"Sorry," I mutter.

He clears his throat and then puts on a surfer-boy accent that I don't appreciate: "'Welcome to your great, big, epically magnificent, cowabunga awesome birthday scavenger hunt! First clue: Our inspiration was shaped like a type of shoe. I was nervous and so were you. Go to the place that welcomes tramps. Bring back a ball—quick!—before you lose your chance. Don't screw this up, Devereaux. Love always, Will.'" Matt drops the imitation, which for the record sounds nothing like Will, who had a nice deep-but-not-too-deep voice and never sounded like an idiot. "Happy?"

I close my eyes. "Repeat it."

He does. Word for word, exactly the same, so I know it's real and that he hasn't forgotten anything. But after that, my heart begins slipping down rib by rib until it winds up in the bottom of my stomach. *"Crap,"* I groan, and lower my forehead onto the steering wheel. "I don't know. I don't know what he meant." I hadn't expected this. I beat my fist against the dash. "Say the last half again," I command.

"'Go to the place that welcomes tramps,'" Matt recites. "Personally I think it's a brothel. Seems like the most logical place for Will."

I sit up long enough to glare at him through the rearview mirror. I've run into a problem, though. Will planned for me to complete the scavenger hunt with him, meaning if I got stuck, he could serve as a backstop. Okay, so he'd probably have made me suffer before showing mercy, but I would have made it to the end. I'd have gotten the prize.

But now what?

Think, Lake, think. I had been so sure that this would be the answer. My methodology. My way back. Everything. But if I couldn't use this, what would I do?

I feel the telltale signs of tears tickling behind my nose and in my eye sockets. I don't want to cry in front of my brother, but I'm not sure I can help it. I keep my head on the steering wheel and try to keep my shoulders from shaking.

Matt sighs loudly, then says, "Italy."

"What?" I push my fists into my eyes and swipe away the tears.

"Italy. Italian food." Matt is mumbling so that I have to strain to hear. "'Shaped like a shoe,'" he quotes. "He means a boot. Italy is shaped like a boot."

I twist to face him. The seatbelt cuts into my chest.

"Any Italian restaurants significant to you?" he says.

A lump rises in my throat. "Yes." Barely above a whisper. "Yes, we . . . had our first real date at Taterelli's."

Matt presses his lips into a line. "Well, there you go. Guess you have your answer."

I watch my brother carefully before finally turning and moving the gear into drive. "Thank you," I say, and I find that I actually mean it.

I see now that the ball from the clue is a meatball—like the one the two main characters, a cocker spaniel and a mutt, share in this animated movie, *Lady and the Tramp.*

Will bought a remastered version of it to show his little sister, Maddie, who we had actually come to like despite the fact that her mother was *Linda*, and Will and I brought popcorn and sour candies and stuffed our faces with Maddie while watching the movie with her, which I think we enjoyed probably twice as much as she did.

A happy memory expands my heart, testing the strength of the arteries and veins that hold it to my chest. We drive downtown to Taterelli's, where I circle the block three times, looking for handicap parking. "You have to be kidding me," I say, leaning over and searching the spots. "Where do they expect us to go?"

Matt scoffs. "Are you surprised by this?"

"Um, yeah." I flick the blue permit hanging from the mirror. "This is supposed to mean something. There are *supposed* to be designated spots."

Matt sighs, like I am so naïve it physically exhausts him. "I don't know if you've noticed, but the world's not exactly designed for people like me."

I chew on the inside of my cheek until it becomes raw, barely listening. By the fifth time that we pass the restaurant's green awning I make a decision to stop in the middle of my lane and turn on the flashers.

"What are you doing?" Matt asks indignantly.

I push the minivan's gearshift into park. "What does it look like I'm doing?" I say. "Getting you out." I wait until a few cars pass and then jump down from the van. Matt's ramp unfortunately unloads from the driver's side and already there are two cars stopped behind us. The first one puts on its blinker and waits for the chance to swerve over into the next lane, which it does at an entirely unnecessarily high rate of speed. I put my hand up as a human stop sign right outside the front of Taterelli's and try my best to look authoritative.

I press the button and Matt's ramp begins to unfurl. "Lake." His face comes into view, contorted into an irritated look, bordering just this side of angry. "Stop, this is—this is—we're in the middle of the road." I'm not used to seeing my brother flustered.

I put my hands on my hips. "They'll wait."

"I don't want to do this," he says.

"Too bad, we already are." I glance over my shoulder. Cars farther back in the line with drivers who can't see what's happening ahead of them begin to honk. "You wanted to come."

"Just park and leave me in the car."

"Uh-uh, no way." I stoop and march up the ramp, swivel his chair, and begin backing him down into the street.

The street has erupted into a cacophony of honking horns by now, and even my cheeks are going red at being the cause of the holdup. Still, I manage to get Matt's wheelchair onto the blacktop, but then run into an additional hang-up when I have to bump his wheels up onto the curb. I watch the back of Matt sway clumsily in the chair as I hoist the apparatus onto the sidewalk.

I wipe my forehead, which is slick with sweat, and rest for just a moment with my hands on the rear handles of his wheelchair. The honking escalates. "Okay, God, I hear you!" I shout at them. The air outside the restaurant smells like cooking oil and marinara sauce. "Wait here," I tell him.

"Lake, wait—" But I'm already sprinting back to the van. "Okay," he calls after me. "But if you can't find me, I'm having a beer at the bar down the street."

Very funny.

I retract the ramp and throw the car into drive, this time heading a few blocks over, and find a parking spot about a five-minute walk away.

I hustle back to my brother with the sun burning my skin. Downtown shoppers and beach tourists step around where I've left him on the sidewalk, most with sour looks on their faces. A woman pulls her young child's wrist closer to her and I catch her saying, "Watch out for the nice man." And see Matt roll his eyes in response. I stare after her, wanting to yell at her that my brother isn't the bogeyman for goodness' sake, he's just a boy in a wheelchair, but find myself thinking twice because sometimes he is sort of scary. At least to me.

"Gee, Lake," he greets me. "Thanks for leaving me in the center of a busy sidewalk. Super swell of you."

I grit my teeth, feeling disproportionately exhausted from the day already. "I'm doing my best, Matt." But then I see it. The stairs up to Taterelli's and no ramp. I am positive that on my date with Will a fact like that wouldn't have registered. Taterelli's sits in an old historic district of downtown. I scan the storefront and find no suitable way up.

"Shit," I say.

"Shit," Matt agrees.

I close my eyes and take a deep breath. "I'm going for help."

It takes me no effort at all to climb the six steps. A blast of cool air greets me in Taterelli's, where the inside of the restaurant feels three shades too dark.

"Can I help you?" A hostess comes into grainy focus.

I'm looking around at the restaurant. I haven't been here since . . . since Will. It looks exactly the same. Dark-red curtains. Tiny candles on each of the tables. Fresh long-stemmed roses sitting in a vase atop a grand piano that's being played by a guy in a gray suit and cufflinks.

"Would you like to see a menu?" asks the hostess, politely.

She holds out a laminated booklet. I know that if I open it, there will be a list of entrées way too expensive for any high school kid.

"No." I hold out my palm and push the menu back in her direction. "My brother. He's in a wheelchair. See, we were trying to come in, but there's no ramp. I need help getting him up. Please, can you find someone? Preferably someone big and strong," I say, eyeing her silky blouse and waif arms.

Her mouth forms a dainty O of surprise. "Of course, of course. One moment." And she disappears down a dimly lit hallway.

After what feels like an eternity, the flimsy-armed hostess returns with two young men in grease-stained T-shirts and rolled-up sleeves. They introduce themselves as Antonio and Teddy.

Frustrated by the wait, I usher Antonio and Teddy outside, where my brother sits with his head bowed over his lap. "Matt?" I venture.

Matt lifts his head. Sweat is dribbling down his nose and from the hair plastered to his temples. There are droplets in his eyelashes and he's squinting and blinking and can't seem to open them all the way to look at me. His hands rest uselessly on the armrests of his chair.

"I brought help."

Matt's mouth turns into a sneer and I feel more than see him harden. "And they're supposed to what? Snap their fingers and magic me into the restaurant?"

"No." I take a deep breath. I can't help being embarrassed by the way Matt acts in front of other people. "They're supposed to carry you."

Antonio and Teddy hustle to either side of the wheelchair and position their hands on the handlebars and through the spokes of the wheel.

"Not a problem, buddy," says Teddy.

Matt's eyes snap into focus. "No. Lake. No. This is humiliating. I'm not a— Whoa." The wheelchair teeters into the air. "Stop manhandling me, *buddy*. Put me down. Right now."

Teddy and Antonio share a look. Teddy nods and they lower Matt to the ground again.

"I didn't think you got humiliated," I say.

His jaw clenches. "Leave me here. I don't care."

Teddy's eyebrows swoop up, questioning.

"Come on, Matt." I groan and tilt my chin to the sky.

I watch as a familiar darkness spreads over Matt's face, slowly, like a building storm. His Adam's apple bobs up and down, a sign that I recognize to mean he's shifted from uncomfortable to in pain. Because despite not being able to move from the chest down, his whole body can still wrack him with agony any time it damn well pleases.

I shouldn't have brought him out here. I don't know how to care for Matt. I don't even know how to talk to him.

"Please, Matt." His gaze is stony. "There's air-conditioning in there."

He stares up at me through his lashes. After a long moment, he nods. "Fine."

Teddy and Antonio make soft grunting noises as they spirit him off the ground and carry him into the restaurant like he's royalty. By the time his wheels touch down, Matt's using some very creative curse words.

Antonio disappears back into the kitchen the first chance he gets, shaking his head. "May I show you to a table?" Teddy asks, though.

"Christ, Lake." Matt's chin is squished against his chest. "My goddamn eyes."

"Right." I glance around and spot a napkin on a place setting at the first table in the fancy dining area. I quickly grab it. The silverware clatters noisily to the table. "Here." I come back and gently lift his chin with my fingertips. I then dab the corners of his eyes, his lashes, and his eyebrows, where the sweat is still trickling, until it stops.

When Matt is able to fully open his eyes again, I'm caught, level with his gaze, staring into the gold-flecked irises.

"Thanks." Matt's voice is soft.

"Yeah, um, no problem."

"So," Teddy interjects.

"Right, yeah." I stand up straight and press the napkin to my own damp forehead. "No table. We're not ordering any food. I don't think, anyway." When Teddy looks confused, I soldier on. It was just like Will not to care how completely embarrassing and out of my comfort zone this whole interaction might be. "My boyfriend came up with this scavenger-hunt thingy." I think I see Teddy's smile falter for a split second. "For my birthday. I think this is one of the spots, but I'm not exactly sure what I'm supposed to do here."

"You're supposed to bring back a ball," Matt says. "Her name is Lake. Lake Devereaux."

Teddy raises an eyebrow. "So, you must be the famous Lake, then."

"That's me. Well, except for the famous bit. I'm the nonfamous Lake Devereaux. Hope that's okay."

"She's just being modest. This little lady has completed the *eleventh grade*," Matt says in the slowest and most condescending tone possible.

"Boyfriend, you said?" Teddy tilts his chin away from me and studies me out of the corner of his eye.

"Um, yeah, that's what I said." There's a pause. "Why? Is something wrong?"

Teddy blinks and shakes his head. "No. Sorry. He just came in with someone."

"Hippie looking? Lots of jewelry? Offbeat clothes?" I say.

He cocks his head. "No, I don't think so," he says. "I think I would have remembered that. Anyway, I just thought—well, it doesn't matter what I thought." My heartbeat quickens because it doesn't sound like Penny, which means it might have been someone else. Another girl. But we didn't hang out with any other girls. Teddy nods abruptly and spins on his heel. "Right. I'll, uh, be right back." And he vanishes in the same direction that Antonio has.

I tap my foot on the carpeted floor, and since I don't want to think about the someone that Will came in with, I decide to snap at Matt instead. "Do you have to be such an *ass* to everyone?"

"Oh, the eleventh-grade comment? I'm sorry. I just

thought the twentysomething bus boy should slurp up his drool given that, I don't know, you're still in *high school.*"

"He wasn't drooling."

"Please, Lake. You know what effect you have on people," Matt mutters and glances away. "Your friends. School. Everything's so easy for you. I mean, I'm your brother and all and trust me, the whole thing makes me want to vomit, then aspirate my vomit so that I can vomit again, but even I know, the pretty thing . . . it works for you."

I grind my teeth together and cross my arms. "You're an idiot" is all I can muster.

Because I know I'm pretty. I have known since the first moment I walked into St. Theresa's and met Harrison and Peng. But to imply that I have friends because of the way I look is ridiculous. Hurtful, even.

Unbidden, though, and despite my best efforts to ignore every sign pointing me back to it, Will's secret posts echo through my mind: *Well, when you said it, did the ugly parts show through?* And it's as though someone has socked me in the stomach with a baseball bat. Again.

Maybe that's why I'm confused when Teddy reappears holding out a Styrofoam takeout container. "What's this?" I ask. Or it could just be the fact that Teddy is holding out a Styrofoam takeout container, since that in itself is pretty weird, considering I didn't order anything.

"A meatball for the lady." Teddy grins, but his grin folds when he notices Matt staring hard at him again. Teddy shifts his weight on his feet. *Lady and the Tramp.* I was right. The two dogs have a fancy dinner and nudge the meatball to each other between their noses. It's oddly touching, even for someone like me who doesn't like dogs.

Will, of course, adored dogs. Then again, he didn't have a scar on his hand from where one had bit him, so that made it easier.

"And this." He hands me an envelope. On it, Will's handwriting spells out my name, and then underneath it: *Clue 2*. Seeing Will's writing after his death feels eerie. I can't stop staring at it. I consider asking for more information about the someone with whom Teddy saw Will. Could it still have been Penny, just in less free-spirited clothes? But instead I gingerly pick up the envelope and press it to me.

Teddy offers us a close-lipped grin and then takes his leave.

"Right, well." I suck in a breath. "I guess I'll pull the car around so that we can cause another traffic jam."

"You're not going to read it?" Matt asks.

"Not right here." I stuff the envelope in my back pocket. I feel too exposed here. Maybe it's the idea that perhaps Teddy had been checking me out after all that makes me uneasy. I don't know. Will hasn't been gone a week.

God, this is all so confusing.

I notice that Matt's stare could burn an ant alive.

I roll my eyes. "I'm not backing out of my promise. I'll read you the clue and you can come with me on the next one. I didn't leave you out on the sidewalk or in the car, did I?"

"So you haven't escalated to the level of abusing cripples. Whoop-dee-doo." But even with his head tilted down, I can see the faintest smile threatening to peel open the seams on his perpetual scowl. "Hurry back."

I do. I speed walk to the van, my hands trembling slightly as I work to jab the key into the ignition. The clue in my pocket feels like a bomb waiting to go off. Another stop. Another memory. The same Will? I don't want everything to change. But since the accident it's as though I can feel the ground gradually shifting underneath me. One way or another, things are going to.

I pull the van around the corner close to the curb and turn on the hazards. To my surprise, when I return, Matt is actually talking to the hostess.

"A total shoo-in." His eyes twinkle up at her. "You know, I don't get out much, but as far as I'm concerned, I bet they'd put your face on the cover."

"There's a *cover*?" She kneels down so that she can be on the same level as Matt.

"Of course. Hair, makeup, wardrobe, the whole works. I bet they even let you keep the clothes. Is that a thing girls care about?"

"Um, yeah!" She claps her hands. "Are you kidding me?"

"A-hem." I scoot closer. I raise my eyebrows at Matt, who swallows a grin and slides his glance sideways toward the door. I smile and thank the hostess, and I get the sense that she feels very proud for having entertained the boy in the wheelchair while he waited.

I lean close to his ear as I push the chair out of the restaurant. "What, is there some kind of moratorium on relentlessly mocking that you're observing, or were you just that enamored with Miss Taterelli's over there?"

"Oh no," Matt whispers back. "No moratorium. It's not my fault she actually believes that there's a contest for the most interesting food service employee and that she should enter it. She asked where to find an application."

I can't help it. I laugh.

Teddy and Antonio reappear to carry Matt down the stairs, and the loading of Matt into the van goes much more smoothly than the unloading. We ride in silence past the empty tourist shops that sell beach towels and sand buckets while the envelope containing the second clue rests conspicuously on the center console, waiting to be opened.

# chapter eighteen

## 1,094 DAYS

"Where are we going?" On the starlit road in front of me, Will stands up to press his full weight into the stiff pedals of the fat-wheeled Huffy bikes that we stole from Penny's garage. "If I'd have known we were making a cross-country road trip, I would have worn real shoes," he says. Like mine, Will's feet are sliding around in a pair of flip-flops.

I listen to the sound of chinking metal and the whir of spokes. We're following Penny's lead, each chasing the flutter of her white-blond hair like it's a comet. The air is warm and dry. I'm still wearing my bathing suit top and jean shorts from this afternoon. Specks of sand stick to my legs and between my fingers and toes. It's the end of our first summer together. Next week I'll be turning fifteen and Penny and Will have already been bugging me about what I want to do for the big day. But I don't care as long as it's with them.

"On life's journey, faith is nourishment!" Penny calls back.

"Is that from *Star Wars*?" Will asks.

"Buddha, you idiot!"

"Well, I don't think Buddha banked on having to ride on a banana seat," I say, trying to ignore my chafing thighs.

Our laughter fills the darkness of the empty road. My skin is electric. We told Penny and Will's mothers that we were staying over at my house tonight and we told my parents we were crashing at Will's. Nobody bothers my parents on account of the fact that they think my mom and dad have their hands full enough with Matt. But Penny stuffed blankets in the basket on the front of her bike and she tied a cooler with a bunch of snacks to Will's, which is probably why he's whining so much.

We're biking away from shore, uphill, so that sometimes we have to get off our bikes and walk beside them. "Did I tell you I used to have asthma?" I say to them, still huffing and puffing.

Penny scrunches up her forehead. A gauzy tunic covers up her bikini. "What do you mean 'used to'? Asthma doesn't just, like, go away."

I shrug. "Mine did."

"Weird." And then she comes to a full stop. And Will nearly runs his front wheel over the back of her ankles. She lets her bike crash on the side of the road. Will and I share a look. "I think this is it," she says. "My dad used to take me here as a kid to camp." This surprises me a little, since Simon Hightower is a tech-nerd who works at a fancy tech company and treats the family's gadgets like the FBI or internet hackers could be trying to survey them at any moment. In other words, he doesn't exactly scream *outdoorsy.*

But I suppose he does scream *good dad.*

I feel jealous of Penny because I used to have a dad like that too, but the jealousy is gone in an instant. Only a silvery sheen of light cascades over the rocky landscape that butts up against the road. A ragged wooden sign reads: CAT MOUNTAIN STATE PARK. "Do you see that?" she asks, tilting her face up to the sky.

*"Ummmm . . ."* Will scrunches up his eyes and stares up in the same direction, spinning around like a dog after his own tail. "I'm gonna go with *no*?"

"It's a full moon."

"So?" I say.

"So, it's the last full moon of the summer. That's when dreams are born." Her eyes are shining, filled with excitement and light, both of which are contagious. "We had to do *something.*"

Will and I learn that the something involves gathering up by the armful the small stash of supplies we've brought and tramping off the road into the baked terrain.

The ground is uneven. Penny takes out a battery-operated lantern and I trudge after it to the sound of crickets. Will and I walk shoulder to shoulder. He's still shirtless from our day spent scouring the beach for sharks' teeth to add to Penny's collection, and the light bounces off his chest.

Weeds strangle the path and get caught on our flip-flops. Will catches me by the arm more than once to stop me from face-planting. It's not until we're nearly on top of it that I see the cave. A low rocky cliff, pierced by a dark opening, forms an open jaw in the stretch of landscape before us.

Penny's lantern swings as she turns to face us. "It's an old cougar den," she says. "Don't worry, it's been abandoned for, like, a billion years. My dad said most of the bones are fossilized."

I pick my way over the rocks to the opening. The seeds of adventure and the unexpected are blooming inside. "Cooool." The word blows out, long and amazed. "Bring the light over here, Pen."

I stare at the ground until the light pools around my feet. There, a pair of curved white ribs lies in the red dirt. I bend down and run my hand over the length of bone. The cave is shallow. The glow of the lantern easily reaches the back wall of stone and we drop our belongings at the cave opening.

Will shows us half a paw print preserved in the mud, and he shows a gopher skull that he finds to me but not to Penny, because he thinks it might upset her. Ever since Will's dad moved out, Will's started to go quiet for a few hours, sometimes even a day, at a time. If I watch him closely, I can tell that he wants to *go dark* now, which is the name I have in my head for this mood of his. When the words run out and we have to wait for our Will to come back.

I think maybe that's why Penny wanted us to come out here. So I hope that she's right and there is something magical about the full moon.

Meanwhile, Penny is spreading out a threadbare blanket on the ground. She sets it in the center and makes us sit around it cross-legged, like we're in kindergarten. I wonder about the time and whether it's after midnight yet. "Now." She lingers on our faces individually for a couple of seconds each. "You guys have to promise not to laugh." The backs of Penny's hands are resting on her knees, palms up to the cave ceiling. A choked giggle sticks in my throat and I put my fist over my mouth to clamp it in. Penny shoots me a Penny version of a sharp look, which is sort of the same as being scolded by a cartoon version of a baby bunny.

"How about we promise to *try* not to," Will says for the both of us. The dimples in his cheeks deepen in the lantern shadow.

"We're here for a friendship ritual," Penny presses on, and fishes in her bag.

Will holds up a finger. "Let's make that a tentative promise, then." There's a crackly smile in his voice that makes me glad Penny believes in the effects of things like lunar phases and gravitational pulls on people.

She straightens her posture and stares at Will as sure and steady as if she were queen of the cave. "Are you in this trio or are you out, William?"

"I'm in," I say, quickly.

"See? Lake gets it."

"But she *started* it." He points to me.

I push his hand away. "Real mature, *William*."

Penny tugs her tunic down over her thighs. "You guys already know this, but you two are my best friends." *Uh-oh,* Penny is already starting to tear up. This could be rough. "Will, we've been friends forever and, if it wasn't for you, I'm pretty sure everyone at school would just think I was a weird hippie or witch or something, but no offense, it's nice having a girl around."

"A *little* offended," he says, cocking his head.

I shove his shoulder and he topples over onto the blanket. "Penny, *continue*," I say.

"Right." She holds a knife out to us. "So this."

"Christ, Penny," Will says, dramatically dusting off his elbows and reseating himself. "If you've been doing all of this to murder us, I have to give you credit, you've really been running the long game."

"I'm not planning to kill you, but if you don't cut it out I reserve the right to change my mind." She flashes a sweet smile. "*Anyway*, as I was saying, ancient civilizations have been doing blood rituals to seal relationships for, like, thousands of years." Her voice lowers to nearly a whisper. "The rituals are sacred, for only the deepest bonds. I don't have a brother or a sister," she says. "You guys . . . are my blood." I can see the ropy veins in her throat tighten. Her eyes are shining.

And all I can think is that I used to have a brother that I tried hard to keep until it burned me up inside, and when he finally wanted me—*if* he finally wanted me, because I've made my choice and now I'll never know—there was nothing left of our relationship but ash. I swallow down the memory of Matt's face after he recited the movie times to me, after he told me about the pelican. I swallow down my own broken heart, rough and jagged as if made out of glass, chipped to pieces every time I reached out to him. I wonder if it could have been different between us. If he had tried sooner and I had tried longer. I . . . just wonder.

"Then let's make it official," I say at last, voice catching on one of those glass shards.

Will doesn't even make another joke. He offers us each a hand to pull us up. Penny's gone all trembly and the knife is shaking in her hands.

"Are you sure about this?" Will asks, and he's instantly the Will I'm used to, the one I like best. When I had to watch Will and Penny from afar, I noticed how he cared for her gently, the way he would a baby bird, scooping her into the nest. I didn't quite understand it until I knew Penny too. She's strong and brave in her own way, but if Penny is to be Penny, sometimes Will and I have to be there to hold the world at bay. Now that I'm no longer watching from the outside, I've noticed something about Will. He's at his most magnetic when he's *doing* things for other people, and I wish that I didn't feel what I'm feeling when he gently presses his hand between her shoulder blades and looks Penny squarely in the eyes.

She nods. "It's just the thought of the blood." She laughs softly at herself. "Probably should have considered that." Her eyes close and she must mentally travel to a different place, because her features ease. "I wish sometimes that I was as brave as you." And then her piercing green eyes are staring straight at me.

I wonder what it must be like to feel the whole world stampeding around inside your heart. "You're braver," I say, and mean it.

She pinches my cheek like an old grandma, teasing me. "You're pretty even when you're lying," she says.

Will goes first. "Cheers," he says. He holds his hand up in salute. After that, he takes the tip and drags it across one palm straight through the crease that fortunetellers call the lifeline. He scrunches his nose, then closes his hand into a tight fist and wipes the blade over his shorts.

I take the knife from him. I don't have to think about it. I dig the metal straight into my flesh until I feel something hot rise to the surface, and I fold my fingers into a matching mushed-up ball, same as Will's.

Last is Penny. Her teeth dig into her lip. She holds the knife all limp so that it couldn't cut a wet a noodle if it had to.

"Pen," Will says so tenderly, it microwaves my insides into a puddle. "Pen, you don't have to do this. It's just symbolic."

I'm not sure what makes her do it, but she resolves then and there to. She cuts the line the worst way—while staring at it. Then she drops the knife in the dirt and looks at us, wide-eyed. "I did it," she says. "I did it."

My own hand stings, even worse when I try to open it so that the breeze can touch the open gash. I close it right back up and hold it close to my heart.

"We have to make the covenant," she says. "Now, before our cuts dry up."

We grow still and watch Penny swipe her shoe to smooth a spot in the dirt. "Swear," she says, "that no matter what, the three of us will always be friends. Swear that we'll be there for each other. Even if in college I go through some weird pixie-haircut phase and move to Mumbai or Lake starts hanging out with the skaters and grows dreadlocks."

"Hey! That's not me," I interject, but Penny shushes me.

"Once our blood mixes, we'll be bound forever," she says. "Swear."

"Swear," I say.

"Swear," says Will.

Penny stretches her arm out over the ground and lets two drops of her blood drip onto the dirt. Will and I both follow suit. Our blood mixes, forming a damp blotch on the ground.

"Make a wish," she says, like she knows something magical about full moons for sure and not just for maybe. "Make a wish on the moon, but don't tell a soul." She returns to her bag and pulls out scraps of paper and pens, Mary Poppins–style. She hands me one, and each of our bloody thumbprints appears on the page. "That was for us, now this is for you." Will gets a scrap too. "The universe demands balance."

I stare at the page and think about balance and how a year ago I was losing it all, crumbling away piece by piece like a sandcastle built too close to the sea. Somehow the events of the last few months have led me to a cave of bones where I can sit beside my two best friends and watch them worry over their wishes. I rest my chin on my knee, hoping to lock down the dorky swell of emotion. But I can't help feeling that if I'm a sandcastle, I'm finally being built farther up on land by Will and Penny together.

I write my wish and don't tell a soul for fear that it won't come true.

# chapter nineteen

## *15 DAYS*

"What's so wonderful," says Dr. McKenna, the sound of her voice snapping my attention on like a light switch, "is how present your love for your friends still is. I want you to try to think about that bolstering feeling of overarching love in your life when you feel yourself getting bogged down with grief, okay?"

I blink and look up from my fingers, which I've been knitting together in my lap. How long have I been talking? I glance up at the clock.

She waits several beats, and when I say nothing else, she closes her notebook gently and presses it into her lap. "Thank you, Lake. I believe that's all we have time for today."

"Oh. Yeah. Sorry," I say, a little bit embarrassed, but her smile is warm and unbothered. I haven't told her about the scavenger hunt or about how I know the wishes, even my own forgotten one, are waiting at the end of it. She might have understood why I needed them, but then again, she might not have. In any event, she briskly ushers me out of her office.

Time is money after all, I think drily, before realizing this is something Matt would say to me when I was a kid. Back then he'd lean over and share these quick observations and it made me feel grown-up, the way the two of us both knew something that no one else in the room did. Of course, he still makes the side comments, it's just that now they're mean and I'm often the punch line.

On my way out of Garretson, Smith & McKenna, the door opens abruptly before I can reach for it, and the edge knocks me in the forehead. I yelp, clutching the center of my skull.

Strong hands grasp my shoulders and steady me. "Lake? Whoa, are you okay?"

I lower my hand and stare up into a face cut in half by a strawberry birthmark. "What's the saying? Adding insult to injury?" My laugh is forced and limp. As though my month could get any worse.

Ringo chuckles. "Sounds like you'll live."

He lets go of my shoulders and, for a hairsbreadth, I have a quick pang of wishing that he hadn't.

I miss Will, I remind myself. It's the missing Will that makes me crave contact. *Any* human contact.

I rub again at the spot where the door knocked me. "Do I have a mark?" I ask, without widening the space between us.

He squints, one eye shut, and studies me. "I think you have quite a ways to go until you can compete with this." He gestures around the side of his face.

Despite myself, I smile. "I thought you'd already left today. Later appointment?"

He shakes his head. "No, I just went for a walk. Finished up an hour ago."

"Still with the late ride?" I ask. I imagine his mom on the couch watching her soap operas and sipping out of her Big Gulp and it makes me angry.

He folds his hands dramatically over his chest. "My cross to bear."

Another person comes through the door. Ringo and I press our backs against opposite walls to let them through, and I have this annoying sensation, like an adult has just caught us making out. I clear my throat and nod toward the exit. Ringo follows me out into the waning sunlight.

"So how are you feeling?"

I touch the tender spot on my head. "Fine, fine—I was just being dramatic. I mean, I seriously doubt I'm concussed or anything."

"I meant about your decision."

"Oh, right, that." I bite my lip. "Swinging wildly between heaving into a paper bag and total denial. Honestly, it feels like I'm living in, like, a great big hourglass and the little granules are falling on me faster and faster until I'm pretty sure I'll suffocate."

"Healthy."

"Yeah, well, my cross to bear, right?" I mean it to come out as a quip, but the moment the phrase leaves my lips I can tell it sounds more like a jab at Ringo.

"You . . ." He takes a sudden and deep interest in his tennis shoes. "Haven't texted or anything since the coffee shop. Did I do something?"

"You?" I can't help it, I laugh. "No! God, you're, like, the only sane person I know right now." What with my parents, who I can hardly look at, I feel so guilty—even though I shouldn't feel guilty, but I do feel guilty—and then, of course, there's Matt and Will's parents and Penny's too: if I had to spend time in a room with one living person, it would be Ringo. I determine not to study the implications of that too hard.

"Sane?" he says. "You might want to take a look at where we're standing." He glances back in the direction of Dr. McKenna's office.

"That's just geography," I say. "I've been kind of busy."

"Oh, then . . ." Apparently there is more territory to cover with those shoes, since Ringo goes for another look.

"Matt told me the first clue."

Creases form in his forehead as he looks up at me. "So you're on your way. Good for you."

"Sort of," I hedge. It feels good to be having a real conversation, one without a hidden agenda, but it's been nearly forty-eight hours and I still haven't opened the second clue. I thought that starting the scavenger hunt would make me feel better. And it did, visiting Taterelli's, remembering the early days of my relationship with Will, only it hasn't drowned out the other needling worries swirling around in my head. The words I read kept surfacing at all the wrong moments.

*Like I'm constantly on stage performing the part of great guy . . . maybe I'm just a phony. . . .*

Instant nausea. Because, see, the thing is that the Will I know *is* the Great Guy, he doesn't just act it. But if I'm being 100 percent honest, the scavenger hunt itself and all my birthdays before have a way of feeling like evidence of a performance now. I just always thought Will relished the showmanship. After all, parts of that personality were there before his dad left. He was outgoing and made everyone love him. Then Penny and I worried during the whole my-father's-secretary-is-having-his-baby fiasco that he would become quiet, sullen Will. But he recovered, right? And Will Bryan was bigger than ever and he was mine.

Here's the truth: a guy that makes a show of being a great boyfriend *is* a great boyfriend. What I can't wrap my head around is the fact that it might not have been genuine. And if it wasn't, then I'm stuck right in the middle, following one of the stage pieces, playing out a scene that Will didn't really want to be acting in any longer. "I haven't exactly figured out the next clue," I say. Then again, I think, maybe the last few days are just messing with my mind. "Ringo?" I say, and I already know that I'm not thinking through what I'm about to propose next. "Will you go to a shiva with me?"

He raises his palms to me and shuffles back a couple of steps. "Ah, Lake, sorry if I gave you the wrong impression, I'm not really into kinky stuff like that." But his eyes are squinted into moon-shaped crescents, so I know that he's joking.

I put my hands on my hips, tilting my head. "It's a Jewish tradition for when someone dies. I don't understand the exact details. It's for my friend, Penny. . . ."

Ringo's eyes don't leave mine for a second. A lock of his hair falls into the lashes of one eye, and I have to clench my hand into a fist to fight the urge to gently push it back off the purpled skin and into place. Luckily, he does it for me. "She was Jewish?" he says.

I feel a pang at the use of the past tense. I wonder how

many times I've used it myself in the last few days. "Penny? God, no. She worshipped, like, Mother Earth, pretty much. But her parents are." I get the distinct feeling that Ringo doesn't want to go, which only makes me want him to more. "There will be food and drinks and—"

"Lots of people I don't know," he interrupts.

"Well, yes, that, but . . ." I deflate. "That was extremely weird, wasn't it? Me just inviting you to a shiva. I don't know what's wrong with me. I don't even know if *shiva* is a *noun*." I run my hand over the top of my head. "Sorry." But the idea of not having to go alone felt like someone throwing me a life raft, and the thought of going with my parents felt akin to going in a life raft—but one loaded down with two tons of cement and emotional baggage.

Ringo rubs his chin, tosses his head and groans. "Sure," he says.

"Sure?"

"Sure, I'll go."

"To the shiva?" I brighten. "Because you know it's basically a funeral, right?"

"Not the traditional third date, but what the hell."

I blanch at the word *date*. "I didn't mean it as a . . ." I say slowly, thinking, Will, Will, Will. Will the leaver of epic voicemails, Will the best hand-holder, Will the boy I love.

Ringo lifts his eyebrow. "Lake, relax. I know. It was a joke." My shoulders slide back down the length of my neck just a bit. "Flattering reaction, though." He peers down his nose at me with a gentle smirk. Ringo accompanies me to my car, and I don't even mind that he's probably coming with me out of pity. It's worth it to have him be there.

Ringo drives. He insists, but it's not like I put up much

of a fight. He hums intermittently, and it's a nice distraction from the road. In between he tells me about the Beatles and how when he was in middle school, playing their record *Abbey Road* was the only thing that kept him from wanting to blow his brains out. I can't tell if he's serious.

But it's when he lists the band members that I startle. "Ringo Starr is the drummer's name? But I thought you got the name Ringo because of... well..."

"Because of the ring around my eye? It's okay, Lake. I'm aware that I have a birthmark on my face." I flush. "And you're right. That's how I got the name." He cracks his knuckles over the wheel. "But," he says, brightening, "it's also how I discovered the second-greatest Ringo in history." He shrugs. "You know what they say, if you can't beat them..."

I don't have time to process this because we're pulling up to Penny's house and the van we're pulling up behind is my mom's. I didn't want her here. But she is here. And that means she has unilaterally decided I can't handle this on my own and that instead she will come rescue me with her loaded boat of cement and painful words between us that go unsaid.

Only I'm not on my own. I'm with Ringo. And I wish none of us had to be here.

# chapter twenty

## *15 DAYS*

Penny's house is two stories and made of yellow stucco. Unlike ours, the lawn is always perfectly maintained by Tessa, a natural gardener, and Simon, who put his techie senses to good use, installing a hypersensitive automated sprinkler system of which NASA would be jealous.

A friendly WELCOME wreath adorns the pale-blue front door. The rest of the yard bears all the remnants of Penny. Her kooky wind chimes dangle from one of the branches next to a hummingbird feeder. At the corner of a well-maintained flowerbed, Penny built a rock garden. It's only a few square feet, but Penny claimed it had perfect feng shui.

I pass the Penny artifacts and every bone in my body goes flu-cold achy. I've been so caught in my fog of sadness that I haven't quite fully realized how much of it was specific to missing Penny. Now that I'm here in the presence of so much Penny-ness, though, the loss is breaking into me like a wave.

"You okay?" Ringo's hand finds the small of my back and I worry that it's the only thing holding me up.

Outside the house there sits a pitcher of water. A man is entering right before us wearing a yarmulke. He bends to wash his hands in the pitcher and then lets himself inside. I look to Ringo for guidance.

"We don't want to look disrespectful," he whispers.

I nod and dip my hands into the cool water. Without thinking, I run my wet hands over my cheeks. It cools the heat rising in them and quiets some of the discomfort. I nod and we let ourselves into the home of Tessa and Simon Hightower.

"I probably should have worn black, huh?" Ringo says into my ear. We both stare at his purple Clemons University T-shirt. He does stand out. And not just because of the T-shirt.

In the foyer, black cloths cover the mirrors. I scan the mourners gathered in the living room for my mother but don't see her. An elderly woman with silk pulled gently over her gray hair shuffles over to greet us. She extends a bony hand to me.

"Lake, dear," she says. I recognize the voice, though it's been over a year since I last saw her.

"Grandma Adler." I take her hand, which is as cold as her veins are blue. I cup it in both of my own, hoping to warm them. Grandma Adler is Penny's grandmother on Tessa's side. My own grandparents had all died by the time I was five years old, but visits from Grandma Adler became a treat for both Penny and me. Seeing her brings tears to my eyes instantly.

She reaches up with her free hand. The skin on her thumb feels papery thin as she wipes away the trickle running down my cheek and says something softly to me in Yiddish.

"I would have come sooner if I'd known you were here," I say, starting to turn to introduce Ringo but feeling the empty space behind me just before I do. He's gone. The swell of panic has subsided now in the company of Grandma Adler, and I tell myself that I'll find him. Later.

She pats the back of my hand and begins leading me into the living room. I'm not sure I'm ready to go in, but I walk beside her, holding onto her elbow to support her. "I would have come sooner myself," she confides. "Tessa is not honoring *k'vod hamet.* Penny should have been buried right away. But Tessa won't hold a funeral. She won't allow burial rites. We didn't even know Penny . . ." Grandma Adler pulls a crumpled tissue from her pocket and dabs at her nose. "We didn't even know she had passed away."

I try to keep my steps and breathing even. It's nothing I couldn't have predicted already, but to hear the lengths to which the Hightowers have gone, hoping for my resurrection choice, sends pain searing through muscle and bone, where it continues to burn.

"It was her cousin Halina who saw the accident report on the news." I've been avoiding the news for that very reason. "Rabbi Fisch informed the rest of the family, and I told Tessa we are sitting shiva and I won't hear another word. Here"—she takes a torn black ribbon from a basket resting on a side table—"put this on. We have to honor Penny however we can."

I glance around for Ringo, worried that maybe he decided to leave after all. I'm trying to stand on sea legs and, suddenly, it doesn't feel like an eighty-year-old woman is going to be enough to keep me upright. The Hightowers have turned their backs on the rituals of their faith. All because of me.

As if by necessity, Mom appears next to me. Before this moment, the thought of her intruding on my space with Penny's family seemed like it'd be a violation. But at the moment, I don't think I mind. She has on her usual odd mash-up of clothing that she puts together whenever she's forced into social situations—an unflattering peplum top six seasons old paired with slacks too baggy in the leg, and kitten heels. "Lake, honey." She runs her hand over my hair. "Mrs. Adler, I'm so sorry for the loss of your granddaughter. *Hamakom y'nachem etchem b'toch sh'ar availai tziyon ee yerushalayim.*"

I gawk at her in surprise. "What does that mean?"

It's Grandma Adler who translates for me. "'May God comfort you among all the mourners of Zion and Jerusalem.'" She nods. "Thank you."

"If you'll excuse us," my mom says to Grandma Adler and leads me away.

"How do you know—I don't know—*Hebrew*?"

Mom's smile is sweet and sad. "When you've experienced tragedy, Lake, you want to help others who are experiencing it in whatever small ways you can." We weave through the other mourners. "Tessa and Simon are lucky to have a community surrounding them." Her voice is wistful. I glance up long enough to see a canvas portrait of Penny propped up on an easel. I recognize the photograph. I took it. It's Penny in our spot. The cliff overlooking the point where the three of us—well, at least Will and I—jump. Penny sits cross-legged on a rock, meditating with her eyes closed. Her pointer finger and thumb are pressed together, the backs of her hands resting on her knees. The pink sunset behind her turns her blond hair into a golden halo.

I swallow hard, surprised that Penny's family picked *this* picture to display. The Hightowers are kind people, but they're very by the book—PTA, expensive Tommy Bahama shirts, that sort of thing. I always got the impression that her parents thought that the free-spirit, whale-saving, yoga thing was just a phase, a stop on Penny's way to law school as opposed to a monastery in Tibet. I knew better.

"Mom," I say, careful to keep any anger out of my voice because I'm not—angry, that is. "I didn't ask you to come."

"I know," she says.

I'm about to explain why when I notice a slim girl who I immediately recognize crossing the room toward me. Maya's long graceful legs carry her to us in a few easy steps, causing me to lose my train of thought entirely. She weaves her fingers together and clasps her hands below her waist. "I'm sorry for your loss," she says to me. Her dark hair is swept back by a shiny gold headband. She offers my mom a close-lipped smile, then dabs at her nose with a crumpled tissue. It could be my imagination, but I think Maya may have been crying.

Mom beams down at her. "I'll let you girls chat for a

minute." She shrugs and it comes across cutesy and falsely conspiratorial. I want to throw up.

"What are you doing here?" I ask.

"You're not the only one broken up about Will's death... and Penny's," she adds, almost as an afterthought. She crosses her arms, tucking the hand with the tissue beneath one armpit, and looks off to the side.

Her comment annoys me for reasons that I can't quite pinpoint. "You hardly even knew them," I say.

She sniffles. "I knew Will. Maybe not like you, but I knew him. Both of them, I mean," she adds. The hairs on the backs of my arms prickle, but before I can reply, her eyes flit skyward and she says, "Relax, I go to Penny's parents' synagogue. I'm not here to lay claim to"—she sweeps her hand over the room—"any of this, okay?" Maybe I was being paranoid. "Look, Harrison told me you came to talk to him about that stupid ChatterJaw thread. And I just wanted to say that he means well. Harrison, I mean. Really, he does. He feels like he has to, I don't know, watch over everyone." I think of how seriously he's been taking his lifeguarding duties and how I might have underestimated him. "It can be really sweet. But this wasn't his place. He should have minded his own business and he certainly shouldn't have posted about what he read on ChatterJaw." At this she blows a long stream of air out from her jutted lips.

I narrow my eyes. "He mentioned that you were against me knowing about that thread in the first place," I say. "Why?"

Maya pins a stray hair back underneath the metallic band. "I told you. He doesn't have the full story."

"And you do?" I ask, not quite sure why I'm pushing Maya on this so hard, but feeling my bloodhound senses going ballistic.

"No," she says. "I don't. Just like you don't have the full story about us." My stomach tightens. I assume she's referring to Harrison and her, or . . . is it something more than that?

That's when I start to notice the uncomfortable amount of scrutiny I'm receiving from onlookers all around, casting furtive glances over plastic cups. Words die on my tongue. People are looking at me. I hear someone whisper, "That's her best friend."

Is that what they said?

Maya glances over her shoulder. She seems to sense it too.

My ears prick at the mention of my name. Yep, that's definitely what they said.

My jaw clenches. Unexpectedly, Maya reaches down and squeezes my hand. "You'd better go find your mom," she says. I nod mechanically. She lets go of my palm. I push through the crowd, but now snippets of conversation reach me with every step.

"Resurrection . . . is there a chance?"

"Apparently the girl's boyfriend was . . ."

"Any other hope?"

That last one is followed by a sullen silence.

My heart trips faster and faster. Out of a cluster of people, Mom yanks herself free and clasps both of my arms and stares into my eyes. "You doing all right, kiddo? You look a little green."

A smooth black dress interjects itself in front of me, followed by a charcoal-gray suit.

"Tessa." My voice cracks. I realize I have never stood in the same room as Mom and the woman who treated me like a daughter when my own mom was too busy with Matt. I wonder if my mom is coming to the same realization too. "Simon," I say. I'm wishing that I'd come to visit them some other time, when I didn't have to be here in front of all these people.

"Lake, sweetie." Tessa wraps her arms around me and pulls me into her breast. Her perfume smells like roses and cinnamon. "Your arm." She unclasps me and latches onto the cast around my elbow. Her expression is pained. "Does . . . does it hurt?"

I turn the cast over. The weight of it still rests in her hands. "No, not too bad, really. It's fine." I gently extricate it from her grip.

"It's kind of you to come," Tessa says to Mom.

Simon clears his throat and ever so slightly fills his chest with air to increase the heft of his presence. "We're . . . uh . . . we're sorry about that, Lake. And about Will, of course. We're . . . very, very sorry."

And then it strikes me. They feel responsible *to* me, like Will's dad said. Penny was driving. In everyone's eyes, Penny caused the accident. And yet, they hadn't held the funeral, they hadn't done the burial rites.

I wish I could be anywhere but here. I look to each side, eager to feel Ringo hovering next to me like a security blanket, but he's vanished and what I'm left with is a chill. And the initial relief I felt at first finding my mom here is evaporating.

I crane my neck back to see if I can even catch a glimpse of Maya in the room, wondering if this would be a comfort.

The whole experience in all its strangeness is already taking on the quality of a dream to me. But she's faded into the black outfits too.

"It wasn't Penny's fault," I say, turning back and forcing myself to accept that what is happening right now is reality. I wish they could know how badly I want to bring their daughter back too.

"Actually," Simon says, imposing his figure in my path so that there's no escaping even if I want to, "we were hoping we could talk to you about something." The strain in his voice is unmistakable. He looks nervously to my mother.

"Maybe now's not the right time," she says. If it's possible, she manages to grow taller beside me.

*Where is Ringo?*

Penny's parents share an "adult" look. "Lake," says Simon, ignoring my mom's protest. "We know how close you and Penny were—*are*— We never had another child, but you two were like sisters. Heck, you practically are sisters."

"That's enough," my mom says. "She's only a child."

I stiffen and step away from her. *"What?"*

"You're only a child." She turns back to the Hightowers. "I know you're suffering, but this isn't fair to put on her."

Anger hardens, scratching my throat like a ball of steel wool. "Since when has that ever stopped you?" I say.

"Lake." Her voice is a warning. She shouldn't worry. I'm not going to spill the big family secret. But she's just as bad as the rest of them. "I'm only trying to help."

I fold my arms across my chest and refuse to look at her.

"We want you to take our car," Tessa jumps in. She's wringing her hands together, stretching her fingers from the back knuckles out. "And we have about five thousand dollars we could offer you."

"Tessa . . ." Simon warns. "We discussed how we were going to go about—"

She presses on. "We can probably get a little bit more. We're not very what they call, I guess, *liquid* right now. Our assets, I mean. And I know time is of the essence, with your birthday coming up. But please, Lake. We'll do whatever we can. You have to know we're good for it. Just give us time. Name your terms."

I'm bright red with shame for her. For Tessa of all people to cross the line from crass to flat-out illegal—I never would have expected that in a million years.

I hear a man yell as though it's coming from a dream—or a nightmare. Will's dad appears in the center of our clump of bodies. "I can't believe you people."

Mourners turn to stare. The rabbi puts down a deviled egg. I count the seconds between heartbeats. *One . . . two . . .* And then Ms. Bryan is there too. *Three . . . four . . .*

"This shiva is for Penny," Simon says sternly.

Logan doesn't hear or doesn't care. "Jolene, they are trying to *buy* Lake's resurrection off of her."

My mom flails her hands. "No one is doing anything. Lake is leaving." The color has returned to her cheeks. Bright-pink brushstrokes.

"Stop it, Mom," I say, pulling my arm away from her.

Ms. Bryan spins on Tessa. "How could you lower yourself to that, Tessa? *Pay* her? *Really?* We'll call the police on you. We will tell the bureau about this. Don't think we won't."

Tessa's eyes bug like she's been holding her breath too long, and she bursts out, "Then Lake would lose her resurrection altogether! Then where would we all be?"

"I can't believe you—" Ms. Bryan's shirttail frees itself from her skirt.

Tessa bares her teeth like a cornered animal. "You think I don't know about your little dinner with Lake?"

Ms. Bryan wraps her fingers more tightly than I'm sure she means to around my elbow. "Lake, we know your resurrection can't be bought. You loved Will."

"Oh, stop your manipulative bullshit, Jolene," Tessa snaps.

Mom puts herself physically between the two women and holds out her hands. There are no more seconds between heartbeats.

"Stop," I repeat, but this time to Penny and Will's moms. "You two are friends. *Best* friends."

No one hears me, though. *No* one is paying attention to me at all.

A sob escapes Tessa and it sounds like a drain coming unclogged and then there's a lot of water. Everyone's grief is spilling out onto me and it's bigger and pushier than my own, and I want to scream and run until there's space enough for all of my sorrow. These people really think that I don't want Penny and Will and even my older brother back enough for myself? Do they think I want to be the best, if not only, option to get their kids back? It makes me sick. But no one else from our nice private school would even consider using a resurrection choice on anyone but family or close to it.

In the midst of the shouting, there's a tug on my wrist.

I look over to see a face cut in two and a pair of eyes that look comfortingly lopsided.

I let him drag me from the group of adults, who don't seem to notice me leaving, but I don't let him lead me away from the house and from the yelling. Instead, we wrap our fingers in each other's and I pull him up the stairs. I wish I could pick up the phone and call Penny. I imagine her listening to how fucked up this whole week has been. Matt. Will. Her parents. She'd know what to do.

I am pretty sure that I am crying, though I don't pull my hands away to check. I only know that my face is hot and that my nose feels stuffy. "What happened to you?" I ask with a hint of accusation.

"I was giving you space," he says as if in echo of the exact words I was thinking moments earlier. Space for my sorrow, space for me. But I don't think I want that space from him.

We walk down an upstairs hallway decorated with framed school pictures of Penny in chronological order from kindergarten all the way to eleventh grade. I stare at the blank place on the wall for senior year. And then I sink down to the carpeted floor and moan into my hands. "They don't think I miss her," I say. I rock, hugging my legs and pushing my kneecaps deep into my eye sockets until I see stars bursting in my vision. The pressure squeezes out tears that flow faster and harder. "They don't think I'd give anything to have her back if I could."

Ringo has sunk down next to me. He hasn't let go of my hand. I struggle to breathe through my stuffed-up nose.

"I wish I'd gotten to meet her," Ringo says.

"But"—sobs are still erupting out of me at short intervals—"if she—were here—we never would—have met."

He hums and I pry my face away from my legs far enough to see him studying a photo of Penny with braces, circa seventh grade. "You keep forgetting we already had."

I let the meaning of his comment go unexamined. I am too tired. I let Ringo's hand go too, though I'm thankful that it had been there to lead me away. With Penny and Will, I didn't need anyone else. Ringo couldn't understand that. The three of us were different. Special. At least I thought so. After a time, I push myself upright. I can feel the tears already crusting on my skin. I take soft footsteps into Penny's room, like I'm walking onto holy ground. It still smells of incense, and the longing in me presses out against the borders of my skin, throbbing.

Carefully, I touch her belongings. Seashell necklace. Moroccan scarf. Honey lip balm. *Penny.* I try to imagine the words she'd say if all this were over and she found me at the cliff. She'd look at me and know what I'd been through, sucking the week's worry in like she could take it all back from me. Together we'd talk about Will every day. She'd weave a basket out of palm fronds or something and we'd send parts of his memory out into the ocean and she'd know exactly the right words to say.

My fingertips land on a well-worn spiral notebook. I hesitate before flipping through it. I'm flooded with thousands of Penny's words all gathered up like an answer to a prayer. I hesitate, checking over my shoulder to see Ringo squinting at a framed picture of Will, Penny, and me with our tongues out, all dyed red from cherry slushies. I slide the notebook into my purse along with the lip balm and zip it closed. Finally, it feels like I have a piece of Penny to carry around. I relax for the first time since I entered the Hightowers' house.

"Over here, Ringo." I cross the thin rug to the window, wedge my fingers under the the edge of it, and jiggle open the frame. I turn to gesture for Ringo to follow.

"Look, I know you're going through a rough time, but jumping? Not the answer." His head is cocked to the side like a bemused dog, so I can tell he doesn't think I'm actually suicidal. But he still doesn't appear to be keen on following me out an open second-story window. Sensible. I can respect that.

So I demonstrate by hoisting one leg through the opening, then the other, and soon he can see that I'm crouching comfortably on the roof. It takes only another moment's hesitation before he joins me.

"Welcome," I say, taking a seat on the sandpapery shingles. "This was our spot. Mine and Penny's." The view is of the backyard and of overflow parking of the attendees from the Hightowers' synagogue. Weird. Never in my worst nightmares did I dream of coming out here and looking down at . . . this.

"It's, uh, cozy." Ringo's hip is pressed against mine. We're hemmed in by the slope of the roof beside us and the edge below. "So what exactly are we doing up here?"

"There's oxygen up here," I say, somberly.

Ringo shakes his head. "You really should get some help with that oxygen addiction of yours."

I nudge him with my elbow. "Penny and I used to sunbathe out here. Or sometimes when I slept over, we'd sneak out the window and fall asleep. I know, I know, it *sounds* dangerous, but we'd hold hands so that if one of us began to roll off, the other one would wake up to save her." Ringo pulls one eyebrow up. "Okay, so, it wasn't, like, a foolproof plan. But no one died, right?" We both go silent.

I chew the inside of my cheek, searching and thinking—for what, I'm not quite sure. In the end, I start weighing whether or not to tell him this next thing and then find a strange compulsion to do it. "We tried pot up here. Just once," I add hurriedly. "It was dumb. Penny got this joint from some guy in her yoga class." I rest my chin on my bent knees, embarrassed now that I've begun. "I'm not even really sure it worked. We felt, like, a little, I don't know, *fuzzy*. Penny said she hated it. I thought she was just being dramatic." I turn my cheek to my knee and peer at Ringo. "You ever tried it?"

Ringo snorts softly. "I'm more of a 'Just say no' guy."

I remember how mad Will had been when he found out we'd tried it without him. I wanted to explain to him how, once we were dating, I owed Penny her own special things so that she stayed *mine* too. I needed them both. Will and Penny, Penny and Will. *The universe demands balance*, as Penny would say.

"Okay, then." I bump my shoulder into his. "You tell *me* something."

"Like what?"

"A secret." I bob my head to add a silent *Duh*. "I told you one and now you have to tell me something. That's the way it works."

"Excuse me? Referee?" He mimes looking around. "I believe I've been entered into the game against my will."

"Well?"

He sighs and runs his fingers through his hair. I realize that I really like his hair. Or at least I notice it a lot. Ringo has nice hair. Why am I thinking about his hair? This has to be the most anyone has ever thought about *hair* in a thirty-second period. *Lake . . .*

"My real name's . . . Christian." This snaps me out of my hair haze.

*"Christian?"* I roll the name over my tongue. "Christian . . . as in feeding the multitudes with loaves and fishes, walking on water, resurrecting on the third day Christian?"

"At least one of those fits."

I form my fingers into a makeshift picture frame, squint one eye closed, and view him through the diamond-shape opening. "Nope." I frown. "Doesn't fit. *Christian?* Are you sure?"

"Pretty sure."

"That's a lame confession anyway. Your *name*? Try again, please." I lift my chin in defiance. At eye level, a group of palm fronds rustles in the wind.

"One for one," he says. "Those are the rules."

"And here I thought I was in charge of the game." Below us, a few mourners trail off to their Mazda Miatas and Mitsubishis. Two women clasp each other in a long hug. "Okay, fine." I take a deep breath and watch Ringo out of the side of one eye. "But I have to warn you. After this one, I'll have taken a decisive lead on the scoreboard." He nods once for me to continue. "Okay." I take a deep breath. "Sometimes," I say, "I hate my brother. Like really hate him. I think he's a jerk. More than a jerk. A world-class villain. An asshole."

"And you called *my* confession lame?"

I hold up one finger because I can tell what he's thinking: What siblings don't argue? But that is so not the case with Matt and me. "I hate my brother. I think he's a jerk and . . . he's in a wheelchair. Yep, everything's paralyzed from the neck down." I eye Ringo sideways. I see the corner of his mouth tug. "I know. You're not allowed to hate people in wheelchairs, especially not your brother, but I swear," I continue, clenching my fingers into a tight fist, "sometimes I don't even believe that we're related. Now who's the jerk?"

Ringo plays with the laces of his shoes. I'm waiting for him to tell me what a heartless, insensitive little girl I am, but instead he says, "I tried to remove my birthmark. I mean, not personally. I had surgery." He shakes his head and throws a pebble that he found on the roof off the edge. "All this talk of how I'm so *okay* with it. The birthmark is *part* of me. I'm *Ringo,* for God's sake. And here I tried to get it removed. I wanted to be normal. Just to know what it's like. Now I just have these stupid scars." He turns and points to a spot near his temple. I see them now—three raised and jagged lines, kind of like a burn, branded on the skin. It looks painful. "Guess who just moved to the top of the leader board."

I don't know what to say. The confession is sad—heart wrenching—but his face feels like a puzzle that I can't figure out. Maybe his face feels that way to him too.

Sadness stretches out between the two of us. I notice that it's less heavy when we're here sharing it together. It makes me want to stay with him forever, perched on the top of my best friend's roof. So I do what I have to in order to stay. I add to the sorrow with another offering of my own. "What if it's not just Penny and Will?" I blurt out.

"What if what's not just Penny and Will?" Ringo blinks as though coming out of a daze.

"My decision. Who I'll use my resurrection choice on. It may not only be . . . between two people."

Ringo sits up a little straighter. A warning dings quietly inside my head. "Who?" he asks.

Am I really ready to betray my family like this? Just this small piece of information places another crack in the foundation of our family's pact, our code. But does it matter anymore? I'm not resurrecting Matt. It won't happen. They'll be responsible for nothing. Jitters crawl up my arms and around the back of my neck.

"You first," I say to buy time, and it's like placing a quarter into a slot machine. "You owe me another confession, and hold on, hold on—I know what I want it to be." His mouth closes. "Tell me why you visit Dr. McKenna." I clasp my hands under my chin to wait eagerly for the answer.

Ringo presses his lips together, starts to speak, thinks better of it, then finally begins. "Let's just say I have Mommy issues."

"Come on. That's way too vague."

"So was yours."

"Touché."

*Mommy issues.* His mother seemed to be a special brand of awful. I hate her on his behalf, the way she leaves him at his appointment for hours at a time and won't look at him or get off the couch. All I know is that at least in some ways, Ringo's just as messed up as I am, if not more, and again I get the sensation that I'm sharing the weight of my sadness with someone, and I like that.

From the roof, we watch birds flying home to their nests for the night. The breeze picks up and it's as though the wind, like an invisible paintbrush, is gently sweeping the sunset colors across the sky. The warmth of Ringo's body next to mine feels comforting, the way warm sand does after a swim in the ocean.

After the accident, I felt like I'd been stripped bare and left alone to weather the elements, but here Ringo is and I have to admit—even though I don't want to—that life, in this minute, feels tolerable.

I find the back of his hand resting on the shingles and place mine over it before knitting my fingers between his. "So, do all moments have Beatles songs?" I ask. "Or just certain ones?"

"The memorable ones do."

"And what if there's no perfect song? For that moment."

"The Beatles always have the perfect song. For every moment. Trust me."

"Then tell me this one."

"You already had your question."

"What song is it?" I insist.

This time he tilts his chin like he's listening to a melody. He doesn't move his hand. "Too cheesy if I go with 'Penny Lane'?"

My face lights up. "Penny has her own song?"

"One of the best," he says.

And I'm about to ask him to sing the Beatles for me, when a clang at the window behind us makes me jump. Logan Bryan has grabbed the back of Ringo's shirt and is yanking him back through the window. I have to acknowledge that for a split second I saw Will latching onto Ringo and it took the breath clean out of my lungs. Maybe that's why it takes me a second to react.

"Let *go* of him!" I screech, grabbing onto Ringo's ankle.

"What do you think you're doing?" Logan's face is red and splotchy, but he releases his grip on Ringo, whose shirt is now stretched out around the collar. Logan is huffing and puffing and his hands are on his hips, like he's recovering from running a mile.

Ringo rubs his neck and looks at Mr. Bryan. "Who are you? What is your problem?"

"I'm her boyfriend's father, pal." He thumbs his chest. "You do remember him, right, Lake? Your boyfriend, *Will*?"

My mouth falls open at the accusation in his tone. "Of course I remember Will. What are you talking about?" Logan hasn't cooled down from the confrontation downstairs, or if he has, the sight of my fingers entwined with Ringo's must've got him heated right back up again.

"Really? Because you look pretty comfortable up here with—" It's then that I see Will's dad take in Ringo's face for the first time. "Him." The last word lands with a dull thud, his anger tempered slightly, replaced with something uglier and a little meaner. "Is he *that* easy to replace, Lake?" There's a special emphasis on the word *that*, which I'm sure isn't lost on Ringo. "He loved you."

Shame burns through me like a fever, but there's anger there too, ripe and ugly. "How . . . dare you," I say to my surprise—and clearly to Ringo's. "What do *you* know about love?"

Logan looks like I've smacked him. I might as well have. I rise to my feet on the roof and stand staring down at Logan, the small man on the other side of the window. "He"—I point to Ringo—"is the only person who will even listen to me. You guys are down there acting like monsters and . . . and . . ." My foot slips. The sole of my shoe skids on a shingle. My kneecap cracks onto the roof. I grab for something solid, but it's my plastered arm that reaches out and I'm skidding. My shin launches into thin air.

I scream. Images of the car crash sneak in. A river of blood. Two legs and pale white bone.

The skin on my inside forearm peels up like an orange rind and I jerk to a stop. Ringo is scrambling from the windowsill, skidding butt to heel down after me. His hand closes over my wrist. I'm panting. I rest my forehead against the rough surface. Shaking, shaking, shaking.

And then it's there. Another image. A different one. Like double vision for my heart:

*Slick rocks bite into my palms. I crawl along a pile of them. Sea spray rockets into the air in great plumes. Someone's behind me, calling my name. "Lake! Lake!" And when I look back it's my brother standing on two legs. But I don't listen. I love the roar of the ocean like I love the sound of my own heartbeat and I can hear it best out here on the jetty. Best when I stand and tilt my head back, close my eyes, and let the ocean boom around me.*

Slowly, the terror quells. I lift my face. Ringo won't let go of me. Behind him, the spot in the window is empty. Logan's gone.

# chapter twenty-one

## *14 DAYS*

I wake up sore and hours before dawn. The scabs on my wrist are stiff beneath the bandages. Mom didn't come in to check on me after the shiva. I wonder if she's mad that I yelled at her. Dad came to sit on the edge of my bed last night. He stroked my hair while I pretended to be asleep and cried into my pillow. He might have known I was bluffing.

The black outside is still thick. I was dreaming about Will coming back to me. He would give Penny a eulogy at her real funeral, one that would be funny and bittersweet and would make people laugh and cry in exactly the right places. He would shower me with flowers and thoughtful cards. Maybe we'd get married after college and have Maddie over for sleepovers with her friends.

Even at night, I feel the minutes ticking by—*tick, tick, tick*—leading up to my eighteenth birthday. I pull my bare feet underneath me and stand up. Sleep is out of the question.

Propped beside my mirror, I spot the ignored envelope.

"'Clue Number Two,'" I read softly to myself, pinching the edges between my thumb and forefinger. I've been saving it, holding onto the untouched seal, scared to open it. I press it to my chest. I promised Matt I wouldn't open it without him. But it's late.

Quietly, I push open the door to my bedroom and pad down the hallway. I've always thought that the ocean sounds louder at night. Here, it thunders through the walls when I pass by the great room. Through one of the windows I can just make out the ghostly form of the jetty marker, cast in gray by the nighttime that is punctured by a spray of stars.

I tread through the house, the floor cool against my toes. At Matt's door I raise my fist to knock. He'll be sleeping at this hour. I hesitate, then slowly turn the knob and tiptoe inside.

"Who's there?" The question is instantaneous.

I freeze. For a moment, I consider creeping back out the way I came without saying a word. It's not like he could follow me.

"It's me." My voice rasps. "Lake. Sorry, I didn't mean to wake you." I slink farther into the room until I'm standing at the foot of his bed.

His eyes gleam in the darkness, staring straight up at the ceiling. "You didn't."

"It's the middle of the night, Matt."

"Aren't you observant."

"I just mean—"

"You just mean what am I doing staring at the ceiling in the middle of the night when I'm supposed to be sleeping? Well, Lake, this might surprise you, but my days aren't exactly filled with the sort of stimulation that tuckers me out and sends me crawling to bed exhausted but satisfied from a hard day's work. But after Mom and Dad are sick of me, they put me to bed. Once I wake up, here I am till morning. And, since you asked, it doesn't help that now the sole purpose of my legs and back is to torture me with pain that makes me want to peel the skin off my face, only I can't even take up skin peeling as a pastime because—oh yeah—my hands don't work."

I curl the envelope in my fist selfishly, wishing I hadn't come. "So you just lie here in the dark like this?" Matt grunts. "For how long?"

"It depends on when I wake up. I'd guess four or five hours."

I feel sick to my stomach. "Matt, we have to tell Mom and Dad."

"Christ, Lake." Matt sighs. "It's—it's not a big deal. It's not every night. I don't need you or anyone else feeling sorry for me, okay? I was just . . . venting. Now tell me, to what do I owe the pleasure of your company?"

"I couldn't sleep. So I was just thinking and, well, I saw the envelope and thought we might open it together."

"*Hmmph*, you sure it's not already opened?"

"I swear. It's not." I tap the crisp envelope on my palm. "Still sealed." He's quiet. I take that as a good sign, a sign that he's interested. "May I turn on the light?" Matt makes another noncommittal noise that sounds enough like a yes to me, so I flip on the lamp.

He looks frail stretched out in the center of his bed like that. I watch the mound of his torso crest and fall. His knees form two shallow hills under the sheet. I nervously crawl onto the foot of the bed and wait for him to yell at me to get off. To my surprise, he doesn't.

"Well?" he says, peering down his nose at me. "Are you going to read it or not?"

"Right." I run my finger through the seal. The paper tears. I pull out the card and swallow hard before I begin. "'Clue Two,'" I read. "'Atlantis was the theme of the night, dress, tux, roses, the mood just right, Go to our place and ask for the key. There you'll find the next clue from me.'"

"Can this guy get any lamer?" Matt scoffs.

I stare at the words, read them over again.

"I mean," he continues, "what's wrong with a card and one of those little heart necklaces—you know the silver ones?—girls your age seem to like so much? Something less . . . showboat-y."

I wince at the implication that Matt doesn't know he has made, that all this really is just for show. Instead, I look up. "I know this one. I *actually* know this one!"

I guess Matt finds this sufficiently interesting to stop his silver-necklace vent dead in its tracks. "Where is it?"

My shoulders droop. I play with the fabric on the bed. "I don't want to tell you."

"That was the deal. I give you the first clue. You include me. That was it, Lake. Those were the terms."

He doesn't have to include the subtext. That I don't keep up my end of bargains. That I'm a cheat. A fraud. Disloyal. A girl who breaks promises. Even the important ones. Especially the important ones. But this is different. I'm just too embarrassed to tell him how.

Yet.

"I'll bring you," I say. "But you have to promise not to

laugh, ridicule, mock, or pretend to throw up. Deal?" He resumes looking at the ceiling, stonewalling me. "Those are the terms."

"Fine," he huffs as though the inability to mock is a huge compromise. "Deal."

"Great. Let's load up."

*"Now?"*

"I'm sorry. Did you have something better to do?"

Matt weighs less than I do.

I'm surprised at how light he is in my arms as I lift him and set him in his wheelchair. The landing isn't graceful. I don't have Mom's help this time and I'm sure that I've hurt him somehow even though he doesn't say so.

The van part's easier this time at least, and I make sure not to park in any gravel.

The clock on the dash now reads 4:00. I cut the headlights and we're left in the fluorescent glow of the Seaside Inn. "This is it," I say. I've been growing more and more anxious the closer we got. This is not a place I had ever hoped to visit with my brother, one of the exotic dots on the maps that the two of us used to talk about going to before the accident—the Forest of Knives, Longsheng Rice Terrace, the Great Blue Hole of Belize—but here we were.

"It's a motel," he says from the back.

"It's a *nice* motel." I peer out the windshield at the squat two-story inn painted a faded blue. Rows of doors stare out at us. At one end stands a small office with a VACANCY sign in the window and big script letters fixed to the top letting us know that this is the Seaside Inn. Even though it's actually a couple of miles from the sea.

"Why did Will send you to a motel? Does he want you to get bed bugs?" Matt wrinkles his nose.

"Because," I say, unbuckling. "It's significant to our relationship." I go around the side of the van and press a button, and the ramp drops down.

"I thought we were going to a ballroom or something. Like for a school dance. 'Atlantis was the theme of the night,'" he recites. "Sounds sufficiently cheesy for high school."

"It was. A school dance, I mean." I roll Matt backward until his wheels are flat on the asphalt. "Sufficiently cheesy too," I admit.

Even though I know he can do some maneuvering himself, when I push Matt toward the office, he doesn't complain about the help.

*Go to our place and ask for the key. There you'll find the next clue from me.*

A cowbell clangs overhead when we enter. A man with a walrus face and a sweaty yellow button-down looks up from a crossword puzzle. His hefty jowls give way to an eager grin. "Welcome, travelers. What can I do you for? We're offering garden-view queen-size beds for thirty percent off this week. And"—he hides his mouth behind his hand conspiratorially—"if you drive a hard bargain I could probably throw in some free Wi-Fi."

"Thanks." I try to look grateful. "But actually, we're not here for a room. We're here for a clue."

The man's blond eyebrows pinch inward. "A clue?"

I've been hoping he'd know right away what I was talking about. It feels silly to explain. "Yeah. See, my boyfriend, he came up with this scavenger hunt for my birthday. I'm on the second clue and I'm positive he meant for me to come here. He told me to ask for a key and that would lead me to the third clue."

"Well, I'll be." He lays the pen down over his crossword puzzle. "A real-life treasure hunt."

"Yeah," says Matt, pouring on his tricky sick-kid charm. "It's a real humdinger, isn't it?"

I slap the back of Matt's head and smile back at the man, who points to Matt and walrus-grins back. "Sure is, kid, sure is!"

When he stands up, his stool screeches across the floor. "Loretta's the day manager. She might have left a note or something. Let me check in the back." The man trots his girth to the back, where I hear rummaging around.

"What?" Matt answers my glare. "I'm just saying. I have not seen a doozy such as this before. *Nosireebob.*"

I snort. Just a little.

"What room did you say?" The night manager calls.

"I—I didn't." *Ask for the key.* Right. Will expected me to remember the exact room number, because of course he would remember it. I think back to that night. We'd been dating seven months. I wore a strapless pink dress. My mom had taken me to the mall a week before. She never took me shopping. Between Matt, my private school tuition, and my parents' dwindling bank accounts, there was really no room for frivolous purchases. But this dress she'd bought me wasn't on sale. It hugged my hips and had what felt like a thousand rhinestones on the bodice that shimmered when I walked. I adored it like I hadn't adored anything that I'd ever owned. I felt beautiful and that feeling was reflected in the way Will looked at me.

I pictured the night. We'd dropped Penny off at her

house first even though mine was closest. We'd grown accustomed to this routine ever since Will and I had started dating. She didn't say anything when we both gave her hugs and made sure she got inside, but I think she knew what was about to happen and was too nice to comment. That was Penny for you.

I close my eyes, remembering how my palms were sweating when we pulled into the parking lot. My heart beat quicker than a hummingbird's as I waited for Will to come back with a key. And I kept thinking how I loved that dress.

"I'm not sure of the room number," I say. "But it's on the first floor, the third door from the right when you're facing the building."

More shuffling. A few G-rated substitutes for curse words. "Nope, I don't see anything." He lumbers back to the counter. "Ah, now, don't look disappointed like that. I can't stand to see it from you both."

I look down at Matt. He has his lower lip jutted out in a deep frown. "What are you, Tiny Tim?" I mutter through clenched teeth.

"Is the room, that one that I described," I say. "Is it occupied?"

He arches and peers into the back room, squinting his eyes. "No, no, doesn't look like it is." Now it's my turn to look pitiful. Not that I feel guilty. If he knew the whole story, he'd feel *plenty* bad for me.

He scratches his head. "I suppose it can't hurt for you to take a quick look-see," he says.

He goes back to retrieve the key, then dangles the flimsy credit card–size thing in front of me. "Say, what are you doing here in the middle of the night?" he asks. "This isn't the boyfriend, is it?" First I see him glance at my bulky cast and bandages. Then he looks down at Matt. I have a grudging respect for the lack of judgment he shows about the fact that my beau might be in a wheelchair.

"No!" Matt and I both shout at once.

The man holds up his hands. "Sorry, sorry. None of my business. We just don't usually get much excitement this time of night and now here we are with a real live treasure hunt."

"Sure, yeah, well," I say, sliding the key from its spot on the counter. "You know what they say—'the early bird gets the worm.'" My patience for this sort of banter is waning, so with a few more pleasantries, we take our leave of the portly night manager of the Not-So-Seaside Inn.

"You know," Matt says, as I wheel him down the covered first-floor walkway. Cheap aluminum blinds are drawn over each window. The only noise is the freeway and the whir of a vending machine fan. "My mind is starting to paint an unpleasant picture as to why we're here."

"Then you might want to tell your mind to put down the brush."

We arrive at the third door from the right. The same nerves that I felt that night all rush in on me at once. It takes me two tries to get the key into the lock. It clicks open.

A blast of musty air greets us. I push Matt's wheelchair over the threshold and onto the thin carpet. The room smells like a damp towel. "This is it."

I don't know what I expect to feel when I walk into the room. Worse, I don't know what I do feel. Basically a bunch of emotions muddled at once, the way a thousand colors would mix together and form only an ugly, muddy brown.

"You did it in a motel room," Matt says thoughtfully. "How original."

I am praying that Will had already hidden the clue inside the room for me to find. Will Bryan was an orchestrator, never a procrastinator. And this was his magnum opus.

I leave Matt to rest where he is and cross a few feet over to sink onto the striped duvet of the room's queen-size bed. "We're in high school. It's all we could afford." Which is true, but it also hides some of the truth too.

I remember walking in the night of the dance, how all the rose petals leading to the bed couldn't mask the damp-towel smell. But Will was Will and he was in host mode. He was also in grand romantic gesture mode and, to him, this was the grandest of them all.

He'd chilled champagne that his cousin Jeremy had bought for him. He'd brought bubble bath for me to use in the shallow shower-bath combo inside the tiny bathroom with the scratchy towels. I loved him for all these things and more. My first time wouldn't be like other girls' first times. It wouldn't be in the back of a car or in some dude's basement while I listened to make sure his parents weren't home. Mine would be different. Special. It would be with Will, who, being Will, would make sure it was everything.

But that night, when I let him unzip the back of my hot-pink dress, I felt like an actress playing a part. The roses, the champagne, the bubbles—I recall a single moment when I was curled next to him beneath the sheets feeling like, sure it was so romantic, so thoughtful, but it was also so *much*. We were kids, weren't we?

Matt scans the room. "I guess it's not the worst place." His voice has gone husky and he clears his throat.

"Yeah, well, it's not the back of a car at least," I say, noting the puke color of the quilted duvet.

He emits a soft snort. "I'd take the back of a car." We both fall silent. I watch my brother carefully, studying him as he stares down at his lap and presses his lips together. "Or, you know, anywhere." His nose twitches. "You know I never . . ." Matt says without looking up. Pink patches crop up on his sharp cheekbones.

Startled by the change in conversation, I feel my own cheeks flush. "Oh," I say, trying hard not to sound totally grossed out. Instead, I pick my feet from the floor to sit cross-legged. "No, I didn't—I mean, I wasn't sure."

He shakes his head, slowly, still staring at his lap, where his too-skinny legs dangle off the chair. "It's embarrassing."

My eyebrows pinch together. I pick the threads on the duvet. "It's not *embarrassing.*"

"I'm a twenty-three-year-old virgin. It's pathetic." He wets his lips before speaking. "I just thought I had plenty of time, you know?" he mumbles.

"Yeah," I say with an unexpected strain in my voice. "You should have. Had plenty of time, I mean. I'm . . . sorry."

His eyes snap to mine. He studies me in his typically intense Matt-like fashion, then nods slowly. "Yeah, okay, um, thanks."

I chip at the two-week-old polish on my toenails, sprinkling the bed with aqua flecks.

"Mom gave me a pack of condoms for my seventeenth birthday," he says. "Can you believe that? Told me Dad was going to come by and give me 'The Talk,' but he never did. They're probably still in my nightstand. I wanted to get a girlfriend, though, someone I was actually comfortable with and knew wouldn't, like, laugh at me when I took my—well, when, you know." His mouth twists to the side. "Like you and Will, I guess."

I swallow. "Yeah, like me and Will," I say sadly.

Matt glances at me again and then quickly off to the side. Away. "It's fine. It's . . . it's whatever. It's . . ." He rolls his eyes and sighs. "It's just that, I guess I've always wanted to know, like, how . . ." he begins. "I mean what . . ." He huffs. His face has turned blood red.

"What it was like?" I finish for him.

His teeth are set on edge, but he jerks his head yes.

"Right, um . . ." I scratch the back of my neck. "You really want to know?" I squint. "You do realize I'm your sister."

"Yes, we've met," he says, flustered. "But I don't have a ton of people to ask these things to. Unless you count Mom and Dad, in which case I think sister seems preferable, don't you?"

I sweep the confetti bits of polish from the bed. "Okay, yeah. I guess so. . . . It was . . ." I search for the right words. Magical? Meaningful? A regular after-school special in terms of protection? "Short," I confess. Matt snorts. "But really sweet." I toss a pillow at him. It misses.

*"Sweet?"* Matt wrinkles his nose.

"Yeah, I mean, I think you have to wait for the sweep-you-off-your-feet, animalistic-desire kind until you're at *least* in your twenties." I am only sort of joking. "But it was with someone who cared about me and cared about how I felt about . . . about all of it." I know this alone was more than a lot of girls in my school got. The truth is, though, I'd never thought about it much. It was something I knew was going to happen eventually. Will and I loved each other. So if it didn't happen that night, it would have happened the next month or the month after that. Will and I were inevitable. "It only hurt a little. At first."

"Was it all it's cracked up to be?"

I frown. My heart has hurt so much, I don't think it knows how to hurt anymore. Everything's gone to shit. And not just for me. Matt's asking his little sister about sex. And I'm actually wishing he could get to have it.

"I think it could be," I say honestly. "Eventually."

Matt's lips twitch. "Okay, then, that's, um, educational."

He clears his throat and I realize I've fallen silent. I look away. I can't stand to feel what I'm feeling, which is sorry for him. "Matt," I say, lowering my head to peer down to him at his level. "Are you sure that you can't, you know, have it?"

He closes his eyes and I watch the swell of his chest. In. Out. In. Out. "It's complicated."

My eyebrows lift. "So, that means not a *no* then."

He smirks. "It means it's complicated."

I dig my front teeth into my bottom lip and embrace half a smile. "Matt Devereaux. You've been holding out."

His mouth is pursed, dark hair hangs around his chin. There's a sparkle to his eyes that I haven't seen there in a long, long time. "Shall we find that next clue?" he says.

"Yeah." I clap my palms onto my knees. "Let's do that." I crawl off the bed and survey my surroundings, trying to think strategically. If Will were to hide the clue here, where would he hide it?

I know Will would have expected to be here, helping

me find the clues. I imagine him saying "Colder, colder—no, warmer" like I was a toddler and gleefully clapping his hands when I got "hot."

He would have hid it somewhere, though, where the staff wouldn't clean or look, somewhere a scavenger hunt clue could go unnoticed. Finally, I open the mini fridge, run my hand through the freezer tray, and feel a hard square resting inside a plastic baggie.

I slide it out and hold up the envelope: *Clue 3.*

# chapter twenty-two

## *596 DAYS*

"What do you wear to a death party anyway?" I ask, tugging open Penny's dresser drawers. I begin pulling out clothes and dropping them on the carpet beside my bare feet. Soon, the floor is littered with sarongs, long gauzy dresses, and tribal pants, none of which I could appropriately wear to a party.

Penny lowers her rear end from the downward dog position. "I was planning on wearing this." Penny's sporting a long printed skirt and a white knit sweater that hangs off one shoulder. I stare critically at her.

*"What?"* Penny demands, flipping the magazine closed. "What's wrong with what I'm wearing?"

I blow my bangs out of my eyes. "Nothing, it's fine. It's just . . . very you. Which of course I love." I put my fingers to my lips and blow Penny a kiss. Aside from her favorite pair of yoga pants and a bathing suit, Penny has absolutely no form-fitting clothes.

"Okay, I'm going to stick to black," I say, pulling the outfit I brought from home off Penny's bed and stripping my shirt off to replace it. I duck to view my reflection in her vanity while I braid my hair in a long plait down my back. "It just seems on-theme, doesn't it?"

"We're not going to a funeral, Lake." Penny pushes her feet off the ground and raises them in a headstand, revealing a pair of bright-blue underwear. The top half of her forehead turns red. "We're going to the part *before* the funeral." I shudder at the reminder. My first death party, an "underground" gathering where someone agrees to die on the eve of someone else's eighteenth birthday in order to be resurrected the next day. It's supposed to be a rush for the resurrection holder to have the experience of ending a life, and some death groupies believe that they'll actually come back more spiritually connected with their killer once resurrected. Since suicide and assisted suicide are strictly taboo, death parties are always hush-hush and the deceased's untimely demise must be presented as an accident. I can't believe I'm really going to one.

"Besides, black is so boring," Penny finishes.

"Gee, thanks." I fasten a few wisps with a bobby pin. A black cut-off T-shirt skims the waist of my black jeans, exposing my belly button whenever I lift my arms too high.

"Scratch that," Penny says. "We've only got five minutes before Will gets here. You look great."

Penny returns to upright and comes to stand next to me in the mirror.

"Okay, seriously." She holds the edges out on her sweater. "Is this not okay?" She turns to the side. "I picked it out kind of specifically for—I just picked it out special," she finishes in one breath.

I spin from the mirror to face her. "Seriously. You could wear a potato sack and still look like a *Sports Illustrated* model. Minus the boobs." I grin wickedly.

Penny crosses her arm protectively over her chest. "Hey!"

I lean over to apply blush to the apples of my cheeks and glance sidelong at Penny. I know that's not how she meant to end her sentence.

I take a few extra minutes at the mirror knowing that I'll see Will Bryan any moment too. We both freeze at the sound of a running engine outside. Penny rushes to the window, opens the blinds with her fingers, and peers out. "He's here," she says.

It's just Will, I remind myself. Will is your friend.

But I can't contain the guilty smile that's creeping up the corners of my lips. What's more, I'm horrified when I turn to see Penny wearing a matching one. We both swallow our smiles at the same time.

Penny shakes out the pleats in the long, flowing fabric of her skirt. She turns to me with a now serious expression. Her delicate hand wraps around my wrist. "Lake, are you sure we should be going to this thing?" I can feel my pulse beating fast against her fingers. Because I'm not at all sure.

Outside, there's the scuff of footsteps on the sidewalk, followed by the doorbell chime. "I don't know," I hedge. "But... I think we already are." I squeeze her shoulder. "Come on. It'll be fine."

Together, we traipse to the front door. Standing on the doorstep is Will Bryan. "Your chariot awaits, my ladies." He grins. A wad of gum is stashed between two rows of perfectly white teeth. A kind of electric energy causes Penny and me to shift our weight too much and knock elbows. He tucks his hands in his jeans pockets and rocks back on his heels, chuckling softly.

*Our* Will Bryan. My stomach turns itself into a pretzel each time I see the gentle bump at the top of his nose and that sandy-blond hair that hangs down over his ears. My heart tugs. The problem is, I don't know how Will stopped being *just* Will and started being *Will Bryan*, boy whose full name I like to repeat in my head over and over.

Penny takes shotgun in Will's old Pontiac and I convince myself to feel only the smallest pang of jealousy when I have to crawl into the backseat. I can hardly hear their conversation over the roar of his engine anyway, and after ten minutes or so I tune out and stare through the window at the straight line of dark ocean horizon as it passes.

Finally, Will's wheels land off the paved road with a thud and I jolt to attention. I sit up straighter now and lean forward to peer through the windshield. Ten minutes earlier we left the coast behind and headed inland, where the terrain quickly shifted from cute beach town to country.

The night sky is black as an ink stain out here. Will guides the car through a grass lot. Bugs dart in and out of the beam of his headlights. At the edge of the line of parked cars, a two-story house sits beside a thick, crooked tree that bends over the roof like a broken finger.

Some kids are streaming into the house, while others mill on the wraparound porch. The closest house appears to be half a mile away.

"This," Penny says, "is kind of creepy."

Will leans into the steering wheel to peer out the windshield. "It's a *party*."

"Where someone *dies*," I say. I can't believe the three of us are doing this. On the one hand, I feel a thrill to share the experience together. Our first grown-up party. A death party, no less. It's wild and dangerous, the kind of thing we'll be talking about when we're adults and looking back on our crazy teenage years. On the other hand, the thought of seeing someone die up close is terrifying. What if I get sick? What if I have to look away?

But then my eyes land on the back of Will's head and the strong arch of his shoulders where they slope up to his neck and I know I wouldn't want to be anywhere else.

He finds an empty patch of lawn beside a pickup truck and parks the Solstice. The rumble of the engine stops and we pour out of the car. There are more people here than I thought there'd be. We pass cars double-parked in places as we walk toward the house.

As we mount the porch steps, the music shifts from a dull pounding beat to an actual melody. A large boy with a shaved head and skin folds on his neck that resemble a bulldog's sticks out his arm, blocking Will's chest as he tries to enter.

"You on the list?" he asks.

Will's face pales. "What list?" It was Will's idea to come to the party tonight. I cast around, noticing all the kids who look at least two or three years older than us.

The pseudobouncer performs a once-over on Will, Penny, and me. "I'll take that as a no."

Just then, though, a red cup held high makes its way through the crowded doorway. "Hey, hey, hey." Jeremy crashes through. His cheeks are slack even when he smiles.

Will's mom has never kept a tight rein on her basement tenant, even if he is technically family. He slings a sloppy arm over Will's shoulder. "Ronny, this is my little cuz. And his friends." He sweeps his free arm to encompass all of us and, in the process, sloshes beer on my shirt. I jump back, but Penny keeps me from toppling off the porch.

"They're cool?" Ronny's long forehead, made longer by the shaved head, wrinkles and he lets his lower lip hang out in a tough-guy pout that really does make him bear a striking resemblance to a dog. I thumb the toothy scar on my hand and decide that I dislike Ronny on principle.

Jeremy leans over Will to get closer to Ronny. "That's Matt Devereaux's sister," he says in a stage whisper. I bite my lip and try to blend. Why had he said that?

"Matt, the-kid-that-got-paralyzed Matt?" He squints at me as if he's trying to see the resemblance. He shakes his head. "Shitty luck," he says. "Matt was cool. Tell him I say hi, will you?"

I nod and look away without saying anything. I will most definitely not be telling Matt anything of the sort.

Jeremy's eyes brighten again and he waves us in. "Come inside." He tugs Will's head into the crook of his armpit and tousles his hair. "Look at you." He glances back in our direction. "Two dates. You're such a pimp."

My stomach clenches. I don't like that Jeremy—or anyone—might see Penny and me as Will Bryan groupies. It had never occurred to me until this moment that this might be the public perception.

Will doesn't correct his cousin, and Jeremy's feet swerve as he snakes through the crowd of people playing Beirut in the living room and Flip Cup in the kitchen. Will steadies him.

Jeremy points out the keg sitting on the kitchen counter and tells us to help ourselves before mercifully wandering off in the direction of the patio. Will watches him go and once he has disappeared returns his attention to us.

"Shall we?" He reaches for a stack of red plastic cups.

Penny holds up her palm. "Not for me. I seriously doubt the beer here is gluten free."

Will fills cups for the two of us like he's a professional bartender. He sniffs the contents, then knocks back several large gulps. "Okay, that's actually disgusting," he says. "It's like drinking horse piss." This isn't surprising since the last and only time we've had anything to drink was when we paid Jeremy to buy us a six-pack of wine coolers, and those tasted like lemonade.

I cautiously dip my tongue into the beer. "Gross. Maybe we can just use them as props." Most of the people in the crowd are holding identical red cups. "Helps us fit in."

Will takes a few more cautious sips and then scrapes his tongue against his front teeth.

"I have to go to the bathroom," Penny says, bobbing on her toes.

"Already?" I ask.

"I can't help it," she whines. "I drank a whole bottle of iced green tea before we left. Lake?" Penny asks. She's already starting to walk away. "You coming?" Her brows pull together expectantly and my palms go instantly clammy.

I look to Will. "I—*uh*—" I love Penny with all my heart and what I'm about to do is a total violation of girl code. Even though we haven't said it, I am almost 100 percent positive that we both like the same guy. It hurts even more because I know Penny would never do the same to me, but

I can't help it. "I don't want to leave Will alone," I blurt. "I think I'll just wait for you here."

Penny's frown lasts only a brief moment and I wonder if she's rethinking how badly she needs to speed off to find a restroom, but she drops it and disappears into the thick mass of people.

After that, Will and I are alone. Well, alone plus twenty-five or so strangers. Relief washes over me. My gaze flits over the crowd. "So who do you think it is?" I ask.

Will leans in close, our ears grazing each other, to hear. "Who do I think what is?"

"The one who's going to . . . you know . . . *die*." A chill races up the length of my spine. I've never seen a dead body before.

Will now follows the line of my vision purposefully. Off to the right in the kitchen, near a dormant fireplace, stands a girl talking with grand hand gestures to a gaunt-looking boy. Will points directly at her. "That one."

I hush him and push his finger down. "Don't point!" He laughs and now takes a real swig of the beer. "Okay, why her?" I ask.

"She seems like she's in desperate need of attention. I mean, look at all that arm waving about." He mimics her gesticulations. "It's so me, me, *look at me*. I figure a girl's got to be attention hungry to go through with something as ridiculous as a death party."

I bite the rim of my cup. The floor is sticky against the soles of my shoes. Suddenly, the music cuts off. The crowd stills. Where's Penny? I search for her multicolored skirt, her silky blond hair, but I don't see her anywhere. A bell chimes three times and a voice whose source I can't locate says, "It's time."

Will checks his watch. "Eleven thirty," he says. He looks at me head-on. I can feel the color slowly draining from my face.

His chest rises and falls in deep breaths. "Lake?" he says, holding my shoulder in place with a tender grip. "I wanted to say, I'm sorry about earlier. About not saying anything when Jeremy... you know, said that. It was stupid. I don't think of you—of us—like that and—"

I'd nearly forgotten about Jeremy's offhanded comment, but the fact that it had been bothering Will since we'd gotten to the party fills every inch of me with longing. Will's been extra sensitive since his dad left them. He's dead set on not turning into him and I respect that.

I lightly punch him in the arm. "Don't worry about it. That's what family is for, right?" My hand falls awkwardly to my side and I shrug. "It's fine." After all, no one's family is as dysfunctional as mine.

He nods. "Okay, then." And after another nod for good measure, he seems to have returned to his normal Will self. "Shall we?" We both turn toward the door. Sweaty bodies are being herded up the stairs to a second story.

Will and I fall in line. Trudging in silence, we pass a gallery of family portraits. I realize I have no idea whose home this is. Once upstairs, I crane my neck and see that the upstairs seems to have two bedrooms and a bathroom accented with frilly yellow-trimmed curtains. I doubt the adults of the house envisioned their home being used as a place to die.

A cold, emptied-out feeling settles in the pit of my stomach. I don't even know how the death will take place. Is there a standard, and if so, what is it?

I try to imagine how I'd choose to go. Overdose maybe. Then I shake off the thoughts as too terrible to process.

We're led away from the bedrooms to a large room that must be used as a game room or some other shared space for the family. Even though it's nighttime, the windows are blacked out with cardboard. Will and I shuffle to the side and, once settled, I scoot closer to the warmth of his arm.

In the center of the room, a petite blond girl with stringy hair sits on a couch. It's not the one Will predicted. This girl's eyes are unfocused. She stares off into the center of the crowd, looking at no one in particular. It's almost like having her ghost already in the room.

My heart bangs in my chest. A boy separates from the crowd and leans down to kiss the girl. She responds only by lifting her chin and kissing him hard on the mouth, letting out a slight moan as she does it. When their lips part, he hands her a bottle of vodka. She takes it by the handle and downs a big gulp.

The boy, whose eyes are black and hard, the features of his face sharp like a skeleton's, turns toward us. He presses the fingertips of both hands together. A smirk cuts through one cheek. "On the eve of my eighteenth birthday, I commit my girlfriend, Matilda Thorne, to death"—he reaches back and touches Matilda's shoulder—"so that she can return to this life anew." Murmurs rise like the wind whispering through branches.

The floorboards creak. A lanky boy with greasy hair hanging down to his ears and rope tied around his wrist for bracelets steps to greet Matilda's boyfriend. He holds a book with its spine cracked open and presses the tip of a long fingernail to the page. He reads, "In front of these witnesses, do you go willingly into the darkness?" I hold my breath and wonder who will take her body to the resurrection site tomorrow. Will the boy's face give away his guilt? Will the accident they stage be convincing enough to save Matilda?

She stills. Her chin is pointed down and, with milky eyes, she stares up at the boy. "I do." There are small gasps from around the room. Her boyfriend's fingers twitch at his sides like spider legs.

The boy with the book turns to him. "Do you commit to rebuild her from blood and bone and to fill her with the lifeblood so that she can be resurrected from the dead?"

Shadows hatchet his face into mean lines. "I do."

The boy closes his book, nods once, and fades into the onlookers like a spirit.

I can't speak. I can't look away. The eventualities stretch out in front of me. This boy could be hit by a bus tomorrow and then where would Matilda be? He could be caught, in which case he'll lose his resurrection choice altogether. Poor, lost, bird-boned Matilda would be dead forever. Gone. Snuffed out. And she wouldn't even get to say good-bye.

My thoughts instantly flip to Matt. Then off to the side, someone hands the boyfriend of the soon-to-be-late Matilda Thorne a plastic bag. I'm holding my breath. The back of my hand rubs against Will's. Our fingers move, then I loop my thumb around his and suddenly we're holding hands. Opposing emotions swirl inside of me, but the one that has most of my attention is a swelling happiness at the feel of our skin touching.

I glance up at him. He tightens his lips into a straight-lined smile and moves closer. He rubs the side of my hand with his thumb. Matilda sways and I know she must have more than that last drink of vodka swimming through her system. The boy places the bag over her head.

I squeeze my eyes shut. This will be my brother someday, I think. We will have to do this to my brother and we'll stage an accident and it will be up to me to bring him back. Anger surges in my veins at the thought. That I should have to keep that terrible secret for someone who hates me for no reason—it turns my head feverish. And when I open my eyes again, the weight of it feels all wrong. Matilda is puffing into plastic now. Puffing and puffing and then suddenly her eyes go wide. I startle as her hands shoot to the bag digging into her neck and try to tear at the material. Her legs kick straight out and then she smacks her feet hard against the floor. Her back arches. I see the ridges in her throat like the spine of a reptile. Her boyfriend tightens his grip, twists the plastic tight in his fist, holds it fast against the base of her skull. She writhes. Her face swells. Arms and legs move less, less, less. Breaths get slower and slower. The boy's eyes are shining with interest. I feel like I'm going to be sick.

Without thinking, I push my nose into the rough fabric of Will's shirt. He doesn't let go of my hand, but instead rests his chin on my hair. I don't know if his eyes are open or closed and I know I won't ever ask. I wait until the bell chimes three more times. That's when I know that, until tomorrow, Matilda is gone.

It's only one day. But it's still one whole day.

The mood is somber as we file back down the stairs. White lights dance in my vision. My palm stays pressed firmly to Will's and a surging pride and warmth mixes with the leftover horror from upstairs.

At the bottom of the stairs, we find Penny waiting for us. Her complexion has turned translucent and she appears shaken. "I couldn't find you—" And then she notices Will's and my hands curled together. "Oh," she says, blinking. Her cheeks light up a fluorescent pink. "Oh," she repeats. Her hand brushes across her forehead like she's checking for fever. "Um, yeah." She tucks a quivering lip behind her front teeth and tries on a smile. "Great, then. Here . . . you are." And, at once, it feels as if Matilda Thorne isn't the only thing to have died up there.

# chapter twenty-three

## 13 DAYS

Matt and I are home before sunrise, so early that our parents don't even know we've been gone. I lie on my bed, head fuzzy from lack of sleep. I've been reading a couple of pages from Penny's notebook every day. It's the closest thing I have to talking to her and sometimes, when I'm especially tired or worn out from crying or can't shut off my brain, I can convince myself that she's written certain passages specifically for me. Like:

*Better than a thousand hollow words*
*is one word that brings peace.*
*Better than a thousand hollow verses*
*is one verse that brings peace.*
*—Gautama Buddha*

I read the words softly under my breath, finding a crumb of peace in them, if for no other reason than that the quote is in her handwriting.

*Suffering, if it does not diminish love, will transport us to the farthest shore.*
*—Gautama Buddha*

I trace the loopy letters one by one, wondering why Penny chose it to write down.

*A man should choose a friend better than himself.*
*—Chinese proverb*

I did. For the past nearly four years, I have known that if I have a superpower, it is the ability to choose the very best of friends.

On other pages, Penny wrote her own thoughts, transcribing them onto the page with lovely, colorful turns of phrase, often testing out a few lines only to cross them out and decide on others:

*I'm afraid of being left behind like an old doll that Will and Lake have become too old to play with. Every time they leap from the cliff, I'm left frozen in place, ~~too scared to ask them to stay~~, too scared to follow.*

I slip the *Clue 2* envelope between the pages and close Penny's journal. With each passing day, I feel more like I'm living in a snow globe that's been tossed upside down and shaken left and right. There are sides to my friends that I never knew existed, angles that I've never been in the position to see, maybe because I was looking from too close up. I want to be close again, even if it means only seeing the parts of them that are familiar. Now I worry that the farther I get from the car crash, the more they'll feel like strangers to me.

I'm mostly too tired to move. Grief has this way of making me exhausted even when I've barely moved a muscle. Soon, I find myself navigating to a streaming music service application on my phone. I punch in the Beatles. Dozens of songs pop up. I scroll down and find "In My Life," a new song that Ringo texted to me just last night. I hit *play* and the melody begins. I listen to the song twice straight through, enjoying the tune more on the second go-round. It's the first verse that I like the most. I play that a third time. John Lennon sings about the memory of his friends and lovers, some of whom are dead and others living, but nevertheless he loves them all.

Eventually, though, my stomach growls and I'm forced to venture into the kitchen to forage for cereal and half a Pop-Tart. Matt is watching television—morning news anchors interviewing a best-selling author—which he almost never does. He looks up and gives me a covert grin, like we're sharing an inside joke. I purse my lips, and realize that I'm holding in my own smile.

Last night we were spontaneous. We ventured out in

the middle of the night and no one knew but us. It's the sort of thing I imagined doing with my older brother when I was a kid. Secret adventures for milk shakes or the perfect tater tots. Camping. Memories that never became memories because they never happened.

Mom brings in the mail at ten o'clock and there's a letter for me in a government-issued envelope. I stare at my typed name peeking out from the envelope's plastic window.

"Aren't you going to open it?" she asks, breaking the silence that has been metastasizing between us. We both know what's inside the envelope and I don't want to open it.

But since ignoring it won't make it disappear, I slowly turn it over and rip open the perforation. I find three neatly folded pages inside:

Dear Miss Devereaux,

With your eighteenth birthday approaching, we would like to confirm your time slot on Monday, August 24 at 11:00 a.m. to complete your resurrection choice. Please fill out the Application for Resurrection form provided herein or arrive at the Trifeca Resurrections Division, Trifeca County Courthouse, Third Floor, Suite 3300, twenty minutes before your designated appointment time.

Two government-issued forms of identification will be required at check-in, such as a driver's license, birth certificate, and/or valid passport. A complete list of acceptable documentation is available on the Bureau of Healthcare Research & Quality website, www.hrq.gov/resurrectiondocs.

Instructions for resurrection candidate drop-offs may be found on the back of this letter. All drop-offs must be made within twenty-four hours of your appointment.

If you are forfeiting your resurrection choice, please check and initial the box below.

Sincerely,

Luis A. Valdez
Director of Resurrections Division
Trifeca County

I finish reading. My mom doesn't need to ask what the letter says. She doesn't look at me either, and I don't care if I caused the rift between us or if she did, but it hurts to have her disappointed in me.

How did everything get so screwed up? Penny and I were going to be best friends until we were eighty and we were going to sit on our rocking chairs together and knit wacky-colored oven mitts. Will and I had a plan.

I was going to keep my promise to my family so I could wash my hands of my brother forever. But now nothing feels right.

The secret smile Matt and I shared moments earlier has been forgotten. He too knows what has arrived in the mail, and he stares out at the jetty with his mouth sealed. I wish for a crazy second that I could talk to him about this, explain to him what I'm going through, but then I remember who he is and what we are and instead I just want to punch a hole in something hard. I want to curse and drive too fast and listen to music so loud that it shakes my organs.

Back in my room I text the only person I can talk to, Ringo.

The paperwork came, my message reads.

I'm relieved when the response is quick: Neville's in twenty?

I'm there in ten, arriving before Ringo. The smell of coffee beans and soaked tea leaves acts as an instant stress reliever. Kai and Vance are tucked into the corner, Kai's legs thrown over Vance's on one of the small love seats, and they are both plugged into their headphones. Vance nods at me and it's not dismissive, more like he expects me to be there the same as any of his other friends.

There are remnants of the rest of the group—strewn magazines, Simone wearing a black apron and clearing tables—but the main vibe seems to be: intermission. I like the more relaxed connection of the group . . . or at least I find it intriguing. Penny, Will, and I, we were usually attached to one another like we shared vital organs. For instance, we had this running joke that if one of us had to be absent from a group hangout we'd call, "No secrets!" Because no one wanted to be left out.

The thought makes me sad. At the end of this, there will be only two out of the three of us left and the secrets will stack up first by the tens, then dozens, then hundreds, until we don't even think about it anymore.

This time, I order coffee willingly, but not from Simone, who intimidates me. I still add an extra dose of cream and sugar to the cup. "What's up, Lake?" Duke looks up from a glowing tablet screen at a table.

I clutch the warm mug between my hands, the steam rising up to my nose. I glance around. "Mind if I take a seat while I wait for Ringo?" I ask, feeling a little bit proud of myself for being brave enough to ask so easily.

Duke has on a short-sleeved black-and-gray bowling shirt that might have been in style sometime last century. Emphasis on *might*. "Please, allow me." For such a large boy, Duke's surprisingly both graceful and agile as he jumps out of his seat and sweeps a chair back for me. Slightly self-conscious at the gesture, I take a seat beside him. "I'm watching Margaret's computer and bag," he explains. "While she runs an errand. If anything happens to her laptop she'll gouge my eyeballs out with ice cream scoopers." I laugh. "I'm not joking," he says. His jowls are floppy and serious. "Nah, I'm joking." His face volcano erupts into a brilliant grin. "But wait, am I?" Serious again. "No." I cock my head, totally perplexed. No, he's joking? Or no, he's serious? But then he shudders as though he really is contemplating how it would feel to have his eyeballs served in a sugar cone before at last grinning wickedly at me again. I realize at once that I should probably immediately give up making any sense of Duke Ellington at all.

"Lake, may I be blunt?" he asks.

I set my mug down on the table, nearly choking on a hot sip of coffee. "Sure, yeah, please."

"Good." He trains his large brown eyes on me. "What are your intentions?"

"My what?"

"Your intentions. With Ringo." He straightens the collar of his shirt, then rests his meaty elbows on the table.

My hand knocks my coffee cup and liquid sloshes into the table between us. "Oh! No!" Duke isn't fazed. "Ringo and I are just friends."

Duke rubs his lips with two fingers. "Relax!" He swishes

his hand through the air. "Oh man, you should see the look on—did you think I was serious?" He leans forward and presses his hands to his knees.

"Yeah." I wipe the back of my mouth. "Kind of."

"Good, because I am." I look at him sidelong, unable to tell whether Duke is messing with me again or if he even considers any of this messing around at all. "What I mean to say is: Are you going to hurt him?"

I take another sip of my coffee. "I told you. It's not like that. We're not romantically involved."

Duke grins. "What does that have to do with anything?"

I frown. Does the loss of Penny hurt me any less than the loss of Will? Romantic love is just one kind of emotion on equal footing with others. I think about being hurt by my brother too. One kind of emotion and one kind of pain surrounded by a dozen variations. "Nothing, I guess," I say, remembering what Kai said about Ringo being fragile.

Duke lays both of his hands out in front of me on the table. "So the way I see it is, if you have to choose between hurting Ringo on the one hand and not on the other, I would go ahead and choose not."

I roll my eyes. "Obviously." He shrugs in response.

"Maybe obvious and maybe not."

"And what about if he hurts me?" I challenge.

He leans forward and cups his hand around his mouth as if he's about to tell me a secret. "That's when I borrow Margaret's ice cream scooper."

"Deal," I say. And I like Duke because I don't think he's actually antagonizing. He cares about his friend, fiercely, and I can relate to that. Only Duke's clearly not as insular about it as Penny, Will, and I were. He's the big guy checking IDs at the door. And I think I care about Ringo too, so I don't know, maybe my ID needs to be checked.

"Are my services no longer needed?" Ringo leans over my shoulder so close, I can breathe him in. I blush, but then he picks up my mug and slurps some of my coffee. He wrinkles his nose. "That concoction you have there is going to kill you. Like, it's literally going to give you diabetes, Lake."

I pull it back from him. "Hey, I'm just starting to like coffee. Back off."

We leave Duke to guard Margaret's belongings, and stake out one of the sofas with the overstuffed arms where I can cradle my mug against my chest and almost pretend I'm three or four years older than I actually am, a college girl with everything figured out. Ringo props his arm on the back of the couch and hikes his knee onto the cushion so that we're facing each other dead on, inches apart.

"I don't know why I'm here," I admit suddenly. "I know there's nothing that you or anyone else can do. I got the paperwork, though, and the walls, they started pressing in." I wrap my arms around myself and squeeze. "I needed to pull the rip cord and get the hell out of my house, you know?"

"More than you can imagine," he says.

"My birthday. It's so soon." I moan and drop my forehead into my open hands. "How am I ever going to choose? I can't. I can't possibly. It's—it's in less than two weeks." Ringo shifts his weight and looks off to the side. "Did you know that? Two weeks!" Our knees are nearly touching, but he pulls his away from mine ever so slightly. I almost wouldn't notice if he didn't seem to be developing a twitch over the eye with the red patch over it, the one that made him Ringo and not just Christian. "The paperwork," I continue. "It's so clinical."

"Yeah." He scratches his nose. "I, uh, I remember."

"Two forms of government-issued identification. Resurrection candidate drop-off. Hello, we know what they mean—dead body. Dead person. And—" I rest against the cushion, feeling lightheaded. I'm watching the puzzle pieces of his face. I still see the birthmark when I look at him—I can't help that—but the more I'm with him, the more I see just Ringo. I do wind up focusing on the unmarred half, the full eyelashes that brush the smooth skin and frame his cool blue eyes, the dark eyebrows, interesting for how much bolder they are than the color of his hair. It's strange that in some ways I'm pretty sure the scarred port-wine stain on his skin makes the right side of his face all the more striking and beautiful. But I'm waiting for him to jump in, the way he did at Penny's shiva. It's like I came for a fix of Ringo comfort, but he's not dealing all of a sudden.

"What?" I ask. "Why are you looking at me like that? Why aren't you saying anything?"

He sighs and runs his fingers through his hair. "I thought you came to talk."

"Yeah, but not to a brick wall."

"About that." He rolls his neck. He looks physically uncomfortable and I wonder if we should change seating. "I've been thinking maybe I'm not the right person for this. . . ." He must note my dropped-jaw expression, because he trails off. "Or something."

"What are you talking about? Did I do something?" I pin my gaze to the cream swirls in my coffee.

"I, um," he starts. "Shit, Lake, okay, I need to tell you something."

Here it comes. I don't know what the *it* is, but I wait for another collision, another impact to knock me off my feet, to break my bones, to finally break me.

He checks over his shoulder as though to make sure no one is eavesdropping. "You see, I'm not exactly an unbiased listener," he says. "Not the way you think I am anyway. I think it's only fair to tell you that . . . I used my resurrection choice." He plays nervously with the scar on his temple.

My eyes grow wide as golf balls. "*You did?* Why didn't you tell me?" Questions start to pile up like water from a spring.

"Because I was embarrassed, I guess." He catches himself worrying over the scar and pulls his fingers away to spin an empty saucer on the table between us. "You've met my mother."

"I'm not sure I would call that much of a meeting, but sure," I say, tucking my heels underneath me.

He takes a deep breath. "My mother is resurrected. By me."

"Oh." I'm confused. "But . . . she doesn't seem very . . . grateful."

"*That* would be an understatement." He picks at the frayed hole in his jeans. "It's, well, it's complicated." When he talks, it's with the reluctance of somebody wrenching words out of his throat with a pair of pliers. "Look, all I can tell you is that you think what you're going through right now is the problem, that choosing is the issue. But resurrection isn't necessarily the solution you think it's going to be." There is an edge to his voice that I don't recognize. It's a piece of him that doesn't sound fragile at all, but instead forged in a part deep inside him where there is red hot anger that can turn nice, soft feelings into steel.

His words feel like fingernails tearing at a spot in my heart. I can tell he wants to stop talking about it, to leave it at that, but I can't. "What do you mean? You got your mother back."

He grinds his jaw back and forth. Then he puffs his cheeks out, exhaling for what seems like an eternity. "My mother was a professor. She argued against the ethics of resurrection her whole life. She built an academic *career* on her opposition of it. Not just that, but she really believed in what she said and wrote. When she got sick with cancer, I swear, she was proud. She could finally put her money where her mouth was. She would die and that would be it. She'd put into practice what she had advocated in her academic career. She'd go down as one of the greats. I think she thought she'd be like Socrates or something. A fantastic mind that wasn't fully appreciated until after her untimely but noble demise."

He shakes his head thoughtfully. "It probably could have been cured, you know. Her cancer. Seventy-five–percent chance. That's what the doctors said. But she wouldn't do chemotherapy. She wouldn't do anything." There's a lump forming in his throat. I watch the veins pulling tighter, tighter, tighter, and when he swallows it looks like he's fighting down a mouthful of screws. "Then in the hospital... she looked so tiny." The memory is etched on his face. "I held her hand as the cancer ate her from the inside out, but there was this light in her eyes, like she was excited to go. To leave me. I don't have a dad, I could have been put in foster care. I had a few friends then, but nothing holding me together, plus this big, giant, well, *thing* on my face that I've had since the day I was born and . . . and still she wanted to go. I—I couldn't stand it. She had the doctors pull her off any form of life support early, before my eighteenth birthday, just to prove a point—that she could be resurrected but had chosen not to.

"I stayed in the hospital for three days with her. She screamed in pain for hours at night but wouldn't let the doctors give her anything that might prolong her life. It was the pain that killed her in the end, actually. She had a heart attack. I was furious at her."

I set my coffee mug down on the ground beside the sofa and scoot closer. "That must have been awful," I say and think about how Dr. McKenna first told me that there are no magic words, just regular ones that fail us when we need better ones to say what we feel. But at least I have to try.

"Believe it or not, my mother—'Mom' back then—had this brilliant and crazy fun mind. She invented games for us with nothing but a few strings and a half-empty box of checkers, that kind of stuff. When I was a kid, those things were huge for me because I only knew Smelly Ellie and, well . . ." We both smile at that. "I loved my mother. Afterward, it turned out that she'd provided instructions to me about how I was supposed to publish this paper that she'd written. Her great manifesto, I guess. I couldn't even read it. A month later, when I turned eighteen, I turned in a resurrection application with her name on it. She hasn't spoken more than a word at a time to me since."

"But, you're her son."

"She's a proud woman and she hates me for ruining her legacy. I can see it every time she looks at me. Honestly, it's all been such an ordeal. I feel like just knowing about the possibility of resurrection or the nonpossibility of it—it—it made it impossible to move forward with anything until after it was all over and everything was totally wrecked. I started going to therapy. I thought that it would help to talk about it. Most days it does. My mother ignores me most of the time. Forgets to pick me up. Or maybe she means to leave me, since that was her original intention. I don't know."

"So, you think if you hadn't resurrected her, that everything would have been fine? But that would have been so unfair to you."

"I think the very existence of resurrections at all created a mess that no one, including me and anyone else, is equipped to clean up. Resurrections were just there, looming over us, and the idea of them didn't leave us any room to heal, if that makes sense." Two sides of his face. Two ways his life could have gone. Just like mine. "Using my resurrection destroyed everything. I just think you should know what you're dealing with." The edge has returned. Sharp and forged hard as steel.

I stare at him, shaken, because the only thing I can think of is Matt. What Ringo's mother did was cruel. Who cares about an academic career when it comes to the people you love? But what he says about the mere existence of resurrections stops me dead. Without them, how might Matt's life have been different? The very idea of the resurrection has been looming over Matt for years, keeping him from healing.

I have never thought to wish away resurrections entirely—especially not now that Penny and Will are gone. But I can't help feeling ill. Because for the first time, I consider that if the thing that could save my two best friends didn't exist, my brother might have stayed my brother, even if he couldn't walk. He could have changed. In other ways. He could have been the old Matt.

Back when I was first learning about quadriplegia, my research turned up all sorts of people with his condition. Ones that had gone on to get married, have children, become activists, travel. Why *couldn't* Matt have been one of them?

The answer seems obvious now: because of me.

Competing emotions war in my head, swaying me, pulsing against my temples until I have to reach up and press my thumbs into the sides of my skull. "Ringo," I tell him, ripping myself from my own problems to deal with the ones that have just been laid bare in front of me. "You're the kindest, least selfish person I think I've ever met. Aside from Penny, but don't feel bad." I let out a sad laugh. "Because you're basically competing with a saint there."

Me. My resurrection. Mine. Matt can never allow himself to get better because I exist and so does my choice. I push the thought back hard with every ounce of strength that I have. I cannot feel guilty about this. I have to be strong.

His mouth quirks. "I'll try not to be too offended."

I close my eyes, open them, and take a deep breath. "I don't think you could have done anything differently." I want to tell him the reasons for my own family's dysfunction too, because I want to make him feel connected. But I can't.

He stares at me seriously. "I could have chosen not to resurrect her." Then he breaks and looks down to readjust his position on the couch. "I just want you to know what you're dealing with."

"But . . . it's different, right?" I say, not wanting to sound dismissive but wanting him to see. "Your mom didn't want to be resurrected." I pick up my mug and find that my hands are shaking and I don't even know why. The liquid in the cup is tepid and I swallow it down while pulling a face.

"How do you know what your friends want, though?" he says.

I pick at the side of one nail absently. "I think that's why I have to find the wishes," I reply. "So I know."

He doesn't look away from me. Not for a second. Not to blink. His demeanor reminds me of a more human version of Matt, and I wonder briefly if it's their shared familiarity with being stared at that gives each the ability to look into other people long enough to make their insides turn into writhing earthworms. "I think you know you're placing too much faith in them," he says.

But he doesn't know what he's talking about because he doesn't know Will and he doesn't know Penny and neither of those things is his fault. It just sucks that he was stuck with a sorry excuse for a mother instead of a best friend and a boyfriend who could create a family out of fossilized bones and a few drops of blood and the light of a full moon.

# chapter twenty-four

## 589 DAYS

I could list all the things that I love about Penny Hightower:

The jangle of her bracelets that lets me know whenever she's near
Her capacity to love
The way she cries when she thinks of dolphins getting caught in tuna nets
The hemp necklace she spent a week making and which I managed to lose less than two days later (she didn't get mad)
How she's not embarrassed to be scared of little things like spiders and heights, but not afraid of big things like what's going to happen after high school
Her advice

But right now what I love most about Penny is sitting on her roof and the sparkly twinkle in her eye when she turns on her side and tells me she has a crush on Noah Ramsey.

Her pale hair fans out from underneath the elbow crooked to support her head. We're both in bikinis and her skin is turning red around the triangles of fabric covering her chest.

I turn on my side to face her. "Noah Ramsey? You're sure?"

"I know. Weird, right? I mean, I'd never really noticed him before. But he's heading up this food drive for the middle school, which is really admirable, don't you think? And I don't know." She smirks. "He has nice eyes."

I try to picture Noah Ramsey's eyes. They've certainly never stood out to me as noteworthy, but I want very badly to believe that they're nice. Really nice. Nice enough to make someone forget about another boy's completely, no-second-guesses-about-it nice eyes.

Come to think of it, Noah's eyes may be blue. With dark, full eyelashes. Yes, I think that's right. I bet those *are* nice eyes.

"So I asked him to go to the beach with me tomorrow," Penny says all casually, like she has ever asked a guy on a date. Ever.

"You asked him *out*?" I push myself up on my elbow and gawk at her, because even though I want this to be true, a real friend can't let this pass by unexamined. And I'm a real friend, I remind myself.

"You could act a little less surprised." She shuts her eyes and points her face up to the sun. Her mouth quirks.

I lower my shoulder back to the spread-out towel. Boys

at St. Theresa's have been invisible to Penny and me since I first started school there, except for Will. *Noah Ramsey.*

"He said 'yes,'" adds Penny.

"Obviously." I snort. Every guy at St. Theresa's would sell a kidney to go out with Penny.

"So . . ." Penny doesn't open her eyes, but continues to bask. "How are you and Will?"

My abs tighten. It's been a week since the death party and Penny and I haven't discussed the demise of Matilda Thorne or the fact that Will and I were holding hands.

"Is he a good kisser?" Her voice is classic Penny. Light. Floaty. Sweetly optimistic.

I bite my lip. Relief is already washing over me. "I wouldn't know," I confess.

Penny reaches over and pinches my side. "Well, you'd better get on that, Dirty Devereaux. Because I'm going to need details. Stat."

I just nod, smile, and let my heart fill up like a hot-air balloon.

This, I tell myself. I have to remember this. I reach my pinky over and hook it into Penny's. No matter what, I will never let myself forget that just because I don't make out with Penny—assuming Will and I ever make out, which I'm pretty certain we will, and soon—doesn't mean our relationship is any less important.

I want to cut through my skin and hand her a piece of my beating heart so she knows that everything is going to be fine between us. Always.

"Penny?" I say, knowing that what I'm about to tell her will amount to the same thing. "If I tell you something, can you promise not to tell anyone, not even Will?"

"No secrets," she says with a smile.

"Secrets," I say to the sky. If I stare at it long enough I can forget a world exists below us at all. "Just this once. Will couldn't keep it and it's too important."

I turn my head to watch her. She shimmies, adjusting for comfort on the roof shingles. "Okay, yeah, anything." She squeezes my pinky.

"I'm going to resurrect Matt, Penny."

She abruptly lurches upright, gives me a confused look, then flips onto her belly. She props her chin up on her criss-crossed forearms. "Matt's not dead." Her voice is low.

"Yeah, exactly." I've finally done it, I've betrayed my family. I've told the big, hulking secret that has been pulsating like a fever blister inside the walls of my home. And I don't feel bad about it. "My parents promised him. So that he would stop trying to kill himself."

She bites into her forearm, holding in a yelp. "Matt's tried to kill himself?"

"Only if you count every chance he gets."

She turns serious. "You should have told me."

"I couldn't. It . . . could ruin everything."

She nods, then shudders.

"What?" I demand.

Her eyebrows swoop up. "I'm sorry, it's just, the whole idea, it's unnatural."

"My parents helping my brother commit suicide? Yeah, it's disturbing."

She hums softly. "Or . . . you know, maybe it's *all* of it."

For the record: Penny went out with Noah Ramsey exactly twice and claimed that he kissed like an iguana.

# chapter twenty-five

## *8 Days*

I'd be lying if I said that the conversation with Ringo hasn't been bugging me. Not just about his mom, which is depressing, sure, but about Penny and Will.

I've gone to the coffee shop three times since Ringo told me that he used his resurrection choice. Sometimes I chat with Margaret about the books Matt used to read me because it turns out she's a huge fantasy nerd too. She even has a C. S. Lewis quote tattooed on the inside of her arm, and I think in a different life she and Matt probably would have made a good couple. I finally did get the chance to ask her about the other address in the ChatterJaw thread and she's been going crazy trying to uncover who it is. I think it's become a point of pride for her to figure it out, because she says the user's IP address is guarded and encoded, like they are protecting matters of national security. She asks if I know anyone who would have that kind of capability and I tell her that I can't think of anyone except for her.

On the other end of the spectrum is Simone. It turns out she and Ringo went on a couple of dates last month, so she's the least friendly of the bunch to me, but I gather that she's sharp-witted, bitingly funny, and militant in her defense of both feminist ideals and Virginia Woolf, when she's not working behind the counter or bussing tables anyway.

Much of the time spent at Neville's, I share a set of headphones with Duke Ellington while he loads playlists onto my phone, mostly of Beatles songs that he thinks Ringo would like me to know by heart. I've learned most of the lyrics to "We Can Work It Out," "I Want to Hold Your Hand," and "Blackbird" and like to surprise Ringo by singing bars from the songs at random. I get a kick out of the way his face transforms, how his eyebrows lift a full centimeter when I catch him off-guard with a new verse that I've memorized, how he occasionally takes my hand and twirls me around and stops me by the waist before spinning me back out again.

Mostly, I like the distraction of the coffeehouse crew. It's so different from Penny and Will. Everyone comes and goes as they please and no one worries about things like secrets being told when they're not around.

I realize now that some of the pain I've seen drawn on Ringo's face isn't just an illusion created by the birthmark, it's the real, raw kind of pain that bubbles up to the surface like water in an unwatched pot. That's one of the reasons I enjoy surprising him with the song lyrics so much. It's fun to see that pain evaporate, if only for a second.

He's more honest about it all now and that weirdly helps

us both. I've started to think about pain the way I think about lifting a heavy sofa—it's easier to move around if there are two people carrying it, one at each end.

It's the other thing, though, what Ringo said about knowing what my friends would want. It's been weeks since I last saw Penny, but I've begun to imagine a new version of her: Penny with flawless skin, no scar on her elbow from where she cut it on a broken pool tile, an altogether even more gorgeous, more perfect Penny. Would she be comfortable with that? Because nothing about resurrections is exactly . . . *organic.*

I haven't been mentioning any of this to Ringo. Instead, in quiet moments, when I don't have the distraction of the Neville posse, I scroll through the internet idly searching through various forums and opinion pieces on resurrections. The web Buddhists tend to have split views—some see it as unnatural, others as reincarnation. None of these people speaks for Penny, I know.

I'm at home, waiting, waiting. Matt has the kind of appointment where they look at him and tell him he's still paralyzed. Okay, I don't actually *know* what goes on at these appointments, but he has one, which means that I have to wait until Mom finishes carting him back and forth from the special wing of the hospital for people who've had really, really bad things happen to them. Like Matt.

At just after eleven in the morning I hear the van door slide open outside. The sounds of voices, followed by those of Matt's wheelchair and Mom's footsteps, filter inside. I have to admit that I've been avoiding Matt ever since I received the resurrection paperwork, but with just over a week left until my birthday, I can't waste any more time, time that I truly can't afford.

Once I know that he's alone, I'm patient for only a few minutes before barging into Matt's room. "Matt, I'm opening the third clue," I say, brandishing it.

I expect this to elicit a reaction. What I find is statue-Matt. I'm semi-used to this version of my brother because he can go unnaturally still, but this time Matt's chin hangs down onto his chest and he doesn't move. He isn't wearing headphones or playing an audiobook or even an album of classical music. He's just sitting there. "Do we really need an announcement?" he mumbles without lifting his head.

I walk over to sit on his bed and tap the envelope. "Still sealed, see?"

"Lake, I don't have time for this."

I hold the envelope at the edges and peer down at it. "But it's almost my birthday," I say.

He squeezes his eyes shut and then opens them wide, like he's trying to wake himself up, but he keeps staring down, down, down and won't look at me. "Yeah, I'm aware."

Like everything with Matt, the words are laced with double meanings not lost on me. But I press on. "So I want to finish the scavenger hunt."

And the thing that's bothering me is that Matt isn't even bothering to be Matt. Especially now.

"Then finish it," he sighs.

This makes me feel a slimy kind of cold. "We made a deal. I promised to bring you along. On every single stop. You were very specific about that part." I tap the edge of the envelope against my palm, testing the edge. "I'm making good on that promise." There it is. I leave an elephant-size opening for him to call me out. But he doesn't and my stomach flip-flops like a scummy dead fish.

"Maybe later," he says.

I set him up perfectly. Slam dunk. I haven't kept any of my promises, why start now? I could write the insult for him. So why doesn't he go for it?

I soften my tone. "Did you get bad news at the doctor's?" I ask. "Are you . . . are you dying or something?"

A huff. "Nope, Lake. Going to live for a long time. Good news," he says with a healthy dose of sarcasm. "My body can keep ticking along like this for about thirty more years, so . . ."

"But thirty more years," I say. "That's not very long. That can't be right."

He stares, stares, stares out the window. "It's plenty."

And I'm worried by the resignation I hear in his voice. I fidget and turn the envelope over in my hands. It feels so light now. "So," I say. "So nothing has changed, though. So, so . . ." Resolve tightens in my belly. "So no maybe later. Maybe *now*. You wanted to come. You're coming." I feel a burst of annoyance. What makes Matt think he can just give up? It's not even my birthday yet.

"Lake—" His tone isn't even mean. Or angry. Or anything.

My knuckles turn white, fingers clenched onto the envelope. "Matt—I—I—don't be like this. *Please*." I stomp my foot just like I'm twelve again. I've gotten used to the idea of Matt coming. Why is he trying to change it up on me? What gives him the right to say it's all over?

He looks at me for the first time. Messy hair, clean-shaven, thin, hollowed-out cheeks. We stay there for five long seconds. I watch him for signs of the old version of my brother or any version of him that I recognize. But to me he looks small and alone and sad.

And then Matt says, "Okay." No explanation, just "Okay."

"*Okay?*"

"Okay."

I nod and feel a slight swelling sensation pressing out at my ribs. I swallow it down so that, without further hesitation, I can slide my fingernail under the flap and tear open the envelope.

"'Clue Number Three,'" I read. "'By now you must think your boyfriend's awfully clever. Outside of where we learn, you'll find your next endeavor. Here we all share the spot together. Hummus, ham, peanut butter, and rye, our love's forever.'"

Matt lets out a long, exaggerated breath and drops his head. "Wow. Wow, wow, wow. That is *so* much worse than I thought it'd be. *Hummus? Peanut butter?* And they say romance is dead." There is still no humor in his eyes, or any scorn for that matter, but at least Matt is still showing signs of life.

"Don't forget about the ham," I say, barely registering how much easier it's becoming to laugh at Will.

We arrive at St. Theresa's in search of the fourth clue when the sun is high in the sky and threatening to tip over toward sunset. The empty school is lovely at this time of day. The centerpiece of campus is a quaint chapel with a white steeple stretching up into the sky. Dozens of classroom buildings encircle it and, at the bottom of a short hill, there's a bright-blue swimming pool.

I know the third clue will be somewhere around the lunch table that I shared with Penny and Will during the school year. It's been the same one since we first became friends.

*Here we all share the spot together . . . our love's forever.*

The words have been playing in my head over and over. *Our love.* And Will had chosen our lunch table, a fact that Matt naturally found hilarious, as the third stop on the scavenger hunt.

I've wandered back to the ChatterJaw thread too many times to count. There have been no updates from them. Not from the person I know to be Will and not from his nameless muse.

No updates, though. Just the leftover words and the thoughts that sink claws into my back that I can't shake.

I roll Matt down the deserted pathway made of bricks that were purchased by, and printed with the names of, past St. Theresa's graduates. Next year, I'd have a brick on the path. But would Will or would Penny?

Or . . . or would neither?

*No.* I stuff the thought down, down, down. Everyone wants something from me, everyone wants to change my mind. I have to follow the path I've laid out for myself. It's the only way to the truth. I need to find those wishes. They're the only way I'll really know who Will and Penny were when they weren't attached to me.

I watch the back of Matt's head. He hasn't finished high school. He hasn't even gotten his GED, although the state would have made certain accommodations for him had he wanted to try. He didn't. Or more likely, he wouldn't. Even though he's listened to more books than are in an entire school library.

I listen to the sound of the wheels over the bumpy surface, content to remain silent. There's so much to think about and I know that I'm reaching the end of it all. I'm lost in my own head when Matt tells me to stop.

His voice echoes against solid walls and glass windows. It'll be another week and a half before students return to the school. The emptiness surrounding us is eerie.

"What?" I jerk the wheelchair to a halt. "What's wrong?" It's my automatic assumption now that something must be tragically wrong. This more than anything else seems to have become a constant in my life.

"I—I want to do something," he says.

This isn't what I was expecting. "You want to . . . *do* something?" If there's one thing I've known about my brother in the past few years, it's that he absolutely never wants to do anything other than die, and I'm not helping him do that, so I'm nervous to ask, but I do anyway. "What?"

"It's stupid," he says. "Actually, just forget about it." Even though my brother can't move, sometimes I can see the motion he'd make just by listening to his tone. Usually the gesture would involve giving me the middle finger, but today it'd be more like waving me off.

I sigh. "Matt, we are on a great, big, epically magnificent, cowabunga awesome birthday surprise scavenger hunt. How much more stupid can it get?"

"I thought maybe it'd be cool to be onstage for just a second. You know. Just to see what it felt like to graduate. Because I never got to do that." He spits this all out at super speed. Faster than I've ever heard him talk, and even then, it sounds like each word pains him. He was noticing the bricks too, I guess. I suppose we're all feeling a bit nostalgic this week. "But it's dumb," he concludes.

"It's not dumb." I rest my cast on the back of his wheelchair.

"It is. Graduation's not about the stage. I know that." His head droops and already it's like I'm watching the life drain from him.

"I bet it's a little about the stage," I say, teasing, and I can't help imagining Matt in a cap and gown. But the Matt I picture is walking and grinning, still tan, still my brother. Although generally a jerk and a half, Matt is still the smartest person I know. He deserves to be on a graduation stage. "Come on," I say, standing up straighter. "I have an idea."

"Lake..." He protests without really protesting. I pick up speed, wheeling him down the curved path, around the outside of the chapel to a dome-shaped building marked KLATZENBURG AUDITORIUM.

*"Voilà,"* I announce with a flourish of my cast-encased arm. Suddenly this seems brilliant. Matt said I needed closure. That's why I've come after the clue. Now I'm not the only one searching for my bookend.

"It's closed, Lake."

"Give me a second," I say. I then give each of the doors a quick tug. "Wait here." Then I go around and tug on the back and side exits. They're all locked. Determined, though, I go back around to the front, where I take my keys out of my pocket along with a couple of bobby pins. I crouch down in front of the doors and work to finagle the locks. I stick a bobby pin in one of the jagged holes. I jiggle a half-inserted house key. Each time I listen for a promising rattle. When I think I hear one I tug on the handles some more. But they don't budge.

Okay, I admit, I'm starting to panic. It was a harebrained plan to begin with. I thought I'd get into the auditorium, find a spare cap stashed in the stage's wings. I imagined myself pushing Matt across the stage and moving the tassel for him and pretending to create thunderous applause. I thought I could do this and it might mean something. But that's as far as I've gotten. I was so eager to do something that meant something to him, that might make up for . . . for what I was going to do—or rather not do—for him, that I pushed ahead before I thought it through.

"Lake." Matt's voice is deep.

"Just—just one second." I bite on my thumbnail. "This always works in, like, movies and stuff." It was so ridiculous of me to think it was that simple. This wasn't the movies. If this were the movies, my brother wouldn't be paralyzed and my friends wouldn't be dead and my boyfriend wouldn't have a secret self too important to tell me about.

"Like, what's the point? Like, none of this stuff is who I am on the inside." Will's words tumble through my head. I wish for them to stop.

"Lake, let's go."

"No!" I have my hand pressed to my forehead now and I'm pacing. "There's got to be a janitor here or something. Hello?" I call out. "Hello? Is anyone here?" Silence. I don't know why this matters to me. Only that it's the one thing that Matt's ever said that he wanted aside from my resurrection choice and coming on this stupid scavenger hunt, so I thought that at least this I could definitely give him. This one thing.

"Lake!" This time he shouts so loud that it makes me jump and I quit pacing. "Christ, you insensitive little . . ." He trails off. His tongue is stuffed between his teeth, seething. Meanwhile my mouth goes dry. "Did you really think wheeling me across a *stage* was—going—to—fix—*anything*?" He drags out the words and I feel like he's dragging me along with them. But his voice is no longer deep. It's strained. And I have to think that maybe it would have fixed something.

"I just wanted to try." I sound so small.

Out here it's like we're the only two people left. Birds chirp and land on a nearby roof. Shadows stretch out, trying to swallow us whole.

"You have made me suffer for days on end with this will-she-won't-she bull and now you are desperate to clear your conscience over it. Well, stop it. You don't want to use your resurrection on me." He lets the bomb land. I wait for it to detonate, to see if it still feels like the truth or if maybe it's somehow, over time, morphed into a lie.

I direct my words at the pavement. I don't know what's made it harder to tell Matt that I won't resurrect him, not now, not ever, but saying it out loud has started to feel about as easy as tearing holes through my skin. "It's complicated."

"Astrophysics is complicated. I am your brother."

"No, you're not," I snap back. "*My* brother died five years ago. I don't know who the hell you are."

I can practically see the red outline of a hand having slapped him across the face. Never had I expected one of my remarks to land. We both know that this one has and it leaves us wide-eyed and blinking at each other.

Matt breaks the silence first. "Go get what we came for," he says softly.

My forehead is blazing hot, but I obey. Behind me, I sense Matt wanting to crawl out of his body. It's so saddled with limitations. It's so dependent on everyone else around him. He's a prisoner to me, to my parents, to all of us.

I want this all to be over. That's why when I find the fourth clue hiding underneath the lunch table I tear it open and read the contents and don't bother waiting for him at all.

Because, who even cares anymore? I'm already a promise breaker.

Aren't I?

# chapter twenty-six

## 7 DAYS

*Lake, you'll find your prize by light of the next full moon.*

*Wait! Wait! Not yet! I promise, you'll learn the location soon.*

*This year your birthday happens to fall on a night that's quite auspicious.*

*Look out for your invite and follow the directions to uncover all our wishes.*

I don't tell Matt that I've already opened the envelope. By the time I return to him at St. Theresa's, he's wiped his face blank again and makes a point of acting unfazed by my remark. Instead, he makes several jabs about my driving and then claims he's too tired to have dinner. So I guess we're both keeping things to ourselves.

After I've gone to bed, Mom comes into my room and sits down on my bed. I quickly stash Penny's journal beneath the comforter. I notice Mom doesn't have a magazine in hand and find that I sort of wish that she did, even if only for old times' sake.

She has her hair pulled back in the white shell barrette. It's not worth being mad at her any longer.

"Lake," she says. It's been too long since I've heard a version of her other than one who's exhausted. "What are you doing with Matt?"

"What do you mean?"

Her fingers are long and bony and if you pinch the skin above the knuckle it takes a long time for it to go down. I watch her play absently with the folds on her hands. "I mean that you've been taking him on outings, spending time with him. Why?"

"Because he asked me to."

"Asked you to what?" she says.

I sit up and use my toes to tuck Penny's journal farther beneath the covers. I have a one-minute debate about how much to tell her and then decide that it doesn't matter. I can tell her or not and it won't change a thing, so I do what's easiest. "Will set up this scavenger hunt for my birthday," I begin. "He wanted me to get to the end of it because . . . because it would tell me something. Because it's important, what's at the end. Matt made me promise to bring him along on the hunt."

Her mouth twists as if she's fishing around in there for the right thing to say. I think she finds it. "Sometimes grief makes us hold on to things tighter than we otherwise would and search for answers where there aren't any," she says. It reminds me of one of Penny's Buddhist quotes, transcribed carefully in her handwriting.

I stare down at the remnants of chipped polish on my toes.

"When your brother got hurt, I showed up to the occupational therapy wing of the hospital every day. I would wait for doctors outside their offices. I once drove three hours to speak with a doctor who had already written me to say Matt's case was hopeless and that he would never walk again." It's strange, but I don't remember my mother doing this at all. "I held his feet and would mimic the motion of walking, praying that his legs would remember. I held on for a long time, I searched for answers, but there weren't any. Do you know what I mean?" But I think maybe she hasn't stopped hanging on, she's just changed what she's hanging on to. Matt's resurrection.

"Dad still bikes, though," I say. "Miles and miles, and you think that's healthy."

"Dad's biking . . . it's a coping mechanism. It's different. He's not looking for anything out there on the road. He just does it and then he comes back better. The answers for him are in the act itself. It's not a crutch."

I nod, but don't know how I will be able to tell the difference between a coping mechanism and a crutch.

Before she leaves, I want to ask her one thing: *Will you still love me if I don't resurrect Matt?* But I can't bring myself to say it out loud and the question becomes just one more thing to die between us.

When I check the calendar I discover that, as I suspected, the next full moon isn't until the eve of my birthday. I check the mail and my inbox and my phone and even ChatterJaw for signs of an invitation even though I know I need to put it out of my mind until the day before my birthday, but it's hard to shake the sickening feeling that one may not arrive at all.

I sink my head into my knees. There's a week until the full moon. When I find the wishes, I'll probably have only hours left before I have to make my final choice and turn in my application for resurrection. Hours and then minutes and then nothing. And I have to pray the pieces fall together—*snick-snick-snick.*

But worry is sinking in, pulsing in rhythm with my heart. What if my mom and Ringo are right? What if I'm holding on too tightly? Worse—what if the wishes don't say anything important after all?

There are questions that have been nagging me, questions that maybe it's time to start getting answered. I feel for Penny's journal resting underneath the comforter and pull it out. Finding the wishes has always been about trying to uncover what my two best friends would have wanted. I need to make sure I have all the information I need before the clock runs out.

I send two texts, make a plan, and then turn out the lights on the beginning of the end of my countdown: seven days to go.

# chapter twenty-seven

## *6 DAYS*

The sun is so strong and bright, shining directly into my eyes, that it throws the figure standing by the side of the road up ahead into total silhouette. Seashell gravel crunches under the tires as we edge off the asphalt and pull over in front of it.

"That him?" Ringo says from the driver's seat. I've taken to letting Ringo drive me anytime he's around. It's easier on me this way, especially now that I'm seeing him more often. A couple of days ago, I listened to stories about his mother, about how she used to serve ice cream for breakfast on Fridays and rent foreign films with subtitles nearly every Sunday night before the school week began, and I think I understand something about him just a little bit better.

Then there are things that I will never understand, like how so soon after Will's and Penny's deaths Ringo and I could have managed to create our own inside joke, something stupid about percentages and honesty and the back of my jeans, but still it makes us laugh. It makes *me* laugh. And when I see him, it makes the beginning of this day just bearable enough to keep going.

I squint. The light shifts behind a row of palm trees and then I can make out the broad-shouldered figure of Harrison Vines.

"Yep," I say, feeling like I've unwittingly entered the Twilight Zone. I roll down my window. "You ready?" I ask him. I'm surprised to realize that the surfer-boy-haircut-and-board-shorts look that I've been completely used to because of Will and all the other beach-bum guys at school looks a bit silly to me now—like a caricature—so at odds with Ringo's style of coffeehouse cool. I look over Harrison's shoulder to where his house, a one-story home with lawn chairs set up in the front yard, stands set back from the street. I expected his family to be wealthier. Wrong again, I guess.

"It's been a couple of years since I last saw my uncle," he says, climbing into the backseat and sliding over to the middle.

"No time like the present for a family reunion," Ringo remarks, startling Harrison. Ringo twists back and extends a hand. "Ringo Littlefield, moral support," he says by way of introduction.

Harrison returns the handshake, but he freezes when he sees the dark stain on the top quadrant of Ringo's face. Harrison looks down and licks his lips and takes Ringo's hand without looking him in the eye. "Harrison," he says. "Nice to meet you." Then to me, "I didn't tell my uncle we were bringing anyone else."

"Yeah, well, Ringo's my friend, and I need a friend right now. So your uncle's just going to have to understand. And so are you," I add. The idea of leaving Ringo behind twists a knife in my gut. "Plus, Ringo has some personal experience with resurrections," I explain.

Harrison glances into the rearview, where Ringo's forehead is partially reflected. "You don't look resurrected," he says. It's not exactly a compliment. If Ringo had been resurrected, the lifeblood would have slipped through the cells, including those discolored on his face, most likely leaving the skin smooth and undamaged.

"Thanks," Ringo says with an edge to his voice. "And you don't look like a horse's ass, and yet..."

I flinch. With me, Ringo has always been self-deprecating, the first to point out his physical differences and embrace them. This is a different side of him. I turn and glare at Harrison.

Harrison squares his shoulders and pins them to his seat back. "Sorry, sorry," he says. "I only meant... Look, I was just making an observation."

Ringo grunts. "It's my mom," he says. "The one who's resurrected."

Harrison nods. "I'm sorry to hear that."

Well, this trip is off to a great start, I think, though I don't regret my decision to bring Ringo along. An hour-long car ride alone with Harrison would be too weird even for this month.

"Maya couldn't come?" I ask, trying to lighten the mood.

Harrison shrugs, stretching out his long suntanned legs. "I don't know, I didn't ask her. Why?"

"I—I don't know—" I get an embarrassed flush in my cheeks. Will, Penny, and I always asked each other everywhere. It was an unwritten rule. Sure, sometimes Will would have soccer practice, or Penny would have family dinner, but the separations were always involuntary.

"It's fine," he says. "I think she and her friend were working on programming some crowd-sourcing game she likes where you get rated on, like, the outfits you put together or something." He leans his head back on the head-rest. "*Glad* to get out of hearing any more about that, if you know what I mean."

I try to laugh but can't help feeling that something about what Harrison says has caught me and needled its way under my skin, where it itches like a small, bothersome tick. Nerves, I think. I'm just letting my nerves get the best of me. Because the truth is that I'm unsettled by the idea of visiting the commune.

And so we drive in relative silence. We hug the coastline. Signs of our beach town, with its pastel condos and tourist shops, fade, replaced by a shoreline that grows more rugged with each mile. Patches of European beachgrass sprout from between rocks, and the brown tendrils of wrack that collect near the road help to form dunes along the upper beach. On the side of the road opposite the vast stretch of ocean, acres of farmland unfold. We pass groups of chocolate-and-white cows munching in the fields and the occasional spotted pony.

Harrison watches his phone for directions, finally telling Ringo to turn left at a rickety road sign that reads ZYLE LANE. Ringo sits up straighter.

On either side of the dirt road on which we've turned are bunches of sticks standing together like totems. We pass them every thirty seconds or so. I twist my hands around the door handle and lean forward to see farther over the dash.

"Have you been here before?" I ask Harrison quietly.

"Once," he says. "I was a lot younger. The last time I saw him, my uncle came to visit us at home. It's better that way, I promise."

The first person we come upon is a man, walking barefoot with his back to us in the grass and dressed all in white, linen pants and a tunic. His gray hair is pulled back into a wiry ponytail. We slow down as we pass by. The man doesn't look over at the lone car pulling up beside him, and then we pass and he continues wandering along the roadside seemingly without noticing our intrusion at all.

"There's a general store. You'll see it. That's where we go first," Harrison says. "It has the only phone in the whole commune."

Up ahead there are groups of dwellings. Doublewide trailers have tented canopies extended off the side. Around them are a few freestanding wooden cabins with lopsided shingles. Men and women mill around outside, each wearing a matching tunic and pants. Everyone seems to be moving at dream speed, slow and unhurried. A girl pumps water from a hand well into a bucket on the ground.

"Wouldn't it be easier to just, like, book a weekend at a day spa?" Ringo asks, sneaking glances as he drives at the odd assortment of people gathered outside.

Harrison snorts. I crack a smile. "Did your mom join a commune?" Harrison asks.

"Not unless you count the cult of Big Gulps and soap operas," Ringo answers, then adds more thoughtfully, "But yeah, she did change. After, I mean."

"Look, there it is." I point up ahead. A classic pickup truck is parked in the dead grass outside a large aluminum shed in front of which is a hand-painted sign that reads GENERAL STORE.

We pull off and park near the pickup. The first thing I notice is how quiet it is. The three pairs of our shoes sound like draft horses clomping through the dry dirt. We walk in. There isn't much "general" about the store. There's one bookshelf and on it a few items from a first aid kit—gauze, scissors, medical tape. Near it, on the floor, is an ice chest. Somebody has written *Please replace the scoop* on the top.

Harrison greets the white-clad man who is sitting on a stool reading a book with no title on the cover. "Hi, we're looking for Coyote Blue," he says.

*"Coyote Blue?"* Ringo repeats too loudly, and I jab an elbow into his ribs to get him to shut up.

The man's teeth are bright against his dark skin. He has beautiful almond-shaped eyes and tight curls of black hair springing from the top of his head. "Coyote?" He says this like he's just waking up. "Coyote," he repeats. "Yes, one moment. I'll send a messenger. He's expecting you?"

"Yes, he should be," Harrison says. "We called yesterday." He points to the lone cell phone sitting atop a counter, plugged into a generator.

The man slides from the stool soundlessly, bows slightly, and then disappears out a back door. The three of us are left to stare at one another.

"It used to be Darrell Vines," says Harrison. "Commune members change their names as part of their rebirth."

"And the best he could come up with was Coyote Blue?" I say.

"He's changed too," Harrison explains while I wander

to the bookshelf and turn over the small pair of scissors and wonder what anyone would do out here if there were a real accident.

Shortly after, we see the long shadow of someone who is crossing behind us, without hearing the person who casts it. We turn to see a man in the uniform of the commune, again without shoes on, which must explain some of the members' ability to move without making so much as a whisper of noise.

"Hello, Harrison." Coyote's tone is cool, but not unfriendly. The man is strikingly handsome—eyes as blue as glaciers, hair a blond spun from golden thread. It's easy to see the resemblance between him and his nephew, but unlike Harrison, who feels bulky and grounded, Coyote seems to hold himself lightly on the earth, as if he's not subject to the full force of gravity.

Harrison hesitates, like he's not sure whether to hug him or bow or back away slowly.

I step forward, saving him. "Mr. . . . Blue. I'm Lake Devereaux and this is my friend Ringo." Coyote's eyes dash over Ringo's countenance but don't linger over the deep-red shading there. "Harrison arranged this for me."

Coyote's smile has that looking-down-from-heaven air to it that feels both condescending and comforting at once. "Yes, he provided a few of the details." Though his eyes passed over Ringo, they are boring into me, scanning me over and over and not in a creepy-hitting-on-me way, more like he's searching for something. He stops, smiles again. "Should I show you around?" he asks.

We traipse after him, a herd of noisy tourists.

"Get many visitors around here?" Ringo quips.

I notice that Coyote's arms don't swing at his sides when he walks. "Not usually," he replies matter-of-factly.

Coyote leads us through a wide de facto boulevard between the rows of houses. "We make all of our food here on the compound." He points to raised planters where green plants sprout in the dirt. Each residence appears to have at least one. "We parse out what each family will grow and we share the produce."

"What about meat?" Ringo asks, trotting behind us after pausing to peer into a square planter that has baby pumpkins growing inside. "And dairy?"

"There are no animals on the commune," Coyote says, evoking a chill on the back of my neck, like an icy hand.

"You mentioned families . . . ?" I venture. I can't imagine that there are many wholly resurrected families—not even many parent-child pairs. The likelihood would be too small.

"Ah, yes, well, you'll see," he says. "This is my home." He gestures to a trailer on our right. Large sheets are tied to wooden poles propped up to create a canopy on one side. "Come in and you can meet my daughter."

I raise my eyebrows at Harrison. *Daughter?* I mouth as Coyote squeaks open the screen door.

Harrison shakes his head. "My cousins are alive. I don't know."

I swallow hard. We scale a step stool into the trailer. It's crowded with us all inside. The decor is a wash of tan and brown. "Starshine," he calls into the back. "We have guests."

I take a seat on a faux-leather bench. There is a watery stew boiling on a hotplate nearby. My arm presses into the sticky skin of Ringo's beside me.

A girl materializes from somewhere in the belly of the

trailer. She is younger than I am, I would guess no more than fourteen. She has fiery-red hair and a pale face oddly free of freckles, given her complexion. Starshine has the posture of a ballerina, but it's obvious at once that she has none of the confidence or presence of one.

From the corner of my eye, I see Harrison grip his knees more tightly. "Your daughter's name is Kate," he says to Coyote, stiffly.

"*Darrell's* daughter's name was Kate," says Coyote Blue. "Coyote's daughter is Starshine." He looks at her proudly as she stands pressed into the corner with her hands folded at her waist. I offer an awkward wave, not sure what to do. My brain has started to scream, *Cult! Cult! Cult!* Yet my heart has started to sense the peeling shell of a creepy old man. "Starshine died when she was only eleven." He says this like it's a good thing and it turns my spit sour. "The best I can tell, she was killed by her stepfather, who found her sometime after she had run away, though she doesn't remember so it's really all just hearsay. She was homeless, begging on corners. A pimp thought she had promise and had one of his girls use her resurrection choice on Starshine and she was brought back to life to become one of his working girls when the time was right." He raises his eyebrows disapprovingly. "I noticed her on one of my trips in," he says, referring to life outside the compound. "And I brought her here to be my daughter."

I feel Harrison flinch again.

"But... why not live with your real family?" I try.

Coyote's lips form a straight line. "Starshine, would you get our guests some soup?" She obeys like she's someone used to obeying. For a second, I think that he's going to avoid my question. "There's no place for me with my family anymore. I've died and been reborn. My family doesn't *grasp* that. Besides, my first-life wife—Harrison's aunt—had already fallen in love by the time that my daughter, Kate, used her resurrection choice on me."

Harrison jolts, nearly knocking a bowl of soup from Starshine's fragile hands. "She never did anything with that guy. She waited for you. We all did. She waited for you so long that he married someone else after you were resurrected. And you didn't even want our family."

Starshine hands Ringo and me small bowls of the soup along with a pair of dented metal spoons.

Coyote narrows his eyes at Harrison. "I don't expect you to be able to understand." But as he says this he switches his stare to me and I feel guilty that I've made Harrison go through this for me.

I take a sip of the scalding soup and jerk back. The mixture tastes like dirt.

"Do you feel different?" I ask him.

"Stronger, smarter, more pure," he replies.

"Do you remember dying?" I say. Starshine turns her shoulders away to stand over the hotplate and stir.

"It was a long process, dying of pancreatic cancer, so yes, I remember every excruciating detail up until the last day of my life. Then it's blank. I was a part of the Other for two full years before I was reborn." Again, I detect a hint of pride and I wonder if, here, the amount of time spent dead carries with it some twisted badge of honor.

The quiet presses in on me from all sides. Coyote is able to go as still as Matt. And there is nothing natural about Starshine, though I feel a pulse of sympathy for her.

By Coyote's account she had no place else to go. I wonder what her name was before all this. I wonder whether she had anyone to love her. Most of all, I wonder if she'd be better off dead.

Unease creeps up my back, onto my neck, until it reaches my scalp. Ringo has been strangely quiet beside me, but he never wavers or stands to leave and for that at least I'm grateful.

When the conversation dies, we all tumble out of the trailer, nearly on top of one another, so eager are we to escape the muted chambers of Coyote Blue with his dreamy, thousand-mile stare and his daughter who's not a daughter and the muffled peacefulness that makes the hairs on my arms stand on end. Once out, I look up to a blank slate of blue sky and feel it confining us, like a ceiling.

# chapter twenty-eight

## 6 DAYS

We drop Harrison off at his house, I thank him, and he says something like, "What are friends for?" and I'm pretty sure that I've accidentally become friends with Harrison Vines and that I don't even hate it.

After that it's just me and Ringo in the car. I relish the return to civilization, with the seagulls squawking overhead and the *boom-crash* of the ocean and the tourist shops with their sidewalk sales that draw in women with white shopping bags. We drive down Pineapple Avenue, through the heart of the town, past a statue of a sailor kissing a flapper girl.

The entire ride back I've been trying to speak, been trying even to *think* about the things that we saw. About our encounter with Coyote Blue and with Starshine and the eerie quiet of the commune. And about how I hated it all. Every single thing about it.

I attempt to sort through the reasons why a person who

has been resurrected would choose to join a commune. Is there actually a spiritual transformation that takes place during the dying process or is it only the perception of one? Or worse, do the commune members merely wish for a transformation in order to place some meaning on their deaths that was never there in the first place?

I picture the serene faces, all twisted illusions of people. I think I'd rather be dead than live in a commune. But Penny? What would she think? She cried over an injured bird. She thought the full moon was magical. How would she perceive the shift that she inevitably would make in the natural order if she were to be resurrected?

I worry.

I worry that she would be tempted to seek meaning with people like Coyote Blue. It's a concern that clenches me in the gut and won't let go as I start to imagine Penny in linen, face smoothed to unnatural perfection and unflinchingly serene. She wouldn't cry for birds or for whales or for anything. Would Penny stay my Penny or would she become . . . something else?

I hate the thought of her going to live somewhere I can't and wouldn't follow. If she were tempted by the empty, meaningless spirituality of the commune, my resurrection choice would have been wasted.

When I think about the experience of the commune, the same word keeps slipping into place: *unnatural.*

I swallow down the meaning of this like a dose of cough syrup, but my throat still itches, itches, itches, and I want to say something that I'm nearly too scared to breathe.

What if I've made my decision? It feels impossible. Wrong even. But I suspect that I've felt it the entire drive home, percolating through my bones, hardening into a choice—yielding a name now balanced on the tip of my tongue.

My palms sweat.

I tell myself that there is no good resolution but that I will do the best I can with the information I have.

"Ringo?" I'm holding my breath and squeezing my abs tight to try to hold together the pieces of myself that I have left. "I think I'm going to resurrect Will," I say. "I don't think Penny would like it. The whole resurrection thing."

We turn onto Lemon Drive, then Orange.

Ringo seems to have given up speaking, like it's a sacrifice for Lent. But then he finally says, "Oh." And nothing else.

"That's all you can say?" I respond, really and truly kind of pissed.

He pushes a little harder on the gas pedal. My stomach lurches and I grip my fingernails into the stiff stitching of the seat.

The pedal pushes closer to the floor. We go fast, faster, fastest. I watch the speedometer dial climb the outside of the circle.

"Right now, yeah."

His face is calm, but I notice his fists clench almost imperceptibly around the wheel.

Fear threatens to crush my windpipe. My heels are bearing into the floorboards. "Can you . . . can you please slow *down*, Ringo?"

I squeeze my eyes shut, but the effect is that I feel like we're going even faster and I can't see where we're going, which means it could be anywhere. I am barreling. Too much. Too quick. Waiting, waiting, waiting for impact. I brace myself. So tense. I cannot move.

"Slow down!" I shout. Eyes still shut tight.

And this time, he listens. He eases off the accelerator. "Sorry," he says, flatly, but I can't help the deluge of images that flood in at the sense of panic. They layer together one on top of another, coming, coming, quick, quick, quick—*blond hair, red blood, glittering glass, white bone, crushed metal, limbs, intestines, open flesh, suffocating, ocean, dead*— I gasp, tearing myself from the sinkhole of frightening pictures.

"Lake?" he says. His hand is on my leg. I'm shaking my head. I can't look at him. "Lake?" he asks again. And then I hear the *blip-blip-blip* of the blinker and we're curving to the side and coming to a stop. Horns honk. Cars whoosh by Ringo's door. But he has pushed the gearshift into park and we are no longer moving.

He turns toward me. I'm shaking violently. Ringo leans across the center console and wraps his arms all the way around me. His nose is resting in the nook between my shoulder and my neck. His mouth is warm there. "I'm sorry, I'm sorry," he says, this time with real concern. "Are you okay?" he asks. My teeth chatter so much, they might chatter right out of my mouth. Ringo pulls away and ducks his head down to look into my eyes. I drink in the marine blue and trace the intricate edges of his birthmark with my own eyes, like it's a map back to the present. He holds one of my shoulders firmly and strokes the back of my head with his other hand. "I didn't mean to scare you. I didn't mean to, Lake." He watches me until I nod and then he pulls me into him again. He presses my nose into his shirt collar, tucks me into him like a doll. He is much more solid than I thought he'd be.

"I'm fine." My words are muffled.

I feel his head above me shaking back and forth. He doesn't let go and I don't try to move. His Adam's apple bobs sharply and I think I feel a slight tremor in his chest when he says, "'Anna.' The Beatles, they knew what they were talking about when they covered 'Anna.'" He only holds me for a moment longer, squeezing me once tightly before letting me go. Then he wipes his hand over his face, shudders some emotion free and drives.

At the Southshores complex, I watch the back of Ringo's head disappear into his apartment and I think that I want to cry. How can a heart be full and empty all at once? I wish for the days to pass. I wish I could wake up and for it to be the day after my birthday. Lately, there only seem to be wrong turns and I'm taking every single one of them. I'm forced to replace Ringo at the wheel and drive the distance back to my house, slowly and cautiously, always on the lookout for a silver Lexus.

I try mentally repeating the same thing I told Ringo: *I think I'm going to resurrect Will. I think I'm going to resurrect Will.* I try not to think about the other side of the coin. Cause and effect. Push and pull. Life and death. And the person whose face I'll be choosing never to see again.

The sun is warm. I slide Penny's journal out from its hiding place, grab a towel and sneak out onto the beach behind our house. Salt water sprays up between the jetty rocks. I think about walking out there, the way I used to when I was younger until my parents forbade me from scaling the rocks, but I spread my towel out on the gray sand instead. My toes dig ten holes in the beach.

Penny's journal keeps me company next to my hip. I imagine carrying her with me this way, adding to the notes she kept with some of my own observations. I could tell her about college and how I hold a Save the Whales run each year in her honor. I can explain to her about Ringo. Lines and words would fill up the page and maybe somehow they'd reach her.

Or maybe they wouldn't.

The thing I'm hoping to feel as I'm sitting out here, watching the waves lap just short of my feet, is peace. Or at least relief.

If I've decided Penny might not want to be resurrected, then that should be it, shouldn't it? That should be my decision. It's finished. Six days to spare.

But if it's peace I'm looking for, it's hiding well. I start to build a sandcastle as a distraction. I burrow my hands in the damp, sticky grains, hollowing out a place for my structure. Matt and I had spent so much time making sandcastles when we were younger, we'd practically become master architects, at least when the medium was sand.

I keep it simple. Four cylindrical towers that I form with my palms. I dig a tunnel through the middle one, then use drippings to make spindly turrets on top of each.

My mind merely turns down the volume, it doesn't shut off. Happy thoughts should include thinking of Will, what our faces will look like to each other when we see each other for the first time since the crash, how I can lie in his bed again with the sheets pulled over our heads, how I can wrap my hands around his smooth back and let him warm me like a space heater, how our love story won't have an end.

I will have to tell him about Ringo and about Harrison. Eventually I'll need to ask him about the ChatterJaw thread too.

It turns out that turning the voices in my head to a lower volume helps. There's room for happiness and it's seeping in like the rising tide as I work. The last thing I do is build a wall of sand around my completed castle, as tall and as sturdy as I can make it, so that the water won't sink my work into oblivion.

ChatterJaw and Ringo and Harrison and the absence of Penny and the relationship between Will's mom and Tessa—these are all things that we can deal with later, together, which is the way that we've dealt with everything for the past four years.

I sit back onto my towel and pull Penny's journal into my lap. I open it up. The sight of her handwriting hits me with a fresh wave of pain, the deep-down throbbing kind—but I'd expected it, more or less, and so I turn to the back half where I'd left off and I begin reading, like she's talking to me one last time.

I don't know how long I've been reading against the backdrop of the sea, which is becoming choppier and noisier, and the flecks of salt gathering more thickly on my neck and lips—thirty minutes? forty-five?—when I cross a line that I have to reread: *I'm a mosaic made from sharp edges and broken things,* I read.

The page begins to quiver between my fingers. I wrench my eyes onto the next line, and the next:

I'm a mosaic made from sharp edges and
broken things
As long as no one looks too closely—not
even me—none of the ugly bits show through
Those parts that want to smash love and
tear holes in hearts
But I'm still made up of the broken things
Even if nobody knows
I still feel them
Ripping into my soul

*Thud-thud-thud* goes my heart, *thud-thud-thud.*

I lose count of the number of times I read through the page. There's no attribution. Nothing but Penny. *Thud-thud-thud.*

Make it stop. Because I know the lines. I know the words. I know where I've seen them before.

What had Harrison said to me the first moment that he told me about the ChatterJaw thread? I know. He'd said he was pretty sure the two writers had gone private. That my Will had gone private. And now I know who with.

# chapter twenty-nine

## 152 DAYS

I watch Penny and Will walk away until they disappear through the hospital-wing doors. The slaps of their flip-flops stop and I'm left alone again amid the sound of heart monitors and IV drips.

Maybe it's my own fault. After all, they'd asked if I wanted company. I could have spoken up then. But the problem is, I didn't want them to ask. I didn't want to be the one to tell them not to go without me. I wanted them not to be able to *fathom* going without me.

But of course they could. It was spring break. Their choices were (a) a water park trip we'd been planning for a month, or (b) sit in a hospital waiting room for six hours with nothing to do.

And yet I still find myself with this gnawing feeling that I wished they'd chosen to stay. I take a sip from the milk shake they brought me as a consolation prize, but it doesn't even taste good now, which is saying a lot, since I've been munching on food from the hospital cafeteria for the entire week of spring break so far.

Five whole days while Penny and Will have been out enjoying the time that we should have *all* enjoyed together. I scuff my shoe against the white tile floor, letting myself wallow for another few moments in my great, big helping of bitter pie.

"Lake?" Mom pops her head out of one of the rooms while a nurse in pink scrubs is slipping out. "What's taking so long?"

I slouch toward the door and slink in past her. "I don't know why I have to be here anyway," I mumble.

Mom goes rigid. She abruptly closes the door. She snatches my elbow and pulls me in the way she used to when I was five years old and in trouble. "Your brother is in pain, young lady," she hisses, as if trying to prevent Matt from hearing. "This is the least you can do."

Spittle lands on my cheek. She's right. I'm ashamed at my attitude. But instead of erasing all the other nasty feelings that are swimming inside me, I just add shame to the internal cesspool of emotions already there.

"Sorry," I say quietly.

Her fingers release the fleshy part of my arm and I rub at the spots dramatically, like she's really hurt me.

She runs her hands over the front of her jeans and stands up straighter. When was the last time she went home? Two days ago? Before even then? I can't remember.

I follow her into the room, where my dad is snoring in a chair and Matt's lying in the same spot he's been for the past five days. In a hospital bed.

His breathing is labored. An infection rages in his lungs. His face is red and feverish. His pupils move slowly to focus on me. "Oh," he rasps. "It's you."

I shrink back a step. *See,* I want to scream, *he doesn't even want me here!*

"Didn't mean to break up social hour," he says with a snarl.

"You didn't. They just wanted to stop by to see how you were." Lies.

"Did you tell them my back's still broken? Did they want to help change my bedpan? Or how about my underwear?"

I hug my elbows. "No."

"Oh, shut up, Lake. Stop acting like I'm the freaking big bad wolf and you're scared of me. Nobody feels sorry for you, you pathetic, petty excuse for a human being."

My mouth drops open. It's the meanest thing he has ever said to me. His words have the exact opposite effect from what he intended, because I feel sorrier for myself than ever. I sniff in quick breaths, trying to stave off the tears that have begun to bubble up on the rims of my eyelids.

This time when Mom touches me, it's gentle. "He's in pain."

"Of course you're pandering to her." Matt stares up at the ceiling now. His breath is coming in seething fits. It's strange to see his body lying completely limp. A normal person would be writhing in pain. Clenching their fists. Kicking their legs. But not Matt. He has to marinate in the hurt and I guess that's why he tries to spoon some of it onto me. "I swear. If you weren't good for a resurrection . . ." he says.

And I can feel the hatred in those few words as clearly as if they were a spike shot through my back. The tears won't stop now. I don't understand why he hates me. I don't understand what I did to deserve this. I tried. So many times I tried to reach out to him. He forgets: he was the one who rejected me.

All I know is that being here is making me miss out on the last spring break I have with the people that actually do care about me—Will and Penny—and so I can't help it. I hate him right back.

# chapter thirty

## 5 DAYS

I decide on a plan. Or at least the beginnings of one. I try not to feel bad that I'm actually going to need Matt's help.

I knock on my parents' bedroom door, but there's no answer. Instead, I hear voices coming from the study. The voices sound angry, angry enough to bring my dad home early from work, I realize.

I creep toward the closed doors until I'm close enough that the sounds of angry voices arrange themselves into words I can understand.

"That's why I'm telling you." My mom's tone is shrill. "She needs to know." I stop breathing to hear better. The end of my mom's thought is drowned out by the booming sea outside. I plant my foot another step closer to the door.

"That's not your call to make." My dad, unlike my mother, keeps his voice even, like this is a conversation he's rehearsed over and over again. Have they had this conversation before? "It's against his wishes." I feel the hair rise on the back of my arms and then a little prickling sensation as I realize that the "she" they're talking about is *me*. "This whole thing. It's about choice. Isn't that what we decided together? You know what we have to do. We have to stay the course."

This isn't the first time I've heard my parents argue about Matt's resurrection. Of course they never seem to bother to include *me* in the discussion.

"We're their parents, Peter." I move closer to the door.

"We are. But Matt's not a child." Dad's raising his voice now. "He knows what he's doing."

"You're wrong. Everything's different after what's happened." She's pleading now. My throat feels scratchy. "He's going to make himself a martyr and you're going to let him."

"He's our son. We owe him this much." Dad's voice has the air of reluctant finality. He's tired. Tired of bills. Tired of taking care of my brother. Probably even tired of me.

"We're not going to *have* a son after all this!" Mom says. "Not unless we do something!"

I swallow.

"I'm finished with this discussion." I hear his fist come down on something solid and wooden, like the desk.

"Tell her, Peter. This is on you."

Tell me what? That I *have* to use my resurrection choice on Matt? That they'll disown me if I don't? Or that they'll drag me into the office themselves and force me to write down Matt's name as the resurrection candidate?

Or is there something else? Between Will, Penny, and my parents, I'm beginning to feel as though I've been living my life constantly in the dark, as though everyone knows things that I don't.

Heavy footsteps come from the other side of the door. I have just enough time to take a few steps back, so that it doesn't look like I was hovering, before my dad emerges from the study. He's already in the process of buckling the strap of his bike helmet under his chin

"Hi, Dad." He jumps. He hasn't had enough time to rearrange his face. It looks exhausted and drawn, like he's stayed up all night, and his hair is tousled.

"Lake." His voice grates.

"I was just coming to look for you and Mom," I say. I try to make my eyes wide and innocent looking: *You've seen nothing. You've heard nothing.*

My dad's lips purse and I can tell he's trying to gauge the situation for himself. When did I get here? Do I know he and Mom have been arguing and, if so, do I have any idea why?

I forge on, not wanting to give him enough time to sort this last bit out. "I wanted to let you know that I'm going to take Matt out for a while, if that's okay. We'll need to borrow the van."

His hairline lifts like he's questioning, but then he nods repeatedly with a faint smile on his lips. "Sure, sure. I think that'd be really nice, Lake."

Another pang of guilt, because I'm responsible for planting that look of hope there. Me. But I'm not the only one here holding back. And it looks like nobody is going to tell me anything unless I figure it out on my own.

So it's up to me to fix that.

# chapter thirty-one

## *4 DAYS*

"You have one hour," Matt says the moment I raise my fist to knock on Ms. Bryan's door. "Anything longer with Jeremy and my brain will literally melt."

I peer down at my brother, surprised that we're side by side, let alone speaking to each other, after what happened at St. Theresa's. When I asked for his help, I was expecting to have to negotiate, although what I could offer him that he would want at this point, I don't know. Instead, Matt agreed to come willingly. Almost too willingly. I try to convince myself that the reason was my comment about his not acting like my brother, and that I finally, against all odds, got to him. But with Matt, it's not ever that simple.

But I don't have time for games or reverse psychology. "Oh, come on, Jeremy's not that bad," I say. "He used to be your friend, you know."

"That was before he turned into a huge stoner loser."

"He's not always a huge stoner loser. Besides, I'm sure he's not dying to hang out with Captain Sunshine over here, either."

"Gee, thanks."

"Well."

"One hour." Matt sets his jaw and glares at the door, like he might see right through it if he tried hard enough. When was the last time he hung out with anyone his own age? I wonder. It has to have been years. Maybe even pre-accident. There's a glisten of sweat on his cheeks and, if I didn't know better, I'd guess that he was nervous.

"Okay, okay, fine. One hour." I knock on the door and it swings open right away, like Jeremy had just been on the other side waiting for the formality of the knock.

"Welcome, Devereaux-ses—Deveri?" Jeremy chuckles to himself. "Sorry, I don't know the plural."

Matt looks up at me and lifts his eyebrows. I put my hand on his shoulder, a gesture the meaning of which I hope he registers with his eyes, even though he can't feel it. "Thanks for having us, Jeremy."

"Come in, come in." He steps aside. "Jolene is at work or whatever, but she said she's glad you're here. Make yourselves at home, *mi casa es su casa*."

"Except it's not really *'su casa,'* so . . ." Matt says. I jerk his wheelchair to warn him not to be rude and then push him after Jeremy into the kitchen. And just like that, we're in.

I have to remember to breathe.

"Dude, it's been forever." Jeremy holds out his hand as if for a high five. It hangs for a second in the air until he realizes his mistake and redirects it to sweep through his uncombed hair.

"Yes, well," Matt begins, "I suppose it's not terribly convenient to—" I kick the wheelchair hard. Matt stops and clears his throat. "I mean—yeah—good to see you too."

"So . . ." Jeremy rocks back on his heels. "This, uh, this is more awkward than I thought. A lot of bummer energy going on in this room." He holds his fingers out in front of him as if he could feel it.

My eyes go fishbowl wide. There's a long pause.

But then something happens. Matt tilts his head back and laughs—like, really laughs. Jeremy peers down his nose. His mouth quirks into a quarter of a grin and he says, "Really? That? Okay . . . Hey, well, actually I do have a collection of Tolkien action figures. You want to see?"

Matt looks at me. "He has a collection of Tolkien action figures."

"I heard." And the thing about Matt is that sometimes it's hard for me to tell whether or not he's mocking, but today it might be hard for him too. Because I think he probably really does want to see, even if he doesn't want to admit it. He forgets—there was a reason he was friends with Jeremy. And there was a reason that Jeremy was friends with him.

"I'll bring them up," Jeremy says.

Watching them, I nearly forget why we're here. My cue. Matt gives me a meaningful look this time, and I get it.

"Great." I clap my hands. "I can see you two have a lot to catch up on and, hey, don't let me stand in the way. I'm just going to be upstairs. Ms. Bryan said I could help myself to a few pictures of Will's in case I want to make something memorable for . . . for after." I gulp down the lie and try to digest it. I hike my thumbs over my shoulders, pointing upstairs. Jeremy stares at me all grouper-mouthed. I don't think he expected to be abandoned this quickly. "So . . ." I finish ungracefully. "I'll be back."

*One hour,* Matt mouths.

"In an hour," I add.

Both boys look palpably relieved. I check the time on my watch. *One hour,* I repeat to myself and clomp up the stairs.

After a short walk down the hallway, I find that Ms. Bryan still hasn't touched Will's room. The only difference is that I'm now catching whiffs of that un-lived-in smell. Like an attic. Light flooding in from the window catches specks of floating dust. The space feels emptied of Will.

I force myself to pause at the center of the room and take a deep breath. I'm here for a reason. Penny's dash of prose, the ChatterJaw thread, the fact that my boyfriend and my best friend might have been talking to each other—*really* talking to each other—behind my back. Thinking about it, even in the abstract, is like pressing on a bruise. I keep circling back to the possibilities each time thinking, *Yep, it still hurts.*

While I'm here, I decide to spend at least some of my time poking around.

The closet feels like a logical beginning. I throw open the doors and am hit with the pungent scent of sweaty sneakers. On the floor, tennis shoes and flip-flops are piled in a heap. Rumpled shirts are thrown over hangers and scrunched into cubbies. I kneel and push the mound of shoes to the side, uncovering a kid's baseball glove, a detached surfboard leash, and a beat-up cardboard box.

I pull the box into my lap and flip open the lid. There are stacks of papers, each covered in drawings. I hold one up to study. Like the others, it's been done in colored pencil.

It's a picture of a pelican perched on a channel marker, a fish hanging halfway out of its beak. Everything seems to still, even the thoughts swirling in my head. I didn't know that Will drew so much. I'd seen doodles in his notebooks, but nothing like this. And yet he'd mentioned it in the thread. He'd mentioned it, but never to me. I don't understand why the people I love keep parts of themselves buried, like it's a treasure they don't want to give me the map to.

I set down the pelican and choose another. This one's of Penny's Jeep. The sketch is detailed and I can tell by the eraser marks that he took pains to get the wheels and roll bar just right. Tears fill my eyes because I still can't believe the Jeep is gone. The Jeep and everyone who rode inside it.

On the back of the Jeep is another drawing. I recognize it instantly as one of Penny and me. I'm whispering something in her ear. Her eyes are closed, but she's smiling.

I press the picture against myself. It's comforting to be holding what feels like a piece of both Will and Penny. But none of the rest are helpful: there are cartoons, pictures of waves, scribbled attempts at various animals.

I fold up the picture of me and Penny and pocket it. Then I shove the box back into the closet and turn to the rest of the room. *Where next?*

I slip a few photographs out of their frames, because I told Ms. Bryan I would. I will make copies. I will make something with them. I will.

But they're not why I came. I hate how I feel in this moment, which is completely crazy—like one of those jealous girls who's constantly snooping through her boyfriend's phone.

I could still turn back. I could choose not to know. I

could decide to trust him. I could leave it forever and maybe someday a long time from now I'd actually convince myself that I'd forgotten. I chew on one of my fingernails.

I pause and listen for any signs of trouble downstairs. There are none. And meanwhile, my conscience is at war. I've always respected Will's privacy, but of course I've had no reason not to.

But this is important. Without this, I'll never have the full picture. And I will live an eternity without knowing what it was that I truly decided and who it was decided for. The computer cord snakes from an electrical outlet to a cabinet built into the desk where I find Will's laptop.

I take a seat on the rolling chair parked nearby and slide the computer onto my lap. The machine emits a quiet hum as I open it up and hit the *on* button. The generic geo-patterned background fills the screen and up pops the little box asking me to log in. I know this one because I used his computer for homework sometimes when we were hanging out. I type in the name of his favorite baseball player and add his birthdate at the end. My eyes are wide and darting around as I launch the web browser. I've come this far.

When the e-mail page loads, I again type in the same password. An error message appears on the bottom of the screen. I type it again. Another error. This time I check to see if I'd hit caps lock or something else I wasn't supposed to. Nope. I'm typing the password with such care that I know I've done it correctly.

The password, though, has changed. When did Will change his password? He's had the same one for as long as I can remember. I know, because one time when he was flying to New York for his mom's family reunion he asked me to check him into the gate early because he'd forgotten to and his phone was acting up. And then there was that time he needed to know if he'd remembered to e-mail a biology assignment. Little things like that. Always the same password. We trusted each other. One hundred percent.

Except here I am staring at an error message. I set the laptop down on the chair and begin to pace the room. He could have been hacked. But no, I would have known that. The password could have expired. Mine never expires. He could have forgotten it and had to change it.

None of these reasons feel right. I stare at the computer like it's something radioactive. If there was any question about whether I was going to snoop through Will's personal files, it's gone. All semblance of rationality has fled the building. Will wanted to keep something from me. It was no accident.

There aren't even tears when I think the next part. I'm beyond that. It's open heart surgery with no hope of recovery.

Because it was Penny.

And I don't know what to do. I will never know what to do, not ever again.

I spin on my heel, thinking nothing but feeling everything amplified. If emotions could be loud, mine would be deafening. I want to know why, why, why, why, but there is no one left to tell me.

"Damn it." I kick the waste bin beside Will's desk and it goes *clang-bang* onto its side, spilling crumpled papers and chewed-up erasers onto the carpet. "Damn it, Will! Damn it, Penny!"

I feel like I have been sprinting for weeks and all of a sudden look down to see that I'm out of runway with nowhere to go. I don't want to live inside my own body. I want to take my fingernails and claw my way out, but I can't. And in the next moment, I don't even know why I had that thought or why I have any thought.

I'm hyperventilating now. I'm not sure when that started. But I am walking around the short track of Will's room with a heaving chest and I can't catch my breath no matter how shallow the pumping of my lungs becomes. I clutch the side of the bed, clutch the quilt that, of course, reminds me of him.

I jerk my hand back. My knees quiver. I turn and sink to the floor with the bedpost at my back. Breathe, Lake, I command myself. In and out. Now. Do it. Breathe. Unlike when I had asthma, my lungs try to obey, working hard to slow down, to find a rhythm.

But what now?

I press my phone into my forehead. Nothing coherent comes to mind.

Except that I wish someone were here.

Which makes me think of Ringo. Which makes me think of "Anna."

And I find myself pressing my thumb to the screen and punching "The Beatles" plus the song name together into the search function of my phone. I just want one single thing to make sense and I also hope that maybe Ringo is right, that there is a song for every moment, and that perhaps I can borrow his for now.

I hold the speaker next to my ear as the song begins with a midtempo guitar and drums. I close my eyes and listen while attempting to drown out every other thought. The beat is deceptively happy. My lessons with Duke Ellington have taught me to tell the voices apart and it's when John Lennon first takes the microphone that I know that the melody is only a façade.

Anna comes to the singer asking him to set her free. Anna believes that another boy loves her more than the singer, so rather than state his case, the singer tells Anna to go with the other boy. He sets her free. "Go with him," Lennon sings.

And I hear Ringo's message. Go with Will.

And I'm hollow. I stare at nothing in particular. Ringo is trying to give me what I want, but how is that possible, when not even I know what that is anymore? I might not want to be set free. And does being set free mean I have to go with Will?

I have no clue whether I'm doing the right thing, but I type out a text to Ringo. *I need to talk to you.* I send the message. Then add: *and Margaret.*

My abdomen clenches. Then I'm nearly jumping out of my skin at the sound of a soft knock on the bedroom door. "Uh, Lake?" Jeremy hovers in the doorway. His eyes are red and bloodshot and his mouth droops open. "It's been an hour." He sounds embarrassed.

Look natural, I tell myself. Nothing to hide. "Thanks, Jeremy." I smile warmly. "I'll just be one more second, 'kay?"

Even in Jeremy's clearly impaired state, I notice him scan the room, and maybe I'm paranoid, but I can't help but feel it's with a bit of suspicion. "All right," he says. When he doesn't move to leave right away I think that he might wait for me, but after an uncomfortable silence, he fades into the hallway and then I hear footsteps pounding down the stairs.

Quickly, I grab an old shirt out of Will's closet, wrap it

around the computer, and tuck it under my arm. *The shirt is a reminder of Will,* I'll tell Jeremy if I can't stash the computer in the back of Matt's wheelchair fast enough. That should do the trick.

With a final glance back, I steal the key to my boyfriend's private life and all the things he may or may not have hidden from me—and leave.

# chapter thirty-two

## 4 DAYS

I drive faster than I should toward the coffee shop, faster than I knew I was able to, as fast as I've driven anywhere since the car wreck, fast like I don't even care about it, fast like there was no car wreck in the first place. Fast because *everything* is a wreck.

I glare into the rearview mirror without letting my foot off the gas a single inch. "I don't know if you can tell, Matt, but I'm having a major life crisis right now and *you* are high."

"A little." He chuckles. "Like on a scale from ground floor to airplane. I'd say I'm no higher than an office building, though."

We should be there in seven minutes. So my world should hold up for at least seven more minutes. "I didn't say anything about smoking pot," I snap. "That wasn't part of the plan."

"But you didn't *not* say anything about it either. Wait," he says, tilting his head, "is that what I mean to say?"

"It was implied!"

"Maybe *your* plan wasn't my plan. Did you ever think of *that*?"

I roll my eyes. *Six minutes.* "You're impossible."

*"Im-poss-ee-bluh,"* he says in his best French accent. "Besides, you should relax, Lakey Loo. I'll be dead in less than a week. Who cares?"

I step harder on the gas, willing the minutes to cut in half. Ocean, condos, marina, all blur across the window. "You don't know what you're saying, Matt." I dismiss him.

"*Dead.*" He laughs and I wish I could punch Jeremy in the mouth. What was he thinking letting my brother smoke pot? "Man, isn't death funny? It's just... it's ridiculous. It's, like, it's like this. It's like the only sure thing in life is that we die and yet... and yet... here's the crazy part: we keep being *surprised* when it happens."

*Four minutes.* Another mile and I'll be able to make out Neville's. I turn in my seat to give him a proper withering stare. "Can you *puh-lease* pull it together," I say.

"'Can you *puh-lease* pull it together,'" Matt mimics.

So now he acts like a real sibling. Fan-freaking-tastic.

Green light. Green means go. Go to figure out who my boyfriend was, who my friends really were. Go, go, go. "Oh my god, I'm going to kill you if you don't cut it out," I snipe back at him.

"Well that would work out nicely."

*Two minutes.*

"Stop it," I tell him. My mind is racing with the car and

not all in one direction. Like: What would life be if Matt hadn't gotten himself broken? Would he be a writer? Would he have a girlfriend who he brought home from college at Thanksgiving and on Christmas? Would he have ever played a sport, even if it was only junior varsity? Would we have stayed close? Would we have found new books to read and would we have inside jokes? Would he buy me beer, be a protective older brother, would we have secrets from Mom and Dad? Would I have ever met Will and Penny, or are there no such things as soul mates after all? *One minute.* "You're going to meet some new people in here. Be nice. Okay?"

"Aye-aye, captain."

Yeah, that doesn't bode well.

I choose the handicapped parking spot front and center. Nine minutes at least are added while lowering the ramp, getting Matt's wheelchair onto it, and reloading the mechanism back into the van so that we can lock it. Like with babies, it is definitely frowned upon to leave paralyzed people in the back of your car, but I wouldn't say I don't think about it.

Matt shuts up a bit when he gets inside. Maybe the coffee smell is enough to sober him up. But actually I think that Neville's is the type of place he'd go if he were in that other life, the one in which he isn't broken. As for me, I'm already at home around the tattooed, bespectacled, and tight-shirt-wearing patrons who take notes in their paperback copies of Tolstoy and listen to vinyl records, and I bet Matt doesn't expect this either.

I find the coffeehouse gang in the back corner. My gait slows when I see Ringo. It was just a song, I try to tell myself. It doesn't mean that *I* am Anna.

Except I'm pretty sure it does. And the singer still has feelings for Anna. Does that mean Ringo has feelings for me?

It's awkward enough, after the way we last left things, that we now stop short of hugging, and I'm full of a mixture of gratitude and longing for that. Instead, Ringo introduces himself to Matt. "Hi." Unlike Jeremy, Ringo's too smart to extend a hand. "You must be Lake's brother."

He's wearing a denim shirt unbuttoned over a soft heather-colored T-shirt, a pair of sunglasses hanging from the neckline. Is it just me, or does he look particularly handsome and not at all fragile today? I glance away to stop thinking about it.

"Pleasure," Matt says lingering only a moment more than necessary over Ringo's mismatched face and purpled skin.

I breathe a sigh of relief. "Matt," I say, since my brother is either too high or too dismissive to offer the name on his own. "His name is Matt."

I slide in next to Margaret, who has yet to look up from her computer. "Ringo tells me you wanted to talk?" she says.

My palms are sweating. My knee jiggles. "More like I need a favor." I wince at the word.

*"Ah."* She punctuates with the space bar. "Are we talking party, all in say *aye* or may the odds be ever in your . . . ?"

I wince. "More like *The Godfather,* calling in a . . . favor, that is. A very big one."

"Hand it over." Still she doesn't look at me, but she does flash a quick grin. Her glasses reflect her laptop screen. The rest of Ringo's friends—*my* friends, are they *my* friends too?—seem to give us space, but I cast a nervous smile over at Kai, who offers me a thumbs-up.

"Shit." Matt curses, too loudly. "My buzz is wearing

off." He glances around at all of us, wearing a look of total disappointment. "Is it supposed to be so fleeting?"

"Matt," I hiss. Then, when I realize that there's no way to hide his state, given what he's just said, I add, "No one who does drugs uses the word *fleeting*."

"Guess it'll just have to be this once, then," he grumbles.

Ringo rubs his neck and gives me a *What can you do?* look.

I slide Will's computer onto the table next to Margaret's laptop. She keeps typing with one hand while simultaneously opening the screen to Will's computer. I tell her the password and she makes a grunting noise in response as if this information is completely unnecessary. She's already hooking a cord between the two machines.

"What are you doing?" I ask, peering over her shoulder.

"Downloading some software to this computer. It only takes a second."

My heartbeat thumps. "Will someone be able to tell that it's been, like, tampered with?"

"Done," she says, and untethers Will's computer. "Not unless they really know what they're looking for." She stops typing for the first time. "Don't worry, you're good." She scoots her chair over and then strikes a few keys on Will's keyboard. The blank screen fills with several boxes, each containing typeface too small for me to read. Margaret scans them.

"So, how's school going?" I ask, trying to make conversation, since that seems preferable to all of us watching her hack into my dead boyfriend's computer.

"Okay, I guess." She clicks on one of the screen boxes and scrolls through its contents. "Working on my thesis on resurrection ethics in Asia. Mongolia, China, Indonesia, mainly. The computer skills are coming in handy too. Lets me do a lot of the graphing, charts, quantitative analysis–type stuff. I get some good gigs that way. Professors are always wanting people who are good with computers and then, hello, fellowship recommendations."

Matt scoffs. Loudly. "You think you can learn about resurrections in a classroom? So you can, what, sit there in your ivory tower and judge people?"

For the first time, she stops typing. She frowns at him. "I think I can keep an open mind so that I can learn something," she says, and then she picks back up again.

Ringo leans into my ear. "Did we do something to offend him?"

I don't say anything. I only have room in my head for the one thing and that's for whatever Margaret's going to find in that computer. I'm counting down in my head, but I don't know to what.

"Okay, what am I searching for?" Margaret asks. Her fingers hover, poised for action.

"A ChatterJaw account. A conversation that went private about a month ago."

Margaret lets out a low whistle, but types in whatever it is she needs to type in. A string of subject lines populates the screen. "Anything else to narrow it?"

I chew the inside of my cheek hard, like it's a piece of ice. "Penny," I say.

Five taps. Enter. The list collapses.

"So," Margaret says, folding her arms across her chest, visibly annoyed, "I have to ask: Is Penny the mystery user on the thread?" Margaret had never been able to break through the encryption used by the ISP until she had Will's actual computer to work from. Now I know why.

I nod. "I think so . . . yeah."

She shakes her head. "Well, I have to hand it to her, this girl seriously knew her firewalls." It wasn't Penny, it was her protective techie father, Simon, but I keep my mouth shut because I don't think Margaret would consider this any consolation. "You want to do the honors?" Margaret asks me. She rolls to the side and I take her place.

The surroundings of the coffee shop disappear. From this moment on, it is me and the computer. Tunnel vision. I lick my lips. My fingers dance in the air over the trackpad. This is the last second that I can turn back. I won't be able to un-see it. If this changes anything—and maybe it won't—I won't get a do-over.

But . . . I have to know.

I open the messages like I'm leaping off the high-dive platform. Headfirst and into deep water.

At 9:01 p.m., the conversation goes private:

Twenty Questions

How about we start with five?

Less ambitious, but fine, five

Boy or girl?

Lady ;)

When I'm alone I ______________.

Worry less

Another poem?

I told you, they're not poems

Now you're just being difficult

Maybe I shouldn't have let the ugly parts through

Disagree on premise alone

You've got two more

Why did you post your poem-nonpoem
to ChatterJaw?

The real me needed a place to live in the real world

Does this count as the real world?

I can see it. I can say it. So it must be so

So things are only real if you can see them

or say them, not if they're just inside?

Sorry, you've already gotten your five ;) ;) ;)

That's when the ringing in my ears starts up. I have a vague sense that perhaps someone is saying something behind me. Perhaps to me. I don't really know, though, or care.

That day is only the beginning. There are pages of messages. Pages and pages. I hear Penny's voice in them. And then I hear Will's. But neither is a comfort. And then there's this:

Text me one of your cartoons that you're always telling me about

They're dumb

Cop out

I don't have your number

I don't even know who you are

What would you do if you did know who I was?

What would you do if you knew who I was?

Pray you weren't a child molester or a serial killer

After that

I don't know

I don't know . . .

So put it in a drawing for me

I don't know your number

That can be fixed

267-823-9936

Now you have it. No excuses

There is a pause in the stream of thought and the two talk about other things. I've lost track of how long I've been scrolling. Five minutes? Fifteen? An hour? It's a blur.

I imagine Will at his desk typing. Hitting send.

I just punched your number into my phone . . .

A contact came up . . .

I didn't get anything???

Penny?

Black creeps in at the edges of my vision—darker, darker, darker still. I lean on the table. My head is heavy. I can't look away. I wish I could say that the messages stop. Right then, right there. But the damage is done, so who even cares?

There is no point in wishing. We wished three years ago. We were a family. No secrets.

When I finally look away, my eyes burn like I've been swimming in chlorine. I'm numb while at the same time wanting to scratch the skin off my bones. It's a strange, unreal sort of sensation.

I turn to find that Matt is the only one there. "Where's everyone else?" I ask.

"How should I know?" he asks.

I stand up out of the chair. I want to move. Moving is good. My hand is on my forehead. It's hot. I might even be running a fever. Calm down, Lake. Calm down.

"Well, you were sitting right here," I snap.

The retort changes him, abracadabra. I recognize the hardening of his face. The return to the Matt I've known for the last few years. I register it only vaguely. Like a slight change in temperature. But it's there. Bubbling beneath the surface.

"I'm not a lapdog for you to carry around in your purse," he says.

"Shut *up*." Try to concentrate on your breathing, I tell myself. Because I want to run. I want to take off. Leave him. Be anywhere but here.

"I know what you're thinking," he says. "Look, Matt, look at Ringo, look how okay he is with his lot. Look what you could be if only you tried. You could go by Stiff—no that's not as catchy, whatever—and show everyone how okay you are with it. Why can't you be more like him?"

He goes dark. "This shit is not the same, Lake."

I can't handle one of Matt's rants. Not right now. "Just . . . just let me think."

"It doesn't matter anyway. All this is pointless. Your birthday is in a couple of days and I'll be dead." It's a challenge. His brow is lowered, casting a deep shadow over his eyes so that they practically disappear.

I whirl on him. "Stop reminding me." I raise my voice without meaning to. I hear it echo. Duke Ellington looks up. I whisper at him, *"Stop saying you're going to be dead, Matt."*

"I'll be dead either way." I watch Matt close off piece by piece until his face is as still as the rest of his body.

Just then, though, Ringo reappears with Margaret carrying a tray of four coffees. Ringo stands still. Did he hear Matt? Does he know?

"We have to go," I say. "Thanks, Margaret."

I shove the computer into the back pocket of Matt's wheelchair without caring whether I cause any damage, grab the handles, and start pushing as though there's a gas pedal on this too. We make it out into the open air and that at least begins to alleviate the black dots floating everywhere. I press the button six times in a row, trying to hurry the van into opening up and letting out Matt's ramp.

I don't care if people stare at me. I stuff Matt in the back of my mom's car like he's shipping freight. I am so done with him and with everyone and . . .

As I'm going around to the driver's side, there is Ringo. His eyes stop me dead in my tracks. Of course the tears are now flowing steadily from mine. It's not fair. I have nothing and I'm breaking, but I can't break like Matt, and nobody will feel the right kind of sorry for me because I'm alive and I'm healthy and Will and Penny and Matt, they're not.

So why do I feel like I've just been stripped apart bone from bone?

Will would have chosen her. Eventually. I know it the same way I know that the earth is round and that the sun rises in the east. I know it and I don't think I would have Penny's grace to wait, to be the understanding friend.

*A man should choose a friend better than himself,* she'd written. She shouldn't have chosen me.

"Lake," Ringo says. Unreadable the same way Matt is. I hate the buried parts of people. Why can't everyone put themselves on the surface the way I do?

I want to stanch the blood that is pouring out of my arteries and into the rest of my body. I see Ringo and feel my heart pulsing for him, for all the days that I've thought he was a type of handsome that could never be replicated, for all the times I've wished his hand would linger longer on my knee or on my back, for the long moment when he held me in the car and told me he was sorry, sorry, sorry.

I walk over to him, clench my fists around either side of his denim shirt that hangs unbuttoned, and pull his mouth into mine. I kiss him with hot tears pouring onto my lips and the taste of salt that reminds me of seawater, that reminds me of Will, but it's not Will. It's Ringo and Ringo likes me. I've known he has for days or weeks or I can't remember how long. But I work my tongue against his and smash my nose into his cheek and he smells good and real. *This* is real life.

He wrenches away and I press my fingers into my bottom lip, stunned.

"What are you doing?" he asks. He's not happy.

"Kissing you. You were right. About... about everything."

There is a crease all the way across his forehead, from one side to the other. "What are you talking about?"

"I listened to the song, to 'Anna.' It says 'Go with him' and I know you meant Will, but I don't think it's supposed to mean Will. Not now, not after . . . Will loved Penny and Penny loved Will or if they didn't they would have." I shake my head and I realize I sound like an insane person, but I press on. "I—I just wanted to kiss you because maybe I don't have to resurrect Will, you see. It doesn't have to be him."

He grabs me by the shoulders. His chest is rising and falling fast. His eyes flit between mine like it's hard to take me in all at once. Then his eyes leave my face altogether and they look past me to the van where Matt is waiting. "At Penny's you said: What if there was a third option for your resurrection choice." I don't say anything. Penny knows my secret. Penny is dead. "Matt said in there that by your birthday he's going to be dead. You're saying not Will. I'm guessing not Penny. You're kissing me. You're acting crazy. You're saying that this is because of everything *I* said."

He heard Matt.

"So here's what I think. *You* would help Matt kill himself? You would—you would do that—and—then . . . ?" He blinks. "And that's because of something *I* said?" He pinches the bridge of his nose and I wish he'd hold on to me again, even if out of anger. "Resurrections ruined my life, Lake. Have I not made that clear? Why do you think I'm in therapy twice a week? Because it's *fun*?" He spins away from me and circles back. "This is sick. You are acting sick. Every part of this, the way you're doing this, the way you're treating me, like I'm a security blanket to make you sleep better at night, it's sick. I keep trying to convince myself otherwise, but it's clear you don't really give a damn about what I think or what I've gone through. I thought you got it, Lake. I thought you were coming to it on your own, but look around at what's going on in your life and why it's going on. Ask yourself

# chapter thirty-three

## 3 DAYS

I cry all the way home. Matt and I don't say a word to each other. We both have too much on our own minds and also, I feel like I've taken a bath in boiling water.

Everyone I love has been picked away from me—Will, Penny, Matt, my parents, Ringo—and without them I'm not sure how there can possibly be anything left.

Mom must sense something's wrong because she's waiting for us, and I leave her to take care of Matt, pushing past her to get inside and to my room. I read an article once explaining that sick animals hide when they're ready to die. I imagine myself hiding beneath the covers and never waking up.

Instead I fall asleep at some point, but it's a fitful sleep and I keep having dreams about losing my virginity, about holding Penny's pinky, about Matt falling so far that he never hits the bottom and about Ringo— *What are you missing, what are you missing, what are you missing?*

Hours and hours later the tendrils of morning light come for me, snaking their way into my bed and peeling my eyes open against my will. My eyelids are crusty. There are dried salty streams coating my cheeks, and my face is swollen.

The world is still here, though. My mattress is soft underneath my weight. Sunshine bathes the landscape. The saliva in my mouth is sour and stale and my stomach grumbles for food. In the last month I've learned a few things about grief, and my least favorite one is that the universe doesn't quit turning just because a corner of it is crumbling.

I'm nauseous this morning, but not terribly. Actually, I wish I was sicker so that I could curl myself into a ball and melt into the bed. Time is stupid and weird. It never moves at the pace I want it to and it makes things better, even the worst things, even if only by a hair, even if just enough to get up, for instance, even when I don't want it to.

At the door of my bedroom I listen. The house is quiet. Safe. I tread carefully into the kitchen and pour myself a glass of milk. The house is so silent, it sounds like there's static electricity buzzing in my ears. Through the window I see that outside the day is bright and windy. Gusts whisk the ocean into frothy whitecaps. The rocks spout white, as if the jetty were a giant whale.

Is Ringo right about me? Am I sick?

On the beach below, half of my sandcastle wall is still intact, but only the back section. The tide has eaten through the center of the sand wall and swallowed parts of each of the towers, which now stand lopsided, ugly, and sad, the roofs caved in on all of them.

My boyfriend is dead, Penny is dead, my brother is paralyzed. Will and Penny's families hate each other. Harrison's uncle is a lunatic. Ringo's mom is alive but not living. My parents can't hold on to two ropes that are pulling in opposite directions and they can't get over what happened to Matt, maybe not ever. I have a choice that's unfairly huge. I am not God. Hell, I'm not even class president. I'm just a seventeen-year-old girl and I didn't sign up for this.

I try to retrace the steps to the first moment when my life started falling apart. Looking back now makes my current circumstances seem all but inevitable. For five years, I've been breaking too, just like Matt. From the first moment I woke up and I wasn't in the same family as my family anymore and I quit talking to Jenny and I skipped soccer practice and changed schools and Matt hated me.

I repeat that again in my mind. Jenny. Soccer. Changed schools.

And again.

Jenny. Soccer. Changed schools.

And Matt hated me.

My gaze collides with the jetty and I start to add a few things.

Asthma—*poof!*—gone. The summer I turned hot. The way Coyote Blue looked at me.

My brain feels like it's trying to walk through drying cement. *Sludge, sludge, sludge.* But I have to keep going.

I turn my hand over and study the silver scar from where a dog bit me when I was fourteen and a half years old.

My fingers carve through my hair, holding it back in a makeshift ponytail and then releasing it. *No*, I think. I start doing the math in my head. When I was thirteen Matt was seventeen. Seventeen years old.

My mouth and ears tingle. *No, no, no.*

I set down the glass of milk gently so as not to make any noise. In the living room, I scan a gallery wall of pictures of our family. "She needs to know"; I hear the memory of my mom's shrill words. I replay the dreams of the car crash, the ones that had morphed into something more, something real, *something* to do with Matt.

Our photographs look like those of any happy family. I lean in to study a group of pictures from when I was in seventh grade. There is a close-up shot of me smiling from the stage of our winter choir concert. I have a bumpy complexion, not unusual for a seventh-grader, but by my fourteenth birthday, just over six months later, I look like the fresh-faced "after" picture of a teen acne commercial. I had always thought that I'd just gotten really lucky in the puberty lottery, but the shift in perspective makes me look harder. Any clue. Any confirmation.

And then it's there. At least I think that it is. I take the first photograph off the wall and squint hard at it. On the right side of my neck, there appears to be a slight discoloration, a shade darker than my skin. A blotch that could nearly be mistaken for a shadow. I could be imagining it, but I really don't think that I am. Not this time.

I yank another photograph off the wall and I see it, in a picture of me where I can't be any older than fourth grade. I have a very faint birthmark. I feel a sensation like someone sliding an ice cube down my back as I walk, nearly in a trance, to the bathroom mirror, turn my chin to the side, and peer closely at a perfect patch of skin on my neck with not the faintest mark to be seen no matter how hard I look.

"Tell her, Peter. This is on you."

# chapter thirty-four
## *1,645 DAYS*

Jenny says I can't go to high school without having had my first kiss. I don't even know if I like Jenny. Mom says friendships will change as I get older and I think she's talking about Jenny. She had the first boy-girl party when we were in fifth grade. Mom wasn't a huge fan of that idea and wouldn't let me go. Things are different now, though, because I'm thirteen.

I'm thirteen and there's a boy in my room. Not just any boy, either. Isaiah Fox. That's his real name. He's only in eighth grade and he already sounds like a movie star.

I'm not stupid. I know he doesn't want to study geometry. If he did, I don't think he would have shut my door when he came in. Or sat on my bed.

It's entirely possible that I'll have a heart attack in the next five minutes.

He's sitting on the foot of my bed looking exactly like a boy named Isaiah Fox should. Honey-brown skin. Eyes the color of dark chocolate. Hair cut thick and close to his scalp.

Rain is splattering against my bedroom window, drowning out the sound of the ocean.

Isaiah's missing the ragged rope bracelet that he wears on his right wrist, the one I've always admired, but that's because he tied it around my wrist yesterday during fourth period.

I tug on the frayed bottom edge of my shorts, wishing that Jenny hadn't convinced me to cut an inch off them, since they've started to ride up into my crotch.

"I don't bite," says Isaiah, patting the spot beside him. I sit down but leave a small space between my leg and his. "Cool room." He makes a show of looking around, even staring up at the ceiling fan. Given that this is probably the least cool part of a not very cool room, I'm starting to suspect that he might be nervous too.

This revelation does me no good and I just stare at my lap.

Over the course of the school year, Isaiah and I have said very little to each other in terms of actual, out-loud words. We pass notes in class. Mainly games of tic-tac-toe, made-up mazes, and hangman. In groups, we stand near each other. Sometimes he pokes me, or steals one of my books and makes me pretend-wrestle him to get it back. Then there was the one time he called me and I had to tell him dinner was ready even though I'd already eaten, because the silence on the line was so deafening, it made my skin crawl.

Still, it is physically impossible for me to be anywhere on

my school's campus without keeping one eye out for Isaiah. And now here he is, in my room, because he said we should study for our geometry test together.

"I'll get my book out," I say.

He grabs my wrist before I can stand. "My sister taught me how to tell fortunes," he says. I stare at my hand cradled in his larger one. "Want me to tell yours?"

*Our hands are touching, our hands are touching, our hands are touching.*

"Sure." I tentatively look up and meet his eyes. Dead on. No pretending that we aren't two inches away from each other's faces. His breath smells like cookies.

"Hi," he says quietly.

"Hi," I say back.

And that's when it happens. He kisses me. His lips press into mine and his tongue is cool and rough as it wiggles its way in a circle around my own. He is still holding my hand, but neither of us moves anything but our mouths. And I'm thinking this is actually kind of fun. Weird, but fun.

Then the door behind me flies open. "What is this door doing shut?" My mom's voice has a *You're in trouble!* edge.

I startle. Who can blame me? My mom has just walked in on my first kiss, but it all happens too fast. I make a strange choking noise that comes out as a snort while at the same time clamping down with my teeth and pulling away.

"Ouch!" Isaiah jerks back, his fingertips pressed to a red spot on his lip. On his chin is a disgusting, gooey wad of saliva that I'm pretty sure was hocked from my throat as a result of the great snorting fiasco.

"Lake Marianne Devereaux." The edge remains in her

voice as she enunciates each syllable in my name. "What do you think you're doing in here?"

Isaiah has stood up. He's wiping his mouth and then he swipes his fingers through his hair. His shirt rides up so that Mom and I both get a view of his stomach peeking over the edge of exposed boxer shorts.

Congratulations to me, because I must be setting a world record for the reddest face in the history of the planet.

"I'd better be going." Isaiah angles his body so that he doesn't touch me when he passes on his way out. "I rode my bike."

Mom slides over to let him past without a word. It's raining—pouring, actually—and she doesn't even offer him a ride. I guess that's because his house is only a couple of blocks away, but still.

"Sit back down, young lady."

Hot tears are already soaking my cheeks and I'm not entirely sure whether they started before Isaiah left or after. "Screw you." I shove past her.

I have never, ever spoken to her that way and I feel feverish with shame. The shame only fuels me, though. I want to get away from her, from this house, from myself if I could.

"Are you okay?" My brother, whose legs are slung over one arm of the couch, looks up from one of his fat books with tiny print.

I don't answer. I head for where I always head when I'm upset—the jetty. The rain is screaming down from the sky, leaving craters in the beach. My feet don't sink, since the storm is turning the sand hard. I've always loved the beginning of hurricane season for the afternoon thunderstorms and now, even more so, since the rain serves as the perfect camouflage for my stupid, embarrassing tears.

The sea is a moody gray as I kick off my sandals and pick my way onto the jetty rocks. Whitecaps dot the seascape, and the ocean crashes through the rocks, sending up plumes like flare guns.

The rocks grow thicker together the farther out I get. There's no longer beach on either side of me. The seaweed smell disappears and what remains is a purer, saltier scent that latches onto my skin and soaks through my shirt.

The wind whips around me. Anger and embarrassment still surge through my veins, pushing me out toward the lamppost. I watch it, aim for it. The storm blows a wave sideways into the jetty and my foot slips. I catch myself with my hands, now crawling on all fours. Nearly to the tip now.

The foundation of rocks has narrowed.

"Lake!" I turn back to see my brother waving his arms. He's saying something else, but the wind is blowing in the wrong direction now and the words get lost.

*Shut up, shut up, shut up.* I squeeze my eyes shut tightly. I bit Isaiah Fox. I spat on Isaiah Fox. And my mom used mom-voice in front of Isaiah Fox. I had the worst first kiss in the history of first kisses and now all I can think is, Leave me alone.

*Everyone, just leave me alone.*

This is what I'm thinking the moment I see the swell. But by then it's already too late. The ocean looks like it has a monster moving underneath its surface. As it grows closer and closer the monster's back rises, pushing the sea into a mountain of water. I'm frozen on the jetty for a second too long before I move, scrambling over the rocks on all fours. The monster wave rears up, bucks, and crashes. The force rips my hands, stinging from the salt, off the rock.

My ribs drag over the edge of the jetty and I'm plunged back first into the water, with time for only a short drag of breath that fills my lungs no more than a quarter of the way. I can't tell which direction is up.

I'm being dragged down by an invisible current. Down, down, down. My arms and legs beat wildly. I force myself to count.

Thirty seconds. Thirty seconds without a breath. Push, Lake. Push and stay alert.

I quit counting.

I keep thinking I'm close to the surface, but just when I think I should break free, I don't. There's only more water. More and more and more. The undertow is fierce and wild, tossing me around like a marionette.

There's a darkness creeping into my vision that has nothing to do with the ocean.

I am such an idiot. So stupid. What was I trying to prove?

This is a strange thought to have while drowning, but there it is. I will my legs to keep kicking, but I can already feel them becoming soggy and slow. Then my arm sweeps against something. My fingers grasp and I feel it. Skin, fingers, slippery. I reach for it again and again; there's hair and bone and muscles.

*Please, please, please.*

I'm wrenched out of reach. My mind screams with alarm. In that last moment, I can't stop my mouth from opening. I can't stop myself from sucking in a deep breath. And I can't stop water from pouring into my throat and tearing through my windpipe.

I can't stop anything. Because I'm dead.

# chapter thirty-five
## *3 DAYS*

"Why didn't you tell me?" I imagine how I must look standing in the doorway to my brother's room, arms limp at my sides.

My parents and Matt are huddled together. My dad leans on the window seat, wearing regular, non-Spandex clothing. Meanwhile my mom perches on the edge of a chair pulled closer to the group. Dad straightens and positions his hands under his armpits. "Tell you what, Lake?" There's the flash of a lie there.

"I remember . . ." My breath trembles audibly. "Dying." The three of them are speechless. The funny thing is, I always thought my parents were secretly on my side. Like they knew Matt was unreasonable, but they had to take care of him because he was their son and that's what parents did.

Wrong. They were never on my side. The three of them

had their little secret club. Keep-away from Lake. Just like Penny and Will.

I swallow hard and take a step into the room. After all, I ought to be invited now. I know the secret password.

I was dead.

"Is it how you . . ." I start to ask, "how you became paralyzed?" I'm speaking only to Matt now. My big brother. "It is, isn't it?" I nod quickly, almost frantically, for him to confirm.

Matt's gone expressionless.

"Stop it, Matt." My volume is beginning to rise. "Stop it. Don't go blank like that. Answer me! Is this"—I point insensitively at his wheelchair—"because of me?"

The tension in his jawline gives him away. "Anyone care to explain what's going on here?" he asks, boxing me out again.

My dad remains sitting back, studying me with his arms crossed.

"I didn't tell her," Mom says defensively.

"Why? Why would you tell me Matt fell out of a tree? Why would you let me do all of this?" I think about how I've been traipsing around with Matt, solving idiotic scavenger hunt clues, and I feel sick. There is one day standing between me and my eighteenth birthday. What if I had found out after?

Dad speaks first. "What happened the day of your accident happened." *My* accident. It hasn't sunk in yet. Not *Matt's* accident. *Mine.* "Matt wanted you to have a normal life. He didn't want what happened to him to be for nothing. He made the decision that he didn't want you to feel guilty."

I narrow my eyes. "He must have had some help getting there."

"It was me, Lake," Matt interjects. "Don't blame Mom and Dad."

I know everyone expects me to gush this big apology, to thank Matt for trying to save my life and for giving it back to me when he couldn't, but that's not what I feel. That's not *at all* what I feel. "You wanted to hate me," I say. "And you made me hate you."

Because now all I can see is what could have been. He could have told me. We could have accepted it and then my dad's words would have been true maybe. Yes, I would have felt deep pain that I'd caused this accident, but we would have had to accept what happened and we would have had to deal with it head-on. Instead of one big hurt, we let it fracture into a million pieces with sharp points and razor edges. Would Matt have hated me if I had known? Would I have grown to resent him? It's too late to ever know what it would have been like to have the chance to heal.

Matt's eyes turn sad in a way that I haven't seen since we were kids. "Not at first. Maybe a little. I don't know. But don't pretend you didn't cut me off too."

"I did not." But when I look to my parents I can see that they both think there's some truth to what he's said. "How?" I demand. "How did I cut *you* off? I tried to read with you. I tried to watch movies with you. I researched outings. I reached out to you over and over and you wanted no part."

"I needed time," Matt says, calmly.

"I gave it to you."

"You made a new family, Lake. You had Penny and Will. After that you didn't need much else," Matt says.

The memory of Matt and the movie times and the way I left him hanging to be there for Will sits heavy and undigested in the pit of my stomach, but that doesn't stop me from attempting to shove it all the way down to where it will never be reachable. "And what about this new family?" I point at the three of them. "What was I supposed to do? Be alone forever?" I scream. "Excuse me for wanting someone to want me. For wanting something just a little bit real." I tug at the roots of my hair. "Joke's on me, it's all just one big freaking façade, it turns out. You guys. Will. Penny. All of it. Even me!" I am shouting into faces that don't understand me. I am shouting at myself because *I* don't understand me. Not anymore. How can I be one of those people, one of those *things*, like Coyote Blue. How can I have been dead?

No wonder everyone abandons me, hates me, doesn't care about me.

"But whatever it is I am, it's because you made me this way!" I shriek. Matt winces. "I wish you'd never resurrected me." I pull at the collar on my shirt, stretching it out on the neckline. "And you know what I think?" I am seething now. I want to hurt things, and why not? I shouldn't even exist. "I bet you wish I were dead too, don't you? Because you only resurrected me so that I would resurrect you. Bet you're regretting that now, huh? You think I don't realize now that I was only good for one thing to you people and now I'm not even good for that?"

It's only when my mom starts crying that I stop yelling at them.

"Matt's going through with it, Lake." Dad says, wrapping his arm around Mom's shoulder. I'd already known this, deep down, that nothing would change my brother's mind. He's paralyzed and it's because of me. "It'll happen tomorrow night. At a death party."

A full night earlier than the traditional birthday eve. Are they trying to force my hand? To cover their own tracks by making it less obvious what perverse game they're playing? They're asking me to give up on my friends. My friends who lied to me. My parents who lied to me. It's all too much.

"How—" I stammer in disbelief. "How do you even—how do you know about those? No." I shake my head. I'd been prepared for something terrible, but nothing like this. The shock hits me like a bullet shot point-blank.

"We didn't," Mom admits. "Or rather we didn't know that they actually happen in real life. Matt explained them to us."

"Then you should know how disgusting they are," I spit.

"I don't want Mom and Dad to be involved or face any repercussions," Matt says. "They've kept their end of the bargain." I can't help hearing this part as an accusation. "I don't want them to make any other sacrifices. Since I can't do it on my own, this seems like the best option."

I stare at him. Hate radiates off my skin. I was so stupid to have thought things were changing between us.

"And we agree, actually." My father's mouth forms a grim line. This is when I notice the dark circles that bruise the skin underneath both of my parents' eyes and I wonder how many hours they've stayed awake at night thinking about sending their only son off to die without them. "Jeremy's picking him up tonight."

"*Jeremy?*" I repeat. "When the hell did you—when did you talk to Jeremy?"

Matt holds my stare. *No.* I can't believe I drove him

there, that I helped facilitate this. So that's why he was so willing to have his play date with Jeremy, so that he could talk him into this stupid charade. Jeremy, who has lived as the black sheep in his cousin's house for years, who has always marched to the beat of his own drum, who has always had his own ideas as to what is right and fair.

"I'm not doing it." I cross my arms and jut my jaw out like a little kid. "I don't know what you have in mind, but the whole point of a death party is that the person with the resurrection choice assists in the . . . in the . . . Look, I'm just not participating. In any of it."

There are tears in Mom's eyes and her lower lip looks shaky.

Dad nods. "That's fine, Lake."

My lips part.

"Cripple exception." Matt smiles. He actually smiles. "I'll have help one way or another. Most people feel bad for cripples."

Each of my family members looks like a stranger to me. I wish they were strangers. I wish I'd never been born or that if I had been, not as a Devereaux. I hug myself, then rake my nails down the backs of my arms. Enough, enough, just enough of this already.

"Lake, your brother is going to be dead tomorrow."

Tears flood my cheeks. I can hardly breathe. I lift my chin. "Good," I say, because I want him to hurt the way that I hurt. "Maybe . . . it's better that way."

# chapter thirty-six

## *2 DAYS*

This is a mistake.

Part of me hoped Jeremy wouldn't text me the address when I asked. After all, I hid in my room when he came to pick Matt up, borrowing my mom's van for the occasion.

Last chance to say good-bye. Last chance for good-luck wishes. Last chance for prayers: each of these thoughts crossed my mind when my dad came to knock softly on my locked bedroom door. The words that I said when I last spoke to Matt—shouted at him—ring in my ears. Despite my best efforts, most of the anger and contempt has gradually seeped out of me bit by bit. What's left over is a sickening sense of dread.

I didn't answer my dad's knock. I stayed curled on top of a nest of blankets while my brother left to do the unthinkable.

Except all I could do was think about it. I had to, and after I finished thinking, I wound up here. At Matt Devereaux's death party. Welcome to the world's most morbid sideshow act, folks. Now, who brought the popcorn?

The guy controlling crowd flow at the front of the house doesn't give me a hard time when I give him my full name. Apparently word travels fast here. Everyone expects the sister of the boy in the wheelchair who's dying to be in attendance. Everyone but me, anyway.

The house is modern, with floor-to-ceiling panes of glass, white walls, and colorful art that looks like a five-year-old painted it. This type of event draws a more *dramatic* crowd—kids who like to wear all black, outline their lips in maroon, and dye their hair—but this party seems to be even more thick with the goth cliques. They look out of place posing on the sleek concrete floors and congregating around the crystal-blue pool lit up with floodlights.

My nerves feel like a system of sparking wires and I flit in and out of groups of people talking, drinking. There are Jell-O shots in the kitchen, a keg on the outdoor patio, and a couple of boxes of pizza open on a set of lawn chairs.

Very few of the faces look familiar, even though a lot of the partygoers appear to be my age. I see a couple of girls from my school sitting on a counter with their heads tilted toward each other, laughing. One of them lifts her chin and smiles at me when I pass, but we don't exchange any words.

For the most part, I can float around like a ghost and no one notices the former dead girl haunting their party. I still can't wrap my mind around the fact that I'm resurrected. Now I don't know where to turn. Should I go live in a commune? Do I need to change my name to Blossom or Karma or Rainbow Bright? None of that feels like me, but I don't even know how I'm supposed to feel anymore.

I wish to be anywhere but here, and then I tell myself not to wish for anything. The full moon is tomorrow, but still no invitation has arrived with the location of the final destination in my birthday scavenger hunt.

I take a seat on one of the lawn chairs next to the pizza boxes. There's a slice of pepperoni left over, but I don't have any appetite for it.

I rock in place. I don't want to be here, don't want to see this, want to leave, leave, leave. I want Will here so that he could scream his head off at Jeremy for letting something like this happen. But there's only me.

Then I'm scanning the party for my brother when Jeremy walks by. I jump to my feet and snatch his wrist. "Hey!" I say. He stumbles from the force of my grasp. "What do you think you're doing?" I ask.

"Going to get a drink," he says with his typical drawl. His T-shirt is wrinkled and his hair looks predictably slept on.

"With my brother, you idiot." So much for diplomacy. "Who do you think you are?"

He shoves his hands into his pockets. "Look, Lake, I think you just need to chill for a second."

"Chill? *Chill?* That's your big advice? Chill. God, you're an even bigger slacker than Will thought you were." Jeremy doesn't look particularly offended. "Who asked you to get involved, anyway?" I continue.

"Matt did."

People are starting to take notice of us now. Probably wondering why I'm freaking out.

"I think that's the guy's sister," I hear one onlooker murmur.

I lower my voice and step closer in to Jeremy. "You realize what this means for Will, don't you? What the point of all this is?"

Jeremy shifts his weight and scratches the stubble on his cheek. "I realize that Matt was a good friend before all this, and that he should have some control over how or whether he lives his life. I don't know what you're going to do, Lake." His eyes are clear when he says this. There's no red in the whites, no sign that he's been smoking. He looks the most together that I've seen him in years. "That's up to you. But your brother has made it clear that he's finished living like this no matter what. I believe in self-destiny. I didn't try hard enough to be there for him before." He shrugs. "I guess I just want to make up for it." He gives me a pointed look and then he slopes off in the direction of the keg.

I stand there, numb, while whispers gather around me. This moment is surreal. My brother will be a spectacle. The entertainment of the night. The disabled boy who wants to die. And everyone will watch.

This place, this party, it's all the things my brother has grown to hate, but he's willing to be here because he wants out of his body that badly. He'll even risk never coming back. The craziest part is that I thought things were changing for us. The past few weeks, was it only my imagination or were things really getting better? I could swear I've seen glimpses of my brother, the one who read to me, hiding behind the boy who felt trapped in his own body. I know I have.

My throat clenches until it's nearly sealed shut. I don't want to miss him anymore. Just as I was starting to get him back. This has nothing to do with what I choose and everything to do with Matt and what it means to die like this. This will change him, not fix him, and I'm scared—*terrified*—that I'm witnessing the last few minutes of knowing the boy I grew up with.

I need a drink, so I make my way into the kitchen, where I find bottles of liquor lined up on the countertop. I grab onto the neck of the vodka bottle and pour some into a plastic cup. I don't bother with a mixer before I knock back the clear liquid in one gulp.

The alcohol burns my throat. I cough and sputter, once again drawing the attention of the people around me, some of whom snicker at me for not being able to take a shot. I don't mind. The burn helps. I like the way that I can trace it all the way down to the pit of my stomach, where it seems to take at least some of the spark out of my short-circuiting nerves. I pour myself another. And then one more, this one slightly bigger, so that it takes me two swallows to finish the whole thing.

By the fourth, I don't cough when the vodka goes down. The burn has transformed into a warmth that coats my insides.

"There he is." One of the girls who laughed at my alcoholic ineptitude points subtly for the benefit of her friend with too-black hair and a nose ring. The comment's not directed at me, but I look anyway.

*Matt.* My heart squeezes. Jeremy is positioned at the back of his wheelchair, pushing him toward the outside patio. I check my watch. It's 10:30 p.m. My brother's hair has been cut, washed, and combed. The skin around his chin is just a tiny bit pink from a fresh shave. He has let Dad dress him in one of his button-down shirts with a tie looped through the collar. Long dress pants cover the pair of emaciated legs that dangle onto the wheelchair stirrups.

My first step is uneven and I find myself focusing to resume a straight line. I swish open the sliding glass doors to meet my brother.

"Matt," I say.

He cocks his head in that appraising way that he has, but there's a slight tug of amusement at the inside corners of his eyes. His signature scorn is gone. "Already celebrating my untimely demise, I see."

I realize I'm still holding the bottle of vodka. I set it slowly down next to me.

"Not funny." I try to focus on the warmth in my belly to keep the nausea at bay. "Matt, I have something to say to you and I want you to listen." Matt opens his mouth, but I hold my hand up and he stops himself. "What happened to you is balls."

"What?" He squints up at me.

"What happened to you is balls. Balls!" I say more loudly. "I mean," I say, remembering the words that had helped me, "like it really, truly sucks. World's largest Hoover-vac suckage. Universe's biggest black hole. A giant deep-sea octopus with a million bazillion tentacle suckers. That kind of suckitude." I thought I'd run out of tears. Boy, was I wrong. "In all this time, I haven't once told you how cosmically unfair your life is and I'm so, so sorry." I'm choking on sobs and thick, syrupy mucus unleashed by the vodka.

Matt stares at me, mouth agape.

"I'm so sorry, Matt." Impatience is scaling up my insides. Stay with him, I tell myself, he's listening. "This doesn't feel right, though." I gesture at the whole party and everyone who I know is watching me. "Please, I know, but . . . but you're my brother. Please, Matt. This doesn't feel good to me. Does it to you?"

Matt's voice is soft. "It's okay, Lake. It'll be over soon. It's . . . it's . . . it's okay." He glances over at the glittering pool. "The quadriplegic accidentally drives himself into the pool. A real tragedy." He wears a wistful quarter smile. No sarcasm. "But quite poetic."

"No, Matt," I say softly so that I'm sure no one else can hear. "No, I know what it's like to drown." I shut my eyes tightly. Maybe if the memory had been mine all along it would have faded with time. The edges would have worn dull and I wouldn't feel like the air is being slowly squeezed from my lungs all over again. Matt is going to die. The pressure of the water is going to set fire to his lungs. It's going to drive him crazy until he can't stand it anymore and he opens his mouth to take a breath and, despite knowing that he's surrounded by nothing but wetness, he'll be surprised. He'll think there's been a mistake and it won't be over nearly as fast as it should be. And there will be no turning back.

"I've missed you," I say. "I've missed you for all these years. My brother. The one who built canal systems in the sand and read to me about talking lions. I missed you like you'd been dead for five years. But you never died. You're still my brother. It's my fault for not realizing it before. And this . . . feels wrong. It *is* wrong. Please, Matt. I don't know if being resurrected changed me, but I don't want the person that you are, the one right this second, to die. And I don't think I have it in me to use my resurrection choice. So please, I'm asking you not to leave me with that choice. You don't want to go through dying. I can absolutely promise you that. So don't. You can have the life you should have been living all along. I know that you avoided looking for it because of . . . because of me." I take a deep, shaky breath. And rest.

The arches of his eyebrows collapse, his forehead crumples, the corners of his mouth twitch downward. I want to throw my arms around his neck because he's there, my brother, my brother is there.

And then the music cuts off. A bell chimes three times. No, no, no. It can't be time. Not yet.

As if reading my mind, Jeremy reappears. "It's go-time, buddy." He nods at me and wraps his hands around the wheelchair handles.

"Matt, tell them," I say.

Matt gives me a smile that doesn't reach his eyes. "We've come too far, Lake," is all that he says. That layer of sweat that coats his forehead, it's the only thing that gives him away. I watch in stupefied silence as Jeremy takes him from me. The crowd thickens all around, putting bodies between me and my brother.

There's roaring in my ears. The sadness in the room feels infinite. This is happening. There will be pain and then there'll be nothing.

I should be stronger for my brother, who watched me die and broke his back trying to save me. I should hold his hand, comfort him, but the booze has turned me spongy and my legs are practically useless.

Through a space in the audience, I watch Jeremy stand up straight. "I commit—" His voice cracks and he has to push his fist into his mouth to recover. "I commit my friend, Matthew Devereaux, to death." Again, his voice rises in pitch. It's uncomfortable watching him. There's none of the hard-line joy that I witnessed at my first death party. Jeremy touches Matt's shoulder robotically. Matt stares at the rim of the pool.

Somebody should have given him a drink, I think. Too late. Too late. It's all too late.

"So that he can return to this life anew."

The crowd comes alive with muttering undertones. Matt looks up from the pool. He turns his head and stares straight at me, like he can see that I'm hiding here. A coward. Matt's never been a coward.

I shrink into myself. Then I actually stumble backward.

I hear another boy's voice, more confident. "In front of these witnesses, do you go willingly into the darkness?"

I can't stand to listen to another word. I turn my back to the pool, to Jeremy, to my brother, at which point I accidentally careen into a goth boy in a black skirt and army boots. He catches my elbow and I use his shoulder to balance, afterward pushing off him like a boat shoving away from a dock.

My feet crisscross over each other. The vodka swirls around in my head and makes my cheeks tingle. The thing I want most is to get away. I knock one of the fancy abstract paintings crooked on my way out of the cold glass tomb of a house.

Feeling for my keys in my pocket, I click the lock button

so that the car horn blares. I locate my car parked down the street. How long has it been? A minute? Two minutes? Three? Long enough to have no one left?

The second I sink down onto the leather seat, I dissolve into sobs, the kind that send violent tremors through my body, like I'm being electrocuted.

I manage to shift the car into reverse. I tap the bumper of the car behind me before I put the car into drive. It lurches as I switch between the accelerator and the brake. At last I free my car from the parking space. I barely push my foot down on the pedal, almost idling down the deserted street. I can hardly see. There's no such thing as windshield wipers for the drunk and crying.

Three blocks down, a stop sign seems to pop out of nowhere. I slam on the brakes and the wheels screech to a halt. The nose of my car is nearly a car length into the intersection when a pickup truck whizzes past, honking.

I drop my forehead to the steering wheel. My whole body has erupted in shakes and quivers. I shut my eyes and picture the explosion of the Jeep's windshield. Crystal shards raining down on blacktop. The piercing sound of screams and the deep-blue sky.

Another car swerves to miss me. I peel my face from the wheel and let my foot off the brake. Driving as slowly and as carefully as I can after far too many vodka shots, I pull into an alley beside a gas station and dial the number of the only friend I have left in this world—*if* I have even that. Then I curl up in the backseat and wait.

# chapter thirty-seven

## *1 DAY*

I wake up to the sound of knocking and peel open my eyelids. A nose is pressed against the car window, smearing the glass with puffs of fog.

"You guys can't sleep here." The man's voice is too loud. I squint up at him, confused. Sunlight sears my skull. The man has a too-tan face the color and texture of leather, with black patches of balding hair plastered to the sides of a melon-shaped head. "Can't. Sleep. Here." He taps on the glass. The gold chain around his neck glints in the sun. "Do you hear me? You've got to leave."

I groan and push up on my elbow.

*"Oof!"* The thing I push up on grunts. "Watch it."

Rubbing my head, I see that the thing I've been curled up on isn't a thing at all, but a person. Ringo to be exact. He has one eye pinched closed and is using a hand to block some of the light.

I pry myself from the nook between his arm and chest, realizing as I do that it was surprisingly comfortable and I want to go back to that cozy nest because right now my brain is swelling and contracting and in grave danger of busting out of my eye sockets.

"We're going, we're going." I get myself to a fully upright position and wave the man away. "Just give us a second."

He grumbles and shakes his head at us before lumbering back toward his gas station.

I don't think I've digested even an ounce of last night's liquor, considering I can feel it all sloshing around in the pit of my stomach and at least a portion of it crawling up my throat. I take a deep breath and try to think of things other than the dumpster overflowing with beer cans and discarded cheese nachos and anything else that may make me want to hurl.

"Hi," I say, patting my head.

Ringo has a red, splotchy imprint of the car door pressed into the unmarked side of his face. "Morning." He stretches his neck and I can tell that his sleeping position wasn't nearly as snug as mine, but I'm too hungover to feel bad.

"I thought the plan was to drive me home?" I try not to sound annoyed.

"It was, but by the time I took a cab and got here, you were passed out in the backseat." I must look confused, because he adds, "I don't know where you live." His left cheek dimples in an apologetic smile.

"Right." I rub my palms into my cheeks, hoping to wipe away any runny makeup. "The details got a little fuzzy last night."

"Do you want to tell me what's going on or am I supposed to guess?"

I spot the puddle of my drool on his shirt. "I'll tell you," I say. "But do you think I could have coffee first?" The headache still pounds at my temples.

Ringo lets me wait in the car while he runs into the gas station. He comes back with two extra-large cups of coffee—of questionable quality—bottles of water, and a bag full of cookies, chips, crackers, and beef jerky sticks. I take careful sips of the water and sniff at the coffee before taking a small bite of cracker. He waits, patiently.

I wipe crumbs from my face and stare into the bag of snacks. "I know you don't want anything to do with me," I say.

He sighs and drops his head into his hand and rubs at his temple. "I'm here, aren't I?"

"Yes," I say. "Against your will."

He holds out his wrists. "Do you see cuffs?"

"Do you think we could take a walk? I could probably use some fresh air."

There's nothing scenic to look at as we stroll side by side along the shoulder of the road. "Thank you for coming to get me," I say, watching our shadows cross into each other as we walk. "I know you're expecting me to say I'm sorry." I sip the coffee in my hand. Neville's is so much better.

"It probably couldn't hurt."

"But I'm not really sure I can say that, at least not exactly in the way that you want me to."

"Oh," he says.

"What I mean is, I'm sorry for using you for my own comfort without really being there for yours. That was... crappy of me." I let another sip of coffee burn the roof of my mouth. "I thought . . . I don't know what I thought. But jerking you around wasn't fair."

When we're approaching an orange road sign that marks a dead end, I sit on a curb and am pleased when he sits next to me, close enough so our shirts are touching.

"Not a bad start," he says.

My knees are bent up high and I rest the cup on my right one. "But then there's the next thing. And this is the hard part because I don't want you to hate me," I say. "But I found out something yesterday." I take a deep breath and blow it out. It reminds me of Penny. "The accident that turned Matt into a quadriplegic. I . . . died in it. He brought me back. I'm resurrected."

Ringo turns and stares at me. He stares and stares and stares. My cheeks turn pink, like his stare is the sun. "No wonder you're so hot."

But when I dare to look over at him, he has the same sly smile on as when I first saw him in the waiting room at Dr. McKenna's. "Hey!" I say. "I wasn't exactly a monster before, if I recall."

Ringo goes serious. "This doesn't change anything, Lake."

Now it's my turn to say, "Oh." My heart pounds in my chest, something it wouldn't be doing if it weren't for Matt, Matt whose body gave up hours ago at the bottom of a pool. The wave of queasiness hits me hard and fast. I sway and clutch my hand to my clammy forehead.

Ringo catches my elbow. "I still think resurrections ruined my family. I still think they're twisted. And that people are people, not gods. I still think all of that stuff."

I listen, but as I do I pull myself up to sit taller, because I'm glad to be alive. Sure, my head is throbbing, my heart has broken a thousand times, and I've drowned in the ocean and in my own tears, but I've also made blood promises and laughed on rooftops and jumped off cliffs. In the last few weeks alone I've met Margaret, Simone, Kai, Vance, and Duke Ellington and become friends with Harrison Vines. "I understand that's how you feel," I say, trying to speak his language by borrowing from Dr. McKenna. "When I first found out yesterday, I hated myself. I didn't want it to be true. Especially not after visiting the commune. I was sure I had changed and that there was something fundamental about me that made Will love Penny, Matt hate me, and you want to have nothing to do with me." I train my eyes on the ground to say that last part. "But, I don't know, I've been resurrected for five years now, and the more I think about it the more I think it's people's reactions to being resurrected that can change a person. Your mom's. Coyote Blue's. Mine even. I know it's hard to extract one from the other. Impossible for most people probably but—"

"But . . . I don't wish you were dead." Ringo wraps his fingers around my hand. I don't dare breathe. "At all." He holds up a finger to keep me from talking. "And, well, if I don't wish you were dead, then that means that I must be grateful to Matt."

"Matt's dead," I say. "He had a death party last night and he's dead." My extremities go numb as soon as I say it. It doesn't feel real. The only thing that feels real is the pounding in my temples.

Ringo's head droops for an instant, but he doesn't let go

of my hand. "I get it," he says. "You need to do what you need to do."

"And then what?"

"And then I'll be right here waiting." I feel my pulse in my throat. "I mean, not right here," he says, "but like, figuratively speaking, you get what I mean, right?" But we're moving closer and my lips fit easily into his. And finally the kiss seems to loosen the ties to Penny and Will that had been tightening painfully around my heart for nearly a month. I'm able to breathe for the first time in days, and what I breathe in is Ringo.

# chapter thirty-eight

## *1 DAY*

"Hello?" I drop my keys on the foyer table after having dropped off Ringo. I've finally fully recovered from my hangover. "Hello?" There's no answer. I turn left down the hall. I pass Matt's room. Empty. My heart tugs, but I don't cry. It's real now. "Mom? Dad?" I call. I push the doors open to the study. No one's there. "You don't have to worry," I shout. My voice echoes against the walls. "It's all going to be fine now." My new resolve doesn't stop my nerves from sending tremors rippling through my hands. I'd hoped it would be easier once I'd made my decision to resurrect Matt, but it's not. I think all I can hope for now is that this resurrection will be better for our family now that we're all being honest about it. The world feels too empty without Matt in it.

I pick up the pace, checking rooms left and right, until soon I'm jogging through the hallways. The sound of the ocean is gentle outside. "Anybody home? Where are you guys?"

They aren't in their bedrooms. Or on the patio. What if they were worried when I didn't come home last night? What if they're out looking for me? I feel a surge of guilt for putting them through more than they already have been.

It's only when I enter the kitchen for the second time that I spot the note. I slow down. My blood thunders against my eardrums, a sense of dread building as I approach the letter cautiously.

It's instinct that makes human beings afraid of snakes. And it's the same impulse that leads me to fear the letter. Because I've already spent time dealing with the world as I believed it to be. There shouldn't be a note lying there on the counter beside the refrigerator. There shouldn't be. But there is.

And when I pick it up to read it, this is what it says:

*Hi Lakey Loo,*

*Mom's agreed to do the physical writing here, but trust me, otherwise it's all me. Got it? Just pretend she's not here. (Sorry, Mom—see, I actually made her write that! And this!) Okay, I'm done now. We can continue.*

*I think I should begin by saying, I'm not dead.*

*Yeah, I'll let that soak in for a second.*

*A few more seconds.*

*Has it soaked in yet? I hope so, because I think we need to keep going. Time is of the essence, after all.*

*Before you think I'm speaking metaphorically in some weirdly cryptic and annoying Matt-like "joke," I'm not. I don't blame you for thinking it, though. But for real, I'm actually alive. I have a pulse and everything. Yes, Mom cried. Dad pretended not to cry. We'll all meet up and talk about it soon enough. For now, I'm at an undisclosed location with both of them, which means, unfortunately, you're on your own, sis. But more on that later.*

*Because the second thing I think we need to address is why.*

*So, I don't know if you've noticed, but for the last couple of years I've been a huge dick.*

*That was a joke. In case you couldn't tell. Mom has very serious handwriting. I'm just now noticing.*

*Right. Back to me being a dick. Some of this is understandable. I mean, I'm a quadriplegic for god's sake! But the parts that were directed at you aren't. Lake, in no way was my getting paralyzed your fault. It was an accident. You didn't mean to slip. You were only thirteen. And, well, the rest was just bad luck.*

*But I was and am honored to be your big brother and I wanted nothing more than to deserve that title. That's why I jumped in. That's why I was so grateful to be able to bring you back. It's too bad that ever since that moment I've been doing everything in my power to lose the privilege of knowing you.*

*My life is hard now. I can't deny that. But I made it harder and worse, not just for me, but for everyone. Which, when you think about it, is ridiculous considering that was the exact opposite of what I was originally trying to accomplish.*

*Back to the why. I don't deserve to be called your big brother right now. And I don't deserve your resurrection choice. Two other people have spent the last four years earning your affection. I know you. I've watched you grow up. There's a reason you loved Will and Penny so deeply. Choose the person you need the most. That's not me anymore.*

*All right, now for where I am.*

*I can't tell you. I know, I know, forgive us one more secret, will you? See, I have no doubt that you would have used your resurrection choice on me because you're a way better person than I've ever been and if you knew where I was I worry that you'd try to convince me to allow you to choose me. No can do, Lakey Loo.*

*I'm taking the first step on a journey to find a little redemption in this body. I found a place that's going to give me more opportunities. Mom and Dad are on board and I'm actually a little excited. I may even be a writer or a professor after all this.*

*So here's where we are: I can promise you that I'm going to try hard to be a better brother. You can think of this as my grand opening. Big Brother! Open for Business! What I can't promise is that I'll be around forever. But I will make the most of whatever time here that I do have.*

*That's all. I'm done. We'll talk very soon. For now, you have an important decision to make. Good luck!*

*With love,*
*Matt*

I stand gaping at my brother's words, sure that I've misread them, that this is some kind of trick. But they're here in black and white. Maybe that's why he chose a letter instead of calling me. If I hung up the phone after this conversation, I could convince myself that it hadn't happened. That my brother had died at the bottom of a pool watched by dozens of people.

But he hadn't.

He's alive. My palms are slick with sweat. Nothing feels like it's where it's supposed to be. Up is down and down is up. I'm not sure if I'm standing on the floor or on the ceiling. I don't even know how to feel.

A few hours ago, I let Penny and Will go forever. No graduation. No going off to college together. I watched their futures whiz past me like a zooming car.

But here I am again with only one night between me

and my resurrection appointment and the power to choose has been returned to me. Whether I want it or not.

As if on cue, my phone buzzes. I glance down to see that a calendar invite from Will Bryan has arrived at noon sharp. The final clue.

# chapter thirty-nine

## 45 DAYS

There are few sounds as comforting as the laughter of your best friends. Especially at midnight. Especially out on the beach with the ocean as a background soundtrack.

We're on our backs in the sand, heads together, feet out, arranged like a three-pointed star. Milky clouds drift by in the navy sky above us. We listen to white waves crash into the shore a few yards away.

I'm holding hands with Will and Penny, grinning even though neither one of them can see me.

"On three," Penny says. Her voice sounds thick and partially trapped inside her since she's lying down. "One, two . . . three!"

We each raise our linked arms and swish them in a big arc at the same time as our legs. Our feet bump into each other, making us giggle harder.

"*Ow,* Will, your toenails are sharp," I yelp.

"Seriously, William!" Penny shrieks. "You're like a three-toed sloth over there."

Will spreads his feet even wider and runs his toenails up my shin. "Come closer, my pretty!" Will says in a creepy old-lady voice.

My back thumps against the sand, shaking from silent laughter. "Stop! Stop!" I say, clutching my sides and curling into a ball.

"Quick! Everybody up!" Penny shouts.

We scramble to our feet, brushing granules from the back of our legs and shoulders. Together, we step back to admire our handiwork. Three matching sand angels have been traced together on the beach. The glowing embers of our campfire light our silhouettes in the sand.

"Pretty," I say. Because of course this was Penny's idea.

"Not bad," Will agrees. "Except for that one in the center." He points to the angel that he made. "It looks a little chunky."

I shove his arm. The remnants of our night are scattered around. Chocolate. Marshmallows. Graham crackers. Penny's weird bottles of kombucha.

There's nothing particularly special about this moment, but it feels perfect. There's a swell of emotion inside me. Will's the first one to break away. "Last one in has to lick Harrison Vines's face." *Shoot.* I do *not* want to lick Harrison's face.

So I take off sprinting after Will. Penny and I run neck and neck, our elbows jostling each other, screaming all the way. Will plunges into the surf. Penny's long gazelle legs hit the water first.

"No!" I tumble into the water with such feigned tragedy, I should win an award. And I should actually be way more disappointed than I am, given that I am now going to have to beg my two best friends to please, please, please not make me lick Harrison, which I will absolutely hate doing. But while I wash the sand out from between my toes and under my armpits and around my neck, I can't help but think instead that I'm very lucky.

# chapter forty

## *30 MINUTES*

The sky is clear and coated with starry glitter. I stare up at the full moon and push my bike toward it. My dad's road bicycle zips along much faster than Penny's Huffy bike did and I'm wearing sensible sneakers this time, another plus, but my cast is clumsy on the handles and makes me swerve back and forth across the yellow line painted on the blacktop's shoulder.

The clock on my phone reads just after 11:30 p.m. Ringo's breathing is heavy and shallow behind me and I listen to the spin of our wheels.

Even going uphill, I don't have to stop and walk beside my bike. I press on, letting my lungs burn for oxygen. The farther we go, the less the air smells like the salt of the sea and the more it smells like rain-starved farmland.

Too much has happened for me to believe in magic any longer.

For instance, I know why I don't need my inhaler anymore. It's not an unexplained miracle, I was just dead.

And I've accepted that when Will, Penny, and I wrote down our wishes, we weren't doing it so that by some strange twist of fate I would one day have answers to impossible questions. We were just three kids who loved each other. And that counts for plenty, as Ringo has convinced me.

After all, it's Ringo who has pushed me to finish the hunt, to find the wishes, no matter what he had said to begin with about how I've been hanging on to the possibility of those tiny, hidden scraps too hard.

I hop off my bike while the wheels are still moving and drop it with a *bang-crash* on the side of the road. Ringo skids to a stop behind me. It's so dark beneath his helmet that his face looks one color and it makes my stomach twist uncomfortably. I'm glad when he removes the helmet and I see that it's still him there underneath.

I read the ragged wooden sign. It's barely legible now: CAT MOUNTAIN STATE PARK.

"This is it," I say, reverently, while dumping my helmet on top of the front wheel.

Ringo steps over his turned-over bike. "It's, uh, lovely. Where are we exactly?"

One more thing. I just have to do this one more thing and then what will be, will be and what I'll do, I'll do. "It's the last full moon of the summer," I tell him. "That's when dreams are born." Because I owe Penny the memory of that much.

He takes my hand and I pull my dad's headband lantern from around my neck and onto my forehead. I lead Ringo past the trailhead, where the terrain turns craggy and we have to carefully watch our steps.

I still expect the ground to feel sacred when we enter the abandoned cougar den. Instead, it just feels like ground. Ringo drops my hand and walks around the cave's perimeter. "Whoa, you guys came here when you were fourteen?"

"Almost fifteen," I correct him.

Because we have exactly eleven minutes until midnight if we're to be exactly respectful of Will's plan, I show him the set of ribs mostly buried in the red dirt, and together we search for the gopher skull, but neither of us can find it.

We uncover other treasures, though, like a fossilized paw print and a dead lizard being gnawed to bits by ants.

I watch the clock on my phone as it flips the numbers to midnight. It's officially my birthday.

"What now?" asks Ringo.

"I—I don't know," I admit. I turn on the spot. For several long moments, I worry that Will hadn't gotten to this last part, that the wishes aren't exactly here. I search the walls of the cave and trace my feet over the perimeter—nothing.

"Will, Penny, and I, we did this friendship ritual right here years ago, but—"

"Should we do it?"

I frown and tuck my hands into my armpits, hugging myself tightly. "I—"

Then Ringo nods. "It's your thing. The three of you. You're right."

My shoulders relax, thankful. Yes, he gets it. Almost as well as Will and Penny would have, and for that I'm so fortunate.

Crickets and cicadas scream in the night around us. I walk to the spot where we cut our hands and rubbed our blood in the dirt. Ringo stays close but doesn't touch me. I tilt my head up to the moon—a perfect orb of a frosty silver light. "I don't know," I say, letting my palms clap against the sides of my legs. "I'm stumped."

I think back to that night. It feels like eons ago when the three of us sat here together and vowed to be family. Had we failed? Or am I wrong to feel hurt because, in truth, we had the same issues as every other family?

The spit grows thick and sticky in my throat. I remember how I'd been all alone—or at least it had felt that way—before I met Will and Penny, and how I'd stood in this same spot, bleeding and giddy, feeling as if I'd just won the lottery.

But Ringo is looking over my shoulder. He taps my arm. "What's that?" He points and my heart skips.

"What's what?"

I turn around and, though we are a few feet off from it, see the tip of what looks like a mason jar sticking out of the dirt, barely glinting in the moonlight.

I go over to it and kneel. I push the dirt away with my hands. Then I use my fingernails to scrape more of the dirt off. I scrabble frantically until finally I've unburied enough of the jar so that I can grip my fingertips around the lid and yank it free. I tumble onto my backside, wide-eyed and clutching the jar.

Inside are three scraps of paper, each with rusty bloodstains on it.

"The wishes," I say. "They're actually here." I stare at them, disbelieving. How long have they been here? A month? Or maybe they've been here all along, for years. I'll never know.

Ringo moves closer.

I bring the jar up to my nose and peer inside, like I'm examining insect specimens.

"I'm scared," I say.

"Of what?" Ringo's voice is low and quiet.

"I don't know exactly." I shake the jar ever so slightly so that the scraps dance inside. All along Ringo and my parents have been warning me that I've been holding too tightly to the idea of the wishes. They told me that grief would make me attach importance to things that really weren't important. I'd told myself that Will thought the wishes were important and that's why I had to too. That was reason enough.

I don't think that now. They were right all along, except for one thing. I think the journey—following the clues, searching for three wishes in a jar—made space for Matt and me where before we'd been trapped by resentment, by ourselves, by a history that had been clogged by the end date of my eighteenth birthday.

Ringo rubs the center of my back and gives me a pat and I know that I will want to kiss him very soon. "We've come this far," he says.

I unscrew the top and empty the three scraps out into my hand. I jiggle them until I can make out each of my friends' handwriting without seeing the full message. I know there are parts of my friends that they had purposefully kept buried from me, but at least these parts they'd wanted me to uncover. I select Will's first.

Gingerly, I pull back the edges and read what is written

there, like it's a fortune cookie. "'~~I wish to never turn out like,~~'" I murmur. "It's crossed out," I say. "'I wish to be a hero.'" Followed by a smaller, later scribble that I don't read aloud. It says, *Unlike my dad.* I dig my teeth into my bottom lip. Of course this was Will's wish. It informed everything about him. The grand romantic gestures, the constant effort to be the perfect boyfriend—but at what cost? I wonder how much more quickly he might have moved on to Penny if he hadn't written down this particular wish. I wonder if he would have felt more himself if he wasn't letting someone else define him before he even had a chance to become who he truly was. I drop the wish back into the jar and open up Penny's.

"'I wish to be loved, as much as I love.'" There are red thumbprints crisscrossing the words. Penny's blood. I can imagine fifteen-year-old Penny earnestly scribbling this sentiment. She was so open to the world, in constant danger of taking on enough love to sink her. But Penny loved balance, and whether she knew it or not, the world loved her right back, just as much. Even Will.

Finally, it's my turn. I've been trying to recall what I'd written down on my wish scrap. So much has happened between then and now that whatever is contained of myself in this miniature time capsule I can't touch with memory. So I open it up and I read my own writing. "'I wish for the three of us to be friends. Always,'" I say. I turn my wish over, hoping there is something written on the back. There isn't. I stare at it, blinking.

"Is everything clearer now?" Ringo asks.

I wait. Then I curl up the piece of paper in my fist and drop it into the jar with the other two. "I—I think so. . . ."

# chapter forty-one

## *HAPPY BIRTHDAY TO ME*

I turned eighteen today. I don't think there'll be a party.

Instead, my ankles dangle off of a rock where I'm leaning back, weight on my hands. The day's sun has baked the surface so that my palms are warm against it. Pink, purple, and orange spool from the sinking gold as it dips lower and lower, painting the ocean's horizon with rich streaks of dappled amber.

It's taken me 6,570 days and two lives to get to the place where I could watch the sunset on the day of my eighteenth birthday, the choice of a lifetime behind me.

There's a spot in my chest too deep to reach that aches with a longing so sharp that there are seconds during which I'm not sure I'll survive. But each time it passes and I know the next stab won't be lethal. With any luck, it'll start to hurt less both with time and repetition.

I know for sure now that I'll be haunted by beautiful days. Still, I drink in the one stretched out before me anyway.

I hear footsteps behind me but don't turn. A set of cool hands covers my eyes from behind. "Guess who?" I don't have to. He smells like pine trees with a touch of vanilla. I hold his fingers and tug them down away from my eyes. I tilt my head back and stare up at Ringo's mismatched, work-of-art face. "Happy birthday," he says and pulls two long-stemmed white roses out of his back pocket.

I bite my lip and gently take the stems from him. "Thank you," I say. "These are perfect." I smell each of the roses, then climb off the rock.

Ringo watches me closely. His hand is protective as it guides my elbow and hips. I'll be wearing my cast for another couple of weeks. I'm anxious to get it off, since it itches like a dozen mosquitoes have crawled up inside it.

"Are you all right?" Ringo asks. He doesn't try to hide the concern that shines through in the crinkles forming at the corners of his eyes.

I called Penny's parents this morning and then Will's mom and told them what I planned to do. They all cried, but that's okay. They're only at the beginning of their journey. Maybe they'll go to therapy. Maybe I will too. What I hope is that Tessa and Ms. Bryan will be friends again, perhaps even best friends. And while I know that won't make them whole again, neither would bringing back only one of their dead children.

"I will be," I say.

At the edge of the cliff I've put together two side-by-side pyramids of rocks that each support crosses made of driftwood and twine. The scavenger hunt is over, but this is where it really ends.

I can hear Will's voice in his last message that led me to the wishes. There probably would have been a present at the end. It doesn't bother me that I'll never know what it was. I kneel in front of the crosses that I've built at the cliff we used to jump from. There, I rest a rose beside each, then stand and clasp Ringo's hand in my own.

I think it's true what they say, that misery loves company—Matt taught me that—but it's only because to crawl out of any hole, there needs to be one person to offer a boost up, and another to stick around long enough to help pull the first one up after them.

In the end, I picked the path that led to healing. The best that I could anyway. Matt gave me that. It turns out my brother has made more sacrifices than any human being I have ever known. I don't know when he'll be back. Tomorrow I'll be able to talk to him, once he knows this is over and we can have the space we need to find our way to what comes next.

In the meantime, I hope someday to memorize all the different inlets of Ringo's face like they are spots on a continent I live on. He's become my home in very different ways from Penny and Will, but that doesn't make either any less real. There are a million ways I've been wrecked over the last few years. My new wish is that by facing them head-on, we'll all be better off.

Ringo pulls me closer and rubs small circles on my bare arm with his thumb. My great, big, epically magnificent, cowabunga awesome birthday surprise.

I get another one of the chest pains and have to wait it

out before I can breathe comfortably again. Ringo must feel this, because he squeezes me tighter. I rest my head on him. "Well?" I say. "What song fits the mood for today?"

Ringo turns his two-toned face and presses his lips to my hair. "Today," he murmurs, "*has* to be 'Here Comes the Sun.'"

I breathe in through my nose, out through my mouth, exactly like Penny—my best friend—taught me. "I think I like the sound of that."

# ACKNOWLEDGMENTS

Many authors have what we call a "book of the heart," and this one's mine. I'm grateful to have a team who has adopted it into their hearts as well.

My agent, Dan Lazar, read *This Is Not the End* and became its greatest champion. It has meant the world to me to have someone who so fully understands this book and the characters in it.

Thank you also to Laura Schreiber for always crying while reading the same part that I cried while writing and for an incredibly long, but incredibly thoughtful edit letter that inspired many of my now favorite pieces of the story.

Emily Meehan, Mary Ann Naples, Cassie McGinty, Tyler Nevins, Mary Mudd, Deeba Zargarpur, Dina Sherman, and the rest of the team at Hyperion, thank you for making Disney such a welcoming and collaborative place to create books.

Torie Doherty-Munro at Writers House gave me some particularly smart notes in the early stages, as did Charlotte Huang and Lori Goldstein, who both helped me figure out what this story was really about.

Thank you also to the girls in my book club who read early copies and gave me much-needed encouragement, with a special shout-out to Lisa McQueen and her eagle-eye editing skills.

I wrote the entirety of this book in a fit of inspiration while on maternity leave, so I need to thank my daughter for being an exceptionally easy baby, and my husband, Rob, for supporting me in my crazed insistence on writing, even with a newborn.